THE HARROW SAGA
FROM UNDER A TREE

SPECIAL EDITION

THE HARROW SAGA
FROM UNDER A TREE

BOOK ONE; SPECIAL EDITION

THE HARROW SAGA
SHADOW IN THE FLAME

BOOK TWO

THE HARROW SAGA
CHILDREN AT THE GATE

BOOK THREE

THE HARROW SAGA
FROM UNDER A TREE
SPECIAL EDITION

PHILIP MAZZA

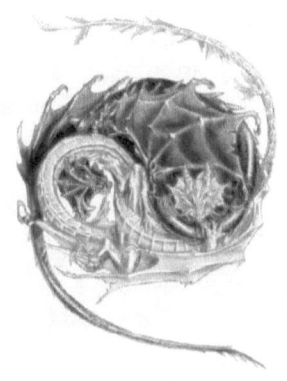

Omni Publishers of New York

www.philipmazza.com

Omni Publishers of New York
ISBN 978-0-9977109-0-8
Printed in the United States of America

First Printing: December 2014; Special Edition, February 2018

Alkar I' Aran - The Song of the Anar Ere

O with a charge like thunder does the Maker hurl brilliant rocks and stones asunder,

With seeds of light sowed in furrows to grow in wonder.

O with a charge that crashes does the Maker stir a furious wind that lashes,

With a storm of fire that swiftly burns souls to ashes.

O who will stand with the stones in hand?

O who will stand to nurture the seeds of the land?

O who will answer to the Maker on his throne?

Hear it not, for the noise and quiet are of the same tone.

About the Author

 **PHILIP MAZZA IS A** novelist with boundless imaginative gifts - a spellbinding storyteller who has created for us a captivating world with *The Harrow Saga*. Born in New York in 1959, Philip received his undergraduate degree from LeMoyne College, where he majored in Business and later achieved his MBA. His career focused on human resources and operations, having held leadership positions for companies, both large and small. He has also served on the boards of several not-for-profits. Now a professor of business at the Madden School of Business, Philip devotes his time to his students and his writing. A writer since a young age, *From Under a Tree* is the first novel in *The Harrow Saga* trilogy. He and his wife enjoy travel and their cat; they continue to live in upstate New York.

Dedication

To my father: On April 2, 2011, a hole in the space-time continuum opened and my father jumped in head-first. As it is said: *He didn't tell me how to live; he lived and let me watch him do it.*

* * *

To my mother: On August 15, 2014, the delicate raven who had perched on my back porch for 55 years decided to spread her wings and lift herself to another realm. As it is said: *A man never sees all that his mother has been to him until it's too late to let her know he sees it.*

* * *

To my grandfather: He gave me the gifts of wine, the sweet scent of a pipe, and the enjoyment of laughter. I know he is gladly turning each page of this book with a big smile on his face.

* * *

To Big Purr and Lil' Man: Together they are on a very special adventure and in a place where they can chase after birds to their hearts' content.

* * *

To Big Grrrr: On December 14, 2017, and only after nine years of life we lost one of our explorers – Drake. We will forever miss our Drake, our cat-around-the-corner who always greeted us with a big purr. We are sure that he is having way too much fun exploring his new existence.

* * *

Listen: The words stopped on April 11, 2007. This is when the master came unstuck in time. So it goes . . .

THE HARROW

Author's Note: Editors have rewritten and edited my Harrow novels since 2014, and yet there were still some lingering errors that needed to be corrected. This was because they had dramatically changed aspects of the story. I have taken some time to edit and restore my Harrow novels to their original form. I have also added new material to take the story further. I want to say that editors do serve an important purpose for authors. But sometimes they can mishandle a good story. This is what has happened here. I am grateful to my publisher who allowed me to restore my novels to their original form, and I thank them for doing so. I hope you enjoy the result.

Publisher's Note: Sometimes the author uses capitalization to add weight of emphasis to objects or places, either as an indirect reference to the proper noun, or as a personification of some greater concept. The author does not use capitalization consistently, so it is fair to assume that much of it depends upon the immediate context of the statement. In some cases, the races receive capitalization when named, but again, this is somewhat inconsistent on the author's part. In many instances, races of the good and righteous are capitalized, while those of the brood are not. This has proved a continuous struggle for the publisher to attempt to create some consistency.

TABLE OF CONTENTS

Author's Introduction 1
Prologue 13

Chapter 1   The Sycamore Tree 19
Chapter 2   The Aina Dur 43
Chapter 3   The Fenri Prince 61
Chapter 4   The Cauldron and Scroll Inn 89
Chapter 5   Blackstone Keep 117
Chapter 6   Tales Upon Tales 157
Chapter 7   Ug'Ghi Otha 193
Chapter 8   Moondancer 233
Chapter 9   The Catacombs 279
Chapter 10   The Hermit and the Tar Malal 319
Chapter 11   Hammer Fief 347
Chapter 12   The Tangle 377
Chapter 13   The Guild Lords 405
Chapter 14   Sgurk Bentgibber 445
Chapter 15   The Draaklel' Daan Defile 473

Appendices

I.   The Great Upheaval 509
II.   Of the Races 519
III. Of Time and the Races 525
IV.   Mystical Tenets of the I' Ra Heru 549

Author's Introduction

INDEED, IT IS TRUE. The story began over ten years ago, on the back porch of my home which overlooks an apple orchard. The makings for a rich epic fantasy were everywhere and a story started to emerge in my mind, until one day it happened . . . the spark . . .

The spark occurred on a dark and stormy day. The rain and wind together dashed against the trees, blew through them, and upon the house with a roar. My wife and I had just finished moving into our new home and were settling in. Our two cats at the time, Lil' Man and Big Grey, were both house cats but enjoyed being outdoors, as all house cats do on occasion. At our old house and now and then we would take them outside and walk them on leashes. They would enjoy exploring the gardens, rolling in the grass, and chasing after butterflies. But with our new house, the backyard was yet unfinished. It consisted of raw field and earth. This made walking the cats quite an implausible proposition. So, until we could get the backyard seeded and our new gardens flourishing, the cats could only stare from the windows and imagine great adventures.

On this rainy day, I decided to open the porch doors to let some fresh air into the house but forgot to slide the screen door shut. A few hours passed when I noticed my mistake.

"I left the screen door open!" I shouted to my wife. "Where's Lil' Man? Big Grey? Where are you, Big Grey?"

My wife found Lil' Man inside, sleeping in his wicker basket. But where was Big Grey?

As I looked out to the back porch there sat the large cat, peacefully, looking over the back yard, watching the rain lash the apple trees and soak into the cracked earth. I carefully approached the cat. I did not want to frighten him off and into the muddy backyard.

"Big Grey, are you alright?" I asked softly with an outreached hand.

The cat turned to me and gave me a meow. He began a big rumbling purr and rubbed up against my hand. I smiled.

We shared a moment on the back porch as we watched the rain fall, feeling the dampness. As the storm passed a light wind chilled the air. In the distance loomed the many apple trees, the leaves rustling in a thousand whispers. I thought about the apple orchard.

Here were secret places, cold and empty.

"You want to go on an adventure? Under a tree?"

Big Grey gave another meow. I reached down and stroked the soft back of the cat rubbing behind his ears. He looked up at me. The great cat was getting old and I could sense hesitation in his eyes.

"Adventures can wait. Come on. Let's go inside now where it's a bit warmer."

The cat breathed in deeply the freshness of the moisture-laden air and was content. Slowly he followed me into the house. I slid the screen door shut behind him.

Spark!

* * *

So, here we are. Many years since that one spark, and since that time so much has changed in my life. My parents are now gone, my career is ending, Lil' Man and Big Grey are on a new adventure, and I've written a novel. Yet, one critical element in my life remains unchanged: I still desire to know more and to better understand myself and that which surrounds me. These are not easy tasks, for life is but a mystery. For some, faith and spirituality are guideposts to understanding life. For others, unfortunately so, life is only understood in death. Some wish to understand life in its entirety and seek the purpose of their existence. Life is thus both an opportunity and a myriad of challenges, a mix of comforts and difficulties. Of course, it depends on how people perceive it.

For me, great understanding has come through my writing. Writing is the method by which life divulges itself. Through writing, I reveal myself to myself, because through my characters, I live many different lives. I experience different emotions, and in doing so explore my feelings toward many different situations. It is this exploration that helps me to better understand myself, others, and the reality in which I live. For you see, life is just that – an exploration

- an adventure - a journey with many paths and stops along the way.

When the end was calling to my father, my journey took a different path. I sat and cried. I could not imagine life without him, his voice, and his sage words. My father was a man who had fought in one of the greatest battles of World War II. He had confronted the worst in mankind, but also experienced the beauty and marvel of life itself. He had experienced and seen so much in his lifetime. Now, on his deathbed, we were in a moment in time where he was slipping away, a generation on the precipice. When my father passed I wrote chapter 8. I was Erol Carrick at the Thorndell as he looked to the valley's southern extremity, a solemn place, a battlefield graveyard. I was the great Carrick as he sat for hours by a lone grave mound. As I wrote . . . it was a "scene of desolation, swept with sighs, washed with tears, and covered with graves."

A few years later my mother passed, and my journey took yet a different pathway. She was such a wonderful spirit who had a great understanding of herself and what life was all about. For my mother, life was family, friends, humor, and faith in the divine. When she passed I was writing *Shadow in the Flame* and found myself with Molly and Elizabeth as they both clutched the Lia Fail stone. The sisters took an amazing ride into the stars and I was with them. During this ride, Molly told her sister, "Never lose faith in me and our love."

This is my journey, a voyage. At times it is a pleasant stroll along a quiet forest pathway. Other times it is on a sea, through a storm-tossed passage. It may follow a predictable route or a tortured course, but always with elements of surprise and discovery along the way. And what's ahead? What's around the corner? Only I can imagine.

Indeed, my writing is a journey of self-discovery, almost spiritual in a sense, and along this journey I find myself exploring and attempting to resolve many riddles. Some riddles, I know, have yet to present themselves. It is a kind of mystery waiting to be solved - who and what am I? This is my journey and as Brows said, "when one is on a journey one takes only what one needs and leaves behind what one doesn't need."

What must I bring with me? What do I discard?

Yet, I am uncertain I may ever fully complete the journey. Perhaps there will be too many stops along the way, slowing my forward progress, or there will be stops ahead I may never experience but should. However, this much I know - as with any journey, lessons come along the way, not in reaching the journey's end.

Like me, as Molly continues her voyage she learns and grows as a person. In the upcoming book *Shadow in the Flame* Molly reminds us of what is important when she ponders, "I guess what matters in life is not so much the various things that come to meet us, and with which we have to deal, as our readiness to meet them."

Yes, I'm finding myself. Can you imagine that? After all these years I'm finally figuring things out. But it remains a slow process.

I'm reminded of something C.S. Lewis once wrote, "There are far, far better things ahead than any we leave behind."

In the end, life is but a journey, we know not how far.

* * *

I am often asked why I wrote the Harrow. Well, besides my journey of self-discovery, the answer is fairly simple. First, it is the only tale I've written that truly captivates me. At every turn, I am enthralled with what could happen next. For you see, there is no greater joy for a writer than the joy of creation. Also, I enjoy telling tales and the art form of story writing. There is no nobler profession than that of the writer - well, perhaps save one - that of the teacher.

It's all about the story because the story matters. Story first. It's kind of like taking an oath. For writers, I think the oath would be - first, tell a good story. Next, I think it would be – to give the story applicability. I use this term because it is a term used, in a sense by Tolkien, who was confounded by those who considered his works an allegory.

For writers, the use of allegory demonstrates a moral or spiritual truth or political or historical condition. Tolkien despised the thought of allegory as it applied to his writings. He hated allegory. He didn't want his stories viewed as references to what may have happened in his own time and life. He wanted the messages to be common so that the reader could apply them to his or her own life. In this way, his writings would be applicable and timeless.

I know of no writer who would disagree with Tolkien. But there are many common stories that we tell that have allegorical meanings. These are especially popular in stories for children because allegories mean to teach some lesson or help the reader understand complex ideas and concepts. *Yertle the Turtle* by Dr. Seuss is an allegory about Adolf Hitler and the evils of totalitarianism. *The Hunger Games* is an allegory for our obsession with reality television and how it numbs us to reality.

If one believes that history repeats itself and that one can learn from the sins and truths of the past, then there is no harm with the perspective of allegory. A good tale is like an enormous puzzle. Each piece of the puzzle, by itself, does not seem to make sense; the shape provides a bit of help but the content is but a blur of color and without specific form. It is only until you properly place all the pieces together that you see the whole picture, that meaning is provided.

Reader interpretation is certainly a factor in deriving allegory from a work, but just because the reader thinks it's there doesn't mean it is, nor does it mean to be the author's intention.

For me, the Harrow is a good story with oodles of applicability.

Oodles.

Now there's a word you do not hear or even see often. Yet, for those who have followed the writings of Kurt Vonnegut you are aware of its use.

In *Breakfast of Champions* Vonnegut wrote this: "I can have oodles of charm when I want to."

There can be no doubt that Vonnegut is one of my inspirations and in fact, you will see a reference to him in my dedication.

Why Vonnegut?

First, let me start by saying that when it comes to fantasy tales one must consider Tolkien an influence. Tolkien is generally recognized as the father of modern fantasy with his epic novels. *The Lord of the Rings*, *The Hobbit*, and *The Silmarillion* are all genre-defining masterpieces. On top of creating thousands of years of history and mythology, he also created many languages. This makes Tolkien one of the best world builders in the history of fiction. Where Tolkien is an influence on so many, we cannot forget those that influenced Tolkien. For you see, nothing is ever new.

Tolkien was a devoted student of history and classical literature and mythology. His tales include smatterings of ancient Greek, Roman, Egyptian, Babylonian, and northern European history and mythology. One only has to read Plato's the *Republic* and the story of the ring of Gyges to understand Tolkien's inspiration.

Inspiration is everywhere.

Vonnegut's writings were inspirational to me. He turned me on to fiction and the power of words. He got me through my teen years. As a young adult, I waited for every new book and ran to the local bookseller to buy a copy.

Even though he did not write epic fantasy fiction, Vonnegut was an author who stayed with you long after you thought you were done with him. You didn't have to be young to appreciate Vonnegut. He taught us that we are what we pretend to be, so we must be careful what we pretend to be. On a technical level, Vonnegut has influenced me. Unlike some, who after brilliant passages seem to get lost in their asides, Vonnegut, no matter how digressive, always arrived at his points of departure, with a light touch.

As I said, it's all a journey with many stops — Vonnegut, Tolkien.

So it goes . . .

* * *

And here we are . . . before you rest the pages of a special edition of *The Harrow: From Under a Tree*. I was surprised when asked to write for the special edition. Readers wanted to know more about the Harrow and I am more than thrilled to provide the extra detail.

But there is a surprise! This special edition contains much of the writings from the original draft! Some enjoyed the opportunity to make changes and trim things out here and there, and tell a writer what is best. Well, this special edition puts many of those trimmings back in. For the fans of *The Harrow Saga*, I believe you will quite enjoy the previously edited content.

So, what can the reader expect? The tale's beginning is very different as you first meet Drogur Vorn the Orc Master. Later, readers will meet Snerv Slog, a malevolent little creature who assists Vorn. Readers will also walk the evil underground fissure known as Esku En' Urra, a place where vile demons are harvested and slaves tormented. Readers will also enter the sacred of all sacred places, the tomb of Ra Carathor, and peer into the glass sarcophagus. I have provided additional information about the Anar Ere, or Enlightened Ones, and of the White Knight, Nim Dagora. There are new insights into Col Shas who is the Jhaer Tystalaes to Dalgaes, how the Professor and Shaer Thol became friends, the relationship between Shaer Thol and Ras Amon, Moondancer's special power, the demon creatures called the Gurtha Naur - all of this and more from the original draft.

I am also very pleased that we are now able to provide the reader with a map of the Harrow and more details in the form of appendices. They reward the reader with an enhanced understanding of the characters, history, and culture of the Harrow. Within the appendices, you will learn the chronology of the Ages: The Age of Fire, The Age of Kings, and The Age of War. You will experience the Sinome A' Eller, or great upheaval, as recorded in the I' Qarma En' Ilya, the Book of Histories. You will also be introduced to the mystical tenets of the I' Ra Heru, the mighty father feline creator of the Ra Cath. You see, when one creates a world, one must first create its history.

There are other surprises as well that will remain unmentioned!

So, enjoy the journey! As it is said, *tu kai a' kai* !

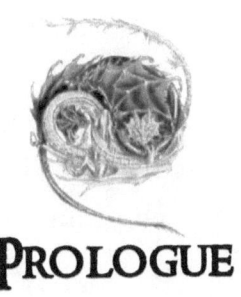

PROLOGUE

IN THE ELVEN KINGDOM of Tir Nan Og, the grand white castle Kaer Tari with its towers and turrets shrouded in the morning mist stood like a gleaming crystal at the top of a mountain. Deep within the castle walls, courtiers and shamans quietly conducted their duties while high above in an imposing spire the great Elf-King Dalgaes, now in the autumn of his life, sat alone in his library. With a warm blue shawl tucked about his legs and a thick leather-bound book on his lap, he sat by his favorite window, looking down upon Eilthir. The ancient city sprawled at the edge of a narrow gorge, surrounded by streams that descended from the adjoining mountains, forming cascades so high that the glimmering city was almost lost in the spray. The city was a magnificent sight, replete with red and orange tiled rooftops, columns and sculptures, and mosaics aplenty. Its walls were encrusted with precious stones and masterly workmanship to the very top. Everywhere, vines and lush greenery dappled with blooms of bright orange and red flowed.

The Elf-King found comfort in what he saw. It stirred memories of the mist of his childhood and of years when everything was ahead of him and endings did not exist. These days, he thought of the past more frequently, with tenderness and fondness, and thought less of the future; for in his youth the future was time immeasurable, but now it seemed finite and nearing its end.

Now, as he neared his final days, life had slowed considerably for Dalgaes who found himself seeking refuge and solace in his library. His hands crippled with age relished the feel of the leather-bound books, and his slowed mind delighted in the words of the venerated writers of yore. The books were special to him for they recalled a glorious time long past, of wondrous travels, of great upheaval and battles, of pain and sorrow, and great exhilaration and celebrations. These were his memories, of a time when he sat upon his white throne and dealt with matters of state. Now his eldest sons handled such matters leaving the Elf-King with time to rest and time for memories.

Indeed, his time in the library was peaceful, reading in the quiet haven, that was until one of his many great-grandchildren would happen by. The little ones loved to climb on the shelves and explore the books, just like he did when he was a child. It was a beautiful day whenever they would visit, and it made him remember the first time he had come to the library as a young boy.

"Great Grandpapa, can I come in?" came the soft voice of a child.

Dalgaes closed the book he was reading and turned to see the library door open ever so slightly. Peeping through the door was the gentle face of an elf-child, wide-eyed and innocent. The child was his great-grandson called Jin Dalhar.

"Great Grandpapa, can I come in?" asked the child again. "Would you tell me a story?"

The great Elf-King's face looked soft with the traces of a kind and useful active life now nearly spent. He slowly motioned with his hand for the child to come closer.

"Why yes. You may enter."

Jin Dalhar tip-toed across the room and sat on the lap of his great-grandfather. With an innocent grin, he looked up at the Elf-King and gently placed a small, soft hand on the aged face. The Elf-King brightened at the touch and gave a gentle kiss to the child's forehead.

Such a pure face as a prophecy, a dream of the future, Dalgaes thought.

"Tell me, my child, what story would you like to hear?" he asked, his voice having a faint tremor.

The child beamed.

"I like the story about the Great War," he said.

"Well now, there were two Great Wars. Which story would you like to hear?"

"Tell me the one about the children who came from under the tree," said Jin Dalhar gleefully. "I like that one."

"Ah yes, I know which story you speak of and it so happens that I have the book here with me." Dalgaes pointed with his crooked fingers to the closed book on his lap, its gold-leafed title on a scuffed red leather cover. "It is called *From Under a Tree* and it was written by one of my good friends. The story includes many of my friends from the past. I am so grateful to have had them in my life, and I miss them very much."

The elf-child nestled in the Elf-King's lap, his arms wrapped around his great grandfather's neck.

"Yes, that's the one Grandpapa, about the human children who came from under the tree and saved the Harrow," he said. "Why do you miss your friends so? Have you not seen them?"

Dalgaes smiled and breathed a deep breath.

"I have not seen them in such a long time."

"Why do they not visit?" asked the child innocently.

"You can say they are on an adventure of sorts, their last adventure. In time, it is an adventure we must all take."

The child gleamed with excitement.

"I so love adventures!" he twittered. "I can't wait for when I must go on that adventure!"

The Elf-King looked at the child whose face was golden and pure. He chuckled.

"Oh, there will be time enough young Jin," he told the child. "This is one adventure you do not want to rush. Always remember, some adventures come to you in time, whether you wish to take them or not. Now, what about that story you asked about?"

"Can you read it to me? Please."

Dalgaes felt the warmth of the child against his chest and instinctively reached out his arms.

"Well, it is a rather large book now. There is so much to tell," he said. "Let us see how far along we can get. Where would you like for me to begin?"

Jin Dalhar looked up at the great Elf-King, his eyes joyful with delight.

"Grandpapa, where all stories begin - at the beginning, of course."

Slowly and very carefully the aged Elf-King turned the pages and started to read aloud to the child . . .

CHAPTER I
THE SYCAMORE TREE

THIS IS A STORY of a different time. Although there were evils and fell beings in the world, it was a fair and green place. The loudest sounds were those of land and air and water. These were peaceful places long ago disturbed by forceful devices, the machines of war, now restored by time to their natural beauty. And war, that which had defined existence for so long, was no longer presented as something necessary, and its necessities and anxieties had ceased.

Oh, there were some, those who little liked fair things, and dark magic was not yet so commanding that could unmake with terrible swiftness the handiwork of the Maker. For the realms of the Shadow were reduced. Demise and decay were largely forgotten, receding into a small dark place, far away. It was a moment in time between the past and the future, where reality seethed with secrets and sins, both past and present.

But time changes things and things change with time. For, as it is said, time is fluid and changes as mankind changes. It brings with it probabilities that are altered by the Maker in a cadence of realities, that come one over the other, like waves upon a shore. One moment reality is familiar; the next moment it is strange, brought about by a great upheaval. Those with understanding, the attendants and messengers of the Maker, know reality is but an illusion, a fleeting glimpse of all that was, and it is changed in a moment.

For this is a story of long ago, of times passed, and times yet to come, of illusions, secrets, and dreams, of a different reality.

As the pure beings of the divine, or Anar Ere teach: *Reality changes with a blink of an eye.*

* * *

Through flame and smoke, the evil tower called Urth' Goroth stood looming, found deep within the southernmost reaches of the Drueger. It was a great fortress built of stone and rock from the side of a mountain, hand-hewn by the dregs of wicked brood that inhabited such a soulless place. Towers upon towers and battlements upon battlements, tall as the surrounding mountains; great open halls as dark as the night, walls of steel and prisons of hopelessness, and massive stone gates barred with dulled steel. This was the place of the Dark Lord, or as he was sometimes called, Szard, or Dark Master, or *Mori Ni* in the old tongue, and from this shadowy place did he rule.

Within the shadows and along the cavernous and icy stone hallways of the tower walked the black hooded Dark

Lord, his face obscured in darkness and doom. Within the coldness, the snarls, grunts, howls, and the scraping of fingers and claws against the stone walls and floors echoed loudly. These were the sounds of the imprisoned, enslaved, lesser creatures of the land, and such noise pleased the Dark Lord. It gave him purpose and fed his insatiable desire for more.

Deeper and deeper he journeyed, through a labyrinth of dark tunnels and passages, until in the distance shone an orange light. Immediately, he could feel the warmth and the smell of forges melting metal that slaves fashioned into tools of war. He took a deep breath. The smell was exhilarating.

"My master," came a deep voice.

From the shadows appeared Drogur Vorn. Here was a huge and hulking beast, an orc almost the size of two orcs, a mountain of sheer muscle and honed for intimidation. His leathery and hairy skin marked his race, his face hidden by a mask made from his father's skull, the Dol Goran. Vorn was a descendant of a race of great orcs, the Ra Orqu, and held a position of superiority for the Dark Lord. For it was Vorn who was Orqu Tur, or Orc Master, as was his father and his father before him, and it was Vorn who alone measured the legions of orcs and ensured that slaves were useful until they withered.

"Are we on plan?" asked the Dark Lord.

"Yes, my master. The forges scream and our numbers grow stronger every day. Soon now, we may unleash the full abundance of foul."

"Good."

The two now traveled together, closer to the orange light, following the stone hall until it became a pathway that opened upon a massive underground fissure called Esku En' Urra. This was a place where the tortured labored endlessly within its depths, overcome by an unnerving sense of immensity beyond knowledge, a frightening scale of vastness. Here was eternal torment and punishment, a hot and dirty existence without escape.

Within this ghastly vision, thousands of forges of great fire roared. They were hollowed stones in which were beds of hot coals. The bellows were the lungs of giant beasts, which blew through reed tubes that entered holes in the bottoms of the forges. The anvils were large, rounded stones, at which slaves squatted as they hammered out blades, hooks, and mace heads. The largest of the forges crafted great pieces of metal that were used to construct grand machines of war and death, devices that would be deployed for the relentless siege on the domains of dwarf, man, and elf.

Vorn pointed far to the distance, to the back of the fissure.

"Look, my master. We are fruitful as commanded."

From within the stone walls, far beyond the forges, brood came to life, gruesome monsters seeping from rock and earth, born of slime and mud, maggots and worms. Hundreds upon hundreds of hideous brood were given life of the baking flames, unseen things even in myths, or the darkest days of yore. Green hides and yellow eyes of bile, foul limbs with razor-sharp talons, hunched backs of muscle, drooling lips, obscene and cruel; and there were others of rotting dark skin and bristle, and red eyes of fire, with yellow teeth that clattered, the sound like metal on metal – the wicked brood forever multiplied.

So it was, after creating hosts of wretched creatures did the vile legions of brood form thousands of wicked battalions. They waited patiently, deep within the great fissure in orderly rows and columns, stretching out like a black, reeking, tremulous swamp. They hissed, howled, growled, and snarled. Then horns blew, and drums rolled like the beat of doom pounding in one's breast, and the army of the damned advanced from the place of unending fire, marching out from the tower and into the blackness of the Drueger.

"I am most pleased," the Dark Lord told Vorn.

"Your pleasure is my wish," said Vorn with a slight bow. He sensed the bitter glint of a smile on the unseen face.

The two continued their walk, now leaving the underground cavern and entering a series of dark tunnels that linked to a second evil tower, which had been rebuilt after the Shadow War, the ancient tower called Ug' Cthuth. The tunnels were lit sporadically by torch; the eerie light revealing sullen shadows against the cold and wet jagged walls.

As they traveled deeper and deeper into the earth, the tunnels became long and narrow. They strode in a single file with Vorn leading the way and along a passage till they came to a stone door set in the wall. The enormous beast extended both arms feeling for the door's edges.

When he had a good grip, and using all his strength, he pushed the door ajar.

"I do not like what is inside here," said Vorn.

"I understand your apprehensions," said the Dark Lord, softly yet confidently.

Behind the great door was a modestly sized chamber, perhaps fifteen feet square. The room was dark and had a foul odor. A bit of light from a torch just outside the room crept into the darkness and upon a strange sight. There within the blackness was a creature of metal and wire, its body human-like, but now dismembered and fragmented. Parts of its torso were scattered about the shadowy place, wires and pieces of metal and plastic strewn about, with a green fluid from the complex mechanism flowing onto the stone floor. In a corner of the room was the creature's head, shiny as though polished.

The creature's head suddenly sprang to life with a thrill of power. It had sensed a presence in the chamber. Vorn was startled. The brute took a step back and growled.

With the sound of gears whirring loudly, the metallic creature opened its eyes and looked blankly up at the visitors; a faint blue light glowed from a light at the back of its eyes.

Click! Clack! Sounds from the creature's head.

"Two of youth, the females will arrive. A jewel of red, one will revive," said the creature, a mechanical voice that sounded strangely melodic. Green fluid oozed from its mouth. Another click and the head moved slightly staring at the Dark Master. "Carefully tread the halls of sanity."

The head then twitched again.

Click! Clack!

It gave a blink and closed its eyes; the sound of gears turning went silent.

Vorn reached down, picked up one of the creature's glistening arms, and tossed it aside in anger.

"I do not like this creature," he said. "I do not know of his people or the land from which he comes. He speaks in riddles. His meaning is not clear."

"There is a truth hidden within riddles. One must simply search for it," said the Dark Lord.

"I was taught that one should fear knowing the truth," said Vorn.

"The fear of knowing the truth can be so powerful that the doses of truth are lethal. But we must always face the truth of a thing. If we fail to do so, then we choose to ignore what is occurring. Knowing the truth of a thing can be frightening and an impossibly difficult matter, but it is something we must always look to achieve."

The two left the chamber. Vorn pushed the stone door back in place. They started back down the dark tunnels together, quietly, until Vorn took leave of his master.

The Dark Lord went gently within the dark passages. In his mind, the creature's words echoed and felt like a huge weight upon his very existence.

Words can have different meanings. Sometimes one hears what they wish to hear.

He struggled against this thought. He knew the truth of the creature's words, what he believed to be the truth; he knew the reality that would come, what he believed to the reality.

The words are my words. I understand them.

He thought of the lands to the west, the expanse of verdant pastures, dense spruce and pine forest, cold rivers of blue waters cutting through granite peaks. He thought of the races that inhabited the lands as weak, inferior misfits - miserable failures of flesh and bone. This was such a contrast to his realm of stark and primal principles, where barren landscapes and grey rock prevailed, and the races were strong and obedient.

Yes, he knew the truth of the creature's words, and it was his truth.

They send two girls and with them the stone. Most certainly, I will make their cities into a wasteland and cast death like a shadow. I will destroy the wisdom of the wise and bring nothing to the learning of the learned. I will cover the sky and make the stars black. I will destroy everything there is and everything there will be.

* * *

In a speck of time and reality, they were children, two sisters named Molly and Elizabeth. They were pure of heart and mind, shielded from the troubles of the world. They were sweetness with black hair, big wide eyes, and a pixie's face. Molly was the older of the two by a couple of years and taller than her sister. She was very practical, and already behaving like a grown-up person. Of course, this sometimes upset Elizabeth who was precocious and prone to mischief.

During the summer the girls would spend some time at the country estate of their Uncle Theo and Aunt Margie. It was always a special time whenever they visited their uncle and aunt. There was so much to do, so many places to explore hidden away from the sight of adults. They enjoyed playing in the acres of lush gardens, and around the massive sycamore tree with its large roots that rose above the ground. Sometimes they would play hide-n-seek around the tree. Oh, and there were butterflies to catch or follow, at night lightning bugs to jar. and if it rained there was the massive house of rooms filled with oddities and trinkets that seemed to have been collected over the many, many years.

The fashion of the grand house was such that it was perfectly suited for play and fun. It had been built in the early nineteenth century and retained much of its grandeur. The house was a collection of rooms that flowed from an enormous foyer with paneled wood darkly varnished. It was richly decorated with a vaulted ceiling, tall columns, and immense stained-glass windows.

The mansion seemed endless in its inner recesses. All about were balconies, arches, landings, niches, bays, leaded glass, plain glass, beamed ceilings, plain ceilings, and cove ceilings. Large wooden doors led out to verandahs and balconies from every room, and many windows provided cross-breezes. And there were books everywhere, thousands and thousands of books. In some rooms, shelves were bulging, and in other rooms, stacks of books covered every available space, including large swaths of the floor.

Molly so loved books and took to reading as many as possible, but there were too many. The girls could smell the history here; it was faintly musty, peculiar, but exquisitely wonderful.

On this one summer day, it was Molly's birthday. She had just turned thirteen, and she and Elizabeth were outside playing far off in a field of wildflowers. The sun started to make its way behind dark grey clouds and the smell of rain was in the air. It got cooler.

"I think it may start raining," said Elizabeth.

"Oh my, come on," shouted Molly. "Let's get back before we get wet!"

But it was too late.

Just as Molly shouted her warning she felt a drop of rain slide down her nose. Off the girls went. They quickened their pace as more rain was felt, first in fat splatters that landed heavily, then finer, harder. Faster and faster they ran, through fields of tall grasses and flowers, over small wooden bridges, and along paths. Finally, they were at the house dashing up the back porch's rickety stairs and into the foyer. The back porch door boomed as it slammed shut behind them.

Once inside the grand house, they could hear the pitter-patter of raindrops against windows. They made it and not too wet!

"Let's find the cats to play with," said Elizabeth. "They weren't outside."

"Okay, but if we find the Professor," added Molly in a rush. "We may find them. They're usually with him."

The girls always referred to their uncle as the Professor. His full name was Theodosius, but everyone called him Professor because he taught at the university. As you would expect from a professor, he spoke in a low voice with long pauses and precise articulation, and he always had a book in hand or nearby, and a pipe of tobacco handy. He was an imperious fellow with long flowing greyish hair and a beard that covered most of his face.

The sisters loved to play with their uncle's two cats, Big Grey and Lil' Man. Big Grey was a large cat with deep grey fur and a small tail. He had light green eyes, smallish whiskers, and a tiny black nose. He was a loving cat who enjoyed having his belly rubbed and was always purring. This led to his nickname - Big Purr.

Lil' Man on the other hand was much different. He was small and thin, about half the size of Big Grey, and was frail, having contracted an illness that would sometimes leave him sick. He was orange tabby in color, short-haired, with a long tail that was almost as long as his body, and at the tip of his tail were three orange rings. He had long white whiskers, a pinkish nose, and orange eyes that seemed to turn black when he was up to no good.

From time to time, the girls would frolic in the gardens with the cats, playacting, pretending to be fairies and sprites, and waving imaginary wands around. The cats would play along with seeming enthusiasm as if understanding what was happening. It was great fun.

"Where could they be?" asked Elizabeth.

The girls looked around the grand foyer. Molly pointed upward.

"They could be anywhere. Let's start at the top," she said.

Up a sweeping wooden staircase, the girls sprinted, to the third floor. Here they each had a spacious room with a private bath. Down a long corridor was a playroom chock full of dolls and stuffed animals and toys. The Professor and Aunt Margie collected stuffed animals and whenever the girls visited the Professor would say that all the stuffed animals were "put to good use." Farther down the hall was Aunt Margie's craft room where she made all sorts of pretty things. She made jewelry out of colored pieces of glass, and small ornate boxes of gold and silver, delicately clasped and lined with dark velvet.

The girls searched each room, nook, and cranny. They found no one.

"Professor?" whispered Molly making sure not to shout. "Are you here?"

"Big Grey? Lil' Man?" whispered Elizabeth. "Where are you two?"

They continued to search and found nothing beyond the lavish furnishings and books.

"Maybe they're lost," giggled Elizabeth. "If we can find the Professor, do you think he'd tell us a story?"

"Maybe, but we have to find him first, and I've no idea where he or the cats went off to. We've looked everywhere."

Exasperated, the girls made their way to the playroom of stuffed animals and other toys. They played until the late afternoon. That's when the rain stopped.

* * *

From the window, Molly saw the storm clouds had left the sky. The sun reappeared and was beginning to dip below the tops of the woodland's tall beech trees. Shadows began cascading about the gardens and stretching up to the house reflecting a transient sun-gleam from the polished copper beech leaves. It was at this time each day that one could most clearly see the splendid outlines of this king of the forests swaying in a gentle breeze.

Molly rushed to her sister.

"Come on!" she said. "There's still time to play outside."

The two girls backtracked their search quickly peeking into every room, then dashed down the staircase and out to the back porch. As they made their way outside, they heard the creaking sound of a rocking chair. They turned to find the Professor on the back porch. Big Grey was by his side.

Of course, the back porch! Molly thought. *Why didn't I think of that?*

The Professor enjoyed the back porch. He would sit in his favorite rocking chair with the two cats usually by his side, each curled up in comfy wicker baskets. He enjoyed the peace and solitude of the place, listening to the birds and watching the flowers in a wonderful performance of unfurling their buds in a rainbow of color. The best part was that he could read for hours while smoking a bowl or two of tobacco in a long-stemmed, curved pipe. He called it his elf pipe, and while he smoked it, he rested the bowl on his belly. He said it was given to him by a dear friend. There were plenty of stories about his elf pipe and fantastical adventures to be told.

The sisters would spend endless hours on the back porch listening to the Professor's stories. He would tell tales of all manner of creatures; and the tales were so strange that he told them only to the girls, because, as he explained, many older folks were unable to believe the truth. When the tales would end the girls would run out to the gardens with the cats and create their own fantasy places. Of course, they would first ask their uncle for permission to play in the gardens, and when they heard "By all means, but please be careful and listen for your Aunt Margie when she calls you for dinner," they would run down from the back porch and into the gardens.

"There you are," exclaimed Molly. "We were looking for you for what seemed like hours. We thought we lost you."

"Hmm . . . I do not think I have ever been lost before," said the Professor with a big smile. He puffed on his pipe. "I am where I am and that's always where I am."

Elizabeth put her hands on her hips and shook her head.

"You're silly," she said.

"Perhaps little one, but I have been right here all the time with Big Grey. You two ran by like a bolt of lightning when it started to rain. You did not even see us."

"We're sorry Professor," said Elizabeth.

Molly looked at Big Grey curled up in his basket but saw that Lil' Man's basket was curiously empty.

"Where's Lil' Man?" she asked.

"I am not too sure. He is probably off on an adventure. There are so many adventures to be had around this place, do not you know."

"Can we go out in the gardens and play and have an adventure too?" asked Elizabeth. "The rain has ended and there's plenty of time before dinner."

"Of course, but remember, today it is more than dinner. I believe there is a birthday cake to be enjoyed, for a special young lady," said the Professor with more puffs on his elf pipe. He winked at Molly and smiled at her. He reminded them, "Be careful and remember to come back when you hear your Aunt Margie calling you for dinner."

But before the girls could run off Big Grey sat up and stretched. He padded over to the Professor and looked up at him with his green eyes. He started a rumbling meow. It was a long and pronounced meow that ended in a series of deep chirps.

The Professor brought himself forward in his rocking chair. He looked down at Big Grey, tilting his head as if to better hear what the cat was saying. He seemed to be intently listening to each sound from the cat. Molly and Elizabeth were amazed. They had never seen him react this way to Big Grey.

Suddenly everything around them became oddly silent. There was no wind, no sound of rustling leaves, nor the cheerful chirping from birds. It was a strange feeling for the girls.

The Professor looked up to the sky.

"It is quiet," he muttered. "Too quiet."

Big Grey gave a few more chirps. The Professor returned his gaze to the cat.

"Yes, it is time," he told the big cat. "I had hoped we could wait another year or two. And no. I do not know if they are ready. But is anyone ever ready?"

He lifted a hand to his forehead in a gesture of frustration, then sat back in his rocking chair and stared off into the distance. Big Grey rumbled a few more meows.

"Yes . . . yes . . . yes . . . I recognize the situation is dire. I understand and I know what needs to be done," grumbled the Professor under his breath. He then said louder in annoyance. "Give me some time to explain a few things!"

"Professor, what is it? Is Big Grey talking to you?" asked Molly.

"What's he saying?" followed Elizabeth.

The Professor again sat forward in his rocking chair. He took a deep breath and took the girls into his arms, gently bringing them closer to him.

"There now," he said turning to each, a slight smile on his face. "It is time for you to go on a special adventure and Big Grey will be your guide."

The big cat sat looking up at the girls.

"An adventure?" said Elizabeth. "How splendid!"

"Well now, splendid perhaps, but you girls will have to be careful. Big Grey is going to take you to a very special place. You will see some unimaginable things and some things that may frighten you. Just be aware of your surroundings, and the situation you find yourself in. But don't be frightened."

"I don't know if I like the sound of that," said Molly. "Frightening?"

"But of course, adventures can be frightening. They can be long and tedious, sometimes frustrating, and sometimes dangerous. They can also be exciting and rewarding. That is what makes them adventures. You see, adventures are wonderful things because they can lead anywhere. I ask - what fun would an adventure be if you knew where it led?"

The girls nodded. They felt reassured by his words.

"Now, before you go off, I have something to give you," he said almost whispering.

He reached into his shirt pocket and pulled out a golden necklace with a red stone pendant. He delicately displayed it to the girls, the necklace a shining gold draped in one hand, and the stone crystal firmly seated in the other. It looked to be hand-cut and polished, a red gemstone strangely shaped like a small blade or fang.

Molly felt drawn to it. She reached for it and lifted it. The jewel was stunning and barely had any weight to it. Its edges were a bit sharp, and she flinched as she ran her fingers over it. It began to glow ever so lightly with her touch. She quickly released the jewel and gasped.

The Professor smiled.

"Do not be concerned with its glow or its warmth," he told her. "It is for you and it has a name."

"A name? What is it?"

"It is called the Lia Fail," he said placing it over her neck, "and it is yours."

"Where did you get it? Did Aunt Margie make it?" she asked, twinkling with delight.

"How it was made is not important, is it now?"

"No, I suppose not," she said remembering her manners. "Thank you, Professor. It's so beautiful."

She again placed the stone pendant in her hand and looked at it as Elizabeth leaned over for a glance.

"It will help protect you on your journey. It is magic."

"Magic?" she beamed.

"Yes, and you will know when to use it. But whatever you do never give it to anyone or anything. Be careful," he said, a seriousness to his face. "The Lia Fail may look beautiful, but it is more weapon than a jewel, and as you will discover."

"A weapon?" she asked. The word made her wary.

"Yes. It has great magic, but only you can use it. You will eventually learn how to use its power. But do not worry about it right this instant. I am sure you have a lot of questions, and they will all be answered in time. Everything will be alright. Trust me."

She was still a bit frightened but did trust him. He had always been so kind and patient and protective of her and her sister. She felt safe with him and knew he would not allow anything bad to happen to them.

"Alright," she said.

The girls nodded.

Big Grey gave another meow. This irritated the Professor.

"Yes, I know. I heard you. You require patience Big Purr!" he told the cat. He turned to the girls. "One more thing: know that every adventure will change you, and this adventure will be no different. It will be change for the better. Adventures bring experiences and experiencing things is part of life. It is a process with no end. But it is important to learn from your experiences and apply your learning to new experiences. Now, I will be waiting for you here when you return. Remember everything I have told you. Oh, and one last thing. Always remember to do what Big Grey tells you to do and you will be safe. Promise me."

Molly looked at him strangely.

"Do what Big Grey tells you to do and you will be safe?" she said, her tone dismissive. "As if Big Grey can talk. Professor . . . really. Whatever you say."

"I am very serious young lady," he said firmly with a stern look.

She sensed his intensity and nervously nodded.

"Yes sir," she said.

"Good then. And always do the best you can do. As a good friend of mine always says – I do what I do and that's the best I can do," he said with a smile. He gave each of the girls a kiss on the cheek. "Go and follow Big Grey. I will be here when you get back. And remember, somewhere, something incredible is waiting to be known."

The girls were excited and ran off with Big Grey into an expansive lawn and field of wildflowers. But Molly stopped. She heard a sound. It was the sound of movement. She turned in the direction of the sound to see the Professor waving from the back porch.

He called out, his voice ringing in her ears.

"Your birthday cake will be waiting for you!"

She smiled and waved back and then turned back to the field. She ran as fast as she could to catch up to the others and, after what seemed an eternity, they reached that part of the gardens where the field crested and a path entered into a lightly wooded area.

* * *

Big Grey led the girls down a path that wound through a small canyon constructed of puddingstone, with natural pockets and crannies. This was the rock garden. Beyond the canyon was a long stream that flowed to a small waterfall, and there were pools fed by springs. Near the pools was a climbing hydrangea that found its way up a stairway of what was called the Lookout Tower which was a tall edifice made of rock.

From the rock garden, they followed Big Grey to the rose garden. Here, they would sometimes play pretend teatime. They would bring out dolls and stuffed animals and have a grand time. "Be careful of the thorns," Aunt Margie would always remind them. But they were always careful. The garden was so pretty with rambling roses covering arched walkways and beds filled with roses of every shape and color. From the pink, red, orange, and white roses, there were also lavender, apricot, peach, orange, and combinations of these. Along the border, fences of climbing and shrub roses provided a colorful background for bedding plants.

Elizabeth struggled to keep up.

"Where's he taking us?" she puffed.

"I'm not sure," said Molly. "Maybe the tree?"

The rose garden connected to a formal garden through great green archways of ivy, one after another. As Big Grey led the girls past the last archway the formal garden was revealed as low boxwood hedges that formed a pattern of five circles. Each quarter section was a garden figure with a central circle crossed by diagonal walks. The Professor called it his "geometric garden" because of all the shapes.

Leaving the formal garden, they found their way to a stone path that led through a woodland garden. Here, there were towering trees and abundant natural shade, tree ferns, and moss-encrusted logs and stones. Butterflies, songbirds, and wildflowers were their constant companions. At one point a rippling natural stream ran through the dense woodland alongside the path. But darkness began to shroud them as they walked deeper and deeper into the woods. A few rays of sunlight tried to force their way through the thickness of the trees but to no avail and soon they had lost Big Grey.

"Where is he?" asked Elizabeth. "This is the second time today we've lost him. I don't see him. Which way did he go?"

Molly looked about. Again, things became strangely quiet.

"I don't know but let's keep to the path," she said.

They followed the stone path to its end where they saw the big cat. He sat at the end of the path where the woodland garden gave way to a large vista.

"Look! The tree," gasped Molly. "I knew it!"

They could see it, a huge sycamore tree just beyond a field of grasses and wildflowers. It stood majestic against the horizon, tall and imposing with each of its limbs discernible against the blue sky. It was massive and beautiful, a thick light orange bark and branches holding dark, broad leaves, rounded and deep green. The sycamore was an old tree, and the Professor often said it had been there since the dawn of time.

Surrounding the tree was an apple orchard. Rows and rows of apple trees glistened ripe with fruit. There were red, green, and even golden apples. It was a beautiful sight.

"Maybe we can play a game of hide-n-seek!" gleamed Elizabeth.

They smiled. They knew Big Grey and Lil' Man loved to play near the great tree. It was one of their favorite places to be.

"Meow . . . meow . . . meow," rumbled the cat.

He scampered off into the grasses. The sisters followed until they were upon the sycamore's sturdy trunk. Huge roots formed flattened buttresses that reinforced the tree, making it impossible for any windstorm to uproot. The natural holes and crevices formed by the roots were dark with twigs scattered about the openings.

Big Grey circled the imposing tree and then turned to the girls.

"Meow. Meow," he rumbled.

They watched as he slipped between two giant roots that reached out from the trunk like gangly legs, disappearing down into the depth of a dark tunnel.

"Meow. Meow," came more rumbles, this time from under the tree.

The air remained deathly still and quiet. They looked at each other, shrugged their shoulders, and followed the cat.

* * *

As the sun continued its slow descent below the tops of the woodland trees, the shadows seemed to dance gleefully up the yielding grass and to the porch edge. The wind came once again as did the gentle bird songs.

They are on their way, thought the Professor.

He took a deep breath rocking in his rocking chair with his elf pipe in hand.

There then came a deafening sound, a hideous screech that shattered through the wind.

"Caw! Caw! Caw!"

Startled, he dropped his elf pipe.

A raven was perched on the porch railing, its feathers a deep black and its eyes a piercing yellow.

It fluttered its wings a bit to steady itself and then turned its head this way and that to better focus on the Professor.

He waved a hand at the bird looking to frighten it away.

"Wretched bird!" he shouted. "Get out of here!!"

The raven defiantly moved closer.

"Caw! Caw! What's done is done, old man. Caw!" it said, almost human words broken through the low pitches of several caws. The perverted attempt at sounding human was terrifying to hear. The bird convulsed and struggled to continue. "Caw! We are not impressed by the human children. Caw! Caw!"

He leaned forward in his chair.

"Return to your evil nest," he said. "Tell your brood brethren that their time can never come."

The bird flapped its wings lifting itself away, the waft of which brought a horrid stench to the porch.

"Caw! Caw! We shall see old man," it said in painful convulsions. "We prefer you humans dead. Caw! Caw!"

It opened its wings, gave a long and loud screech, and in an instant, was gone from the porch.

He stood and watched as the bird flew into the woodland trees, its shadow momentarily spreading darkness over the gardens.

Images flashed in his mind. The most vivid of all was of great evil armies crossing a magical land, of dark creatures ravaging a city on a vast ocean.

They seek the relic, he thought.

Then came an image of Molly holding the Lia Fail.

The stone's magic still has its way with my mind. But its hold wanes.

He thought of the girls and reminded himself of the advice he gave them.

Just do what Big Grey tells you and you will be safe.

CHAPTER 2
THE AINA DUR

THE GIRLS WERE ABOUT halfway down the dark tunnel when they saw a light amber glow flickering in the distance ahead. Behind them, the daylight that had previously seeped into the open crevice had now faded, and the sound of the wind howling through the tunnel was terrifying. The raven that had visited their uncle passed overhead and gave a loud caw, and even though the girls could not hear its horrifying screech a chill came over them for just a moment. After the chill had passed, they continued onward not knowing of the evil that came so close.

As they continued down the tunnel, traveling deeper beneath the giant tree, Molly found the path becoming dry. She reached out and touched the walls. They were smooth and not like bark or tree roots. The glow ahead became brighter as the tunnel brought them to a wooden door left ajar. Molly peeked around the door and then Elizabeth. What they saw was amazing!

"A library," said Molly. "How wonderful."

It was a beautifully proportioned room, finished in dark wood. At one end a fine marble mantel and large mirror surmounted a fireplace aglow. At the other end was an ornate desk and chair. The walls had rows of shelves each stacked with books, side-by-side, and in some places one on top of another as far as the ceiling. There were also several wooden doors, eight in all by Molly's count. Above each were oak panels carved with a series of symbols of what looked like creatures. But there was one door that was different, very different. It was worn, battered, with timbers nailed across it.

Molly looked for Big Grey, finding him in the center of the room standing by a large dark globe. She was glad to see her friend but so much about this place was strange and gone was the familiarity of the Professor's gardens.

"Big Grey," she whispered. "Where are we?"

He hunched his back and stretched forward yawning, then hunched his back again and rubbed up against the frame that held the globe. He scented the spindles of the frame with the side of his head, claiming each as his. He began to purr, the rumble shook the place.

"Come on in and close the door behind you," he said in a deep and impressive voice. "You have nothing to be frightened of. You're safe here."

The girls were so astonished that he could talk that they did not know what to say. They were in disbelief. Molly cautiously entered the room with Elizabeth huddling behind.

"My word! You can talk!" said Molly.

He lifted his nose and sniffed the air sensing the girls' hesitation.

"Well, of course, I can talk," he told them. "I have talked since I was a kitten. But here, here in this place, you can understand my language. You see all creatures were given the gifts of speech and thought by the Maker."

"Maker?"

"What you know as God."

The girls glanced at each other. As they listened to him, they were both struck by the same thought – his voice sounded familiar as if it were natural for him to sound like that.

He moved closer and sat in front of them. His purring became deeper. The girls knelt with Molly gently scratching the top of his head.

"Oh, how I love when you do that," she said slightly tilting his head. "Now, if you would . . . behind the ear," Molly obliged his request. He continued, "Ah . . . ah . . . that's it. Our journey has just started, but first, why don't we rest here a bit and catch our breath before venturing on."

He walked to the fireplace and the girls followed. They sat next to each. He carefully climbed over Molly's legs and nestled in her lap. She ran her hands through his thick grey fur and with each stroke it seemed as if his purr grew louder.

The fire was nice and warm, giving light to the room and casting shadows that curled and danced above them. Molly was still amazed at all that had happened and Elizabeth who was closer to the fireplace was glad for the warmth but increasingly curious about her surroundings.

"What is this place?" she asked.

"We are within a sacred tree called the Aina Dur," he purred. "It is a very special place because of the thousands of books. All of them here contain histories of different places from a strange land."

Molly reached back and ran her fingers along some of the leather-bound books nearest her.

"I'd so love to read them," she said. "You know how I love books."

He paused for a moment to clean. He licked his paw and brought it from behind an ear and forward to his nose, where he would wet his paw and start the process again. He did this a few more times.

"Unfortunately, you cannot read the books for they are in different ancient languages," he told them. "Perhaps one day you will learn some of them. But this place is also something much more than a library. It is also a gateway, an entryway of sorts to and from other places."

"The doors," whispered Elizabeth to Molly. "Ask him about the doors."

He overheard Elizabeth as he started to clean behind his other ear.

"Ah, the doors," he said. "The door you came through leads to the Professor's gardens. The other doors lead to different places set in different times."

But Elizabeth was much too curious a girl, and sometimes too independent. She was not much interested in the comforts of books, but rather the amusements she could discover. She could not help herself. She stood and started to explore the room. She found it very interesting and particularly the door that had timbers nailed across it.

Some impulse seemed to draw her near to it. While the other doors had textural richness and were sturdy, this door had lost much of its color. Its surface was pitted and badly scratched, and its edges were bowed, its hinges rusted.

As she got closer to the door, she heard a tiny scraping sound and a mumble from behind it. Try as she might she could not understand what was being spoken. The language was foreign to her. She leaned forward ever so slightly to peer through the door's keyhole.

"What about this door?" she asked, an eye moving closer to the keyhole. "It's different than all the others. I think I hear something."

"Noooooooooo!" bellowed the big cat.

He jumped up and dashed to the door. He shoved Elizabeth away and began gashing chunks of wood from the door with his front claws.

"Mrrrrrrrw! Mrrrrrrrw!" he roared. "Mrrrrrrrw!"

There came a thumping sound from the other side of the door.

Thump! Thump! Thump!

Using all his weight he threw himself against the splintered surface and gave a mighty roar. He did this over and over until he was knocked to the floor by a startling thump from the other side of the door.

Thump!

The room became silent, and the scratching and whispers behind the door stopped.

"That door must never be opened," he panted, firmly telling Elizabeth. "There are reasons why it is secured in this manner."

They rejoined Molly back at the fireplace as the big cat caught his breath.

"Promise me you will never open that door?" he asked with an especially sharp eye to Elizabeth, "Both of you!"

They exchanged nods.

Elizabeth felt horrible for causing such a ruckus, but the strange door had become a curiosity. She was consumed by a need to find out what was lurking behind it.

"Big Grey, what's behind it? What's the secret?" she persisted.

The cat took a deep breath.

"In time you will know. Just remember your promise to stay away from it. Now, please behave. There will be no more discussion about that vile door."

"I just don't understand. What's so important . . ." started Elizabeth.

But Molly cut her off.

"Elizabeth, please stop it!" she said chastising her sister. "Listen to Big Grey. Remember what the Professor said? You're always getting us into trouble."

"I'm always getting us into trouble?" pouted Elizabeth. "It's always me Molly. Isn't it? How about the time when . . ."

"Both of you hush now!" interrupted the cat. "Do not go running off alone. Both of you, always remember to have someone by your side."

"I'm sorry Big Grey," said Elizabeth reaching out to touch him. He drew closer to her, allowing her to give him a gentle head rub. "It's just that everything here is so strange and I'm terribly curious."

"You're always snooping around," said Molly cringing her lips at her sister.

"Listen, both of you will have to be very careful," said the cat. "Elizabeth, strangeness is not always something to be explored. There are many things you will learn. For instance, while it is true that a person should live if only to satisfy their curiosity, they must do so wisely and without harm to themselves or those they love. Let these words guide you in the coming days ahead."

He moved away from the girls and to the front of the hearth, his shadow flickering large in the room. He lifted his tail and walked across the room to a door at the far end. He turned back to them and gave a wink.

"Are you ready?" he asked.

They had seen that wink before and immediately realized that all had been forgiven. They turned to each other with a smile. Elizabeth was out of her somber state. They stood and ran across the room.

"Where are we going?" asked Molly.

"Well, go ahead and open the door and let us find out," he said.

She turned the doorknob and slowly pulled the heavy door towards her. Its hinges creaked, and dust swirled from the release of air. As she continued to open the door a brilliant light blanketed the library, and a warm sweet, scented breeze tickled her face.

"Remember, there's an adventure around every corner," purred the cat.

Molly shaded her eyes squinting into the brightness.

"Will we be back for dinner? For the birthday cake?" she asked.

He did not respond as they passed through the doorway.

* * *

In an instant, the door shut behind them, and the three found themselves in tall grasses and beneath a giant sycamore tree atop a hill that overlooked a strange land. The girls stood amazed and in disbelief as they gazed out across fields of lavender and gardenia, rich farmland, vast green forests, rivers and lakes, quaint towns and hovels, and far off in the distance, majestic white-capped mountains. At every turn, the colors were vibrant while high above in a deep blue sky fluffy white clouds danced to the melody of a gentle wind.

This was not the Professor's gardens; it was a separate world with a different reality. This location, much more than the Professor's gardens, was breathtakingly beautiful to the girls.

So, this will be the backdrop for our adventure, thought Molly.

Big Grey took a few steps forward in the tall grass. He turned to face the girls; his ears pricked forward.

"This place is called the Harrow, clear to view," he proudly declared. "You can see as far as your sight will take you."

"It's absolutely beautiful," gasped Elizabeth.

"I've never seen anything like it," said Molly.

He then went on to describe their view; the vast fields that stretched from Laurel Glen eastward to Greenvale, beyond which towered the mountains of Mortha, and then southward to Ahlgren and beyond to the Eldor, the realms of man. To the north was Blackstone Keep, the protectorate of the realms of the Harrow, and farther north beyond the mountains of the Thornback the city of Elandrake gateway to Tir Nan Og, the land of elves. Eastward and just past the hills of Thawnybire was Dagda, his homeland, and within its realm at the end of a valley stood the sacred citadel of Katzhu Pu with its four great walls and four great towers. The magnificent fortress was the home of the Ra Cath, the divine felines of the Harrow. He pointed past Dagda, to a range of mountains called the Old Hills, where nestled within its peaks was the cavernous city of Volemill, home to the race of dwarves. Farther east was the North Eldor and the rocky crags of Ragmorok, where the Ra Draug or Fenri wolf-beasts made their home at the Rakl. He paused as he was overcome with happiness. He was truly at peace in this place.

He began to purr.

"Oh, how I never grow weary of this sight," he told them.

Behind them, past the great tree, lay the vast ruins of what was once a great castle that sat on the promontory along with the great sacred tree overlooking the incredible sight. The weathered and torn ruins consisted of massive fragments of stone, worn into strange shapelessness, yet their position made them wonderfully impressive. It was beautiful in its antiquity with moss-covered stone walls that remained regal despite centuries of wear. Old as it was, its surroundings seemed far older.

Above, the girls saw the brightness of a moon, a day moon, translucent blue and white. The moon was much like the one back home except for two startling differences. It appeared to be much closer and was split open, cracked ajar as if ripped apart by another celestial orb.

"Ah, you see the Harrow's broken moon," said the big cat.

"It's so strange," said Molly. "It looks like our moon back home but scary."

Big Grey smiled.

"It is called the Shyjael Tyl," he said, "which means *that which is breached.* And yes, you are correct. It is the same moon as back home, but different in its appearance."

Molly looked at the cat in astonishment.

"If it's the same moon, then what is this place?" she asked. "Such strangeness . . . elves and dwarves and talking cats . . ."

"And wolf-beasts . . ." added Elizabeth.

The cat interrupted.

"In time you will understand," he told them. "This is a very different place, in a very different time. You will need to trust me."

The three stood in silence. It was a moment when all blades of grass, water, wood, and stone, all things were as one. It was a deep, deep silence and oneness that was almost palpable until a hummingbird flittered before them. It first stared at Elizabeth then Molly, darting up and down as if looking for something.

Molly became uneasy at the bird. She instinctively clutched at the Lia Fail tucking it from sight. The bird then darted off. They watched as it flew eastward until they could no longer see it, becoming lost in the darkness of a looming sky.

Molly pointed east in the direction the bird flew.

"There . . . the sky . . . it's a dark grey . . . almost black. Are those storm clouds?" she asked.

"Storm clouds? In a sense, yes," he said. "That is the Drueger, land of the En' Rauko, or worm brood. It is a place of great evil. The dark mountains you see are sometimes called the Crag. It is a place of wretchedness, as it is always night there where wickedness prowls for prey. It is a dismal and dank world with mountains of flesh, rivers of blood, and where the air reeks of death." He turned back looking up at the girls. "The storm you now see grows and moves west bringing with it great evil. The might of all races must now be joined to stop the menace. It is why you're here."

Elizabeth was frightened by the cat's words. She shrank behind Molly. A thought came to her that this adventure would be dangerous.

"Big Grey, stop it!" she sniffled. "You're scaring me."

Molly turned and hugged her sister who crying.

"Do not worry Elizabeth," said the cat. "You will be safe as long as you proceed with silence and alertness, while carefully observing the flow of inner and outer events."

Molly was confused at his words and somewhat angered. They made no sense to her, and yet she knew, somehow, that there was truth in them.

"You're speaking in riddles," she told him.

"It is not a riddle," he said. "It is a lesson like the kind at school. Just remember these words like you do your school lessons. There are many lessons to be learned in this place. Remember them all."

Observing the flow of inner and outer events . . . Observing the flow of inner and outer events, Molly repeated his words to herself, trying to understand their meaning. But she could not.

"I still don't understand what you mean," she said in frustration.

"Do not worry. Just remember them, and when the time comes, they will have great meaning to you," he said. "Now, both of you listen carefully. You will meet many new friends in this place. Many of them know your uncle, and many are my friends as well. When you have friends, you have not a worry ever, and nothing is impossible."

He smiled with a big grin.

Elizabeth brushed back her tears. She thought of Lil' Man. She missed the small cat and wondered where he might be.

Is he in this strange land? she thought.

She looked about and down into the grasses just to see if he was near.

"Where's Lil' Man?" she asked. "We've not seen him. Is he here or back in the Professor's gardens?"

The big cat lifted his nose to sniff the air.

"Ah yes. He is here, in this place, but far to the east, I am afraid," he said. "But do not fret for he is fleet afoot and knows his way around the eastern lands. Now, the day passes quickly. We must be off. We do not want to be late for our appointment."

"Appointment?" asked Molly.

"Why yes," he said. "We have a meeting with several of those new friends I spoke of. They will aid in determining how you can best help. We do not have much time I am afraid. Come now."

He scampered off with Elizabeth. But Molly did not immediately follow. Instead, her attention was drawn to the moon. It was so much larger than the one back home, and it hung palely in the sky. For some reason, it haunted her.

How did it split? Where are we? she thought.

Mesmerized, she could have stood there all day, but the cat was impatient. He returned to her and pressed against her ankles for attention. She smiled and bent to stroke him. She hesitated, looking back at the old tree. She remembered the Professor's words: "Somewhere, something incredible is waiting to be known."

Why did he send us here? In time I'll figure out why we're here.

She followed the cat and took her sister by the hand as the three walked down the grassy hill.

* * *

Lil' Man and his fellow feline companion Chumsey stood upon a mountain cut by a deep narrow valley that plunged to the Foghollow Barrens, and into a desolate place of grasslands stretching endlessly westward through the Eldor and north to Ragmorok. Overhanging the valley and at the fringe of the Drueger was the city of Gortha-Losh, rambling and low, with its decayed towers and battlements, built of stones hewn from the nearby mountains. It was once a city in the realm of the South Eldor but had been wrestled from the race of man, taken in fierce battle many years ago by the brood. It was now a stronghold for evil and darkness. By taking the city, the brood had removed a tactical advantage, for nearby and to the west was yet another stronghold of man, the island city of Chyh-Mehm, surrounded by the waters of Lake Mehm. In times past, an evil force marching from the east wishing to take the South Eldor would be trapped between the two cities. But with Gortha-Losh in the hands of darkness, this was no longer the case.

For the two cats and from such a distance, it was hard to discern what was in front of them. They could see movement, and dark shadows that were gathering just behind what looked to be city walls and near stone gates. Outside the gates stretched flatlands once teeming with meadows and farmland. But now the land was bleak and carpeted with the wiry turf of the downs. The land had been stripped of any value by the brood that now assembled strength in unknown numbers within the city walls.

"Chums, we must get closer," said Lil' Man.

His friend was a larger cat with a furry thick coat more orange than white, a broad and powerful neck and sturdy front legs, and a bushy orange tail with a white tip. He was not as swift as Lil' Man but had keen senses and was a powerful warrior. Both were of the Ra Cath. They were master scouts, and of the Balor, the warrior guild of Katzhu Pu, which served the protectorate of the realms. They were well-known throughout the Harrow for their cunning and knowledge of the terrain, and this was what made them exceptional at reconnaissance.

Chumsey moved closer to his friend.

"Why must we get closer?" he asked. "I don't need to see that there's a swarm of brood below. I can smell their vileness."

A frigid wind suddenly came from behind blowing furiously up over the Crag. The two cats crouched behind some rock to evade the glacial coil.

Chumsey sniffed the ground.

"We should leave this place now and report back," he said. "There's too much darkness here. For the life of me, I don't know why I agreed to accompany you on this mission."

"You agreed because you're my friend," said Lil' Man, "and if I remember your words, 'Because the damn fool needs someone to get him out of trouble.' So, let's get a little closer. Then we can leave."

With that Lil' Man slowly began his descent keeping near to the ground, his tail curled low. Chumsey followed pausing to look behind while routinely sniffing the air and ground for signs of danger.

"We must hurry," beseeched Chumsey. "I'm sensing something but unsure of what it is."

The two cats continued down the rocky precipice to a shallow just below the dark mists that hung over the city. As a crosswind ripped across the barrens, through the city, and up the Crag, the stench was almost unbearable. Chumsey pressed a paw over his nose while Lil' Man crept ever forward, his belly and tail grazing the cold hard rock ground. They came to a ledge where they huddled near each other peering down into the depths of the devastated city.

They could now see the brood gathering in the city below. They saw Cu Sith or Black Dogs, great black beasts, shaped like hounds, but larger than any hound that ever lived, with eyes that shined white in the darkness. There were Fachens, hideous muscular creatures, man-like in stature, and known for their despicable acts, a desire to inflict severe pain and suffering on their enemies. They also saw Trolls, dim-witted brutish hulks with ugly rubbery moss-green hide. They were quite evil and fed on anything that they could catch. There were Firbolgs, a dark-skinned, deformed race of man with thick black beards and long hair kept back. Their legs and arms were badly bent, and they had hunched backs, but they were surprisingly strong. It was said they were remnants of primitive man. And there were Orcs or the Gulguthra in the old tongue. These were large creatures, slightly stooped in posture, with low jutting foreheads, short-pointed ears, snouts for noses, and long, sharp teeth. They had coarse hair that covered green skin and reddish tint eyes.

"I'd guess about four legions of brood. Chums, what do you think?" asked Lil' Man.

Chumsey quickly scanned the city's depraved scene. But he was more interested in leaving the forsaken place than in accuracy.

"Yes, I'd say four legions is about right," he said, still gazing down at the city. He then came upon an unexpected sight. He was bewildered. "By the Maker. Over there! Do you see that? Near the northeast battlements. Do you see them?"

Lil' Man squinted through the wind that had become stronger. As best he could he followed the exterior stone wall to the mountain base where in one corner of the city he saw Ra Draug, or Fenri, huge wolf-beasts of great stature and ferocity. By his guess, there was a full legion of them.

"It can't be," he said. "Fenri? I don't understand. They've sworn allegiance to the forces of good."

Chumsey was nervous.

"Something is very wrong here," he warned. "Very wrong. We must go west, to Mistmere, to warn the others."

Just as he was about to tell Lil' Man they should leave, something grabbed them by the scruffs of their necks, and carrying them, raced across the rock-hardened surface and back up the mountain.

They could not see the creature that had grabbed them, but it was so much larger, and they realized that any struggle was pointless. All they could make out was the bulky coat of grey-brown fur on its large front legs.

Chumsey knew the creature. He turned to Lil' Man.

"Fenri!" he yelled.

But Lil' Man's eyes had gone cloudy and vague and soon shut in a painful faint.

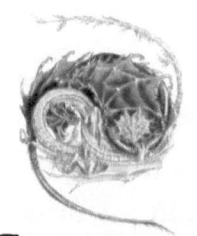

CHAPTER 3
THE FENRI PRINCE

AT LONG LAST THE Fenri wolf-beast came upon a cave, a cleft in the Crag stone opening wide before Chumsey's eyes. Still dangling from the jaws of the Fenri, he knew they were now far away from Gortha-Losh. He glanced at Lil' Man who had gone unconscious several leagues ago. He feared for his friend.

The wolf-beast stepped through a fissure in the rock and into a wide hall, his silent steps taking them deeper and deeper into winding stone galleries until he came upon a room where a small fire blazed. He flung the two cats from his mouth. They slid across the rock floor, hitting against the rough contours of the cave wall.

Chumsey shook off the pain and quickly crawled to Lil' Man who was still unconscious. He wrapped his larger body around him for warmth and licked the wounds where the Fenri's teeth had pierced his skin; much of the white fur near the neck was blood-stained. Lil' Man began to shiver and started a gentle purr. His eyes opened briefly then closed. Chumsey was worried but continued to lick the wounds until the bleeding had stopped.

Watching over was the Fenri, hovering, piercing eyes, a furious snarl. He was very large, with dark grey markings and thick fur, a chest broad with powerful shoulders, and eyes that flashed fire. Across his face ran the scars of previous battles, like badges of honor. He paced and with each step he growled. It was a growl like a menacing thunderstorm in the distance, a drumming of the sky to land.

"Who are you?" he sneered.

Even though the enormous beast was some five paces away from Chumsey, the small brave cat knew there was no chance of escaping, especially since Lil' Man was injured. He hurriedly considered his options but knew there was little he could do or say that would fool or deceive the wolf-beast.

The Fenri knows we are not from the Crag, he thought. *There is only one thing to do.*

He stood and faced the large beast. At first, he was frozen in fear at the Fenri's size, but he mustered all the strength he could and stared the beast down.

"I am Chum Sey Balor El Ta, the youngest of my litter. I am of the warrior guild of Katzhu Pu," he said. "My friend here is Oban Pan Balor El Tar. He is the oldest of his litter. He is of the warrior guild as well."

The Fenri closed in on Chumsey, backing him up against Lil' Man and the cave wall. He glared down at him and opened his mouth, his large, curved teeth thick with saliva dripping over curled lips.

"What brings two puny Balor Guild kitties to the Crag?" he roared. "Tell me quickly or I will make a snack of you and your bloodied friend!"

"We are on a reconnaissance mission, sent by the Guild Lords. We have been tracking the movements of the brood for the past several days."

The Fenri stared intently at Chumsey.

"Tracking? The mighty Balor sends trackers?" he said, baring his teeth.

Sensing the wolf was ready to fight, Chumsey brought his ears back and crouched, ready to leap at the beast.

"Go ahead you brute. Kill us now and be done with it," he hissed, "but by the I' Ra Heru I warn you – I will take parts of you with me to my death bed!"

"Do not look to your creator for help little one. He is not here. He has never been here."

"Perhaps, but after I am done with you, he will welcome me into the light, and I will be honored by Ra Carathor."

The Fenri growled. He slowly backed away from Chumsey while a pack of Fenri appeared from behind the fire. The colors of the wolf pack wcrc heightened, burning until they were an iridescent glow in the shadows of the blaze.

"Captain, we've returned," said one of the Fenri stepping forward. "The brood is on the move from Gortha-Losh. They send scouts west."

The wolf-beast maintained his stare on Chumsey. He moved closer to him, his teeth drawn back over blood-red gums.

"Can't you see?" he told the one Fenri. "I am busy now."

But the one Fenri persisted.

"Do you require anything? Help with anything?" he asked.

The wolf-beast turned to the one Fenri and gave a mighty roar of frustration.

Chumsey recoiled at the sound and cruel fangs. He saw cold anger in his eyes, and his face was set with fury.

Why are they here? Why do they follow the brood? thought Chumsey.

The Fenri quickly turned back to Chumsey with the kind of stare intended to strike fear.

"Grrrrrrrrrrr," he rumbled.

But Chumsey refused to show any fear. He met the stare with a resolute expression of bravery.

The wolf-beast tilted his head a bit, looking down deeply into Chumsey's eyes. It was as if he was trying to look into his soul. Every experience he had ever had was telling him he should be wary of the two cats. His brow furrowed as he debated whether Chumsey was lying to him. But something deep within him made him believe otherwise. All he could feel was extraordinary bravery and spirit in Chumsey.

"My little kitty, there is courage in you," he growled, low and menacing. "More courage than one as small as you should have. It is true what they say about the fearlessness of the Katzhu Pu warrior guild. You are fierce even in the face of horrendous odds. On this day, I have no need for your blood."

Chumsey took a deep sigh of relief.

The wolf-beast turned to the one Fenri and the others.

He shouted out orders, "Bring some vermin for our little guests. The rest of you - back to your positions. We leave at dawn."

"Thank you," said Chumsey.

"I hope Crag vermin is to your liking. It is fatty but it is all we have on this forsaken stone. You may stay here by the warmth of our fire and tend to your friend until he is well. My pack departs at daybreak, but I will leave one of my soldiers to guard your safe passage from this place."

"My friend and I appreciate your assistance," said Chumsey. "But we saw something strange. We saw Fenri alongside brood within the city walls. How can this be? The Fenri are aligned with those of the good and righteous. What's happening?"

The wolf-beast sat back on his haunches and took a deep breath. There was despair in his eyes.

"So, I see word has not reached Katzhu Pu or Blackstone of the treason at the Rakl," he said. Chumsey shook his head. "I guess our allies have forsaken us then. Well, so be it. We Fenri are strong and will survive!"

"Treason, you say. What treason?" asked Chumsey.

"You do not know who I am do you?"

"No. I'm afraid not. Should I?"

"I suppose not. I am Thurir, son to Threch, King of the Ra Draug."

Chumsey recognized the name. Prince Thurir was well known for his prowess as a fighter and his skill in the art of war. It was said he was well equipped to face any threat, and feared by all, even by many of his kind.

"You're Prince Thurir?"

The Fenri nodded.

"I am sorry I did not know."

"Maybe that's best these days," said Thurir, "with everything that's occurred."

Occurred? thought Chumsey.

Chumsey returned to what Thurir had earlier said.

"You spoke of treason," he said. "What treason?"

"Several months ago, my father was betrayed," said Thurir, words slipping from his lips in a whisper, "betrayed by my younger brother, the one called Tharum, who now hails himself as King. My brother's betrayal occurred while I was on patrol with my pack to the northern regions of Ragmorok." He stared off into the cave's darkness. "Upon my return, I was unable to enter the Rakl, turned away by my brother's pack. Of my father's fate, we do not know. Word has come that he was killed at the hands of a dark minion."

A pang of sorrow came over Chumsey as he heard the sadness in Thurir's voice.

"The Ra Cath has great respect for King Threch," said Chumsey. "He is well known as a Fenri of honor and a powerful fighter and possessed of the kindness of hearts."

"My father is my life," said Thurir. "I owe him not only my birth but all my achievements since. He is the master of our proud race, and we revel in our independence. But once he committed to those of the west, agreeing to a pact with the Edainar and the others, something unexpected happened. We were visited by Varul Teardash . . ."

"A Dark Wizard," muttered Chumsey in horror.

He had heard of Teardash, of his failed insurrection against the wizards of the Edainar, and his banishment to the Drueger.

"Varul Teardash," growled Thurir, "dreaded servant to the Shadow that thunders in the sky. I did not want him to enter the Rakl but he cut his way through our packs using sorcery and found an ally in my brother. Soon he became an advisor to my father. I swear on the souls of my ancestors that he held my father under an evil influence, one which I could not break.

"Over time, my father became a puppet under the hands of the Dark Wizard. Movements of our pack legions fell under Teardash's directions, and we saw less of my father. It was as if he had disappeared. Then Tharum declared himself King and banished us from the Rakl. When I received word of our banishment, I attempted to return but was turned away. I decided to fight for another day. We hid within the stone mountains of Ragmorok and watched . . . and watched . . . and watched . . . as pack legion after pack legion left the Rakl. We could not follow them all because they went in separate directions, but we did track most of them to this barren place.

"Little kitty, of this there can be no denial – darkness has returned and it is preparing to wage war against all that is good. It is gathering brood and now with the Fenri will enslave all the races. For me I say, let them wage their war.

For when they do, I will return to the Rakl and take what is mine. Tharum has spread his numbers too thin. In two days, we will return to the stone of Ragmorok and retake the Rakl. I will restore honor to the Ra Draug."

Chumsey thought over what he had heard. The circumstances were indeed ominous. He knew it would not be easy for Thurir to retake his homeland, especially against the power of a Dark Wizard, an entity both revered and feared. He wondered if, instead, Thurir could be persuaded to take a different course of action.

"My friend, you are most powerful," he told Thurir. "You are fearless and ruthless, one who has never spared the guilty, or ever flinched from the shedding of blood. But perhaps your strategy is a faulty one. Many packs may have left your homeland, but I am sure some remain along with a Dark Wizard. You must proceed with caution. It is clear to me that Teardash will hold the Rakl at all costs, and you and your pack are helpless against his vile enchantment. I would say the odds are against you. You once thought better and decided to fight for another day. I would say that holds true even today. There would be no gain in your death or the death of your pack. But some alternative strategies and tactics might produce the results you desire."

Thurir laughed.

"Listen to the great warrior strategist of Katzhu Pu," he said mockingly, frustration gripping his tone. "Where were you when Teardash came? Where were your great warriors when the menace cast his spell on my father? Where were the great armies of the good, or the wizards of the Edainar to defend the Fenri?"

Chumsey understood the frustration, the direct and blunt words. He would not hide from it, nor would he try to assuage the feelings. He would try his best to explain himself, to try to make Thurir understand that he was only trying to help. He would have to tell him the truth.

"Listen carefully to my words," he said. "I cannot speak to the decisions of the past. I can only ask that you look at the reality of your situation. You cannot retake the Rakl. Teardash and Tharum will have at least three legions if not more to protect the Rakl from invasion. Your pack will be torn apart in seconds. The darkness wants the whole of the Harrow, not just Gortha-Losh or Ragmorok. It won't let you or any other Fenri royal bloodline control Ragmorok. This decision has already been made and cannot be altered. I think you know this."

Thurir listened attentively. He understood what Chumsey was saying. It was a difficult reality he had often thought, one he refused to face. He gingerly placed a large paw over Chumsey's, staring off into the fire.

"I have come to realize that when faced with a choice of path," he said, "there is a challenge in listening to reason and emotion at the same time. My father taught me there would be times when I must set aside my emotions. I remember his words. He called it the 'sorting which evens things out.' I know you are right. There is truth in what you say brave cat, a truth I have found too easy to avoid.

"I have been at a loss since our banishment. My anger and frustration have blinded me, and I have avoided how to best direct such emotions. This world of ours has gone mad and it is my nature to do something, to strike back and avenge the honor of the Fenri. It is our way."

"I understand," said Chumsey. "But at times like these, the best offense is sometimes a keen defense. Journey with me and my friend on our mission. We will travel first to Mistmere to warn them of the darkness, and then to the lands west and to Katzhu Pu. There we will gain wisdom and the strength of numbers. Right now, there is little you can do against such odds."

He looked at Thurir and saw the hesitation in his eyes that said it was not that simple. But Thurir gave a reluctant nod.

It was then when one of the other Fenri laid vermin carcasses before Chumsey. Thurir smiled widely.

"I know it is not a tasty stew," he told Chumsey. "There is no shiny rainbow of sweet grease floating on top, but it is all we have. Let us hope for some tastier fare in Mistmere."

Chumsey looked down at the vermin. His mouth began to water.

"This is more a feast than we've had in days," he said.

He turned back to Lil' Man who began to stir as he started to awaken.

"Your friend seems to improve," said Thurir. "Please, eat, and let me hear more of your plans."

* * *

The raven did not have far to go. It rode the stiff winds that swept across the Foghollow Barrens, and there it floated in the air effortlessly until a massive updraft caught it and lifted it up and over the Crag. Once over the sharp whitecaps, it continued southward over the Drueger's wastelands and through the blackened mists until it could see the dark tower of Ug' Cthuth, home to the worm brood; its hardened grey stone surface taking on different shades of darkness as it flew closer. But as the air became heavy, it veered away from the shadowy tower. It made its way deeper into the murkiness and through what now were pitch-black mists until it came to a clearing where a second soaring tower appeared.

Taller than Ug' Cthuth, the black tower Urth' Goroth was an enormous fortress of untold evil chiseled from the sheer sides of a mass of mountains behind it. Made of hard stone and rusted metal, its gates opened to a walled series of battlements and smaller towers within which the sounds of furnaces and forges could be heard. The very top of the tower was ringed with mottled metal posts. At the center, burned a colossal fire that gave off thick smoke and soot that drifted about eerily, crafting a veil of death.

At the tower's base, a long and narrow road led from a gate, lined with spikes atop which were the decayed heads of creatures who either served or rebuked the tower's master. On both sides of the road and surrounding the tower for leagues were pits of black filth and sludge seeping to the surface through fissures in the land's crust. No creature other than worm brood could live near this place for the vile stench and sticky pools were deadly.

The raven circled the summit of the black tower until through the gloom it could see the Dark Lord emerge from the fire, dark and cloaked in a voluminous black hooded robe. It hovered a bit until its master held out a hand for it to perch. Slowly it drifted downward and then fluttered to a gentle landing on the master's gloved hand.

"My friend," said the dark figure, a deep but soft voice, "I am so glad to see you. Tell me, what have you seen?"

"My master, I bring you news of the forces that have gathered against you," said the raven. "Your adversaries assemble across the land to plot strategy, but armies have yet to form. Your reappearance is a point of contention"

The shadowy one was amused and chuckled.

"Oh, my friend they know I am here," he said. "It is just that some are blind to the fact and choose not to believe that I have returned." He brought the bird closer to the cavernous blackness that shrouded his face and whispered, "But tell me. What of the Professor?"

"The old fool sends two children, girls of fair skin and innocence," said the raven.

The master nodded.

"Yes. Does he join them? Did you see the red stone?" he asked.

"The old male human stays behind in his world. From what I could see the children were unadorned."

"Ah, you have served your master well. Now it is time for you to rest."

The evil one gently stroked the bird, once, twice, and then on the third stroke grasped its neck and with a quick and powerful twist, snapped it like a twig. The bird's pain was sharp and burned, but only briefly. It gasped then fell limp in its master's hand.

The dark figure took a couple of steps forward and was at the edge of the summit facing west. He slowly turned his hand over dropping the carcass through the murky mists and into the slime pits below.

He looked up into the dark mists. Far away in the shadows torn by gusts of wind and whirling demon clouds he could see the flitter of a small bird, a hummingbird struggling against the forces to find its master. He could see it hover, holding its body upright, its wings a blur of motion. It tilted flat for a moment then darted off toward him.

Another messenger with news, he thought.

"Ah, my diminutive friend. Come to me," he beckoned reaching out with an open hand. "Come to me. Come to me."

The hummingbird darted up and then down a bit, still struggling against the winds, but eventually found its way into its master's gloved hand.

The bird was excited to be home.

"My master, I have journeyed long and have word," said the bird. "Two human children have emerged from the tree with the fat cat. They are girls, one of which possesses what you seek. I saw the jewel. I saw it. It hangs from the oldest child's neck, red and glorious."

The dark one sighed.

"Thank you, my friend. It is as I expected. Your journey has yielded information most helpful," he said in a soothing voice. He gently stroked the small bird, careful not to hurt it. He then brought it closer. "My friend, you must be tired. Now, rest."

The hummingbird felt its master's loving hands, its heart beating strong.

"Oh, thank you," it said. "I have missed you. I have missed your touch."

"So sweet of you to say such a thing."

The bird settled into the shadowy palm, grateful to be back home, warmed by a soothing caress, which grew deeper and deeper, that is, until a sudden tightening of fingers crushed it into a small heap of bones and feathers.

There was no shriek of pain, not even a gasp, only deathly silence. The dark one swung his hand open, tossing the shattered remains into the raging winds.

The sinister Dark Lord, the Szard, had heard the words he most feared. The Lia Fail was once again in the Harrow having been protected for years by the Professor. He was aware of the stone's power, which, if properly used, could destroy him.

It is as the shiny creature said. A child possesses the stone. But can she learn how to use it? Will she use it? Power is a difficult thing to control.

He turned his thoughts to the Professor. He knew him as a worthy adversary, for he was cunning and experienced in the history of the land, and such a worthy adversary should be addressed with swift dispatch.

But he stays behind and far from my reach. For what purpose? No matter. I have a plan. I always have a plan. The stone will be mine, mine to use.

There came a slithering sound from behind, like the sound of a great snake coiling around a rock. The sound came slowly from the fire, stopping from time to time. It was a sound familiar to the tower's evil master.

"The Professor refuses to face his death," said a haunting voice, like that of an old woman. "The oldest of the girls will be Queen of Ahlgren. My love, you must keep to your plan."

"Yes," he said, "plans within plans within plans."

He stood motionless in thought, looking back at the mountains that crept near the tower's metal crown, then down to the black pits of the Ordraar where the pools of filth bubbled and churned spewing forth a winged creature. It was an eagle. At first, it struggled to wrench itself free from the sticky pits but then unfurled its wings flailing them about casting the black tar-like substance from its feathers. Its wings soon lifted it higher and higher still until it reached the summit and the outstretched hand of the Szard.

"Ah, there you are my friend," said the dark one. "I have a mission for you."

* * *

While strolling down the grassy hill Big Grey described all that lay before the girls, and he answered their questions. He told them that they were off to Laurel Glen, a sleepy hamlet where they would meet with two friends who would aid their journey. From Laurel Glen, they would continue to Blackstone Keep and once there they would have an important meeting with more friends. This made the girls anxious but Big Grey told them that they were not to worry, and everything would be fine.

Near the bottom of the hill, they saw a peculiar fellow, a bobbin, a smallish person shorter than the girls. He was stocky with sturdy legs, wearing red pants with green suspenders and a red plaid shirt. His feet and ankles were wrapped in heavy brown cloth leggings, and atop his head was a flat-crowned straw hat. He had a long nose, and a soft brownish beard, with an appearance more like a child than an adult. On his back was a canvas satchel the straps of which wrapped under his arms. In it were several wooden sticks.

As he started up the hill, he saw the girls. He stopped, staring at them. Of course, they stopped and stared back. He smiled, and they smiled back. They were not afraid. They were more curious, having never seen a bobbin before.

He made his way to them, unknowingly passing Big Grey who was hidden by the tall grass.

"My dear Qinn Farlerstock," said the cat. "It is so good to see you on such a fine day."

The bobbin was startled at hearing the voice. He recognized it.

"Oh my . . . oh my!" he said searching for the cat. "Oh, there you are. Master Sech Tur, it is you. I did not see you in the tall grasses. I was just noticing . . ."

". . . the children?" said Big Grey finishing the bobbin's thought.

The bobbin stared at the girls.

"Why, yes," he said. "I've not seen such tall ones in these parts except for when men visit, and that's not often these days."

He moved closer to Molly looking at her face and then to Elizabeth. He reached up with a hand to touch her face, but she flinched, and he brought his hand back to his side.

He turned to the cat.

"These children are not from these parts," he said. "Are they children of man, the En' Edan?"

Big Grey nodded. He was going to respond but Molly cut him off.

"Wait a minute," she said looking at the bobbin. "What did you just call him?"

"Call him?" he asked.

"You called him something. It was like a name."

He bowed his head.

"Oh, my child, I called our furry friend here in the manner he called me, by his proper name of course – Master Sech Tur," he said.

"Proper name," she said looking down at Big Grey. "You never told us you had a proper name."

The cat rubbed against her legs.

"There are many things I have not told you, as you will discover," he said. "Here, in this place, all creatures have proper names, just as you and Elizabeth have proper names. My proper name is Sech Tur Midir El Tar. Sech Tur is the name given to me by my mother and means grey son.

El Tar means I am the oldest of the litter, and Midir is the cat guild I belong to."

"Cat guild? What's that?" asked Molly.

"Think of it as a group of cats, engaged in kindred pursuits. Here, each cat is a member of a guild. There are four guilds in all. There is a guild of lawgivers called the Midir, a warrior guild called the Balor, a guild of mystics and sages called the Caridwen, and the Belenus which is a guild of healers. The guilds give us purpose, and they define who we are."

Molly remembered he used the word Midir in his name.

"So, you're a lawgiver then?" she asked.

"Oh, our large furry friend is much more than just a lawgiver," said the bobbin. "Dare I say, not a decision is made without his advice and counsel. And we have many other names for our grey friend. Most call him Big Purr or Big Grey. What do you call him?"

"Why we call him Big Grey and Big Purr, too," said Elizabeth.

The bobbin laughed.

"Well, there you have it then," he said. "He is the same wherever he goes."

He decided to rest a bit, gently releasing the satchel from his back, and sitting within the tall grasses. He welcomed the girls to the Harrow and commented on how lovely a day it was and how the lavender and gardenia fields were most fragrant this year. He told them that Farmer Brackenbush was so proud of his crop that he would most likely allow the girls to pick a bouquet of gardenias and lavender if they asked politely.

"My good Master Farlerstock, thank you, but we have no time for that," said Big Grey. "We must be at Blackstone within two days."

The bobbin rubbed his hairy chin.

"Ah, as I guessed," he said, "to talk about the storm no doubt. It's on everyone's mind. Not a day goes by without a tale from the east of black creatures and evil stirrings. I've been told there have even been sightings of an ajatar over Mortha Vale, and at night there's wickedness in the air."

"What's an ajatar?" Elizabeth asked Big Grey.

"An ajatar is what you would call a dragon. Most are known to be evil," he said. "They are much like serpents and cause pestilence and disease. They spew fire and death."

The bobbin had a puzzled look about him.

"Well, if you've never heard of an ajatar you're not from here," he said.

"My dear Quinn, they are the Professor's nieces," said Big Grey.

"Oh, yes, the Professor. There's been talk of him. Folks in these parts are afraid. They fear it's not safe anymore, but they say that the Professor will help us. He always has."

"You know the Professor?" asked Molly.

"Well, of course, I do child," said the bobbin. "He's a good friend and he's protected us for ages."

"He sent us here," said Elizabeth. "For an adventure."

The bobbin thought a bit. He seemed confused.

"Sent you here?" he said. "So, you're children of man, from under the tree." He looked down at the cat. "Master Grey, children . . . to the Harrow . . . instead of the Professor?"

"Qinn, the Professor is aging," said the cat. "He cannot make visits to the Harrow as he once had. My friend, have faith. He knows what he is doing."

"Master Grey, indeed, age is a difficult enemy to overcome. It eventually gets the best of us all. And who would dare to question the Professor." The bobbin looked up at the sky. "Ah, the day moves along at a steady pace and I'm afraid my work never ends."

After a few short pleasantries, the bobbin returned the satchel to his back, hailed the three a fond farewell, and started up the hill toward the tree. They watched as he struggled a bit climbing the grassy hill.

"Well, he was an odd little man," said Elizabeth.

"He was very cordial," said Molly. "I've never seen a bobbin before, and I think I like them. But Big Grey, why does he carry wood to the tree?"

"Master Farlerstock holds a very important position here in the Harrow," he said. "He is the realm's Firekeeper. He is responsible for stoking the hearth in the library under the tree, keeping it aflame and the room warm and bright. So, he must carry wood from the land up the hill and to the tree, every day."

"That sounds like a difficult job. How many times a day must he do this?" asked Elizabeth.

"I do not know. Perhaps, three or four times each day I guess, during daylight and nighttime. Is it difficult work? I suppose so. But his work is essential to the safety of all that is good in the Harrow."

Molly stopped and turned back to look at the bobbin one last time. He had now almost reached the top of the hill and was making his way to the giant tree.

"How so?" asked Molly. "How's it essential?"

Big Grey stared up the hill to the Aina Dur.

"The library under the tree is a trove of ancient knowledge," he said. "The books you saw describe the history of the Harrow, and within those pages, one can find knowledge. Many of the books tell of heroic adventures and times long past, of how wars were fought, or how great structures were built. But there are some books that contain a most dangerous knowledge - spells, incantations, and wicked thoughts of madmen. The fire that he keeps aflame sheds light on all revealing what is good and what is evil. Without light knowledge is distorted.

"What you need to understand is that possessing knowledge does not make you wise. Many men know a great deal and are all the greater fools for it. The greatest fool known to all is a knowing fool. You see, knowing how to use knowledge is to have wisdom. Now, let us continue while we have daylight. We have not far to reach Laurel Glen."

The cat quickly turned from them, not giving them a chance to question him further on the library, the hearth, or the Firekeeper. He continued his way through the fields of lavender and gardenia while Molly and Elizabeth followed.

But the girls had plenty of questions.

"I've been meaning to ask you," said Elizabeth. "If everyone here has a proper name, what's Lil' Man's?"

"Oh, he is called Oban Pan Balor El Tar," said the cat.

She stopped to think. She remembered his explanation of the Guilds.

"A warrior?" she whispered to Molly.

Molly just shrugged her shoulders in disbelief and giggled.

The three continued their journey through beautiful fields and woods, finding themselves on a road that led them into the leafy town of Laurel Glen. To any visitor, it seemed like any other quaint town: narrow cobblestone roads, a pub, bakeries, quiet tea shops, inns, and off the main road were small stone houses surrounded by hedgerows crisscrossing the land. There were ionic porticoes, elms, tavern signs, small-paned windows, flower boxes, and thatched roofs, all guarded by the sleepless sentinel of tall, stone spires through the elms. There was a serenity and quiet beauty about the place.

Upon entering the town, they saw bobbins of varying shapes and colored garb going about their daily business, working, talking about the news, some smoking their pipes while others sat with a drink. There were also cats about the place; some perched on fences or at doors, some walking the streets and some here and there sniffing the ground, while others talked with townsfolk or amongst themselves.

They walked on hoping they would go unnoticed, but it did not take long for the townsfolk to take notice of them, and there were stares and whispers. Many recognized Big Grey.

"Master Cat," said a man with a tip of his hat.

"Master Grey," said another, politely, with a gentle bow.

Cats also noticed him. They would purr and give a slight bow of the head.

"Good day, Lawgiver," they would say.

In passing, Big Grey would respectfully greet each bobbin and cat with a nod, asking how they were doing, and how their children were.

"Good," they would remark. "It's been some time since you visited our town. Glad you are here."

The girls smiled at all this. They realized that he held a place of great importance and respect in this world. They could see it in the way he looked at them and in the way he spoke to them.

"Purr, I just got to thinking," said Elizabeth. "Are all these people from under the tree? I mean do they come from other places?"

"Some do but others are part of this world. Many of the cats you see come from our world, from under the tree, and yet many were born here. Remember, here, all cats are of the Ra Cath, which means they're of the race of felines."

"What about the bobbins?" asked Molly.

"They are of a race native to this place," he said. "You will see many creatures in the Harrow, many of which are native to this world."

"And the birds?" asked Elizabeth.

"Again, some are native, but others come from our world," he said. "The winged creatures are of the race called En' Raama. Do you remember the library and the doors?"

The girls nodded.

"Yes, you called them gateways," said Molly.

"Exactly. The doors lead to other worlds. So, you never really know who is from another world and who is native to this place. I will tell you this; there's something very unique about the Harrow."

Elizabeth laughed.

"Well, if those aren't the silliest words I've ever heard," she said. "Big Purr, *everything* about this place is very unique."

He joined in the frivolity with a chuckle.

"Well, that is most certainly true," he said. "I guess when you first come here everything seems very unique indeed. I have been visiting for so long now I have forgotten what it must seem like to new visitors." He then spoke in a hushed tone, saying, "But there is something I want to tell you, something very important. When you are here, back home, time stops."

"What do you mean?" asked Molly.

"I do not know how or even why, but when you are here for days or even months, when you return home it is as if you have been away for only a few minutes. And there is something else - any afflictions you may have back home disappear while you're here."

"Afflictions?" asked Elizabeth.

"He means like a sickness or disease," said Molly.

"Precisely," he said. "Like with Lil' Man. You know how small he is and how sometimes he becomes very ill? Well, that does not happen here. In this place, he is fit."

Elizabeth thought for a bit.

"Do we stop growing when we're here?" she asked.

"Don't be silly," he laughed. "While you are here time does not stop. Here a day is a day, a week is a week, and so on." He lifted a paw to the sky. "See, there is a sun and at night the moon and stars. So, time moves on and you continue to grow while you are here. But when you return home, you will go back to the age you were when you left. And everything you remember about home will be the same as the day we ventured under the tree."

"I get it," said an enthused Elizabeth. "So, someone could stay here until they get very, very old, and then go back under the tree and when they get home, they're young again, the same age as when they left."

"Yes, yes, that is right," he said. "But most do not stay here to grow old. For you see, as much as those who visit the Harrow enjoy it here, after some time they find that they miss their friends and family and wish to return home. This place is but an escape."

"So, when we get back, we'll be the same age as when we left, but will we have changed? I mean, will we be different in some way?" asked Molly.

"As with everything, our experiences change us," said the cat. "You will remember everything that had happened to you, everything you have seen, and you will grow from it all."

She understood what he was saying.

"That's what I'd like to do," she said. "Remember every moment so that I can learn from it."

He gave a growled chirp as cats sometimes do and they continued down the road.

"Is it possible that some creatures have stayed here forever?" asked Molly.

"I do not know," he said. "I suppose it would not matter, now, would it? I mean does it matter where one grows old?"

The girls did not answer. Molly had never thought about aging, but she remembered something the Professor had told them about growing young. It was a rainy day, and the girls were playing inside. They asked the Professor to play with them. He told them he couldn't since he was growing young. "You mean growing old, don't you?" Molly asked him. He only grinned. "Experience is the greatest teacher of all," he told them. "If you believe that your ability to learn is boundless, you will grow young each day, not old."

"Elizabeth, I think we're growing young," she told her sister.

Elizabeth laughed. She also remembered what the Professor said.

At the end of the main cobblestone road, they came to a beautiful park. They could see trails past meadows, through woods, and a gently meandering creek. But past the park, the terrain became untidy with huge rock formations, caves, and waterfalls. The road became uneven and packed with leaves, dirt, and gravel. Nestled within this tapestry was their destination, The Cauldron and Scroll Inn.

The inn was well-known throughout the Harrow for its warm hospitality and beautiful views of the ancient forest of Cairn Dale. It was a large structure, three floors tall, and made of stone. Deep green ivy wrapped itself about the rough stonework and the windows. A short pathway to the front entry was flanked by cherry trees that bordered the sweep of a groomed lawn and the majesty of the mountains.

"We will stay here tonight then make our way to our destination when the sun rises. Shall we go in?" said the cat.

Elizabeth gave a polite curtsey.

"Why of course Lawgiver," she giggled.

Molly rolled her eyes. She gently pushed Elizabeth from behind and immediately felt the Lia Fail begin to throb. She looked down at it and saw that it was glowing a deep red. She touched it and it felt warm.

She looked at the park ahead and the inn. She felt surprisingly calm. She felt that she was beginning to change in this strange land; that she was beginning to mature and to gain a sense of strength, even during this time of strangeness.

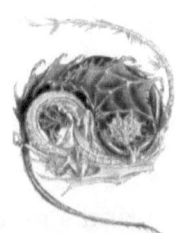

CHAPTER 4
THE CAULDRON AND SCROLL INN

THROUGH THE DOORS AND onto a gleaming reddish plank floor, the three entered the enormous foyer of the inn. From above, balconied arched windows draped in rich fabric overlooked the eclectic space of vibrant walls and whimsical folk art. All about were colorful quilts, quirky patterned pillows thrown about large, cushioned chairs, fragrant flowers, and brilliantly colored pottery that was scattered about on wooden tables. At one side of the foyer, a large doorway led to a smoke-filled lounge, which already was crowded and with sounds of cheer and song. A little farther down was a smaller doorway leading to a paneled sitting room with shelving stacked high with books. Another doorway opened to a dining room with wallpaper of burnt orange and bright blue colors, and a large wooden table with the sparkle of crystal and silver hinting at pleasures to come. There were fragrant flowers, richly layered fabrics, and wall coverings that formed a bewitching backdrop for a wondrous collection of art and antiques. Nearest to them was a crackling fire from a stone fireplace, fronted by comfortable seating and rugs, and above the fireplace was a painting of the original innkeeper, Gorba Gringshek, smiling down approvingly.

A paunchy and jowly bobbin from behind the innkeeper's front desk saw Big Grey.

"Master Purr," he shouted. "So good to see you. Welcome!"

He wore dark pants and a green shirt, most of which was covered by a soiled apron, his belly rounded pertly from the tightly tied apron string.

The cat walked over to the desk.

"Ah, good Master Norba Gringshek," he said. "It is nice to be back."

"You're looking well and fit as always," said Norba.

Big Grey crouched as if to jump, then lifted his head to better judge the distance to the top of the desk. He returned down to his crouch and settled his back legs underneath him, wiggling them a bit, a bit more, until he sprang high into the air, landing softly on the desk.

"Well, as it regards healthy and fit – I am not quite sure about that. I enjoy my food all too much," he said. As Norba rubbed his side, he offered a wink and purred, asking, "And how is your good wife, Porla?"

"Oh, she's fine and would give you her regards in person if she were here. She's in Portmoor visiting our daughter Mora." Norba bent closer to the cat, and whispered, "Last year, another addition to the Gringshek family, don't you know."

"Well, congratulations. How many grandchildren does this make?"

Norba gave a great belly laugh.

"Ha, ha, ha . . . well, I've lost count," he said. "Not enough . . . never enough. The more the merrier, you know, to care for me in my old age."

"Give my best to your lovely wife and Mora. I have not been to Portmoor in some time. Next time I am there, I will see to it that I visit with them."

"Please do. Mora always enjoys your company," said Norba. The potbellied bobbin glanced over at Molly and Elizabeth and with a twinkle in his eyes said, "Oh, and a hearty hello to you fine ladies. Welcome to my fine establishment."

The girls smiled. Molly introduced herself.

"Thank you, my name is Molly," she said. "We're delighted to be here."

Norba gave a huge smile.

"Well, welcome Molly, and I'm glad you're here," he said. He turned to Elizabeth. "And you must be her sister, Elizabeth."

"How did you know?" asked Elizabeth.

Norba chuckled as he petted Big Grey.

"Well, because your friend here made reservations for you at my fine establishment," he said. "Surely you're both famished over your long journey. Eh?"

"Yes, we are!" gleamed Elizabeth with excitement.

"Well, then make your way to our dining room and take a seat. We've already prepared a feast for your enjoyment."

"What do you eat here?" asked Elizabeth.

Norba gave a hearty laugh.

"Ha, ha, ha . . . well, my young lady our feast includes steak, meat stew, mushroom soup, stalks of fresh greens, bread cakes, and a sweet berry pie to tickle your sweet tooth. At my inn, you'll indulge in rich flavors and generous portions . . . and . . ."

"And if you are not careful," said Big Grey, "you will leave forty pounds heavier."

Norba gave another hearty laugh as the cat rubbed up against him.

"Ha, ha, ha . . . and this from the largest cat in the Harrow, who admits to his love of food," he said. "I suppose you're going to blame my fine cooking for your girth."

The cat shook his head with a smile.

"Berry pie?" said Molly in delight, looking at Elizabeth. "Did you say berry pie? That sounds scrumptious."

"Ah, a sweet tooth. Now, no more talk, you two. Into the dining room with both of you," chuckled Norba.

The girls dashed off to the dining room. A booth was already set up in the corner, complete with beautiful tableware, linen napkins, and a feast of exquisite elegance and colossal extravagance. A wooden table was piled with plates and bowls of food, and the girls spent what seemed like hours eating, drinking, and chatting about all they had seen. A bobbin server would emerge with trays of more food as soon as one dish or bowl was empty.

The innkeeper looked down at Big Grey.

"A lot of energy, those two," he said.

"Indeed. They will need it, my friend," said the cat.

He looked over the room in a glance and took in every face. Serving women drifted in and out of the kitchens with food and drink, while patrons were intent on talking and laughing. No one seemed to notice him.

"Have the others arrived?" he asked.

Norba became serious and gave a nod, motioning across the large room to the doorway leading to the sitting room.

"Both arrived late yesterday and have been waiting for you. I told them where you wanted them to be seated. But be warned," he sighed. "The little one is as ornery as ever."

The cat bounded from the front desk and made his way to the sitting room.

"What a surprise," he said sarcastically. "You will look after the two young ladies for me?"

"Of course," shouted Norba. "Good luck with the little one."

The cat smiled at the innkeeper and entered the sitting room, hesitating at the doorway and then moving onward but ever so cautiously. This was a mysterious room, one with magical powers designed to slowly draw the visitor in while leaving the outside world behind with each forward step. It was a room within many rooms. As a visitor first entered, they passed into a moderately large, somewhat darkened room, with paneled walls and stacked bookshelves, the center of which was completely open to a lower level and protected by a railing all around.

He walked around to the back, noticing the many old paintings hanging on the walls, paintings that documented the lives and travels of the inn's many visitors. In the back was a grand wooden staircase that led to a circular room below, centered about a life-size bronze statue of a wizard, and along the lower level edge were antique chairs, and there were artifacts mounted on the walls and even the ceiling, and doorways into more rooms.

Looking downstairs through the railing, he discovered the two friends he sought, a bobbin and a tall man. They were sitting where the innkeeper had instructed, at a table in a cozy alcove with a wood-carved sculpture of the Professor hanging from the wall.

The bobbin saw him. He was older than most bobbins and was smoking a long, curled elf pipe. He had thick bushy white eyebrows, so bushy and large they covered most of his forehead. Even though elderly, he still retained child-like features, soft skin, and calming eyes.

"Ah, there he is now," he gruffed. "Master Purr, what's taken you so long? Time is of the essence!"

"Now, now," said the tall man. "He has journeyed long and is most likely tired, much the way that I tire of your attitude."

The man had a long white beard and wore a bluish-grey cloak and pointed hat. There was a long crooked wooden staff that leaned up against the side of his chair.

The bobbin was agitated, frantically puffing on his pipe.

"Tired? Tired?" he said. "I do not believe the darkness tires or rest. Yet here we wait and wait, and wait, and wait. I ask you: and what do we wait for? Let me tell you. We wait for the Professor and his wisdom. It is a waste of time. We should be marching our armies east while we have the time . . ."

He suddenly stopped talking as his pipe went out. In frustration, he struck a match and re-lit it with swift puffs.

"Thank the Maker your pipe had the wisdom to hush your voice," said the man in a good-natured tone.

Still puffing on his pipe, the bobbin grumbled.

Big Grey made his way down the staircase and jumped on top of the table.

"Some things never change," he purred turning to the bobbin, "like your fervor, and the good wizard's patience."

The man chuckled while the bobbin snarled and bit at his pipe.

The cat was glad to see his two friends. It had been some time since they had last been together. While they continued to banter, he looked at them and his mind wandered.

The bobbin was Tollen Popperdock, or Brows as he was fondly called, for his thick bushy eyebrows. He was a historian from North Sage Barrow and was well-known throughout the lands for his books on Harrow history. But he was also feared by those who were forward-thinkers, for his lucid criticism of what he termed a *move from the old ways*.

The man was the good wizard Fairfax, known by some as Fairfax the Good, or Mirandell in the elven tongue. Of the race called En' Qessirin, or those who possess magic, he was one of the wizards of the Order of the

Edainar, keepers of all good magic in the Harrow and masters of Blackstone Keep. It was Fairfax who had first met the Professor near the sycamore, and it was Fairfax who first introduced the Professor to Brows. The three along with Big Grey and Lil' Man had become friends seemingly bound by fate and blood in a never-ending struggle to rid the Harrow of evil.

"Master Purr! Master Purr!' said Brows startling the cat. "Were you daydreaming?"

"No, just thinking about things."

"He is always thinking," said Fairfax. "He never stops thinking. Unlike someone, I know."

Brows bit down on his pipe stem and grumbled something at Fairfax.

"Well, why don't you tell him?" Fairfax asked Brows. "You are so worried about time. Go ahead, tell him."

Brows took a few puffs from his pipe.

"We have news, Master Purr," he said. "Many days ago, Erol Carrick came from the Aina Dur. He rides his trusted steed Warsinger and brings with him the great falcon Windthrasher. They make their way south to gather the armies of man. War will soon begin. But tell us, what word do you bring?"

"Carrick, you say," purred the cat. "The Professor must have sent for our friend to help. I was not aware of his return, but his wisdom and courage will be most helpful."

He knew Erol Carrick well, Supreme Commander of the armies of the Harrow and friend of the Professor from the real world. He was a man of great stature and a rather striking figure. More importantly, he was a great battlefield strategist, having won battle after battle against the brood in ages past.

Brows pressed. "But tell us. What word do you bring, Master Purr?"

The cat hesitated then whispered, "The Professor also sends allies, two of his nieces."

Brows sat back in stunned silence. He glanced at the wizard, then erupted.

"Nieces? You mean children, don't you? The Professor sends us children?" he asked.

Big Grey gave a nod.

The bobbin was angry.

"Well then, our friend the Professor sends us children! How grand of him!" he said. "Can these children wield a sword? Can they lead armies? Do they possess magic?"

The cat sat up and stared at Brows.

"My dear bobbin, they are indeed children," he said, "and they cannot wield a sword, nor do they know magical spells or incantations . . ."

Brows interrupted.

"Fool," he said in a stern whisper. "The Professor sends us children to fight the darkness! Surely, we are doomed! What we need is . . ."

Fairfax raised a hand.

"Now, now . . ." he appealed to Brows. "What we need, what we require, is for you to be calm. No good ever comes from your agitated state. More than weapons and force, it will take level heads and clear thought to defeat the menace. History has taught us this, and who knows history better than you."

Brows made a deprecating noise and sat back in his chair. He understood the wizard's wisdom and had long struggled to control his zeal, but he remained unconvinced of what he heard. He was always focused, attuned to the words he heard, and ever curious as to where the twisting road might lead. He stole a look at Fairfax who refused to make eye contact.

"Friends, please, let me finish. I have some news of great importance," said Big Grey in a firm whisper. The bobbin and wizard leaned forward to better hear the whisper. "The older of the two children wears the Lia Fail."

Fairfax smiled and nodded. He gave a hearty laugh, making eye contact with Brows. He reached across the table and gave his old friend a nudge.

"There you are, you doubting nincompoop," he told Brows. "The Professor gives us the mightiest weapon of all. Thank the Maker, it has returned to the Harrow. I knew he would not abandon us in our time of need."

But Brows was skeptical.

"Yes, but does the child know how to wield it?" he asked. "Does she have the ability, the strength, or the knowledge?"

"I do not know, but I am sure the stone will help guide her," sighed the cat with a shake of his head. "They are young, but we have few choices here. We must take counsel at Blackstone Keep."

"Yes, yes, indeed, we are expected tomorrow as planned," said Fairfax.

Then the sound of wood splintering caught the three by surprise. The wood-carved sculpture of the Professor hanging above them on the wall began to move, slowly stretching and creaking until its eyes opened. The sculpture had come alive.

It was the Professor.

His eyes darted around the room and then down to the three. He again stretched within the wood as if he were trying to writhe himself free. Cracks widened and there was more splintering until he stilled into a fixed position.

"I do not have much time," said the Professor slowly in a low voice difficult to understand. The wood creaked and cracked with every word. "The Harrow is in peril. An evil brings brood on many fronts. Go to Portmoor. You must retrieve it. Be swift now."

The sculpture stretched a final time and then quickly shrank to its original shape, its cracks closing tight. The sculpture's eyes shut, and the Professor was gone.

Fairfax chuckled.

"His skill in magic improves. He could teach me a thing or two."

"Tricks and illusions cannot defeat the darkness," said Brows. "Only brute strength can defeat the menace."

"Wait," said Big Grey. "Did he say Portmoor?"

"I believe so," said Brows puffing on his pipe. "What do you suppose he meant by that?"

"I think he meant exactly what he said - that we or someone should go to Portmoor," replied Fairfax. "But why? He said to retrieve *it*. What do you suppose *it* is?"

"I do not know?" muttered Brows under his breath. "Always riddles with the Professor. Portmoor's nothing more than a place of scoundrels and half-breeds. What could be there that would be useful to us?"

He was correct. Portmoor was a seafaring town and a trading port, nestled above the hilltops of the Carn. Known for its shipbuilding and trading of goods with merchants from far-off lands and pirates, Portmoor's charm was tarnished by its crime and the fact that most of its citizens were half-breeds, mixed races like man and bobbin. There was little tolerance for half-breeds among the Harrow's races; Portmoor, however, provided them refuge and work, a place where questions were never asked.

Big Grey's eyes widened.

"Shhhhhhh," he implored. "The good innkeeper's daughter is wed to a man in Portmoor. Do not let him hear you."

Brows shook his head and sighed in disbelief.

"And now we worry about the innkeeper's feelings," he said. "How preposterous indeed. The Professor sends us two children, he gives us the Lia Fail which no one knows how to use, and now he tells us we must go to Portmoor as if there is something of grand importance there! Meanwhile, dark armies gather to the east. And all you care about is Gringshek's feelings! I tell you our only hope is the great Erol Carrick."

"Let us see what I can do," said the wizard.

He closed his eyes and attempted to reach out with his thoughts, to touch Portmoor with his magic, but felt nothing at all. He could not gain a vision, nor sense any danger to the city.

"Perhaps, my old friend is mistaken," he said. "The Professor may have foreseen something and misinterpreted its meaning for I don't sense any peril. If there is evil about it is some distance away. Let us keep to our plan and bring this news to Blackstone Keep. From there, our destiny will be charted, and perhaps to Portmoor." He looked at the other two. "What say you?"

Big Grey nodded as Brows waved his hand in exasperation.

They stayed in the sitting room for most of the night before retiring to their rooms.

When Big Grey passed by the girl's room, he gently pushed the door open. The dimly lit hallway yielded enough light for him to see that both girls were curled up in their beds, sound asleep. He could hear their breathing and it reminded him of the soft movement of leaves in a beautiful breeze.

But Molly's sleep was restless and full of dreams with strange and haunting images. She stirred and opened her eyes.

"Big Grey?" she said.

He quietly stepped into the room and by the bed.

"Shhh," he said. "You will wake your sister. Go back to sleep."

He jumped onto her bed and gently brushed a paw against her dark curls, as he softly purred a lullaby.

Rabbits in their holes,
Birds in their nests,
Children in their beds,

And all peacefully at rest.

Come lullaby, come lullaby,
And wrap thee warm.
The Maker has blessed this place
And protects thee from storm.

She sighed and closed her eyes to sleep, feeling safe with Big Grey near her.

* * *

Lil' Man and Chumsey were treated kindly by Thurir and his pack. They had always been curious about the Fenri, and now that they were more familiar with them, they saw them in a different light. They could see that the Fenri were strong, strong in their determination but strong to one purpose in their minds. They were determined to do something good for themselves. They were a noble race.

Chumsey looked at Lil' Man.

"Do you think you are strong enough to travel?" he asked.

Lil' Man nodded to his friend. His wounds had healed sufficiently for him and Chumsey to leave the cave. They set out upon a ledge of black rock that ran out and around with a low-lying brush, dried scattered about. It was night and the moon fought to shine through the Drueger's blackened mists. The wind howled across the Crag gathering strength until it violently swirled bringing with it dust and an acrid stench that stung their nostrils forcing them to turn away. Through the dust and mists, they could make out the grey stone of Ug' Cthuth, the evil edifice of old that had been rebuilt. Farther south they could see a second demon tower looming tall and twisted, from which brood relentlessly marched. The tower spewed forth fire and black smoke, its shadow ominous over the Drueger in a sinister pallet of dark grey and blackness. From the brood's guttural growls, the cats understood the tower's name.

The name drummed across the darkness like a wound that hurt.

"Urth' Goroth . . . Urth' Goroth . . . Urth' Goroth . . . Urth' Goroth . . ."

In the distance, from the east, a faint whistle in the winds was heard. The piercing sound grew louder and louder until it reached a deafening shrill. Suddenly black ajatars appeared overhead making their way west, each harnessed by a Dark Rider, the Uakor Turg, a demon neither dead nor alive, trapped in a world of eternal blackness. The two cats crouched pushing back their ears while the half-faced metal-clad riders struggled to maintain the ajatars in formation against the winds. Their powerful leathery wings beat wildly in a thunderous chorus of death, their shrill keening rent the air, as the mountains seemed to shrink in horror as they bore down on them.

Sensing something, one of the Dark Riders brought its ajatar back and around for one more pass. The Rider surveyed the bleakness below but could not see through the dust. Frustrated, the fiend gave a dreadful wail and flew off never noticing the cats.

"Ajatars, Dark Riders, and Fenri," said Lil' Man. "Evil sharpens its sword within the two towers of doom. Chums, we must warn the western lands of the danger, and with Thurir's help we will gain days."

"But will the Lord of Mistmere listen to us?" asked Chumsey.

They knew the Lord could sometimes be difficult and even obstinate – that his will, like his heart, was as firm as a rock.

"Well, if he will not listen to us," said Lil' Man, "maybe, he'll listen to Thurir."

Chumsey looked about as the night grew long.

"Perhaps," he said. "But I fear his mind may be closed to what he may not fully understand."

Through the dark mists and smoke, the broken moon began to win its battle with the night, as it slowly emerged unveiling a bluish light and casting faint shadows about the rock. A sudden chill came to them as the winds gathered strength and the night air cooled. The Crag was the kind of place that made one long for home.

Within the darkness and gloom, Chumsey's heart grew heavy.

"There is nothing here," he told Lil' Man, "but a desolate wasteland and a never-ceasing wind that laments eerily over broken rock. I miss home."

"I do as well," said Lil' Man. "It would be nice to again feel the gentle grasses of Katzhu Pu on my soft pads."

Chumsey fought back emotions as he thought of the real world.

"I am talking about my home from under the tree," he said. "Oh, how I so miss my human friend. I miss her smile and warm touch."

It was his undying love and commitment to his human friend that held him firm through each challenge the Harrow presented. And it was this same love and commitment that brought him back home.

Chumsey's words stirred thoughts in Lil' Man. He thought of the Professor, the gardens, the girls, his cozy basket on the porch, and of course his best friend Big Grey. But another thought came to him and it brought a profound sadness.

We live between two cold realities, he thought. *At home, we are sickly, stunted, and not given long to live. But here, we escape deadly illness and long for those who love us. Such a cruel decision - leave your loved ones and live; remain with them and die.*

Each day he struggled with this cruelty, sometimes hesitant to go under the tree to the Harrow, and other times running to the tree to escape the pain. He often thought of staying in the Harrow indefinitely. But whenever he did, he became sad for it only made him yearn for those he loved back home.

He looked at his friend who stood before him, perfectly still, a strong, powerful warrior of the Balor, the wind playing with his thick orange fur.

Here is Chumsey of the Harrow. Proud warrior-elite *of Katzhu Pu, brave and courageous.*

But he knew the reality of it all. He blinked and a different vision of his friend came to him. Gone was the proud warrior of Katzhu Pu, replaced by a spindly, hollow-eyed cat with straggly fur, who was barely able to stand or walk. This was the real Chumsey, a cat sickened by disease and ever close to death.

The cruel decisions we must make.

He rubbed up against his friend, forcing himself to concentrate on the task before them.

"Chums, after Mistmere we will get to Katzhu Pu, and away from all this darkness," he said. "Both of us . . . you will see. Everything will be fine. I promise."

Chumsey looked away from Lil' Man and into the dark mists of the Drueger, his eyes swelling with emotion.

"I miss her," he said. "I am not sure this is the best place for us. I am getting tired of it all — tired of running away from things — tired of running away from who I am."

Lil' Man did not know what to say and instead gave a gentle lick to his friend's face.

"There you are," boomed Thurir's voice.

Startled, they looked up to find the large wolf-beast. Behind him, along the inside walls of the cave, passed the shadows of his Fenri pack as they prepared to leave.

"War is upon us little ones," said Thurir. "The forges of the towers bend to the will of the darkness. They fashion machines of metal and doom and destruction while more brood gathers. The time of death approaches."

"All the same, we may have time," said Lil' Man. "The storm hasn't reached the west. There is hope that the forces of good will be joined in time to meet the foe."

"Perhaps, little cat," said Thurir, "but time is a resource we can ill afford to squander. We will take leave of this barren rock." He looked at Lil' Man. "You will ride

Janru, and your friend, my brave one, will ride Talro. We will make our way slowly from the Crag, following close to the ledges until we come to the foot of the mountain where the Barrens stretch for leagues. I will give the signal, and from there we will run like the wind. The flatlands offer us no protection from the brood, so we must be quick. We will run the pack day and night until we reach the west. Our journey to Mistmere begins."

They mounted their Fenri companions nestling into the thick neck fur.

"Keep low," Janru told Lil' Man, "and keep a firm grip for once we see the Barrens our pace will quicken."

Thurir and his pack began their slow descent from the Crag. In time, they made it to the foot of the mountain where it quickly divided itself into four smaller units each with a lead Fenri. Lil' Man knew Fenri packs ran in various formations, the most common resembled a spearhead with three units outlining the head's triangular shape, while a fourth ran behind representing the spear shaft. This was done to protect the entire pack as each unit would be in a strategic position to defend or counterattack against an enemy. If one unit was attacked, another would immediately defend while others would split and run and circle back to attack the enemy. As best as Lil' Man could tell two of the units were small with about twenty Fenri each, while the other two units were larger. Lil' Man estimated about one hundred Fenri in all.

When they were at the foot of the mountain, Thurir gave a quick chirping series of howls, and they were off into the night at flank speed, bounding dark forms over the Foghollow Barrens that stretched cold and empty, a feeling of latent evil about it. They made their way northwest to Mistmere, about fifty leagues away, a journey of at least two days at flank speed. Lil' Man peered through the night but could not see Talro or Chumsey, only the many red eyes of the Fenri shooting through the darkness. The desolation of the Crag was now but a memory to Lil' Man.

A time of darkness approaches, he thought.

He closed his eyes and thought of his cozy basket on the Professor's porch.

* * *

News of Erol Carrick's return swept over the countryside, from Laurel Glen and south through the Strongdale Downs, along the Greenway road, and through the many hamlets and villages of the Greenwood. Atop his mighty black steed Warsinger, the handsome, white-bearded figure sat. He wore the traditional battle garb of the Ahlgren, woven golden and steel chain armor, and over it, a sturdy brown leather cloth and a shiny golden breastplate emblazoned with the Mark of the Tree. In shoulder harnesses, the legendary twin blades glistened - the fire swords. One was named Eligor for an ancient chieftain slain in a battle long ago, and the other was named Ravenscar for the steed that fell with his master.

As Carrick entered the small hamlet of River Bend, he brought the black horse into a slow trot. Crowds gathered along the way as children were hoisted atop shoulders to catch a glimpse of the Supreme Commander.

It was an incredible spectacle, for before them was Erol Carrick, hero of the ages, and his two companions. The mighty Warsinger of the Ure Rokko was a horse of great magnificence, a vision of equine perfection standing twenty-five hands high. With the morning sun on his glossy ebony mane, his strong muscles shone thick and powerful, but with remarkable litheness and agility. Perched on Carrick's shoulder was the majestic falcon Windthrasher. He was a bird of exquisite beauty, with long, broad-based, pointed wings, and a short, dark, hooked beak. The markings on his wings were mostly white with dark spots and carried to his nape, and sides; his bill and legs were yellow; his eyes a chilling burnt orange.

The crowds were quiet but soon erupted in adulation.

"He's returned to save us," shouted someone.

"May the Maker bless you Erol Carrick," shouted another.

"Ride strong to victory," shouted another.

Children pushed through the crowds for a better look.

"Can you see the swords? Can you see the swords?" they asked their fathers. "Can you see them?"

Applause and cheers erupted as men, women, and children shouted their support and placed flowers before the great man and his companions. The very air withered before the noise. Carrick looked over the crowds and faces with delight. But he observed some in the distance, those clad in dark hooded robes, their faces shrouded from view, spies among the faithful. He raised a hand and reared the imposing Warsinger, while Windthrasher opened his wings.

"Good people of the Harrow," he said, his voice rich and deep. "I have returned to bring peace to the lands. Tell all that would hear of my return, whether it be friend or foe, for I care not - the enemy is upon us and will be vanquished!"

The crowd roared in cheer as he bowed his head.

"Peace to the citizenry," roared Warsinger. "May the Maker bless you."

The streets were alive with enthusiasm, but there was a deep-seated fear. Carrick's appearance could only mean there would once again be bloodied fields heralded by the storms from the east. The sounds of hope, joy, pride, excitement, and horror grew louder. With a gentle spur to the steed under him, he continued his journey over the cobbled Greenway road.

* * *

Portmoor was a city that sat on the coast of the Great Western Sea. Some called it by a different name - Donan-Pug in the ancient half-breed tongue - a derogatory name of the place where cutthroats, smugglers, thieves, scoundrels, half-breeds, and brigands called home. It was a city of indescribable threats and dangers, a popular place for outlaws to hide and from which to make their escape to far away distant lands. But it was also renowned for its trade. In days past, traders came from parts unknown to sell their goods and exchange their currencies. But it was not the same now. Fewer traders ventured to the port city and poverty was rife.

The sun was setting behind the Carn hilltops to the west, reflecting a vivid orange off the sea. As the city sat in the soft diffused light, it began to erupt in decadent indulgences and delights. The smell of the sea drifted through the air, and the streets and the people were bathed in a warm orange glow.

On the docks stood the Dock Master, Skag Harwell. He was an enormous man with a stringy, long black beard that he curled into ringlets and tied with ribbons. His arms rippled with muscles covered with tattoos that depicted his many journeys. He was a frightful figure to behold on the docks and thus kept order where lawlessness would easily rule. Not much was known about him, but it did not matter because this was Portmoor.

A blustery wind suddenly came bringing white waves that swelled and bounded up against the ships docked in the harbor. As the wind gained strength and an easterly blow began, Harwell saw something strange - several dark flecks far off on the horizon.

He motioned to his apprentice, a young man named Elban Miragrin.

"My scope," he shouted.

Miragrin raced from the office with a spotting scope in hand.

"Here, my master," he said giving the scope to Harwell.

By the naked eye, Harwell thought he saw many ships but could not determine their size, direction, or speed. He focused his scope and his heart pounded faster; he could not believe what he was looking at. It was an armada of black ships, hundreds of leagues away, heading east toward the city.

"Do you see them?" he asked. "Do you see the ships?"

"Yes, my master," said Miragrin. "Looks to be several of them but I can't make out what kind."

"Any large shipments on the manifest for the next few days?"

"No, my master. Just a few routine shipments."

Harwell paused.

"They look to be headed our way," he said. "Most likely, they'll arrive tomorrow, in the morning, based on the winds."

"Master, are they pirate ships?"

Harwell took one more look through his spotting scope.

"Doubtful," he said. "These ships are black. Pirate ships usually have gilded masts. You'd see a reflection from the sun, like glitter on the horizon. And I've never known such a large pirate fleet."

"Master, if not pirates then who?"

Harwell did not answer. He knew what the sea was bringing, and he knew what needed to be done. Staring at the glowing horizon and clutching his spotting scope he turned to Miragrin.

"Listen to me. We've not much time," he said. "The ships ride a storm. It'll come early in the morn and sweep east on mighty waves. You must go inland to Blackstone Keep, to warn them of the storm. Take Saraanth and leave immediately. Ride through the night and into the next day. Take little rest. At best you'll arrive in a day, perhaps a half more. Once at Blackstone you'll be greeted by guards at the gate. Ask for the one called Galsham. He knows my name and will recognize Saraanth."

"But master, what should I tell him?"

"Tell him I sent you. Tell him what we've seen here. Tell him of the black ships on the horizon. Tell him a storm is coming. He'll know what to do. Now go!"

Harwell shoved Miragrin away. But the young man hesitated.

"What about my wife and children? And her mother is with them!" he told Harwell. "I cannot leave them alone!"

"I'll call on Mora tonight and bring your family to my home. They'll be safe there. Of this, I promise. But you must go now! You must get to Blackstone!"

"What about the city?"

"There's nothing that can be done. The storm will swallow it! No more questions! Now go! Take some provisions from storage, but you must hurry! Go!"

Miragrin ran down the dock and into the office where he packed a small sack of dried meats and bread. He was uncertain of what was exactly happening but as an apprentice was obligated to obey his master's instructions. He grabbed the reins of the magnificent black horse

Saraanth, who bucked and reared, driving bladelike hooves deep into the ground.

Harwell watched as Miragrin and Saraanth thundered into the streets of Portmoor and off to the east. He turned back and stared at the sea where the waves curled and crashed with more frequency bringing a cold mist to the air.

It's a storm alright, he thought. *But not the kind they think.*

Turning from the sea he made his way into the city. With a hurried familiarity and his gaze constantly moving he maneuvered through the labyrinth of pubs, brothels, and hovels, on occasion having to double back to find a new route to avoid a brawl or a street flooded with sewage. It was obvious he knew the city well as he wound his way through the maze of streets until, at last, he found himself in a dark and deserted alley.

He continued down the alley, away from the street noise when he came to a heavy door. He stopped and took a deep breath before gently rapping on it. The door slowly opened, just a crack at first, until a young, portly, bobbin woman with flowing red hair greeted him. It was Mora Miragrin, the apprentice's wife. They and their two half-breed children lived in a simple but cramped hovel.

She was troubled by his appearance at her front door and asked if something had happened to Elban and if he was alright. She was calmed when he reassured her that Elban was fine. She welcomed him into their home

"A storm of fierce winds and rain makes its way from the sea," he told her. "You, your children, and your mother will need to take sanctuary at my home on the city's outskirts, on the high ground."

When she asked if Elban would join them, he told her that he sent the young man inland, to warn those beyond the Carn of the storm. He told her that he promised Elban that he would care for his family.

"I have to be on the docks in the morning," he said. "But when the storm comes ashore take shelter in the basement of my home. There's a hidden stairway behind a bookcase. I'll show you. You'll know when the storm is upon us. The winds will howl, the sound like demons, and you'll hear the screams of those who've not heeded the warnings. Whatever you do, don't venture outside."

Mora trusted Harwell; he was like a father to Elban. So, she packed a few belongings and gathered the children and her mother.

They traveled that night mostly in silence, following Harwell through the maze of dark streets, until they found themselves at his home, near a large tree. He gave them food and water, and clean bed linens, and told them not to worry. When the children were asleep, he showed Mora and her mother the hidden stairway, behind a wooden bookcase that slid quietly along the wooden floor.

"The storm will come in the morning," he told them. "When the skies will darken, that's when you must take shelter. Do not come out until someone comes for you. There's enough food and water in the basement to last for some time."

Later that night, from his bed, Skag Harwell gazed out of his bedroom window.

He thought of Elban Miragrin, of his ride to Blackstone Keep, of the young man's family, now safe and secure in their beds. Then he thought of his deceit and the truth of what would happen tomorrow.

The ships bring a storm. But it's a storm of darkness and wickedness, a doom of evil, a sickening malevolence that wants the Harrow.

An unusually large number of falling stars caught his attention before at long last, he went to a restless sleep with his head upon a pillow drenched in tears.

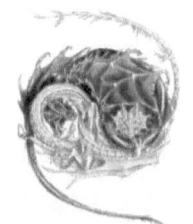

CHAPTER 5
BLACKSTONE KEEP

IN THE MORNING OVER breakfast, Big Grey introduced the girls to Brows and Fairfax. They weren't sure what to make of the cat's friends. Everything Molly had seen since leaving the tree had been unusual, unreal, brilliant, and perplexing - talking animals, bobbins, beautiful landscapes, and now a wizard. Molly was always cautious about things and especially those things not easily understood. She knew this about herself. But everyone she had met along the way on this adventure was friendly and made her feel welcomed including the wizard.

On the other hand, Elizabeth was less timid, believing that you need not be cautious if you follow your instincts. For her, when everything around her was strange, she thought it best to take a deep breath and rush into reckless exploration. She was prone to such behavior, and was prone to taking dangerous chances, often putting herself and Molly in peril. Molly knew this about her sister and always kept a watchful eye on her, especially now before two new friends.

Fairfax looked at Molly.

"Ah, I see a likeness with the Professor," he said.

"Yes, I believe you're correct," said Brows. "It is in the eyes."

The wizard smiled at her.

"You can always tell what is in a person's heart," he said, "by looking into their eyes. The eyes tell a story."

She looked up with eyes softer than mere curiosity. She felt comfortable with him and sensed he was a precious and honorable person. She realized she had a good friend here.

"And what do my eyes tell you?" she asked.

"That you are much like your uncle," he said, "which is a terrific thing to be - smart, observant, trustworthy, passionate - all wonderful things. Your uncle and I have been friends for so many years. I have greatly valued his friendship and am deeply indebted to him for all the kindness and assistance he has bestowed on me and this land. I hope to also value your friendship."

A charming smile came to her, an utterly, effortlessly captivating smile.

"What about our next adventure?" asked Elizabeth. "Where will we be off to next?"

Fairfax gave a hearty laugh.

"Ah! Patience is needed for an adventure," he said. "Wherever it takes us I am sure it will be worth the wait. But it is sometimes best not to be so eager for what may be around the corner. Do you understand?"

Elizabeth looked confused.

"The good wizard, much like your uncle, sometimes speaks in riddles," said Brows. "What he is trying to say is this: when one is on a journey one should only take what one needs and leave behind what one doesn't need."

Molly laughed.

"How silly of you both - one riddle replacing another. Always riddles," she said. She turned to Elizabeth and told her, "What they're trying to say is that we must be careful and prepared for anything."

"Why yes, of course, that is what I said," huffed Brows. "Take with you your curiosity but leave behind your carelessness."

The two girls just shook their heads in dismay at such folly.

Fairfax patted Elizabeth on her head.

"Oh, young one, do not worry now," he told her. "The adventure is only beginning."

The atmosphere in the dining room was warm and friendly, as patrons asked for more coffee or tea, and second helpings of eggs and cakes. Brows asked for three helpings of a bobbin's favorite breakfast meal — honey and mushroom gravy over toasted nuts. The breakfast talk was nice and drifted casually from how well everyone had slept and the delicious food, to the day's journey ahead and how they would be at Blackstone Keep in the afternoon, where they would meet with other wizards. While Brows and Fairfax bickered about what the weather would be like, for the most part, the bobbin was on his best behavior. But the girls intuitively felt more at ease with the good wizard.

When breakfast had ended the girls bid Master Gringshek a fond farewell. The innkeeper was jovial and hugged them.

"See you soon and be safe," he said with a large smile. "Oh, and here's some advice - listen to the tall one, ignore the small one."

Brows scoffed at the remark.

"And who would listen to a pie maker?" said the bushy-browed bobbin.

"We would!" laughed the girls.

Fairfax chuckled and clapped his hands together at the girl's laughter, and the five left the inn with a final wave of farewell.

The sweet morning dew still lay on the grass and the wide, wet leaves of the trees glistened when the five set out for Blackstone Keep. They walked down the short path lined with cherry trees and then took a road north from the inn. The road was cobblestone and led into the Cairn Dale forest. It was an ancient forest shrouded in mystery, filled with layer upon layer of living things, great and majestic trees, and creatures both familiar and strange, all sharing a common purpose to protect the forest from harm. Many woodland creatures scurried about, some frolicking and playing, others looking for food, but all content in the safety and resources provided by the forest. But some creatures of the Cairn Dale remained hidden, terrified of the five strangers not knowing whether they were friends or hunters.

As they traveled deeper into the woods, a carven gloom of crowded trees formed a great cathedral unpierced by sunlight. The air became heavy and dank, and the shrills of birds echoed beneath the leafy dome. Molly was frightened, slowing her pace and ever watchful until Fairfax assured her that the Cairn Dale was not an evil place. He told her that there were many ancient creatures in the forest, some that have not been seen in ages, but all were peaceful. As they continued, they could hear the calls of birds, the rustle of leaves, and the occasional bellow of a stag, all of which gave the forest a sense of peace. After a while, she began to enjoy the part of the journey she was in. Everything seemed peaceful as Fairfax had said and she felt calmer.

Eventually, the trees began to thin, and ahead one could see where the road led from the woodland to an open field. But there the sky was dark, or so it seemed, almost pitch black as if a baneful storm approached.

"How odd," said Molly. "When I look up into the trees, I can make out a glimpse of the sun, but far ahead everything looks dark as if it were night."

Fairfax pointed his staff forward.

"My child, what you see through the trees and brush is Blackstone Ridge, large mountains of black stone," he told her. "From a distance, it looks as if night has returned, but once we leave the woods the sun will be high in the sky, and you will see a most unbelievable wonder."

A twinkle in his eyes made her smile.

Soon, they came to a large forest gateway where the Cairn Dale opened to a vast landscape of golden grasses under the fruitful rays of the sun. From the forest, the road sloped downward, meandering its way through the grasses and to a black stone bridge. The bridge crossed a lake of calm blue waters that surrounded something the girls had never seen - a towering, burnished fortress of black, so large it consumed the horizon.

In front of them was the magnificent Blackstone Keep. It was hewn from the side of massive mountains of the same black rock, the Blackstone Ridge, that loomed in solemn grandeur, its peaks delicately covered in snow. The Keep was an enormous edifice with a central dome, two tall square towers, and long spires that reached into and above the clouds. It was encircled by a high fortress black wall that jutted from the mountains on one side, around the Keep and returning to the mountains on the other. Within its gates thrived a bustling city of buildings, cobblestone streets, and magnificent gardens. The grand structure and its mountain glistened in the morning sun, their surfaces smooth and sheer with angular sharp ridges.

The girls were awestruck, stopping to admire the magnificence.

Fairfax leaned on his staff and knelt before them. From the corner of her eye, Molly saw what appeared to be a birthmark on the side of his neck, blackish, in the shape of a tree. She did not say anything.

"Ah, Blackstone Keep, the sight of this sprawling wonder never fails to thrill," said Fairfax. "Well, what do you think of my home?"

Molly kept her gaze ahead, on the remarkable sight.

"I've never seen anything like it," she said.

"It's incredibly beautiful," added Elizabeth. "What's it made of? Marble?"

"Not exactly," answered Big Grey. "The whole of the Blackstone Ridge is of a black stone, smooth and textured. It's like marble, shiny . . ."

But brows interrupted.

"It is elegant simplicity, young ladies, elegant simplicity," he said, "yet immensely heavy, rigid, and unyielding. In the old tongue, the stone is called darkun ilgot. No army has ever penetrated its walls, and none shall."

"It is not every day one sees a castle born of mountains," said Fairfax.

"It must've taken a long time to build," said Elizabeth.

"Indeed, ages and ages," said Brows.

"It is a very special place, the home to the Edainar," said Fairfax.

"What's that?" asked Molly.

"It is an order of wizards of which I am one," he said. He paused and looked at the girls with a warm smile. "Come, we are close now."

He stood and they started down the sinuous road and through the golden grasses. Along the way, the girls could not take their eyes off the glittering black marvel.

"Who built it?" asked Elizabeth.

The wizard winked at Elizabeth and gave a smile.

"Hmm . . . I think our good bobbin here should answer you, my dear," he said. "After all, he is the historian of the group."

"Yes, why not have the great historian answer this question," said Big Grey, going along with Fairfax.

Brows, not one to fall easily into a trap, quickly responded.

"Well of course," he said with a smirk to Fairfax and Big Grey. "I would be happy to share such enlightenment with those less accomplished in the old ways." He turned to the girls. "You see some do not always appreciate my insights. But I know you two appreciate my words. Don't you now, hmm?"

The girls nodded with a giggle.

They continued their way through the tall golden grasses while Brows told a tale, of ages past when a race of creatures called the Trollock, or mountain trolls, as some would later call them, inhabited the mountains now known as the Thornback. Fairfax and Big Grey knew the history well but listened along with the girls as Brows described the mountain trolls as enormous human-like creatures of great size and strength, much taller than even Fairfax, and hundreds of times stronger than the strongest man.

"History records that some were so tall," said Brows, "that they could touch the stars. Now, I do not know if that is true or not, but it is in the writings of the many historians who came before me. But I digress. The Trollock dwelt high in the mountains where no man or bobbin could reach them. They lived in great mountain cities carved of stone throughout the Thornback. They survived on mutton and snow turnips and would come down from the mountains to trade in fine leather and fur with the kings who ruled the Harrow."

"Kings?" asked Elizabeth.

"Yes, three to be exact," said Brows. "Back then, in ages past, parts of the Harrow were ruled by kings."

"Are there kings today?"

"Only one realm remains from those times – the realm of the elves, ruled by the Elf-King. Sadly, the time of kings has long since passed. Their end was brought about when an evil darkness from the east came over the land, bringing with it pestilence, war, and sorrow. It was a time of great upheaval. The kings amassed vast armies with which to wage war against their foes. Many wars were fought until the Ra Ahtar, or Great War was fought. Mind you, the kings did not look to the mountain trolls for help. The kings knew that the Trollock were a peaceful race without an army or weapons of any kind."

Brows paused for a bit then continued, "But as they were friends of the kings, the mountain trolls wanted to help in some manner. Recognizing they were skilled craftsmen they decided to build three great edifices for the races of the Harrow, to protect them from evil. The great city of Elandrake was forged of great stone for the elves of Tir Nan Og, the golden stone fortress of Katzhu Pu was built for the Ra Cath, and Blackstone Keep, what you see before you, was fashioned from its great mountains for the En' Edan, the race of man. Later, the good wizards of the Edainar would call the Keep home. Each of the structures built by the Trollock soon became large cities as the races sought refuge from evil, in all its forms. But during the Ra Ahtar the three great cities were badly damaged. Now, with Blackstone Keep, the damage was done to the inner parts of the city. The Trollock rebuilt each to its former stature, and beyond."

"Whatever became of the mountain trolls?" asked Molly.

"Alas, our history is unclear. After the Great War against the darkness, some say the Trollock abandoned their mountain cities and migrated to places higher up in the Thornback, places unreachable by man. But others say that they became extinct, an ancient race that could not sustain itself. One thing is known - a mountain troll hasn't been seen for hundreds of years."

"What do you suppose happened to them?"

"I do not know, but I would like to think they are still here with us," said Brows. "They were a noble race and kept everything alive about them. Their hands were as open as their hearts, and their doors never closed."

"You said there were three kings, but that only one remains. What became of the other two kings and their cities?" asked Elizabeth.

Brows hesitated. He gave a glance at Fairfax.

"Go ahead and tell them," Fairfax said with a nod to Brows.

"Well then, as I said, only the Elf-King remains, and he lives in a city called Elandrake," said Brows. "The other two kings and their families were slain by assassins on one night many years ago."

The girls gasped at such horror.

"Entire families?" asked Molly.

"Unfortunately, so," said the bobbin. "In one brutal and menacing night, every possible heir was gone, except the elven king and his heirs as they were protected by magic. It is called the Night of Death and it happened just before the final battles of the Great War. The enemy had planned the attacks for some time in hopes of distracting and diminishing the resolve of the armies of the good and righteous.

"That's terrible," said Molly.

"There was great mourning throughout the Harrow over the loss of two beloved royal families. The time of kings had ended. But the fighting continued and the armies of good and righteous fought with renewed strength. They vowed to take revenge for the murders of their kings. The forces of good prevailed and at the end of the Ra Ahtar, the remaining king, the Elf-King, decreed the Trollocks' gifts of Elandrake, Blackstone Keep, and Katzhu Pu as sacred places belonging to the races."

"The kings and their royal families must've been loved by everyone," said Molly, softly.

Brows gave a nod.

"Indeed, they were," he said. "They were beloved and pleasant in their lifetimes and in their death, were not parted; they were quicker than eagles, stronger than the strongest beast. The inscription on the tomb of King Aulfuren of Ahlgren reads: In death do not weep for me for I will be a bane to another, that he may know not to be proud in my woes; sharing with me in this weakness he will learn wisdom."

The girls were frightened by the tale. They could not fathom the depths of evil in the mind of the nameless enemy. They were beginning to wonder if they liked this place. They did not like to hear about things such as death, or an evil presence that haunted war. The story upset them so much that they were not sure if they wanted to hear any more accounts of this place. But still, they had friends in this world who seemed to genuinely care for them, and Big Grey was always by their side.

Then Molly remembered something, something powerful the Professor once told her.

"There was something the Professor said to me once," she said.

"Ha! What did he say?" asked Brows.

"He told me that history teaches us knowledge and that is something we don't often like to face squarely."

The bobbin smiled.

"He is indeed a wise man," he said.

Molly felt the Lia Fail warm and gently throb.

"Thank you, Mr. Brows," she said. "Thank you for helping us to understand more about this place. Now that we know what's happened in the past, we can be careful in the future."

"Yes, thank you," said a reluctant Elizabeth, still anxious over his stories.

Brows glanced up at Fairfax.

"You are welcome," he told the girls. "And I must say, it is so nice to be appreciated for a change."

Fairfax laughed a deep laugh, his eyes sparkling.

They continued along the road that led ever closer to the black stone bridge. Big Grey was now ahead of the group and the girls ran to him.

"It seems you have grown fond of the children," Fairfax whispered to Brows. "Very unusual for someone of your demeanor."

"Hmm . . . perhaps wizard, but they remind me of myself when I was young - inquisitive and intelligent for their age. And even though I do not understand what the Professor may have in mind, they are after all, what he has given us."

Fairfax nodded and patted his bobbin friend on the back.

"The oldest will mature," he told Brows. "Her intuition will quickly grow. The stone will force this upon her and burden her with great insight."

But Brows gave a cautionary note.

"With maturity and insight comes choices, and many of those choices will be dangerous," he said.

"She will be fine. We have no other choice than to have faith in the Professor."

As they walked the two friends talked of many things: about the Professor and why he had not journeyed from under the tree; about the Professor's instructions to go to Portmoor; about the girls and how they could help; about the Lia Fail and how its power could be used; about their imminent meeting with the wizards, until, predictably, they came to the subject of armies and war strategy. It was then when the girls and Big Grey came to cross the long bridge that led to Blackstone Keep's monolithic stone gates. Elizabeth turned and shouted for them to hurry.

They were soon standing in front of the great Keep's gates. Only the sounds of the gentle lapping of waves against the fortress walls and the chirping of birds from within the massive structure could be heard. From atop the walls, guardsmen recognized the visitors. They shouted an order and there came a heavy dull sound that shook the ground. The enormous stone gates slowly opened, revealing a city with bustling streets, spires, and pinnacles. They entered Blackstone Keep and with another heavy dull sound the ground trembled, and the stone gates were shut behind them.

* * *

Within the great walls of Blackstone Keep, there was movement and sound everywhere; women fetching water, washing clothes, calling to children, and going about their chores; smithies clanging away; children running at play; carts filled with produce for a nearby market rumbling through the streets; and, on hills near the great walls, men working their fields. Blackstone Keep was more than a castle, it was a large city, self-sustaining with markets, shops, farmlands, and vineyards. The city streets were wide, with side guttering, and were kept clean and free of nuisance; no filth or foul matter was thrown on the surface. In some areas, the streets were generously shaded by tall elms, and there were large green spaces abundant with flowers and trees. With Fairfax and Brows leading the way the five strolled through the streets and past the shops and cafés surrounded by wonderful bustling activity, heading for the center of the city, to the Keep itself.

As they made their way through the crowds, a lanky man approached Fairfax and Brows and struck up a conversation with them. He had large hands and a laconic, disarming smile, hollow, aguish cheeks, and a scanty beard. He wore a long blue coat and blue top hat and carried a bejeweled staff.

"Who is he?" Molly asked Big Grey.

"He is called Hadram and is a courtier of the Edainar and servant to the wizards. No doubt Fairfax is telling him of our arrival."

Courtier? thought Elizabeth. She remembered the word from a book she had read.

"It's like a court jester, right Big Grey?" she asked.

"Well, not exactly," said the cat. "Hadram is no clown. He is one of several who attends to the needs of the wizards and is well respected. It is his job to bend not just his actions but his private feelings toward serving the wizards."

Hadram finished his conversation with Fairfax and Brows. He leaned past both to look at Big Grey and the girls.

"Well, Master Purr," he said tipping his hat with a bow, "it's good to see you again. I hope you are well. And of course, welcome to the Professor's nieces. Young ladies, I am Hadram and we are pleased with your presence."

Wanting to show Hadram respect Molly curtseyed.

"Why thank you Mr. Hadram," she said and then nudged her sister who made a quick curtsey of her own.

"Um, yes, thank you," said Elizabeth.

Hadram smiled.

"We must make our way to the Keep, to the Garden Courtyard," he said. "A special meeting is to be convened shortly and your presence is requested."

They continued through the city until they came to a point where the road broadened and was surrounded by tall stone structures that twisted deeper into the city. Finally, the road ended, emptying into a wide park-like pasture with gardens, surrounded by a neatly trimmed hedge, and approached through a simple iron-wrought gate. There the path curved past large oak trees, while the towering Keep loomed in the background.

Hadram opened the gate and they started down the path. Past the large oaks and through a pasture were densely wooded hills with many noble trees, stretching away until meeting the black stone of the lofty wall that surrounded the Keep. Here and there were small pockets of wildflowers that sprang up across the pasture, bright colors of blue and yellow and red and white flowers. It was a glorious sight, calm and peaceful, and the girls imagined themselves spending an entire day walking through the vast parkland, taking in the amazing splendor of the Keep and exploring the beautiful gardens.

Elizabeth ran from the path and into the pasture.

"Come on!" she shouted to Molly.

Molly knew exactly what her sister was up to. She took one step forward then hesitated. She turned to Fairfax.

"Can I?" she asked.

He nodded and gave a smile.

She gleefully chased after Elizabeth following her into a nearby patch of wildflowers. The rest of the group turned to watch the girls.

"Ah, the energy of youth," said Fairfax softly. He looked down at Brows and asked, "My friend, do you remember what it was like?"

Brows packed his pipe and lit it.

"Wizard, you should know better. I was never young," he said taking a few puffs. "I was born ancient."

"Ancient and cantankerous," added Big Grey.

The four laughed.

"But shouldn't we continue on?" asked a nervous Hadram. "They're expecting us. I don't think it's a good idea to keep them waiting."

"Ah, let them wait Hadram," said Brows with his hands on his hip, watching as the girls picked flowers. "The good wizards can wait for a bit while we indulge ourselves."

He took a few puffs of his pipe releasing a sweet scent into the air.

"Yes," said Fairfax. "Darkness may come but we cannot have it take from us such simple pleasures. There is no time like the here and now."

"So be it," sighed a frustrated Hadram.

The girls continued to pick flowers each making a pretty bouquet. They thought the garden was very beautiful and unique.

"It's different than the Professor's gardens," Molly told her sister. "It's more like a field with little structure to it."

Elizabeth agreed.

"But it's just as beautiful as any formal garden," she said.

Molly was about to reach for a huge blue bloom when she saw a little field cricket resting on one of its petals. The cricket's wings and legs were long and yellow. Molly delicately snapped the blue flower from its stem and lifted it, along with the cricket, into her palm.

"Look," she said to Elizabeth bringing the bright cricket closer. "I've never seen a yellow cricket before."

The cricket lifted its wings.

"What are you doing picking my flowers?" it scolded in a woman's voice.

The girls were surprised. They smiled at the fragile cricket,

"Your flowers?" asked Molly.

"Why yes," said the cricket. "These are the Blackstone Gardens, and my name is Elspeth. I'm the keeper of everything you see. These flowers are under my supervision, and anyone who wishes to pick them must first obtain my permission."

"I'm sorry," said Molly. "I wasn't aware."

She gently placed the flower and Elspeth back down in the flower bed. As she did this, the Lia Fail revealed itself from around her neck, sparkling in the sun.

Elspeth saw the red stone and bowed her head.

"Oh my!" she said. "I didn't know I was held by such a gentle touch. Please accept my apology for my abruptness and allow me to sing a cricket song in your honor."

Molly nodded with a smile.

"Of course," she said.

Elspeth began rubbing her legs making a sharp chirping sound, then faster and faster making an even louder sound, and then slower creating a wonderful song. Fast and slow, she created a series of crisp rolling chirps. The girls hummed along. When her song had ended the tiny creature once again bowed before Molly.

"My Queen, did you enjoy my song?" she asked.

Queen? She called me queen, thought Molly. This surprised her.

"Yes, it was beautiful," she said. "But you called me queen. Why?"

Elizabeth was also surprised.

"Her? Queen?" she said. "Oh, you don't know her like I do! Far from royalty, I'd say."

Molly nudged her sister.

"Shhhh . . . be quiet."

"Well, my lady wears the pendant," said Elspeth. "Please accept my apology for not recognizing it sooner."

Molly grasped the Lia Fail.

"Oh, you mean this."

The golden necklace glittered in the sun, the red gemstone reflecting the day's brightness. It became warm to her touch and immediately she felt something strange in her. She became protective of the stone and quickly tucked it back away.

Elspeth gave a quick rub of her legs lifting a gentle chirp into the air.

"Yes," she said, "whoever possesses the pendant is Queen of Ahlgren."

Ahlgren? Ahlgren? I've heard that word before, thought Molly.

She remembered where she had heard it - it was earlier when they approached the great gates when Brows spoke of how Blackstone Keep came to be, long ago when there were three kings, one of which was from the land known as Ahlgren. Then she remembered the tale about the Night of Death, and this frightened her. She became afraid for her and her sister.

What's going on? she thought. *If they think I am Queen, that cannot be a good thing. Maybe we should go back to the tree, and go back home?*

"Can I ask something of you?" she asked Elspeth, feeling a connection to her. Elspeth gave a bow. "Will you come with me?"

"My Queen, I am at your service," said Elspeth.

Molly gently lifted her from the flower petal and rested her on her shoulder.

"Thank you," she said. "There are some things I think we need to sort out." She turned to her sister and motioned. "Come on Elizabeth. Let's go back."

The girls made their way through the pasture and back to the path, holding onto their bouquets. Brows used the flowers and nearby ground ivy and morning glory to fashion a beautiful corsage for Elizabeth. He then did the same for Molly.

Molly pointed to the yellow cricket on her shoulder.

"Look, everyone. I made a friend. Her name is Elspeth," she said.

Big Grey looked up.

"Yes, I see that. My dear Elspeth, it has been some time and it is good to see you again. How have you been?" he asked.

Elspeth gave a slight chirp.

"Well, Master Grey it is so good to see you again," she said. "It has been some time. How have you been?"

"I am well. Thank you for asking."

"Purr, you know Elspeth?" asked Elizabeth.

"Well of course," said the cat. "Everyone knows Elspeth. The beauty you see is due to her fine work. The truth of it is she has given the Professor plenty of advice with his gardens."

"Why thank you Master Purr," chirped Elspeth. "I have heard his gardens are most magnificent."

"Purr, but Elspeth told me something," said Molly, "something that concerns me. She told me I'm Queen of Ahlgren and it's because of the pendant the Professor gave me. Is this true?"

The cat hesitated.

"She is correct," he purred.

Brows placed the corsage of freshly picked flowers on her wrist.

"Why, of course," he said. "You did not know this?"

"No," she said. "The Professor didn't mention anything about me being Queen of Ahlgren. He simply put the pendant around my neck and told me I'd know when to use it. After what Mr. Brows told us about the other kings and their families, well, I don't think I want to be Queen of Ahlgren! I think we should go back home!"

Fairfax sensed Molly's fear. He knelt before the girls and took them by the hand.

"You will have nothing to worry about my dear," he told Molly pointing to the gem. "That stone is the Lia Fail. When a human girl of innocence and purity, like yourself, wears it she becomes Queen of Ahlgren. No harm will come to you or Elizabeth. I'm sure the Professor already told you the secret to that."

She thought for a moment. She remembered what the Professor had told her before they ventured off into his gardens.

"He said as long as we do what Big Grey tells us we'll be safe."

"Well then, there you have it," he said. "I am sure he also told you that here things can be both beautiful and frightening."

Again, Molly thought back. She remembered the Professor's words and felt comforted.

"Why yes. Come to think of it, he did," she said. "But why didn't he tell me about becoming Queen of Ahlgren?"

Fairfax stroked his long beard.

"Perhaps, just perhaps," he said, "he knew it would come up at the right time. Maybe he believed it was best to learn of such a thing here in this wonderful garden. Maybe this is the right time. Now, do not you fret my little one. Everything will be fine. You will see. There is no need to be worried. You have many friends here, and so far, you have met only a few. There are many more you will meet. You will soon see."

Brows took a few puffs of his pipe

"The wizard is right," he said, "and I do not always agree with him. You have many friends in this land, and soon you will learn all you need to know at our meeting. Trust me. Trust in such friendship."

She looked at Brows and Fairfax and wondered if she could trust them. As she looked into their eyes, she could feel the Lia Fail grow warmer, and the Professor's words – *everything will be fine . . . trust me* – rang in her mind.

Trust leads to more trust; fear leads to more fear, she thought. Then a strange and unexpected thought came to her. *Going back is not an option.*

She did not know why the thought came to her. But she knew it was true. The stone continued to warm and throb. She looked at it.

We are too far down the path now to turn back. The adventure – we have to go on.

She turned to Brows, looking at the beautiful corsage.

"Your pipe smells as sweet as the flowers," she told him. "Thank you, Master Brows. Your words are very helpful."

Brows lowered his head.

"Why you are most welcome," he said.

"And thank you too, Fairfax," she told the wizard.

He smiled, a twinkle in his eyes.

She looked around her, at all the smiling faces of her new friends, and felt reassured. But in her heart, there was a vague expectation of difficulties still to come, and deep concern on how she would face each. The stone continued to warm, its pulse almost rhythmic.

I don't know these people, but then again, I feel I do. They need me.

Her thoughts seemed to form in a mature manner, and this surprised her. She was changing. She felt it.

And I need them.

Again, she thought about why the Professor had sent her and her sister to this place, why he had given her the stone pendant.

I know I'm here to help, but how? How will this adventure unfold?

"You'll all help me, won't you?" she asked.

The smiles grew wider as everyone smiled and nodded. Even a slight smile came to Hadram.

But Elizabeth pouted.

"If she's a queen then what am I?"

Brows placed the other corsage he had made on her wrist and adjusted it.

"Well, my dear, if your sister is a queen," he said. "You must be a princess, and I might add a very pretty one at that."

Fairfax stood.

"Well, of course, a princess, Princess of Ahlgren, and as pretty as your sister," he said.

Big Grey rubbed up against Elizabeth's legs.

"Indeed, a grand princess," he purred.

Elizabeth was happy with her title as princess. She often fantasized about what it would be like to be a princess. She had read stories about princesses and imagines them wearing far finer clothes than the ones she wore, as well as gorgeous tiaras.

"Will I have a tiara?" she asked. "That'd be so wonderful."

Fairfax gave a wink.

"We will see little one. We will see," he said.

Hadram was anxious about being late for their meeting. He gave a slight roll of his eyes.

"Good. Let's see now," he said as he began counting on his fingers. "We have a wizard, a bobbin, a cat, a cricket, a queen, and a princess. Now, can we continue, please?"

Brows took a few more puffs of his pipe.

"Well, I think so my good Hadram," he said. "But let us ask the Queen. What say you, my Queen?"

Molly smiled in an uneasy, evasive kind of way. She was not quite sure if she liked being called Queen of Ahlgren. But she was sure of one thing, she did not much care for Hadram's impatience.

"Of course. Let's continue to our meeting before Mr. Hadram has a tantrum," she said.

Hadram slowly closed his eyes and bowed.

"My Queen, thank you," he said.

Elspeth took her leave of Molly and fluttered to Big Grey where she nestled into his thick grey fur.

Hadram led them down the road and toward the massive Keep. They walked in silence until coming to two large wooden front doors of the massive stone edifice. The girls craned their necks to try to view the entire height of it, but it was so tall. Without notice, the massive doors slowly opened revealing a long dark hallway that was lined on both sides with guardsmen. They wore bright red garb and were armed with bows and arrows. At the end of the hallway, they could see a warm light. They continued and as they neared the light Molly felt a warm draft that became warmer and warmer. She knew they were near the Garden Courtyard.

* * *

The morning sunlight revealed the sadness of the Foghollow Barrens, shallow soil and surface rock mostly exposed; a scrubland with groves of stunted pines, gnarled oak sprouts, and tufts of tall brown grasses embedded in a patchy quilt of bracken fern and bare sand. The monotony and scarcity of vegetation was painful as nothing was fresh or vigorous.

Over the bleak terrain, Thurir's Fenri pack held their formation and speed. Ahead, Lil' Man could make out the green grassy hills of the Old River.

We're about halfway there, he thought.

Now with full sunlight, he looked about trying to see Chumsey or Talro, but the images were too blurred in their speed.

Then there came a howl from Thurir.

"Renegades! Aligned with Tharum! Protect the little ones!" he shouted.

Without warning, a group of Fenri came bounding from the north, drooling, growling, and baying, their teeth brandished and ready to attack.

Thurir shouted orders for one unit to join the battle and for the other two to circle back and defend their position.

Then there came another howl from Thurir, more orders. Three Fenri from his unit raced away to points north and west to scout for more attackers.

All around Lil' Man the battle waged. Fenri whirled about clawing at each other as Thurir's warriors quickly overpowered the attackers. With mighty jaws clamped shut, they tore open the bellies of the renegades, scattering their innards about the plains. The defeated Fenri tossed their heads and bellowed, but it was too late as death came over them. In some fights, Thurir's warriors teamed to wrestle the enemy to the ground, with one severing tendons in the hind legs of a renegade, while another ripped at its neck. The snorts of rage filled the air.

Janru and Talro held steady, circled by other Fenri. Lil' Man could see Chumsey holding tight to Talro's neck. It was the first time in hours he had seen his friend, and even though the battlefield was frightening he was glad his friend was nearby.

"I wish they would let me join the fray," he shouted to Chumsey.

Chumsey laughed.

"Are you crazy? You'd be stomped on like an ant," he shouted back.

While Thurir's pack battled, raving and gnashing and growling, their keen fangs making quick work of the foes, the scouts returned. They gave Thurir the information he sought: there were no other enemy Fenri packs about. In a matter of moments, the battle ended; the field was covered with the bloodied enemy, many dead, some barely alive, writhing in pain and gasping their last breaths.

Thurir roared orders.

"Back in formation," he told his pack. "Leave the carcasses for the buzzards to feast on."

Thurir then strolled amongst the bodies of the vanquished enemy.

"For those scum who have enough life to hear my words," he shouted. "Know this — your death is near, embrace it. Remember your betrayal while your souls rot in the netherworld!"

With those words came a celebratory cheer from Thurir's pack. Lil' Man and Chumsey lifted a paw to each other in salute to the victory. They were off again, back in formation, running at flank speed, heading ever closer to the green hills of the Old River.

* * *

Erol Carrick and his companions Warsinger and Windthrasher soon came to the sleepy hamlet of Stag Hollow which was tucked serenely in the hills of the Strongdale Downs. The drowsy air, perfumed with flowers, bathed the old stone-block farmhouses, rambling farmlands, and glades of tall, twisted willow oaks. Unlike other places along their travels, few came out to greet them as here folks were poor, of little means, and were tending to their fields and their mundane daily routines.

Once past Stag Hollow, they traveled off the Greenway road and west over a dirt path to a forest of hemlock and pines. Before entering the forest, Windthrasher spread his wings and lifted himself high into the air, circling above. Carrick and Warsinger followed the path into the forest. Deeper and deeper they went and soon the trees thickened, and the path vanished. With no path to follow, Carrick dismounted Warsinger and led him by the bridle. They wove their way around the trees' neat narrow spires, deeper into the forest. Little sunlight filtered through the trees, rendering it a gloomy and dismal scene.

Warsinger saw a dull glow of white in the distance.

"Ahead. I see it. We are near," he told Carrick.

They followed the glow to an old stone well. Behind it was a small stone farmhouse, abandoned and in disrepair. It was overgrown with vine and thick creepers and dangling mosses. They stood still, their eyes slowly looking in all directions as if searching for something.

The forest became silent, and the air grew cool when a young girl appeared from behind the stone well. She was blue-eyed, pallid with a light glow, garbed in white with a necklace of flowers, and a headdress made of soft green twigs and branches. This was Gallia of the En' Fae, forest muse, goddess of the trees, and known throughout the Harrow as the Lady of the Forest.

Carrick reached back and unsheathed the blades Eligor and Ravenscar. He approached her and slowly knelt to one knee. He bowed his head and laid the blades bare at his side and before the apparition.

"Erol Carrick," said Gallia at a slow and haunting pace, her voice a soft hush of sound that was gently swept away by a light forest breeze. "You have returned to my forest. Why do you visit?"

"My lady," he said in reverence, "I have come for your blessing as a heavy burden is upon me. Darkness has returned to the Harrow."

She moved closer to him. She bent down and placed her hands on the two blades. With her touch they seemed to come to life, radiating intense colors of fire, red and orange and yellow, bright and warm.

She looked at him.

"Gaze into my eyes," she said.

He raised his head and stared into her piercing blue eyes. She moved her hands up the cold steel of the blades and onto his strong hands. He could not feel her touch other than a sharp chill that came upon him. Then he saw fire in her eyes. Within the flickering flames, he saw worries and fear, a battlefield of death and destruction, far and wide, smoldering ashes of bodies, the cloud of evil. She released her touch and stood. He lowered his head.

"Erol Carrick, your burden is heavy," she said. "Darkness is upon us. It has transformed itself into an evil you cannot imagine. I see great armies gathered from across the land and from all paths. I see wicked alliances that have been forged. I see the land in flames. I see cities in ruin. I see blood-stained fields. I see the air twisting like a strong wind, reeking of death."

He looked up at her. There was pain on her face and a lone teardrop slowly escaped from the corner of her eye.

He wanted to reassure her.

"My lady, do not be concerned for I do not fear death," he said defiantly. "I have faced evil countless times."

She took her teardrop and placed it in the corner of his eye. He again sensed the sharp chill of her touch, but also the watery warmth of her teardrop as it rolled down his cheek.

"My beloved warrior, that is the sensation of sadness," she told him. "It is something you have not always felt, but soon will and many times over. Even though you do not fear death, neither does death fear you. Always remember there is one reason to fear death."

"And what is that my lady?" he asked.

"It is a lost opportunity Erol Carrick - the opportunity to say goodbye."

He pondered her words and thought of his lost love. *Merira. How I miss you.*

"You think of her often," she said.

A billow of warmth came and flooded his heart, as he thought about how best to respond.

"I know mere thoughts cannot return someone from the claws of death," he said. "I have walked in death's shadow for what seems like an eternity. I understand its bond and the finite ends of life. I know it can take a life from our reality, but it cannot harvest the memories others have of that life. No, after losing so many friends to war, after losing someone who I loved so dearly, I do not fear the separation from life."

"Erol Carrick, then what is it you fear?" she asked.

"There is one fear greater than the nothingness of the void," he said. "It is the fear of legacy, that which I would bestow to future generations."

She pointed to the well.

"Draw a bucket of water from my crypt," she instructed.

He did as she asked.

"Your men are valiant," she said, "but their numbers alone cannot terrify this fiend. My dear Erol Carrick, do not be so eager for battle, as your success relies on a measure of boldness and caution."

She reached into the wooden bucket and drew water with cupped hands. She then repeatedly pressed her hands together. As she did this, no water spilled but vapors rose like steam and an object slowly appeared. She brought her hands to her mouth and gave a soft blow. Then she opened her hands to reveal a pure white crystallized vial. Inside the vial sparkled a clear liquid.

She handed the vial to him.

"A gift," she said.

He took the vial. It had a fluted shape that sharpened at one end to a hardened point. It felt cold in his hand,

"My lady, you have given me many gifts before. What shall I do with this gift?"

"Erol Carrick, this vial will take you to a place where you will need to be," she said. Ever so slowly she looked around the darkened forest. A look of worry came to her;

he could see it. "You must leave now. The darkness knows of me. It sees all and knows of my power, but it cannot enter my forest. It is watching you. Remember the vial. Remember my words."

She lifted her hand.

"Farewell, my friend Erol Carrick. I bid you peace."

In an instant, she was gone.

The sounds of the forest returned. They could hear the slight rustling of leaves, but they could also hear the soft rustling of the little feet of little animals and the scurrying of small creatures, even in the shade.

He placed the vial in a small leather pouch. Then he and Warsinger left the forest, soon coming to where the growth of hemlock and pine began, where the country broke into open, stony clearings and the path. A rush of air surged as Windthrasher swooped down and perched on his shoulder.

He thought of Gallia. He remembered her words. He remembered the words before he knew what they meant. He remembered the sound of them, and he remembered the touch of her teardrop. Then he became sad as a thought came to him.

I did not say goodbye.

* * *

As the sun peeked through the early morning clouds, the black ships could be seen, no more than three leagues away. Word had spread through Portmoor that the city would soon be under siege. Because of this, the docks were empty, that is, except for Skag Harwell who stood alone, with a strong grip on his sword, and firm eyes fixed on the ships. Behind him, he could hear those hurrying about, fleeing to the east, or taking up arms. Some of those who took up arms began to gather alongside him, with sword and axe in hand, ready to battle the unknown.

As the black ships came closer shrieks of evil shrillness rang from them, echoing over the sea and into the city streets.

"Who is it that we fight?" a yell came from behind him.

"No matter my axe will answer!" another shouted.

"Should we talk terms?" another barked loudly.

Harwell turned to the others.

"There's no fight, no negotiations, no surrender," he calmly told them. "This enemy knows nothing of the protocols of battle. It doesn't plunder for riches. It only thirsts for death. Drop your weapons and run as fast as you can from the city. There's no victory here!"

Another shrill swept into the city as a white haze appeared from the decks of each approaching ship. Slowly, the haze seeped over the sides and onto the sea, crawling its way to the city. The water became deathly still when suddenly a gale-force wind stirred the sea. The haze swiftly bore down on the docks. Stark white shapes began to appear, misty, soaring skeletal figures, darting in and out of the haze, silhouetted against the patch of sunlight and blue sea.

Harwell raised his sword.

"Ghost ships!" he yelled. "Ghost ships! Run!"

But it was too late.

Two shades swirled about him, one knocking him down and tearing at his insides, the other looming like a shadow over him. Images of Elban, Mora, and the children arose in his mind's eye. He allowed the peaceful images to drift through his consciousness until his pain became unbearable. He wanted to scream but already the other shade swiftly descended, engulfing him in a white haze.

The two shades made quick work of him and then sped into the city on the gale wind, leaving his charred remains to smolder on the dock.

The ghost demons were on Portmoor like a plague of locusts, swirling through the streets and into buildings, the unstopping winds hurtling the shades in a maddening whirlwind of death and destruction. The weeping and wailings of the devastated souls ensnared in a dance with death echoed throughout the city which quickly became a wasteland.

* * *

Mora, her children, and her mother cowered in a corner of Harwell's basement, too terrified to cry or move. They could hear the haunting sounds of death and what they thought was the pounding wind of a vicious storm against the house. They kept an eye on the hidden doorway as the pounding deepened, shaking the door almost off its hinges. But they did not move, keeping to Harwell's instructions.

And then it was over.

The winds ceased and the seething water smoothed. The ghost demons returned in triumph to their ships, leaving Portmoor devoid of life, featureless, a place of decay and rubble. The utter silence of the dead city lay like a blanket on the Harrow.

On the docks, a gentle sea breeze began to stir blowing the ashes of the dead about in all directions. The lead ghost ship dropped anchor and lowered a small boat into the waters that made its way to the docks. At the front of the boat stood a tall, dark figure. Within a black leather mask and helmet, piercing orange eyes studied the ruins. The demon's body was lean and well-muscled. It wore studded black steel plates that covered its shoulders, upper body, and shins, and had a long black cloak of armor weave. Strapped to its back was a short broad-bladed sword. This was an Urur Maw, a hybrid of orc and troll and man, bred by the Szard for strength and speed, and trusted to do the evil bidding of its master.

* * *

Within the putrid bowels of the great demon tower Urth' Goroth, the Szard sat in his dark library, near a smoldering fire pit, reading incantations. Always cloaked in black and hooded, he found pleasure in his library, sometimes wandering the darkness for hours, seeking distraction in yellowed pages of history or spells. In this silence, he would devise strategy and deception, of ways to brutalize and torture the innocent, of movements like the plays of a great game of chess. It was this silence that seemed to increase his evil and power, the power to influence, and the strength to see into the many outcomes of fate. But as always silence was meant to be broken, shattered like a stack of withered rushes.

From the shadows came a large Urur Maw called Grimsor. He was Uth' Egoreyr, or Great General of the worm brood.

"My master," said the large beast in a guttural voice. "We've word that the man-general visits with the forest witch."

"Yes, I know," said the Szard, his voice deep but soft. He continued to read from his book. "It is as expected."

The Urur Maw beat his chest with his right hand.

"We'll seek him out and kill him before he can gather his armies," he said. "I'll send brood to destroy the man-general. He'll die a most painful death. You've my promise."

But the Szard was still. That was a strange feeling for Grimsor. It was as though something was wrong.

Then there came a slithering sound and a hiss of breath from deep within the shadowy recesses of the dark library. It was followed by a most horrid voice, like that of an old woman grievously lamenting.

"Oh, it does not know of what it speaks," said the voice. "The foolish creature is too dumb to understand what faces him."

Grimsor was frightened at hearing the voice and stepped back with a gasp. He knew all too well of the creature, a sinister beast of dark magic and power who dwelt within the recesses of the tower, having been loved and favored by the Szard. It was his beloved.

The Szard turned to the darkness and the voice.

"Now, hush my dearest," he said. "The good Uth' Egoreyr only speaks of what he knows."

A snarled hiss sounded from the dismal depths.

The Szard closed his book and looked at Grimsor.

"My dear friend, it would seem you do not understand Erol Carrick," he said. "Oh, you may kill him, but you will never defeat him. You see, he has something many creatures do not have."

Grimsor seemed confused.

"And what is that?" he asked.

The Szard stood and walked to the fire pit. Once there he used an iron poker to slowly stir the dying embers.

"Erol Carrick has conviction and desire," he said, "a deep-rooted set of values and confidence in his belief that he is just and righteous. You see, our opponent is unshakeable. Oh, yes, you can creep up on him and spill his blood, or on the battlefield, you may scatter his armies, and crush his soldiers to a massive, mangled heap of bone and flesh. You can even kill the man himself. But my dear Grimsor - defeat Erol Carrick? Never."

The Szard returned to his chair and continued, "Those before you didn't learn this lesson. For them, war was a game of numbers and tactics. They failed to recognize that war is more a lesson of the encounter, of your opponent, of understanding what drives him." He sighed. "Leave him be Grimsor and wait for him on the battlefield. Leave him be for now and learn your lessons."

Still confused by the Szard's words Grimsor decided it was best to take leave of his master. He beat his chest and left.

Silence returned to the dark library. The Szard sat in the cold darkness and was pleased. He was relaxed and confident in his strategy. It had become clear to him long ago – one can subjugate the enemy without engaging in battle, capture the enemies' fortified cities without attacking them, and take the land without prolonged fighting. He knew this war would be one under the paramount aim of preservation. In this way, his weapons would not become dull.

"Events are in motion that will affect our individual and collective futures," hissed the melancholic voice from the dark depths of the room.

"Yes, my love. I know. It is as we planned."

His designs were more skillfully and deeply laid than the forces of good recognized.

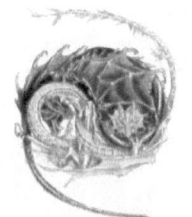

Chapter 6
Tales Upon Tales

ELBAN MIRAGRIN DID AS he was instructed, riding his master's steed Saraanth through day and night. But now as he approached Laurel Glen he knew it was time to rest the great horse. He could hear the trickle of water. They left the road and went through a grove of pine trees, following the sound. The trickle soon became the splashing and rumbling sound of water over rocks as they found themselves at a creek. The water was crystal clear, spilling over sockets of tree roots, and flowing from every tilt and crease and lip and corner until the creek vanished south into more pine trees.

They stood upon a plot of tall grass under the spreading branches of a large oak tree, next to the creek. There they drank the sweet, cold water. It was so refreshing. Elban splashed water on his face and the back of his neck.

He wiped his face with his hands and turned east where he saw threatening storm clouds far off in the distance. He first saw the darkening clouds when they left the Carn, and then again as they passed into Rivers Barrow.

The storm clouds appeared to swirl and swell at times, engulfing the billowing soft white clouds of a peaceful sky, and then becoming a dark green where they would sway and sink and stir up mighty winds, as lightning flashed. At other times the clouds seemed to wane, becoming a light grey, drifting slowly and softly, rolling, lifting, but just as menacing.

There came a crackle of thunder that lit up the sky in yellow and white. It startled him. He immediately thought of his wife and children as well as the ships off the coast.

"Mora?" he whispered.

Saraanth heard his whisper and walked over to him as more thunder roared. He looked up at the sky.

"They are fine. Master Harwell gave you his word and his word is sacred," he said. "I remember a time, long ago, when such clouds and storms appeared."

"You do?"

"Many years ago, with Master Harwell," the horse continued, "on the battlefields of the Eldor and the Crag."

Elban was initially confused, but then surprise caught him as he realized the significance of Saraanth's words.

"You're Ure Rokko, aren't you? You served Master Harwell and fought in the Shadow Wars?"

Saraanth bowed his head and returned his stare to the storm clouds.

"When I think of the past, I sometimes forget the particulars," he said. "But, to your question, the answer is yes. It was a long time ago, and a lot has happened since then. We fought alongside Erol Carrick and the great Warsinger. Day after day we chased the brood, fighting skirmishes here and there. Then came the great battles in the Eldor and Foghollow and Snowwynne, and then came that glorious day when we met the enemy for the final battle at the gates of the dark tower Ug' Cthuth."

The great horse paused and glanced back at Elban.

"Yes, Master Harwell and I were on the fields of the greatest battles that have ever been fought," he said. "We were there with the great warriors and fought with a bloodlust rage and pain in our hearts. Blades slashed and carved through the brood until the ground was covered with thousands of dead and wounded. And when the battlefield became silent, when wisps of steam rose from the bodies of the fallen, it was then that we witnessed the great Carrick bring his two mighty blades like a scissor against the neck of Mauldragw Foulhand. And in one mighty stroke, did he snap off the evil one's head like a twig from a branch. Then it was over. The clouds left; the sky was clear again. So many lives were lost, so much wasted time. To this day Master Harwell keeps a locket of Foulhand's hair, given to him by Erol Carrick. It's a relic of our victory."

Elban stood speechless at the tale. As a child, he remembered his father telling of great battles and triumphant warriors, of the great Ure Rokko horses, of flesh and swords, of the traitorous and evil Mauldragw Foulhand, and of the great final battle at the Crag that led to the release of the evil scourge.

"But Master Harwell has never spoken of this," he said. "Why didn't he tell me of his adventures?"

"He is a humble man," said Saraanth, "strong and silent, proud of his honor and good name, which were never sacrificed to the slightest extent. He finds no glory in war and at the end of it all, he decided to return to the sea, vowing to never again take up arms or talk of the darkness. What was done was done."

Elban looked up at the storm clouds for any sign that they were breaking up.

"I never realized," he said softly never taking his eye off the clouds. "All this time, to think he was there when Foulhand was killed."

"Remember, he does not talk of it because to him it is unimportant. It was something that had to be done. The war was a task that by its very nature excluded selfishness. There was little room for self-seekers. We did not go to war to become heroes. We went to war to clear the sky."

There came another rumble of thunder and a momentary burst of yellow from the east, this time leading to a booming roll that shook the ground. The storm was worrisome. Elban's thoughts again turned to his family.

Saraanth sensed his anxiety.

"We must be on our way for the storm comes and goes as it pleases," he told Miragrin. "It chooses when and where it will strike, and we're at its mercy."

He turned and started back to the road.

The skies suddenly cleared and became a brilliant blue. Together they walked in silence. As they neared the road Elban mounted the great horse, and they continued their journey to Blackstone Keep.

* * *

A storm came with a vengeance to Portmoor, just as Skag Harwell had warned. Its noise was horrific and sounded like howling spirits. Mora did as she was told. She brought her family through the secret passage and down to the basement to take shelter. During the storm they huddled together, frightened of the deafening noises. They waited and waited for the storm to pass, but it raged on. It was only when silence came that they knew the danger was over, that the storm had finally moved away. It was then that Mora took a deep breath of relief.

Is it over? she thought.

She was not sure, so she waited longer until the silence became heavy, almost unbearable. She then decided to leave the basement. She knew Harwell advised against this, but she was too curious, wanting to see what the storm had done.

Ever so slowly she opened the door of the hidden stairway. She gently slid the bookcase aside, and as she did sunlight and dust blew in and down into their basement sanctuary. There was a stench in the air and an uneasy stillness as she looked out at what remained of Skag Harwell's house. The roof had vanished and only a few walls stood. Rubble and splintered wood were scattered everywhere. She turned to her mother and told her to care for the children before leaving the basement, closing the door behind her.

She carefully made her way around the debris and to what had been the front of the house, where a road wound its way up a hill from the city. From this vantage point, she could see the skeletal remains of the city, but even worse yet she could see the smoldering ashes of its inhabitants. She was overwhelmed in horror by the devastation that was now Portmoor, and she was frightened.

This was no storm. This was a greater misery no eye ever saw.

Trouble flooded her mind, and her senses sharpened. She could now make out shadowy images lurking amongst the city ruins, picking through the debris as if looking for someone or something. A breeze brought the growling, guttural sounds of orc tongue along with the pungent smell of burned flesh. Her stomach began to turn. A rush of thoughts came to her.

Something's wrong! Is Elban safe? What of Skag Harwell?

His last words rang through her mind: *Do not come out until someone comes for you.*

Immediately she made her way back through the dust and wreckage and to the hidden stairway. She slid the bookcase back into place, closed and secured the door behind her, and descended the stairs, where the stench of charred flesh faded, and her nausea eased.

"We'll do as Master Harwell," she told her mother, mustering all the strength she could. But there was a tremble in her voice.

The two locked arms and they gathered the children, holding everyone close and safe.

"We'll wait for someone to come for us. Now, let's be very quiet and ever so vigilant," she said.

* * *

Fairfax, the girls, Brows, and Big Grey with Elspeth still nestled in his thick fur came to a great stone archway that led to the Garden Courtyard. Before passing under the archway Fairfax took Molly and Elizabeth aside. He knelt and wrapped his arms around them. With a tilt of his head and gave a big smile.

"The meeting we have been invited to will soon begin," he told the girls. "But before it does, I need to tell you some things. Now, I want you to listen to me very carefully. The Professor sent you here for a very important reason and I am sure he gave you some guidance. Whatever his guidance was, you will want to follow it. But what you need to understand is that you have what may very well be the key to saving this land from a great evil."

Molly placed the stone in her hand. It warmed to her touch.

"You mean this," she said lifting the stone.

"Yes. You have the Lia Fail and that makes you Queen of Ahlgren. This is an enormous honor and privilege. It is something to be cared for, something that one must never take for granted. The same goes for you Elizabeth, as a Princess of Ahlgren. What I want to tell you both is this: most creatures are as variable as the wind, and like the wind one moment they can blow hot and the next cold. Here in this place, you are royalty and as such you must not be like the wind. You must hold true to what you believe is right. This will help you when you're asked to make decisions, help people, and give them wisdom. Much will be asked of you. You must be strong."

She looked down at the stone. She was beginning to think it was more a curse than something coveted. She held the Lia Fail out to Fairfax.

"Maybe I should give this to someone else," she told him.

"No. No. If you did that, it would exactly be what I just warned you about," he said.

"That we can be like the wind?"

He nodded.

She became nervous. She realized she and her sister were much like the wind Fairfax described.

I'm always reluctant to take chances and Elizabeth is good at getting herself into trouble, she thought. *We're not very good at making decisions. They've always been made for us by adults.*

But it was at this moment that she began to gain a greater understanding of herself and the situation around her.

There's a reason we're here. There's a reason why I was given the Lia Fail. Somehow, someway, we're here to help.

Fairfax sensed her apprehension but that she was marshaling an inner strength. His smile widened.

"Do not fret," he said. "Remember what has been said before - you have many friends, and they will help. Let me give you a gift. It is a simple gift, a rule to remember that will help you to figure things out."

"What's that?" she asked.

"Follow what is in your heart. If you remember this simple rule, you will always be true to what you believe in, and you will impart great wisdom."

He could tell both girls were paying attention because they nodded and made eye contact with him while he spoke. He drew them closer to him.

"Now, when we walk through the archway, we will be in the Garden Courtyard, where the meeting will be held," he said. "You will make a lot of new acquaintances from the various races across the land. When the meeting begins each of you will have your own chair. I have asked Big Grey to sit between you so he can answer questions you may have. Remember, this is truly a special place, and you are viewed as very special people. Promise me you will be polite and courteous. Promise me."

The girls looked at each other. They nodded in agreement. They felt very comfortable in his arms. He was their friend. They would honor him, obey him, and if possible, would protect him, and believed what he told them, for he only asked for fair promises and kind treatment. They liked him.

"I think we're growing up," said Molly.

He chuckled.

"Of course, you are," he said. "But do not grow up so quickly as to miss out on all the fun! There is much to talk about and learn today." He handed Hadram his staff and then took the girls by the hand. "Let us go in, shall we?"

Molly looked up at him.

I know him, she thought. *He's of goodness and purity. He looks out for us and wants us to do the right things.*

She grasped the Lia Fail and felt its warmth. Her thoughts again turned to her maturing. She was gaining confidence.

I'm beginning to find my way through this strange world. I feel I can know what's in a person's heart.

Fairfax led the girls to the stone archway. As they passed beneath it Molly saw several designs carved into the stone, none of which made any sense to her. But the designs were quickly forgotten as they stepped through the archway, where they were met by the majesty and grandeur of the Garden Courtyard.

In front of them was a forest of tall trees as far as the eye could see, and it filled the air with the fragrance of cedar and pine. Nestled behind the trees in an opening, was the spectacular sight of a great waterfall. It poured down from Blackstone Mountain's summit and to a lake at the back of the courtyard, churning and frothing the water. Big Grey told the girls the waterfall was called El-Atunya, which meant *veil of spray.*

The girls could hear bird songs that carried like a symphony as the melody of large garden fountains glistened in the enchantment of beautiful flowers. They could see many delightful and whimsical garden sculptures and ornaments. There were birdbaths, gongs, and metal sculptures that inspired and made them smile. To the sides, pots overflowed with roses and lavender lining the huge black walls, as creeping thyme filled the cracks between flagstones on the ground. In front of it all was a large, curved stone dais, upon which sat many chairs. Molly quickly counted them. There were twenty in all. Each was adorned in bright fabric and sparkling jewels, and each was different in size, color and pattern. Some were made of wood and others were made of stone.

Which one is mine? she thought.

Then, a deep voice came from within the forest, and it shook the trees.

"Welcome Queen of Ahlgren and Princess of Ahlgren, nieces to the Professor, and keepers of the Lia Fail," said the voice. "I see you have brought friends with you."

A tall man, white-bearded, wearing a white robe with red silken trim appeared from the trees. He held a golden staff.

Molly sensed magic in him.

A wizard! she thought.

He stood like a statue staring at her. He then took a few gentle steps forward and slowly approached them.

"Molly and Elizabeth," said Fairfax, "I wish to introduce you to Halbierd, Dominar of the Edainar, the Order of Wizards. He is also known as Halbierd of Winter, and is En' Qessirin, or of those with magic."

The girls curtsied.

"Pleased to meet you," said Molly.

Halbierd gave a slight bow and smiled.

"Your majesty," he said. "Thank you for coming here and, I might add, so far from your home. Your presence here is important. I know you have seen many new and peculiar sights along your journey. Please become comfortable with such peculiarity as it marks what is indeed so wonderful about life."

"Thank you," she said.

He then opened his arms in a majestic gesture, and with this gesture, five men emerged from the forest. They were about the same height as Fairfax, and like him, each had long white hair, and a beard, and each carried a wooden staff. They wore long flowing robes of different colors, with symbols sewn into them.

Molly smelled a sweetness in the air.

More wizards, she thought.

Each was introduced. There was Bloomsnare the Green, Glimmershot of Light, Graspin the Strong, and Argannon the Canonical. A fifth wizard stood out. He seemed feeble, bent forward with old age, and required assistance from Hadram. He was Griffinion the Wise. Of course, the last of the wizards was Fairfax the Good.

She looked at each of them and could feel the Lia Fail warm against her skin. She felt at ease with them, that is, except for one, the wizard known as Argannon. There was something strange about him. When she looked at him the stone cooled, and an unknown worry washed over her. She had no idea why.

Each of the wizards took a position in front of a chair with Halbierd at the center of the stone dais. They stood stoic, silent, as others entered the courtyard from the archway.

First, there came a dwarf and two elves. The dwarf was similar in height to a bobbin but unlike a bobbin's childlike appearance, soft-skinned with bright eyes, he was more muscular and rugged. He was a squat man with a long, braided beard, and heavy, powerful arms. He wore layers of animal skins and a leather hat, with a short sword tucked under a brown leather belt. The dwarf's formal name was Ranagul Dithil, but he was called by his last name as all dwarves are.

One of the two elves was dressed in pure white. He was tall, fair-skinned, and had long straight black hair. He was the Elf-King, and his name was Dalgaes. By the Elf-King's side was the second elf. He was slim with auburn hair and wore a mix of tan leather and green cloth. Strapped to his back was a bow and quiver of arrows. This was the faithful elven archer Tinnfierl.

Of the race of man, there were three who followed. A man from Eldor garbed in green and brown was there, and his name was Waywyn I'Kinillel. He had striking features, handsomely chiseled cheekbones, short black hair, a mustache, and a scar just above his right eye. Then there came a man from North Sage Barrow. He was small but stout and was dressed in black wool. He wore a headband around his grey-black hair. His name was Entur Donduin. By him was a man from Ahlgren called Calen Ancorbow. He was a medium-sized man, rugged, and dressed in brown leather.

Another joined the meeting but was neither man, dwarf, nor elf. It was an eagle. It soared high above the courtyard leaving a darting shadow across the dais until it landed in a nearby pine tree. The girls were awestruck by the bird's majesty. Its white head turned and one of its yellow eyes blinked at them. It gave a nod as if to greet them, then unfurled its great black wings and seemed to bow.

"That is Azariel. He is the steward of the En' Raama, or all winged creatures," Elspeth told the girls.

Big Grey looked up at the eagle. Something seemed different with him, but he could not make out what it was. He lifted his nose and took a few sniffs of the air. He glanced back at the eagle, concerned that a yellow eye was now fixed on him. The eagle's talons clenched deeper into its perch.

I will be cautious, thought the cat. *One must always be cautious with the En' Raama.*

Fairfax then formally introduced the girls to everyone. He explained how they came from under the tree and at the Professor's request. When some saw the Lia Fail dangling from Molly's neck, a look of worry came to them.

But when the man from Ahlgren, Calen Ancorbow, saw the stone, he knelt before her and took her hand.

"My Queen, here you see your most trusted servant," he said.

Not knowing exactly what to say but knowing she had to respond, Molly said, "Thank you. I am very happy about that."

Fairfax gave a smile and winked at her. She knew she had acted appropriately. She felt as if she was beginning to understand her role as Queen of Ahlgren.

Ancorbow stood, and gave a deep bow.

Fairfax then pointed the girls to their chairs, one on either side of where Big Grey stood.

"You will know when it's time to sit," he told them.

Their chairs were wooden hewn, smaller backed, cushioned with red fabric, with small green and clear jewels in the backing. They looked comfortable.

The girls stood in front of their chairs, as the others did, and waited. Halbierd then signaled for everyone to sit. The chairs were a perfect fit for the girls and indeed comfortable.

Hadram brought out a wooden table on which sat a large leather-bound book with gold leaf pages. He placed it in front of Brows who reached into one of his pockets and took out a gold inkwell with a hinged lid. From another pocket, he took out a black quill. He placed both on the desk and opened the book to a blank page. Using the quill and ink he began writing, making his first entry as a record of what would transpire.

Molly looked over the dais and saw something curious. There were three empty seats.

Who's missing? she thought.

"My friends, thank you for coming here today," said Halbierd. "I know many have traveled great distances to be here, and we're grateful for your presence. We have much to discuss, matters of serious urgency. Certain decisions must be rendered here today, and actions taken. We will do so without the counsel of those who are not here.

"Know the Professor cannot attend today. He has instead sent us his nieces, the Queen of Ahlgren who is called Molly, and the Princess of Ahlgren who is called Elizabeth. Also, know that the great Erol Carrick is not with us today for he wears the Mark of the Tree and makes his way to join those forces already gathered. Finally, it saddens me to say that the Ra Draug have not responded to our emissaries. Because of this, their seat is vacant."

"Does not King Threch speak for the Ra Draug?" asked the dwarf.

"My dear Dithil, it would seem the Ra Draug no longer have a voice," said Halbierd.

"My people talk of Fenri packs roaming the Eldor and parts of Ahlgren," said Waywyn I'Kinillel, his tone strong and bold. "They say it's like the old times for the Fenri pillage and kill. We've deployed regiments to vanquish any roaming Fenri pack. It seems a black cloud consumes Ragmorok and no one dares to approach the place. If the Fenri find pleasure in the ways of evil, they will be met with deadly force."

"The Ra Cath dispatched emissaries from Katzhu Pu to the Rakl some time ago," said Halbierd. "They have yet to return. We fear for their loss. The Balor Guild has also sent scouts throughout the Harrow and specifically to the eastern lands. Unfortunately, few have returned."

Hearing this concerned Elizabeth. She remembered what Big Grey had told her, that Lil' Man was a scout.

"Lil' Man?" she whispered to the cat. "Is he okay?"

Halbierd overheard her whisper.

"Ah, my good Princess," he said. "You speak of Oban Pan Balor El Tar, your friend. He is fine; of this, I am certain for he is one of the most cunning of the Balor."

The girls found comfort in his words and smiled.

"Thank you," said Elizabeth.

Halbierd looked upon her and marveled at her innocence.

"You are most welcome," he said.

He then paused looking up at the sky. There was a single white cloud drifting slowly across the blue. It was a cloud that looked strangely like a face of a man smoking a pipe. He thought of the Professor and the thought made him smile.

"As I am so often reminded by the Professor," he said, "to understand the *now* we must remember the *then*. So, we will begin with the *then*, the past. You will hear a tale that has been told many times over, that which has been told by fathers to their children, and from the children to their children and so on, and as songs sung by minstrels having kept alive the memory of goodness and greatness and passed down through the ages. And you will hear of tales yet untold."

Halbierd recounted ages past, of bleak times when a darkness claimed the Harrow, when battles were fought, and men died to preserve freedom. The girls were captivated by his tale, their eyes focused on him catching his every word and expression. He told of the Dark Days when storms came from the eastern lands bringing pestilence, disease, and crop failures. He told of orcs and trolls, of black ajatars and other demonic creatures that came from the Crag. He told of times when war was waged against the good creatures of the Harrow. Along with the telling of the tale, Big Grey would provide the girls with additional detail, where he could.

But the tone of the tale changed. Halbierd spoke of a time long before the lust for war and greed for gain seeped into life. It was time mostly long forgotten when the

Harrow was different, and three kings ruled much of the land in peace. In those days, the land of Tir Nan Og was ruled by the Elf-King; the ancient land of Cairn and what is now that land west of Greenvale and north to Shadow Barren was ruled by House Eaniel; and what was then known as Ahlgren, that which lie west of the Old River and to Loch Shore was ruled by House Riorn.

The girls looked at each other. They had heard some of the stories of the kings from Brows, but only how the Trollock built the great structures.

"Peace ruled the three lands during this time, the Second Age, or as it is called the Age of Kings," said Halbierd. "This was when the Edainar was fashioned and before the time of great war. For in that time those who practiced the art of magic, conjurors as they were called, were scattered throughout the land."

He lifted his hand and an orb of white smoke appeared before the dais. The orb was motionless at first, but then it started to spin, faster and faster until it began to slow and clear itself, becoming a translucent blue. Within the orb images of four men formed.

"These were the greatest of the conjurors," he said. "You know the names - Rimprandzist, Gaithitur, Windainn, and Elswilineone. It was Rimprandzist who petitioned King Eaniel of Cairn to bring all the conjurors together, to form an Order where the art of magic could be practiced for good, and where it could be controlled. He knew of the future and of the darkness that would come. The just King Eaniel, in his wisdom, agreed to Rimprandzist's petition, and the Edainar was born of good deeds and intentions. It was said, the greatest of those of the Order would join the Anar Ere upon their passing.

"Over time the Edainar grew as young apprentices entered the Order and were trained in spells and magic. I remember that time fondly. The halls of King Eaniel's castle were filled with many young wizards, and they sat on benches under the great trees, studying together and debating incantations until the bells rang when they would scurry along pathways to classes, their arms full of books and lecture notes. It was a wonderful time. The sky was full of stars then, the trees, and the grass full of voices and secrets, the light of the sun full of warmth, and the air, the air full of magic. It was a time when anything was possible, when anything could happen. It was a time when the world was a much kinder place. But things change. As everyone knows, the castle was destroyed by the En' Rauko during the Shadow War, and the Edainar found its home, here, at Blackstone Keep."

Halbierd continued and told of how some apprentices were instructed by their teachers to travel the land, to learn of new incantations, and to bring the knowledge back, where it was written in great books of wisdom. There was one teacher, a learned wizard named Ras Amon, who instructed his students to scour the land and search for some great work of magic, such as the recovery of an ancient and powerful relic, or the invention of a new and potent spell. But in those days, such things were rare, for only the most experienced and greatest of conjurors could find artifacts or form new spells from pure magic.

"But then came a dark day, perhaps the darkest of dark days when it is said, an apprentice discovered a bottomless fissure born of evil. It was a place that spewed forth the vilest of demons, including most likely, what we now face. From this darkest of places did this apprentice take a relic. He was most proud of his discovery and displayed it before his teacher, Ras Amon. Upon seeing the relic, the great teacher felt the darkness. He pleaded with the student to return it to the fissure. But once something becomes known it is impossible to unknow it. An evil presence within the relic had already consumed the student, slowly eating away at his soul. The darkness was unleashed. The beloved Ras Amon fought back against the darkness, but sadly, was given to the Maker at the hands of his student, and the evil relic was mysteriously lost."

The orb then turned black and shook and cleared itself. Within it formed a hazy image of a young man cloaked in black, climbing great mountains that overlooked a barren land.

Dithil stood.

"Mauldragw Foulhand!" he shouted in rage.

Others stood in defiance of the shadowy figure. Big Grey told the girls that this was a name rarely spoken and then only in careful company, for to utter this name was blaspheme, the name of the person who had brought the darkness to the lands.

"Indeed, the once student of the Learned One," said Halbierd. "He goes by many names - the Accursed, Bringer of Doom, Death Reaper, and Foulhand – the names given to this demon by the many races of the Harrow."

"Draoulilen," said Dalgaes, the Elf-King. "As we elves call him – the Great Traitor!"

"It was he who brought the darkness, the doom upon the land!" shouted Ancorbow. "The trees turned black, and their branches were torn from the sky, and their leaves were strewn across the land. The Harrow was laid waste, and the ravens were sent into the sky. Everything was covered in death and darkness, and it seemed as if the whole world had sunk into the abyss. The only sounds that were heard were the wailings of the brood as they crept over the damp ground to devour their next prey. But he was defeated, slain by the forces of the good and righteous!"

The orb's image then cleared and Halbierd raised a hand, to calm everyone.

Those standing returned to their chairs as the tone of the tale again changed. Halbierd continued. He told them that for ages it remained something of a mystery as to how the apprentice came by the relic. Did he stumble on it? Was the dark magic given to him by another? There was also the question of what became of the relic. Those of the Edainar had never seen it, other than Ras Amon. Halbierd explained that only recently had a spell been crafted by the wizard Griffinion, a variation of an ancient spell long forgotten. Called the Obscurite, the spell provided one critical answer, showing the Edainar images of a most terrifying reality -

that even though Foulhand had been vanquished the powerful dark magic remained.

On hearing this, there was disbelief and great commotion. Many began to talk amongst themselves, sharing their thoughts and fears.

Entur Donduin stood.

"Wizard, what does this mean?" he asked.

Halbierd was calm.

"Master Donduin, it means quite simply that the darkness now before us is the same evil from the past," he said. "It is the same darkness your forefathers fought so many ages ago, the same wickedness that almost annihilated the races. It would seem that Foulhand was but a small part of some greater darkness."

With those words, Halbierd was clear. Mauldragw Foulhand, the Harrow's once great enemy who had been defeated in battle, was but a minion of a darker, more sinister force. Almost immediately, there was tumult on the dais, unease, and an edge of panic.

Dithil again rose from his chair. He brandished his blade.

"What is this evil?" he said. "Let me at it so it can feel the sweet edge of my sword. I will slay the foul wretch and its dwellings will be found waste and desolate. I will not swerve from my word until its dark face grovels in the dust of this good land."

There was a rousing cheer.

Waywyn I'Kinillel stood alongside Dithil.

"Brave dwarf, we shall gather our armies and with Erol Carrick venture to the Crag," he said. "We defeated the menace once before and we shall again prevail! In such a cause, with the aid of providence, we'll come out crowned with success!"

Another cheer rose. But Halbierd's expression changed from one of calm to one of cold, deadly intent.

"Now, now, listen and listen well!" he said. "No blade can stop this evil, and it is far, far away, and deeply hidden in the Crag. And, to my good friend Master I'Kinillel, the truth is now known – the menace was not defeated, nay, the wars of old but diminished the brood and defeated an underling, while the very core of the darkness sat in its lair planning, waiting for another opportunity."

Angered by what Halbierd said, a defiant Calen Ancorbow stood.

"Wizard, do you mean to say my father's death and his father's death were for naught?" he asked. "If this is what you now say then I must take issue with your words."

A flush rose through Big Grey. He had heard enough. He jumped down from his chair and to the center of the dais. Elspeth flittered off and high into the trees perching next to Azariel.

"Stop! Just stop it!" roared the cat. "Sit down, all of you! Enough of this talk! We were invited here to learn of the evil we now face. It is best to hold your emotions, as difficult as that may be. Already the menace the Dominar speaks of has an advantage. While we shout and raise our hackles, the brood grows stronger and makes its way to the west. We see the signs above us, in the skies. If there is a chance to defeat this enemy once and for all, to prove we are warriors of skill and courage, we must do so strategically and calmly, for I fear this battle will be long and hard and test our vigor. The races will not shrink from this challenge. No! They will stride forward to meet this evil wherever it can be joined! Let us build our strength here and now and go about things wisely!"

There was a frosty silence; the only sound was that of Brows, his quill furiously writing what had been said. Those that had stood returned to their chairs.

Everyone on the dais respected the cat. They respected his special knowledge of the law. More importantly, they admired his wisdom and understanding of events. Even the great Erol Carrick was known to seek his advice before battle.

As everyone began to settle, the wizard Griffinion stood. He was sallow looking and oddly bent at the waist. He leaned heavily on his staff, with Hadram supporting him from behind. Taking a deep breath, he lifted a hand, gently motioning to everyone.

"Thank you, Master Purr," he declared in a weak voice. "Clarity exists where before there was confusion. The Obscurite reveals many things to us. We see the tower Ug' Cthuth rebuilt. We see the roads and pathways once known to us changed. We see a dark figure wandering the halls of a second tower called Urth' Goroth. We see the dark one wielding great power and forceful magic that grows more ominous each day. We see a new army of fire and steel marching. We see a raging inferno in the eastern lands. We see an evil, the same evil that was the mastermind behind Foulhand so many years ago."

"But how can you be sure?" asked Donduin.

Griffinion did not immediately answer. He was frail and quick to tire. He took short, clumsily hesitant steps backward, as Hadram helped to guide him gently back into his chair. Once seated, he wrapped his arms around his staff and then mustered the strength to reply.

"It is the same magical signature as before," he said feebly. "I have seen it with my own eyes. There is no doubt."

"As you can see, the good Griffinion is weakened by the spell," Halbierd told them. "It drains his energy and prompts him to often rest. Try as he might, he does not have the strength to completely penetrate the dark veil that shrouds this evil. The Obscurite limits our ability, and the evil is strong. But what we've seen provides a pathway, one we must carefully travel if this evil is to be defeated."

Everyone sat in silence for several moments. They did not know how to react to Halbierd's grave words. Everyone seemed lost in their thoughts.

Calen Ancorbow stood.

"A second tower in the Crag? I do not understand," he said in frustration. "We left no living soul there! And who is this mysterious figure you're referring to? Is it possible that it's a Dark Wizard? Why were we not informed about this earlier?"

Halbierd turned to Ancorbow.

"The Obscurite revealed the second tower but a few days ago," he said. "We thought it best to leave the details for this gathering. As for the dark figure, we believe he is not a Dark Wizard. But unfortunately, the aura that surrounds this entity is far viler. It would appear Dark Wizards are servants to this evil soul, to the master of Urth' Goroth.

"But there is much more my friends, perhaps a connection to what we now face. An orc was trapped and captured by the dwarves of Mortha. The creature was secretly brought here for inquiry some time ago. This orc is different, very different than his brethren. At first, the beast would not speak, but in time it fell to the persuasion of Argannon's magic. Under this persuasion, the beast confirmed that which was revealed by the Obscurite."

"Aye, I helped to bring the creature here myself," smirked Dithil. "But I would've preferred it dead and by my swift blade. I'll tell you the beast is mad with the mind of an orc-child. It wandered through our realm, roaming the hills of Mortha Vale for days. Eventually, it made its way to our mountains. We don't know why it entered our land. But those who saw the demon said it rummaged through hovels and garbage and overturned stones as if it were looking for something. They say they heard it mumbling something in its despicable language, over and over again. Some of our wisest understood the beast's rants. They say he speaks of a 'shiny piece of stone' and that 'it is lost.' The Elders decided to set a trap using a piece of quartz, a worthless bit of stone to our people. When the orc reached for the gem, we netted the beast and lifted it high into the trees where we speared it with a calmative. We sent word to the Edainar. The wizards asked us to bring the demon here. We did so but I still say no good shall come of this. The beast should've been killed, put out of its miserable existence."

Argannon the Canonical stood.

"When the orc came to us," he said, "we brought it to the dungeons deep within the depths of Blackstone. There we tormented him with a torch, the fire striking fear, and anger in him. As this was done, I weaved a series of dark spells that reached into the orc's mind. Within this gloom, I could hear a voice talking to it. I was able to replicate this voice using my magic and speak to the creature with it. I believe the voice to be that of the orc's master. The voice seemed to soothe the creature's pain and tranquility came over him. Through this calmness, he spoke to me as if I were his master."

Molly looked at Argannon as he spoke. She felt the Lia Fail suddenly cool. Her concern with him returned as she again felt uneasy. There was something about him; he was different than Fairfax, different than the other wizards. She could not see into him the way she could with the others.

"We have learned many things from the orc," continued Argannon, "many things that will surprise you, frighten you. He is from an orc tribe of the northern Drueger. As an orc child, he was brought into slavery to the twisted towers by the dark one, the tower's master, the one the orc calls Dark Lord or Szard. As he grew, he was taught to be a fierce warrior. He was also instructed in the many languages of the races. We believe this was done so he could understand our ways, perhaps to infiltrate the western lands. He was assigned to a horde, and was given a special mission, to find the Lia Fail, what he calls the 'shiny piece of stone', and return it to his master. But his horde found him strange, too strange. They deemed him useless. They mocked him and they beat him until he was unconscious. Then they purposely left him out in the wild, alone. Even though separated from the security of his horde, he still faithfully continued his mission, to seek the Lia Fail, that is, until his capture by the dwarves."

"The beast is dim-witted," muttered Dithil. Some on the dais chuckled. "All his kind are like that. They're born with little capacity for learning, never learning much. From one horde to the next, each horde teaching the same things, and the brutes never seem to grasp a single thing."

"A dim-witted creature, as you say my dwarf friend, perhaps," said Donduin. "But does a dim-witted creature learn several languages?" he asked, dismissive of Dithil. "As we all know, there've been few orcs able to master the languages of the west. I suspect there's a deviousness here. The orc should not be trusted."

Dithil muttered something under his breath and gave Donduin a stern look.

But it was Calen Ancorbow, who brought simplicity to the discussion.

"So, the brood searches for the Lia Fail," he said. "They wish to eliminate any and all weapons that may oppose them. And the Dark Lord you speak of takes few chances, instead holding back, maybe to have others do his bidding."

The wizards nodded. Again, silence fell upon everyone.

Molly did not fully understand the direness of what had been said. Instead, she felt strangely saddened by Argannon's tale, saddened for the orc, and how he had been treated. It reminded her of home, of children that did not fit in or did not have any friends, those who were chided, bullied, and made fun of by others. She had never seen an orc and believed such a creature most likely to be incredibly horrid. But she still felt sorry for him, as images of the beast sitting alone in a dark and dank dungeon came to her.

The Professor sent us here for a reason. The stone pendant and the orc, is there a connection? Perhaps.

She took the stone into her hand. It warmed to her touch, and she could feel a gentle throb like that of a heartbeat.

Is there a link with the orc?

She remembered what Fairfax told her.

Follow what's in your heart.

She looked at everyone on the stone dais. She had a question that needed to be asked.

She stood and looked at Argannon.

"Does he have a name?" she asked.

Shocked by her question, the others turned to look at her. But she held firm and maintained eye contact with Argannon, this time not as Molly but as Queen of Ahlgren.

"I'm sorry," said Argannon, returning the stare. "I guess I did not hear your question. Are you asking if the orc has a name?"

She was annoyed at him.

"I think you heard me perfectly," she said. "But I will again ask, just to be clear. Does the orc have a name?"

"Why yes," relented Argannon in a soft voice. "His name is Ug'ghi Otha."

"Well then, I would like to see Ug'ghi Otha," she said. "Please, bring him here to me."

A hush came over the group, followed by a great roar. No one could understand why she would want to see the beast. Ancorbow attempted to persuade her against her request, but she would have none of it. She simply kept her stare on Argannon.

As the Lia Fail continued to warm, she felt she was becoming stronger, finding her way, discovering the path set forth by the Professor.

She turned to Halbierd.

"Is there some kind of rule that prevents you from bringing him here?" she asked politely and over the voices of dissent.

He was hesitant and then bowed in deference.

"If so the Queen decrees," he proclaimed.

She looked at Fairfax remembering the simple rule he gave her before the meeting. She smiled at him, and he returned the smile. A lot of things were becoming clearer to her. The Professor knew exactly what he was doing by sending her to the Harrow with the Lia Fail. She was here to somehow help, and if she were to help, she had to begin to do things her way.

The many voices from the dais tried in vain to shape her conviction, but she remained self-confident in her opinions about ideas and people. The more they tried to change her mind, the greater her resolve grew. She was determined to take her place in this world.

Big Grey raised a paw trying to calm everyone but to no avail. He could see Molly's determination.

She is beginning to change, he thought. *The stone is having its way with her. The child is wiser than we know.*

"She's only a little girl," pleaded Dithil. "She knows nothing of this world!"

But Donduin came to her defense.

"Perhaps, but she has the Lia Fail," he said. "Lest we forget this makes her Queen of Ahlgren!"

Dithil pointed to Donduin.

"I've had enough of this man!" he shouted. "He'd have us put our fate in the hands of a child! A shard of stone doesn't make a Queen!"

Dithil's words brought a gasp from the dais. Ancorbow became angry. Even though he did not understand why his Queen wanted to see the orc, she was the Queen nonetheless and as such demanded respect, even from dwarves.

He raised a fist to Dithil.

"Insolence!" he yelled. "Utter insolence! Is the Queen to be questioned thus by one such as you? Would you desire to have the armies of Mortha wage battle without the Lia Fail, without a Queen to wield its power? Let me remind those here, that she's Queen by the mere fact that she possesses something that we cannot. The Professor has been the Keeper of the stone. He's given it freely to someone he believes deserving of its power, someone he's determined to be pure of heart and mind, and strong of spirit. This is the Keeper's role. Who here will question his decision? Huh? Who here will question his decision!"

Ancorbow looked over the dais with determined eyes. No one moved; no one made a sound.

"I thought not," he said. "Know this my friends: I shall have no mercy for those who refuse to recognize the Queen's duty, her virtue, or her burden. The one who is Queen is Queen to us all and Queen over our enemies!"

Stillness came over the gathering. Ancorbow's words resonated. Dithil, his lips tightly pressed together, took a deep breath, and nodded slowly in submission. All eyes turned to Molly, the Queen of Ahlgren.

She remained standing but did not move. Her face was still, her eyes back to a firm glare on Argannon. She did not trust him, and as she held her stare upon him she could still feel the warmth of the Lia Fail, and it was becoming warmer and the rhythmic throb stronger.

Somewhere, something incredible is waiting to be known. The Professor's words rang like magic in her mind.

An idea came to her.

There is a connection! There is a connection!

She knew what she had to say and more importantly how to say it.

"Enough with all this talk. Bring the orc here," she demanded in a slow and angry voice. "I wish to see him."

Brows leaned over to Fairfax.

"Where is this leading?" he asked the wizard.

Fairfax was intrigued by Molly's resolve.

"I think I may have an idea," he told Brows. "We shall soon find out. But my friend, I believe you may need to nudge the process along a bit."

"Indeed," said Brows. "Nothing would give me greater pleasure."

He stood and faced Halbierd.

"Halbierd of Winter, Dominar of the Edainar - the Queen of Ahlgren has asked to see the orc. What say you?" he asked.

Halbierd thought momentarily. He glanced at Fairfax and saw an unyielding trust in his eyes. He then glanced at Molly. He sensed her strength and a purpose to her actions. He bowed before her with his decision.

"As her majesty commands," he said. He gave the order to Hadram. "Bring the orc before us."

* * *

The rolling green hills and wooded terrain of the Old River greeted the view of Lil' Man and Chumsey, and for each, it was one of the most beautiful places in the entire Harrow. To the north, where the hills met the Elmham River one could see plentiful orchards of various fruits, and west of the orchards a vast forest stretched mighty and majestic with the great mountains called the Old Hills extending across the horizon. The white-stoned city of Mistmere itself lay in the distance, cradled within the valley. In ages past, the hills were used as a fortress by the people of the city, to fend off invaders and the armies of the darkness for they provided an ideal view for spotting intruders.

Mistmere was a grand city of fountains, waterways, grand promenades, formal gardens, and courtyards, of broad walks and wide avenues, languid gardens, and red roses which poured forth the sweetest perfume emitted by flowers. The city was renowned throughout the land for its opulence and wealth. It was so beautiful that it was a city of dreams to which one longed to return again and again, and many a poem and story described its splendors and the grandeur of its architecture, and the glories of its palaces. Every aspect of the city was magnificent, and it had a charm and a grace, and a majesty that made all who beheld it exclaim with wonder and admiration, "This could only have been made by the Maker!"

The two cats lifted their noses.

"Can you smell the flowers? asked Lil' Man.

"No sweeter scent in all the Harrow," said Chumsey.

As they neared the great city something seemed peculiar. They felt as if they were being watched by invisible eyes. It was then when Lil' Man's keen eyes spied guardsmen.

"We are being watched," he said. He pointed with his paw to the surrounding hills and trees. "Rhiorsnan, there, and there, and there."

The Rhiorsnan were the elite guards of the city. They wore forest green tunics with purple piping, and the cuffs of their tunics were also purple, with each wearing a leather helmet that covered the entire head, strapped in the back with large rawhide laces.

Thurir also saw them.

"It is to be expected in such troubled times," he said. "Mistrust is everywhere. We will proceed slowly to not make an action that can be viewed as hostile."

They began their walk over the hills and toward the city. The guardsmen slowly followed them, retreating, and signaling to each other, their numbers growing along each hill. Eventually, what appeared to be a full unit of guardsmen stood before them with bent bows and arrows drawn.

A guardsman of lean stature with a tangle of golden hair underneath a helmet stepped forward.

"State your business," said the guardsman with a slight voice.

Thurir halted the pack.

"We are here to see your Lord," he said.

There was no immediate response from the guardsman. But the cats quickly became uneasy when the sound of an arrow hissed over the grass, followed by a sharp thwack as it lodged in the bark of an old butternut tree.

CHAPTER 7
UG'GHI OTHA

"**WE HAVE NO WEAPONS!**" roared Thurir. "We mean you no harm!"

He realized that a simple signal from the guardsman would send a hail of arrows into the air, killing his pack and the two cats. There was no escape or opportunity for battle.

Lil' Man and Chumsey quickly dismounted their Fenri companions and stood by Thurir.

"My friend and I are of the Balor Guild, from Katzhu Pu," Lil' Man told the guardsman. "This Fenri pack has protected us and leads us to the sacred city."

Chumsey took a step forward.

"We have endured great hardship, traveling many leagues and through the black of night," he said. "During our journey, we saw a great black army to the east, and we fought off a pack of Fenri rebels. We must see the Lord of Mistmere. We wish to warn him of the evil that makes its way west."

The guardsman who stood before them raised a hand. It was a signal to the archers to lower their bows. All fell silent. The guardsman moved slowly towards the three and stood looking at Thurir for a few moments, then down at the cats. The guardsman reached behind the leather helmet, loosened its rawhide laces, and pulled off the covering. Long golden hair fell out in a wavy heap.

Thurir and the two cats were surprised.

In front of them stood a young woman, her face clear, round, smooth-skinned, with a thin nose, and her lips full and soft. She bent down to the cats, her face calm, serene, even glowing, and when her eyes met Lil' Man's, she smiled.

"Oban Pan! I thought it was you!" she told him. "From a distance I was uncertain, but now that I am near, I know it is you! Do you remember me?"

He searched his memory in vain for a living image of such beauty, and then it came to him.

"Yes . . . yes . . . I believe I do remember," he said. "It was some time ago. I remember a little girl with similar features. If you're that pretty little girl I must apologize for I do not remember your name."

The young woman laughed and reached out to gently rub the top of his head. He began to purr at her touch, a tender rumble.

"Oh, Oban Pan, I am that little girl. I am Glaeynd, daughter of Kraneth, Lord of Mistmere. I was sent to Katzhu Pu by my father to learn about the world from the Guilds. That is where we met. We would play together in the great halls. Don't you remember?"

He remembered her now. She was a pretty little girl - twelve, maybe thirteen years of age when they played together. He would often see her during his summer visits to Katzhu Pu. Now, she was no longer a girl, but a young woman, and a beautiful one at that.

"Glaeynd the Young, second in line to the Lordship," he smiled. "Yes, I remember now. It's been a long time. It's so good to see you. I hope you are doing well."

"I am well," she said, "but do not let my age fool you. There is a lot of that little girl left in me. Even though it has been many years since you and I played together you may still find me a worthy opponent."

He chuckled and nodded.

Chumsey turned to Lil' Man in disbelief.

"What is this?" he said. "You played with a human child? I cannot believe what I am hearing. You avoid humans the way we Ra Cath avoid water."

"She was different," said Lil' Man. "She excelled at a rollicking game of hide 'n seek. Trust me - when I had my fill of her, I would quietly take my leave. But the silly girl would always come back for more. I swear to you."

Glaeynd burst out in laughter.

"What's this? Ha, if I remember correctly, it was you who would walk away every time you lost, and it was you who would come back and plead for another chance."

Chumsey threw his head back and gave a hearty laugh from deep within his chest.

"I knew it! Always tilting a story," he teased Lil' Man.

Glaeynd smiled and stood. She placed her hands on her hips and spread her feet wide, like a warrior ready for battle. The wind gently brushed her hair down and around her, capturing the sunshine and reflecting it.

"Friends of Oban Pan," she declared, "you are welcomed by all of Mistmere and recognized as favored guests."

"Thank you Glaeynd," said Lil' Man.

She raised a hand. It was another signal. In response, the guardsmen were gone, hiding in the hills and trees.

"Let us make our way to the city," she said.

She led them to Mistmere. The journey over the hills was not long, nor was the way irksome. They followed a path that led them through the vast green landscape of lemon and orange groves, apple orchards and fields of berries, and vineyards of vines bearing heavily. At every turn, the views were spectacular and the scents were fragrant.

For the two cats, there was something very special about wandering among the trees in the orchards with tall grasses underfoot. They examined the lichens on the trees' trunks and enjoyed the sweet songs of birds. As they peered through a kaleidoscopic display of hues made up of fruits of red, orange, green, and yellow, they could see animals grazing in the fields. It was a place of contrasts and diversity, and everything seemed so fresh and new.

Along the way, Glaeynd told the two that her father had grown weak and belligerent with age. Because of this, her brother was now entrusted with most of the city's affairs. He made her leader of the Rhiorsnan and that put her in charge of the city's protection.

Lil' Man was saddened to hear of her father's frailty. He remembered him as a strong leader, intelligent, not personally corrupt, and a man of considerable culture.

Glaeynd then spoke of recent worries.

"We have seen dark signs across the land, evil signs," she told them. "There is word of black ajatars in the skies, and recent storms have been severe, bringing winds with a wicked stench. Some say the storms are harbingers of a coming darkness. But more concerning has been reports of strangers who make their way to the city under the cloak of night."

"Strangers?" asked Chumsey.

"Yes. We are told they travel from the east and come late at night, just before sleep when the shadows deepen. It is said they roam the streets, hunched over as though bearing the weight of another on their back, looking for shelter. But when the sun rises, they are gone as if vanished in the air. We have searched the city for them but cannot find a trace. Only recently have I posted more Rhiorsnan at the city gates. But since then, all has been quiet."

"Many strange occurrences these days," said Thurir. "We should be careful. Is the city safe?"

"I assure you, my Fenri friend, you will be safe," she said. "My Rhiorsnan captains have secured our city."

"Speaking of Rhiorsnan captains, what about the young man, Twain Boggans?" asked Lil' Man. "If I remember you found him quite appealing. How is he these days?"

He remembered there was much talk throughout the land about Glaeynd and the young man, especially when he became a Rhiorsnan captain. He knew the young man, having met him several times over the years, and he thought very highly of him. Boggans was known as a skilled guardsman, brave, who had a quiet, self-possessed manner about him. He was always courteous to strangers and had a way of making others feel at ease.

Glaeynd giggled playfully. She reached down and tugged at Lil' Man's tail, gently lifting his rear.

"Silly cat," she said. "He is doing just fine, and never you mind about Mr. Boggans."

When they came to the oldest apple orchard, that was nearest to Mistmere's gates, the trees were in blossom. These were the same varieties given as a gift to the Professor, for his orchards. A gentle breeze swayed the tops of the trees and light as perfumed rain fell upon them. Ahead, they saw a wide valley with the misty, white-stoned city glistening in the sunlight.

The city of Mistmere was quite a sight to behold. It was built from the white rock tossed out by a volcano that overlooked it, one of many mountains in the eastern and desolate rim of the ancient mountains known as the Old Hills. Mistmere was bathed in sunshine almost every day, a city lost at the end of jagged crags, with magnificent whisks of clouds that continuously feathered through the top of the valley. It was a city of cycles, a city of layers, and a city of rings; as it grew outward, it accrued rings much like a tree trunk. Unlike other Harrow cities, Mistmere's corners and towers were not geometrically even. Its walls repeated the ups and downs of the hills, forming a picturesque wavy line, like a river meandering through a valley, while its large white towers seemed to float serenely above the trees.

Within the city's many rings were fascinating villages with stepped terraces, ornate fountains, and hanging gardens from almost every rooftop. Streams of water emerged from elevated sources and flowed down sloping channels. These waters irrigated the whole of Mistmere, saturating the roots of plants, keeping the land moist, and providing a veil of mist that blanketed the city throughout the day. Such inspired the city's name.

As they continued, Lil' Man trotted out in front with Chumsey, a tiny gallop that made Glaeynd smile. She was glad to see the cat and surprised at the unexpected encounter. These were difficult times for her, and she thought that perhaps her cat friend might assist her in some way. With him close by, memories of a happier time flooded over her. For the first time in a long time, she felt reassurance against the strains of the day and the strangeness she faced. Even though she had taken well to her new duties, she was still uncomfortable commanding the Rhiorsnan. She felt unprepared, especially with her father's frailty, and relied heavily on her captains. Often, she wondered if she even had the strength to lead.

Such were her worries and secrets. She kept them to herself, hidden behind the facade of a strong female who had learned so many things from her father. She knew that letting others see behind this facade would mean complete and immediate rejection. The damage would be irreparable; it would be the worst possible thing. But she was at least certain of one thing - the enduring friendship of her cat friend.

Strange times like these are best handled by men, she thought. *After all, war and battle are the folly of men.*

Nearing the main gate Lil' Man and Chumsey could see hundreds of Rhiorsnan atop the city's massive white wall. The waning sunlight glinted from their spearheads and arrows. Alongside each perched falcons and eagles, massive birds of prey, their seashell eyes glassy in a daunting stare. The cats slowed their pace just a bit, always cautious with such birds. But Glaeynd raised her hand and the Rhiorsnan withdrew their spears and arrows, and the birds looked past them and into the surrounding orchards.

"Fear not little ones," she told the cats as they continued into the city and through the streets. "No harm will come to you. Of that, you can mark my words."

She turned to Thurir and his pack.

"We make our way to Ewellinoth, the Great Hall of the Lord," she said.

But unbeknownst to Glaeynd and the others, there was darkness below the streets, deep in the city's ancient catacombs. It was a lurking devilishness that waited patiently and alertly, a silent watcher nesting within the black, and as potent as the forces that had fashioned the evil.

* * *

There was grumbling, there was muttering, and there was confusion and much scurrying about by everyone on the dais, except for Molly who sat quietly in her chair watching as the others made a fuss. While some looked at her and shook their heads in disbelief, a few gave words of support. But none of it mattered to her. She was confident and calm, confident that soon everyone would understand the reason for her request, and this would defuse the emotions now around her. Something was changing inside of her. She could feel it, especially when she touched the Lia Fail.

I do not understand how, but things suddenly are becoming clear to me. I know what I must do, what I must say.

For someone not prone to taking chances, she finally came to realize that to solve any puzzle, one must accept a certain amount of risk, a degree of danger. In her mind, all the pieces of this puzzle fell into place for her; she had a plan and knew exactly what she was doing.

I must work on building positive relationships with others. That is important. But will they allow me the time to do so?

"Okay, what are you up to?" asked Elizabeth.

Elizabeth's voice shook Molly from her thoughts. She was frustrated with her sister's question.

"What do you mean?"

"Molls, weren't you listening? They're calling that thing a monster. Why would you want to see a monster? What's wrong with you? It could kill us! They all think you're crazy." Elizabeth then pointed to the Lia Fail around Molly's neck. "It's that thing the Professor gave you, isn't it? I can hear what the others here are saying, even though they're whispering. They say you can't handle its power, that you don't know how to use it. Don't you remember what Fairfax told us before we came here? He said for us to be polite and courteous. I don't think this is being very polite or courteous."

Molly was annoyed with her sister, but she understood what she was saying. It did seem crazy. After all, they were strangers in this strange place, and despite being thrust into the role of queen and given a powerful tool, Molly had no idea how to use it. But then again, as best as she could gather, no one knew how to use the Lia Fail. She remembered the good wizard's words and went about reminding Elizabeth of them.

"Fairfax told us to hold true to what we believe is right," she told Elizabeth. "He told us to do what is in our hearts. That is exactly what I am doing. I cannot expect you to understand what is happening to me, but you have got to trust me. I think I know what I must do. I think I now understand why we are here."

"I don't understand," said Elizabeth. "Why won't you listen to what the others are saying?"

Molly searched for a way to help Elizabeth understand.

"I know how you're feeling," she said softly in hopes to calm her sister. "But think of it this way. Remember our friend Sarah? Remember when she first came to our school? Do you remember how everyone made fun of her, because of how she dressed and that she came from a different part of town? Do you remember?"

"Well, yes," said Elizabeth. "But I don't see your point. That's not the same. Sarah's not a monster."

"Of course, she's not. The point is she was first treated like a monster, in a certain way I suppose. Don't you remember? No one would play with her. Everyone thought she was different. It wasn't until we played with her, and when we started to talk to her that we found out she was just like us. It doesn't matter how a person dresses or where they live. Don't you see? Sarah was just like us – a kid who just wanted to have friends. Now she's one of our best friends. Elizabeth, that orc, how he's been treated - it's like how Sarah was treated. He's been made fun of, and no one quite understands him. But there's something else, something important to all this. I think he holds a key, a key to something that we need if we're to be helpful. I think I know how we can get him to help us."

Elizabeth took a deep breath and looked down. She remained frustrated at her inability to understand her sister.

"Molly, I just don't get it. What key could a monster have? Everyone here says that thing is evil! Shouldn't we believe them?"

Molly was about to answer when a noticeable hush came over the group. At the stone archway, they saw the orc, hooded with a black sack, his feet and hands shackled. Everyone quickly took their seats.

Halbierd motioned the guards to bring the orc to the center of the dais. The brute was prodded and pushed into the courtyard by several muscular guards each carrying a long, pointed spear. Slowly and cautiously, they moved the beast to the center. Molly saw that as the orc shuffled its shackled feet streaks of blood were left on the flagstones.

While everyone was fixated on the orc, from the corner of his eye Big Grey saw that Azariel had disappeared. The eagle had soared off, back up into the clouds carrying Elspeth far away past the Black Mountain.

Strange, he thought. *Why would he leave?*

But he soon got back to what was happening. As the orc was brought to the center of the dais Dithil stood.

"Gulguthra!" he cried out in disgust.

Others also stood and shouted with some drawing their weapons.

"Put your blades away," commanded Halbierd, "and take your seats. I will have order here or I will have no choice but to ask some of you to leave."

Those standing had fury in their eyes, but they did as the Dominar demanded.

"Remove the hood," Halbierd told the guards.

With his face revealed many on the dais looked away or cringed. The orc was a gruesome creature, his forehead was low and jutted forward, and his green leathery face was hideously pocked. His head was bald except for a few tufts of coarse brownish hair over short, pointed ears. He was tall and slightly stooped, and wore a close-fitted leather tunic, with protruding veins that wrapped about a massive and strong body like the bark of a tree. He was a horrid sight, one the girls sickened at as they gazed with a sort of fascination.

Donduin stood and pointed at the orc. There was a look of stunned amazement on his face.

"Look! Look! The creature's eyes," he said. "I've never seen anything like it on an orc!"

"By the Maker!" said a shocked Waywyn I'Kinillel. "Its eyes. Its eyes. They're blue."

Molly strained a bit to look more closely at the orc's face. To her surprise, she saw what they spoke of. The orc's eyes were large, wide, serious, a soft blue - too soft and too blue, perhaps for such a misshapen and horrid beast. She was taken by the beauty of his eyes and forgot everything she had been thinking about. She clutched the warm Lia Fail.

One day his heart will prove to be a thing of rare beauty, she thought, remembering a line from a poem the Professor once read to her.

She did not know why the thought came to her; it just did.

The stone? Did it bring the thought to me? Does it speak to me through my past?

"It's unnatural!" shouted Dithil. "I told you the thing should be killed!"

The orc snarled at the dwarf exposing its canine-like teeth. Dithil raged forward, swiftly unsheathing his short sword. A guard pushed him away as several other guards pulled the orc back, with one guard reaching out from behind, stabbing the beast on its side. A stream of blood poured from the wound. The orc dropped to his knees and howled in pain, a cry that echoed through the trees.

Elizabeth turned away from the sight. Molly was disgusted by the violent act.

"Stop it!" she shouted.

Halbierd raised his hand, and all sat and were quieted.

"The orc was brought to us at the request of the Queen of Ahlgren," he said. "Bring him to her, but safely so."

Calen Ancorbow rose and stood alongside Molly, his hand clutching a lean metal blade stealthily tucked under his belt. The guards turned the orc to face Molly and pushed him towards her. The brute sank in exhaustion. He crawled on his knees towards her and tried to stand but could not. As his body bent crooked under the weight of his toil, sweat dripped from his chin and brow forming muddy puddles on the flagstone. While still oozing blood from his wound, he brought his shackled hands tightly to his breast and gritted his teeth in agony in front of her.

She was saddened by what she saw - not the frailty of the weak so much, but the callousness of the strong.

"You poor thing," she said. "Look how they treat you."

She stood and turned to Ancorbow and asked for a cloth. He reached into his coat pocket, pulled out a white piece of linen, bowed, and handed it to her.

She knelt before the orc. The guards nervously held their positions around him, prepared if necessary to protect her. The other dais members were stunned into silence.

"My name is Molly," she said using the linen to wipe sweat from his hideous face. "I mean you no harm. Do you understand me?"

She stared into his blue eyes with unyielding determination. He gazed back into hers searching for some sign of understanding in her stare. He found it. Slowly, ever so slowly, he nodded.

"I speak the common tongue," he said with a quivering and exhausted voice. "I am Ug'ghi Otha. My horde is from the northern wastelands, of the place you call the Drueger."

Molly continued to clean his face with the cloth. She brought it to his side and placed it over the knife wound, holding it tightly against his muscular frame. She continued pressure against the wound as the cloth absorbed the blood.

"I know that place is far away. But why are you here, so far from your home?" she asked.

"I seek that which is special," he said, "that which my master covets."

"Well, I think we have something in common, you and me," she said with a cautious smile.

Puzzlement flushed over his face.

"What could we possibly have in common?" he said. "You are but a child of the En' Edan, and me, I am an orc!"

"It seems I have what you seek, the special object your master so craves."

His eyes widened with excitement.

"Show me!" he cried.

She carefully placed the cloth on the ground, and slowly unclasped the necklace from around her neck. She held the Lia Fail aloft, dangling the stone before him. The stone began to glow a deep red, and she smiled.

A frightened hush fell upon the dais.

The orc gasped. His eyes widened in amazement, then closed in grief as he wept at the sight of the glimmering jewel. Here, only a few inches from his shackled hands, was what he so desperately sought, that which would make him a hero to his horde and his master.

Molly could sense great anticipation in him but also a modicum of fear in having long last found the stone.

He needs it. He must have it, she thought. *But something tears at him.*

"It is his stone," he whimpered. "I have been trying to find it. I have looked everywhere for it. But you have it. You have had it all this time."

She wrapped her fingers around the stone. She withdrew the necklace and refastened it around her neck where she tucked it back under her clothing.

At that moment, he had seen his destiny but could not wrestle it free.

"It is not enough to make me suffer but you also taunt me," he cried. "You are most cruel, just like all the others. Do you like to see my pain?" He motioned his head toward Argannon. "You are no less a torturer than the grand tormentor who tries to break my spirit."

Ancorbow took a step forward.

"Do not speak to the Queen in this tone!" he said gruffly.

But Molly gave him a slight push with her hand, and he stepped back. She returned her gaze to the orc.

"Your words do not hurt me, Ug'ghi Otha," she told him in a serene tone, "for I know I am no torturer. I only show you what you so desperately want, to prove to you that you and I have something in common. I have what you need, and with my help, together, we can deliver it to your master so there can be peace in this land. Do you know of the passages through your homeland, well enough to guide me and others?"

Some on the dais stood and were about to shout their discontent, but Halbierd also stood and raised a hand.

"Do not try my patience," warned the Dominar.

But Molly and the orc seemed not to notice this. They continued to look at each other.

"Yes. Yes, I know of most of the passages," said the orc softly.

"Good. Then you will take me there."

At once there was an uproar of indignation. Many in the group stood and shouted their displeasure at what Molly had said.

"What is this treason!" bellowed Dithil over all the voices. "The child knows nothing of this place or of what we face!"

Halbierd stood and pounded his staff on the stone shaking the courtyard.

"Remove the orc," he instructed the guards.

They lifted him away, but he kept his stare on Molly. She returned his look placidly, unflinchingly, without any aggression or fear, until he was hooded and gone from sight.

Having restored order, Halbierd turned to Molly.

"I do not know what prompted the Queen to say such a thing to the beast," he said. "But there is one thing I do know - one cannot hear an answer if the question has not been asked." He gave a gentle and reverent bow of his head. "So, I shall ask. My Queen, why did you speak such words?"

Molly glanced at Fairfax who had a slight smile and twinkle in his eye as if he knew what she would say. She returned the smile then bent down and whispered something to Big Grey who nodded and whispered something back. The cat jumped from his chair, arched his back, and with a rumbling deep purr rubbed up against her legs.

Now they will know of my plan, she thought.

"I guess I'll begin at the beginning," she started, as if talking to herself aloud, then turned and faced the dais. "Mr. Dithil is right. My sister and I do not know much about this place. But I do know some things. I know that the Professor wanted us to come here." She was nervous and fumbled a bit, revealing the Lia Fail. "I know he gave me this stone. He told me it would protect me, that it had great power, and that I would know when to use it. He also told me to never give it to anyone." She then looked down at Big Grey and then at Fairfax. "And the Professor said that I should always do what Big Grey tells me."

She paused. She could see that some on the dais were listening intently to her words. But there were others whose eyes seemed to stray to Fairfax or Halbierd as if trying to gauge their reaction to her words.

She glanced back to Fairfax with a hint of a smile.

"We've made many friends since coming here and everyone has been so kind," she said. "Fairfax has been most wonderful, and he's helped to guide us. Before coming into the courtyard, he told us how to act, and one of the things he said was that we needed to hold true to our beliefs. Hearing about the orc made me understand what Fairfax meant. Even in bad times, we cannot act badly towards others. Where my sister and I come from everyone is equal and people are treated fairly. Or at least that's how it's supposed to be. I guess things are never perfectly perfect. But it occurred to me. We shouldn't mistreat the orc. He wants something I have, something I control, something I know I can use in time to help everyone. It occurred to me that if we make the orc our friend, maybe, just maybe he could help us. He could lead us to his master."

She shuffled her feet, looking down at Big Grey.

"The Professor said something very special to me and my sister," and playfully intoned. "He said in his deep voice, 'Somewhere, something incredible is waiting to be known.' When I thought about those words, I knew how I could help." She grasped the Lia Fail and felt its warmth. "If the Professor is correct as I am sure he is, and if this is a weapon and I am the only one that can use it, then I must be the one to face the orc's master, and the orc is the only one that can lead me to him safely. I think that is why the Professor sent us here. That is why he gave me this jewel, to use it against this evil. It is clear to me now, as it should be clear to us all, what I must do to help."

She tucked the Lia Fail back under her clothing and returned to her seat. The silence was deafening but there was a strange rhythmic pounding. She looked about searching for the source of the thumping then realized it was her heart pounding in her ears.

Elizabeth sat stunned and confused by her sister's words while everyone else sat staring at Molly. Fairfax sat back and stroked his beard thoughtfully. Even the sound of frantic scratching against paper by Brows was silenced as he sat pondering Molly's words. It seemed no one wanted to break the silence, even as twilight drew in and the air became cool. Then and without warning, Brows popped up from his chair in excitement. There was a beaming smile on his face.

"I think it is brilliant! Brilliant! Absolutely brilliant!" he gleefully rejoiced. "The child is correct! Do you not see? The orc provides us access to the evil, and the child has the means to destroy it. My friends, we must use this to our advantage. Oh, at first, I had my doubts mind you, about what the Professor was up to, sending us children and all. I thought him completely and utterly mad. But there is genius in his madness." He turned to Molly. "Who would ever suspect a child so innocent to be threatening? And she is small enough, small enough that she can easily slip past the orc hordes. Bravo my child! Bravo! And what courage, I might add."

"You talk of size?" said Dithil. "She's no taller than you my bobbin friend, or for that matter me. Why do we not make the journey then? Hmm?"

"Because we do not possess the stone. We cannot wield its might."

Dithil grumbled a bit.

"I'll admit, there may be some logic to her words," he cautioned, "but the child's plan is reckless. To follow an orc into a hive of evil - surely, she'd face unimaginable horrors and odds - and she doesn't know how to use the stone, that's if she can use it all."

"True enough," said Brows, "but remember what Griffinion told us, that the passages and pathways have changed. The orc would be most useful to us, to help us traverse that evil land. And remember your history. It is said that Aerin did not know how to wield the stone's power until that fateful day on the Ronin Plains. The Maker gave her the strength to do what she had to do, and he will give this young lady the same strength, and when it is time."

Ancorbow stood, a hand over his heart.

"Ah, Aerin, Queen of Ahlgren," he said. "Truth rings through the triumph song of the Ronin Plains, when the power came upon her, through the stone, and thousands of brood were destroyed in a single flame." He bowed his head in sorrow and after some time looked up with tears in his eyes. "Before the Night of Death came and took her from us."

Brows stared ahead deep in his thoughts.

"The demons may have taken her life that night, but they could not take her spirit," he said. "The Queen was wise beyond her years, for before that horrible night she fashioned the Lia Fail into a necklace, a simple piece of jewelry, and thus hid it from her assassins. It is the same piece of jewelry the young girl now keeps, and within it resides the same power."

Dithil became distraught the more he thought about Molly's plan. He was skeptical of it believing the whole thing utter nonsense.

"This is a preposterous idea! Foolhardy!" he said. "This child is not Aerin! Why send her to the Crag without her knowing how the Lia Fail is to be used? She may be Queen, but her plan is disastrous!"

"Aye," said I'Kinillel. "We can't have the Queen of Ahlgren face an evil we know nothing of, an evil even the Edainar cannot define for us. The power of the stone is best used on the battlefield and under the skillful guide of Carrick."

Brows was angered by the words he heard.

"Fools! You are both fools! Carrick cannot wield the stone!" he said. "No one can, other than the girl. The Lia Fail has been given to her by the Keeper. Only she can use it. Do you not know this? Do you not see that these are different times? Griffinion has told us of his visions, of what we face, and it is different, different than anything we've dealt with before! We must use the stone against the evil force itself, against the orc's master, not on the battlefield against brood. We have already made this mistake. We must learn from history instead of repeating the same error. If there is one thing that history shouts to us it is this: do not waste mistakes. We must vanquish the evil at its source."

It was then, when all seemed against her, that Molly thought of the one thing that might make a difference. If she were to carry out her plan, she would need help. She knew this was something she could not do alone, and she knew there would have to be some kind of diversion to keep the forces of evil occupied.

She remembered a game the Professor taught her. It was a game of strategy and deception, where each move one makes is designed to trick the opponent into making a completely different move.

"It is like a fox chasing a hare into its burrow," the Professor once told her. "The fox pretends to retreat while secretly doubling back to the entrance. The hare, believing the fox has run away, then leaves its burrow only to be caught and devoured by the fox."

She knew what she had to say.

"With everyone's help, I'm sure I can do it," she said. "I've not met Mr. Carrick but from what I hear I'm sure he can help. The Professor taught me a game. It's called chess. It's a game of moves against the one you are playing against. You always try to move forward but sometimes you pull back, being cautious of what you're willing to sacrifice, to move forward and gain something. The object of the game is to corner your opponent so he cannot make a move. To be victorious you always have to think a couple of moves ahead and constantly ask yourself a very important question."

There was silence that was until Dithil accepted the challenge.

"And what is the important question?" he asked.

Molly smiled.

"What is the other side thinking about?"

The sweetness of her voice, the delicacy of her expressions, and the strength of her judgment stirred the group.

Fairfax knew what he had to do. He had to take advantage of the moment, to compel the group to make a choice. He stood and approached the center of the dais.

"The Queen bears witness to the path before us," he said. "My good friend here, the great historian is correct. History can repeat itself in the most dangerous of ways, and sometimes with a twist. The Lia Fail is a power only the Queen can wield, and the orc has knowledge of the wastelands, a knowledge we do not have. If the orc believes he is delivering the stone to his master, he may gladly lead us to him. As the Queen has most eloquently stated, we have no choice but to enter into this game she speaks of, this game called chess."

"I think you're mad!" Dithil told Fairfax.

Fairfax turned to him.

"Mad? Maybe I am a bit mad - just as mad as the Professor," he said. "Maybe we're all mad! It makes no difference for if we do not act the Harrow will reek of madness so vile it will be beyond imagination. And my dear Dithil, it will be a madness that will spread to your land. If unchecked this evil will consume the entire Harrow."

He turned to the dais looking at each member with confidence.

"My friends perhaps madness is exactly what we need," he continued. "We now have the power of truth on our side, perhaps for the first time. We know that our armies had only defeated a dreaded minion of a greater evil, a greater evil that still lives and breathes with the sole purpose to destroy all that is good. We also know that the magic of the Edainar only now gains a glance at this evil, an evil it cannot reach even with all its powers. This evil looks to remain hidden, never seeking to fight a battle in the open field. It cowardly relies on others to wage its war. Friends, as difficult as it may seem, the Queen's plan may be our greatest hope for survival. Much has already been set into motion. If there is to be war, why not bring the war to him?"

Again, there was silence as everyone thought about his words.

Halbierd stood with a fleeting look to his right then left, and then addressed the dais.

"So, it is proposed," he said. "We will look to have the orc lead the Queen of Ahlgren to the Crag to face the darkness. What say you?"

Dalgaes, the Elf-King, had carefully listened to everything that had been said, and now clarity of thought overcame him. He remembered the prophecy of the child-savior who came from the tree to rid the land of evil. Had the prophecy come true? Was Molly the fulfillment of it? The idea thrilled him and filled him with a sense of destiny. He stood and raised a hand.

"The good wizard is exact. This path is clear," he said in a stately tone. "The Queen must face the evil, but she will require assistance. I have long studied the prophecies and now believe the time is at hand. The ancient writings tell us:

> When the stone cracks
> at the hand of one so small,
> the might of the axe

into the child's hand will fall.

The lands rejoice
for the great tree is in bloom,
the burden of choice
becomes a fate worse than doom.

Its power so great
that all lands quiver in fear,
the child at the gate
stares at an evil so near.

All lands concede
when darkness fills the skies,
the Queen to decree
a battle fought at sunrise."

Dithil stood and threw his arms up in disgust, giving an exasperated roll of his eyes.

"Enough with the prophecies and their foolishness!" he said. "We dwarves have little use for riddles or interpretations of words written long ago. An end to all this talk of prophecies, now and forever! Don't you see what foolishness it is? My dear Elf-King, with all due respect to you and your kind, do these prophecies tell us about how this evil still lurks, hidden away in the Crag? Have the prophecies foreshadowed the coming of the depraved orc? No! You look to fit words to events and events to words. Tell me this: in what age shall we witness the advent of permanent peace in this land?"

Dalgaes did not respond. He just stared at the dwarf.

"Of course, you have no answer," sighed Dithil, his voice softer, "for the words you speak are but riddles, gameplay for those too afraid to face reality. If we do as the child says, we do so because the reality is before us, not because it's foretold in some ancient book on some dusty shelf."

Dalgaes returned to his chair, calmly folding his hands in his lap, not appearing the least bit angered by Dithil's words. He understood the emotional nature of the dwarf and respected his beliefs. He knew that times had changed, and few believed in the old ways or the fulfillment of the prophecies. For many, the books of old were only fables, bedtime stories for children. But for him, the prophecies were less a guide than a reaffirmation of truth. He was strong in his belief in the old ways and would bite his tongue, for now. There was no use in trying to convince those who did not understand.

"We must be careful here. Let us understand what the good Elf-King speaks of," said Brows coming to the defense of Dalgaes. "He speaks of the truth now before us. The good Elf-King simply points out that the path now provided by the Queen aligns with the ancient texts. Let us not lose the perspective given to us by the past. The old ways ask only that we engage our minds with the prophecies and in doing so contemplate alternate paths."

Dithil gave a flippant wave of his hand.

"The tongue of the wise will enhance knowledge, but the mouth of fools will utter foolishness," he muttered. "I don't say if the words are wise or if they're foolish. I no longer wish to talk of such matters for doing so will just further divide us." He turned at Big Grey. "And what do you say cat? What does one of the great Ra Cath proclaim?"

Big Grey took a sniff of the air and then stared back at Dithil, his eyes glaring at him.

"We are taught that those who set the prophecies aside as of little value suffer great loss," he said. "But I agree – now is not the time for such debate. I think the young lady knows exactly what she is doing. We would be fools to not heed the words of the one who holds the Lia Fail. Doing so would dismiss the past. As Aerin led us to victory so too will this young lady. A game of chess is indeed upon us. Who would dare to disagree?"

"Games are for children," scoffed Dithil. "They don't have any real purpose for us dwarves. They're a waste of time. We find that the only real use for games is to keep one occupied when there is nothing else to do."

"You have missed the point," the cat told the dwarf. His tone was serious, his face expressionless. "Games teach skills that are useful in real life. This is what the Queen speaks of."

The dwarf scowled. "I have never missed a point, cat."

A studied and cautious silence came to the group. Eyes focused on Molly with shadowed thoughtfulness.

"Friends! Friends! We have Fairfax, Master Grey, and Dalgaes who agree with the Queen's path," said Halbierd. He then turned to Dithil with a stern look and slowly spoke his name with stiff lips. "Ranagul Dithil, what say you?"

Dithil understood what was being asked of him.

"Oh, fine then," he said mockingly. "Lest it is said that the dwarves of Mortha stood in the way of the Edainar's latest adventure."

Halbierd lifted an eyebrow

"Good," he said. "I know I speak for everyone when I say we are pleased with your support."

In short order, there was additional agreement by the group, and much to Molly's surprise it was unanimous. They had accepted her plan and pledged to do what and how she wished, and there was much talk as to how to get the orc to safely lead Molly to the darkness. As the meeting closed all promised to share information and cooperate, and it was decided that some would gather the next morning to discuss a more detailed course of action.

Before leaving the courtyard, Fairfax, Brows, and Big Grey met briefly with Halbierd under a large pine tree. As the girls approached, the four quietly ended their talk, each nodding their heads in agreement. Halbierd smiled at the girls and gave a gentle wave. He and the other wizards of the Edainar then receded into the forest. The others on the dais also left the courtyard.

When all was hushed, a somber air and darkness came to the courtyard as over the forest there fell a thin white mist, which softly rolled along on the grass like ripples in a pond.

"I do not like that one wizard," Molly told Fairfax as they left the courtyard, "the one named Argannon. He makes me feel uncomfortable."

Fairfax gazed down upon her with a placid look.

"He is sorrow," he said.

* * *

As nightfall encroached, Fairfax paced the hallways of Blackstone, each step echoing through the deserted corridors. He knew his way, his destination, Halbierd's chamber, but it was still difficult to make his way through the vast darkness. He was not alone. The shadows moved with him; their presence felt more than seen. They were strange to him, seemed to have no purpose, and he did not know why they were there.

He came to the door and hesitated a moment, but then knocked on the door lightly, not wanting to make too much noise.

"Enter," came Halbierd's voice, quiet but strong.

Fairfax opened the door and closed it behind him, then turned to face the Dominar. Halbierd sat in his high-backed chair by a fire, a book open in his lap. He looked up at Fairfax, who stood before him, with a stern look

"What do you want?" asked Halbierd, his voice tense and impatient.

"You know why I am here," said Fairfax.

"I was wondering when the niceties would end," said Halbierd.

"Niceties are only applicable to tender plants and fruit trees," said Fairfax, a tinge of anger in his voice. "We would not be in this moment in time if you had heeded her warnings. Because of your inaction, this world will not be the same again."

"She is not what she seems. Argannon and Glimmershot told you this. Her visions of the future were corrupted by the Tar Malal feline she befriended."

"She came to us, showed us what was to come, but you blocked the path. And those two, they are engulfed in darkness, wallowing in a cruel world. They see beauty in the void, the shadows stretching like fingers to touch their hearts. All you do is close your eyes, losing yourself in the cold embrace of the night."

"What would you have me do?" asked Halbierd in anger and in a sharp, quivering voice.

"Release her!"

Halbierd shook his head.

"You know I cannot," he said with a sigh. "The decision was made."

"Then I want to see her."

Halbierd nodded and lifted a hand.

"A fledgling will be in the hallway. The boy will take you to her."

Fairfax looked at Halbierd, his anger still seething within him.

"The darkness will come for you," he told Halbierd, "and when it does, there will be no one to help you."

The Dominar just sat there staring off into the fire.

Fairfax turned and left the chamber where he was greeted by a fledgling, a boy who took him down into Blackstone's pits. There were no windows, just a set of stairs that wound down into darkness. The boy led him through a maze of long, dark, dank hallways, lit only by the pale glow of candles. They eventually came to a hallway with metal doors on both sides. The boy continued, stopping in front of one of the large metal doors which had a small slit in it through which a dim ray of light could be seen. Fairfax looked over the door and felt an impenetrable magical spell, one he could not break. He peered through the slit and into the room where he saw the young woman, Morna Anya, on a stone slab, cradling the black cat Delotha 'Sil. They were under a deep, tortuous spell cast by Argannon. Fairfax squeezed his eyes in deep sadness.

If only they had listened to you, he thought. *You told them this would happen. You saw the darkness in your dreams. But their bias got in the way. And now the darkness has come for us all.*

"Take me from this wretched place," he told the fledgling.

As they walked through the darkness, back up the stairs, and from the pits, Fairfax had one last thought.

At least she lives.

* * *

That night the girls, Fairfax, Brows, and Big Grey were treated to a wonderful meal in a lavish dining room. It was a cavernous room with tall windows that overlooked the courtyard. Its ceiling was vaulted and oak timbered. There was an enormous fireplace at the far end of the room, its hearth ablaze with a roaring fire. In the center of the room was a large wooden table with chairs on both sides and ends. They gathered at the end of the table closest to the fireplace and after their meal, they talked about all that had happened.

The girls soon became tired and did not wish to remain in the dining room any longer. They bid Fairfax and Brows a good night and with Big Grey withdrew to their bedchamber.

"See," said Molly to the cat as she and Elizabeth turned back the bed covers, "I remembered what you told me. You know, to carefully observe the flow of inner and outer events. That's what I did . . . the Professor and the Lia Fail as the inner event . . . the orc and his master as the outer event."

The cat jumped onto the bed.

"You learn your lessons well," he said with a roaring purr.

The girls slept well that night and cuddled around the cat, except for a time when Molly was awakened by a voice. It was a strange, rhythmic, machine-like voice, or so she thought. The voice filled the dark room.

"I have a message from another time," it repeated over and over again. "I have a message from another time. I have a message from another time . . ."

She rose and looked about the room, which now had become pitch black. There was no one there. But the voice continued, repeating itself, pulsing like a beating heart. She looked down at the Lia Fail which began to warm, a soft glow of red.

"I have a message from another time," said the voice, unfeeling and cold. "I have a message from another time. I have a message from another time . . ."

She continued to search the darkness, looking for some kind of light or shadow, or movement of any kind. Then there came a flash. She saw what looked like a mechanical hand in front of her, shiny and bright, its finger-ends holding an envelope. Her eyes searched for something behind the hand, but only it seemed to extend from the darkness.

"I have a message from another time. I have a message from another time . . ."

She went to reach for the envelope, but the hand disappeared. The Lia Fail turned cold and the voice was gone. The deep blackness lifted. She realized she was dreaming and took in a deep breath. She went back to sleep. The only sound she could hear was the faint wheezing of Big Grey.

* * *

From a chasm deep within the Crag, black ajatars flashed up into the skies, one after another, soaring west high above the clouds, and into darkened mists of storms unseen by their enemy. The long, scaled serpentine forms curved lithely as they flew, sometimes gliding along with the winds while other times using their mighty strength to slice through forceful gales brought about by the darkness. As they swiftly approached their destination, they began their descent, slowly and quietly, each guided by a Dark Rider, until before them, rose the smoldering ashes of what was once Portmoor.

The demons circled over the dead city, their haunting screams piercing the deadly silence of the night.

Below, orcs and other brood pillaged and plundered the ruins. Eventually, the lead Dark Rider of the group spotted an Urur Maw. He raised a hand pointing below and gave the signal to land. The huge serpents landed with a thunderous boom. The Dark Riders dismounted, the sound of their mechanical bodies making a deafening clatter. The steel of armor glared, and their half-human bodies seethed.

Seeing the Dark Riders approach, the Urur Maw grumbled and snarled. He despised the evil comrades as they were favored by the master and believed themselves better than worm brood.

Not much was known about the Dark Riders. It was said that each had been a valiant warrior in times past, rose from the dead by the Szard, and given their iron-clad, mechanized bodies in service to evil. The Urur Maw had heard such tales and most of them, as he knew all too well, were no exaggerations, but ugly truths. He had seen the master scour ancient battlefields calling the dead to life; and, he had seen with his own eyes, the forge masters of Urth' Goroth, toiling over the fires of hell as they shaped the armaments of the Dark Riders' bodies. These were creatures that commanded disdain and the Urur Maw knew firsthand that Dark Riders were ruthless and fearsome enforcers of the Szard's will, dispatched to keep control over his servants. They were the tomb brood, the Uakor Turg, killer of any who resisted the Szard.

The lead Dark Rider approached the Urur Maw.

"What are you called?" it asked in a twittering, high-pitched electronic voice.

"I'm the leader here. My name is Dracor, as given to me by my horde," said the Urur Maw.

"A mere formality," said the Dark Rider, "for we care not for names or titles or creeds for that matter. We have no use for them, they have no charm for us. We care only for substance."

"What is it you require, then?"

The Dark Rider hesitated and took a step closer to Dracor.

"The master demands an update," he said.

Dracor held his ground.

"Inform the master that finding the relic will take time," he said. "This city covers several leagues, and I've but a handful of brood. Perhaps if I had additional brood, I could find the relic more quickly."

The Dark Rider moved even closer to Dracor, the human side of its face decomposed and twisted while the metal side glistened. It tilted its head as a mechanical red eye whirred, focusing on Dracor.

"You've enough brood," droned its mechanical voice. "Perhaps your brood requires an incentive."

"And what would that be?" gulped Dracor.

The Dark Rider's face was now so close to Dracor's that he could smell the stench of unburied corpses on its breath.

"Tell your brood that a most painful death awaits those who do not find the relic," it said with an emotionless mechanical voice.

Then there came a screeching cry of the damned, followed by a thump of wind and swirl of dust. A red ajatar swooped low over them. With powerful strokes of its wings, the massive red ajatar soared a wide circle and returned, where it stopped, hovered, opened its mouth, and gave a raging screech before storming upwards and northeast toward the Thornback.

"Ride!" shouted the lead Dark Rider to the others.

They quickly mounted their black ajatars who gave a sibilant hiss.

Each Dark Rider pulled on the reins, bringing their ajatar's head up with a roar of defiance. The beasts lurched this way, then that, snapping their razor teeth.

The lead Dark Rider turned to Dracor.

"Find the relic!" it demanded.

With the Dark Riders mounted, the black ajatars turned to rear, beating their wings. They rose from the ground and started their flight chasing after the red ajatar into the mountains.

* * *

The red ajatar's screeching howl shattered the night's silence and startled Mora. No one had yet to come for them, but now she heard sounds of someone or something approaching. While her children and mother slept she climbed the stairs and placed an ear to the door and listened carefully.

A Black Dog or Cu Sith, large and shaggy, with a long tail coiled up on its back led three orcs up the hill to what was once Skag Harwell's house. The dog's feet were enormous and as broad as a man's. Its great footmarks were often seen in desolate places, in mud or snow, but it glided along silently, with white eyes that pierced the night's blackness. It did not bark continuously when seeking but gave three tremendous bays that could be heard for leagues.

The dog sniffed the ground. It began to track something, climbing over rocks and rubble, and then bounding up a slight incline and into the shell of the house. Within the ruins, the dog continued to sniff the ground and wander, attempting to connect several scents. It then gave three long howls that shook the ground as the orcs entered the ruins.

Terrified, Mora stepped away from the door shaking her head and holding a trembling hand over her mouth. She felt an evil presence on the other side of the door. She turned to see her mother and children in bed, now awake by the horrific sounds, with her mother clasping the two children tightly to her bosom, her hands covering their mouths, their eyes wide in fear.

The orcs began to thrash about the ruins of the house, kicking over stones and splintered wood, ripping pictures and whatever remained from the walls that stood. Then one of the orcs saw small footprints in the dust near the bookcase. The dog began to sniff around it.

The orc pointed to the footprints.

"Look! Fresh meat," it said, guttural words, mostly garbled.

"Impossible," said another orc. "The city is dead."

The black dog raised its nose at the bookcase. It turned to the orcs with teeth glaring, curved, knifelike weapons, in a lasting snarl.

"There's something here," it whispered.

The orc closest to the bookcase looked at the wooden structure. It placed both hands on either side and readied to rip it from the wall when a sparkle of light caught its eye, coming from a small glass jar on one of the shelves of the bookcase.

"What's this?" said the orc mischievously, snatching it.

The orc held the glass jar up to the moonlight as the other orcs and the dog looked on. Strands of golden hair tied at one end with silk threads glowed from within the glass.

The orc knew what it had discovered and became overly possessive of it. It was his! The beast feared that the others would take it from him. Rage consumed its heart. In one quick movement with his sword, it lopped off the heads of the other orcs. It then turned and thrust the blade deeply into the back of the black dog's neck. The carnage was swift and decisive.

As blood pooled about the orc's feet it raised the glass jar safely into the moonlight with its arms. It gave a terrifying scream.

"Foulhand!"

The name echoed through the dead city.

It frantically dashed from the ruins and down the hill into the city.

As time waned Mora sensed the evil had gone. She returned to bed. That night an uneasy sleep, a sleep with a watchful eye and ear came to her, unknowing that but a few paces from their sanctuary had been a mighty weapon, a weapon that had just fallen into the hands of darkness.

CHAPTER 8
MOONDANCER

THE RED AJATAR FLEW NORTH; there was an urgency in the rapid beating of his wings. Soon he dwindled to little more than a speck in the night sky. But his pursuers continued their chase, flying straight and strong at him. Then out of nowhere, a wind blew with a fierce intensity. It caught his pursuers by surprise, slowing them. The Dark Riders pulled hard on the reins bringing their beasts higher above the winds, then swiftly down again, piercing through the gales and closing in on him.

The demons tried to match the red ajatar's every maneuver, dipping, banking, and soaring high above the mountains. As the lead black ajatar closed in, it took a deep breath and exhaled a long and powerful fiery geyser at him. But at the last second, he snapped his tail in defiance, swinging wildly from the fire. Unharmed, he streaked downward to a thickly forested valley below. In a rage of frustration, the black demons gave a blood-curdling shriek, following him lower and lower still, speeding over the tops of trees. In a bold move, he veered off in one direction and swooped down behind his pursuers. With a quick breath, he released a bright red flame that scorched the tip of one of the demon's tails. He then bolted upward from the valley and over the grey ash slopes of the surrounding mountains. The black demons pursued, cutting through misty clouds and over snowy peaks. But the Dark riders pulled back on their reins when they saw the towering Blackstone Ridge in the distance. The black ajatars slowed, hovered a bit, and then with a loud shriek of rage, turned and fled back to Portmoor.

As the red ajatar continued to Blackstone Keep, he glanced back and watched as the black demons disappeared over the rugged mountainous horizon.

They think that they're so smart, he thought. *They should know better than to try to . . . chase after me. For I am En' Carad!*

He laughed to himself.

* * *

The two cats and their Fenri friends spent a peaceful night in a large chamber in the Great Hall of Ewellinoth. Glaeynd provided them with plenty of food and a warm fire. Two woven baskets stuffed with heavy wool blankets were placed together near the hearth for Lil' Man and Chumsey. Over a hearty dinner of roasted mutton and vermin stew, they recounted thrilling tales of their journey over the Foghollow Barrens and their victorious battle over the rogue Fenri pack. In jest, Lil' Man boasted that their victory would have come sooner had he been allowed to fight. At this, Thurir snickered and remarked that their tiny companions did well by instead providing moral support.

Everyone laughed and one Fenri even exclaimed, "Maybe the little ones should lead the next fight!"

Then, and to the great pleasure of all, servers brought the stems and leaves of giant nep, as it is sometimes called, or catmint as it is commonly known. Everyone enjoyed the stimulant, including the Fenri who found that it calmed their tired muscles. They rubbed into it, rolled over it, pawed it, chewed it, licked it, with some even playing with it. After some time, many fell asleep on their nep, thankful there were no more fearful battles to wage.

* * *

At daylight, the two cats and Fenri prepared to meet the Lord of Mistmere. After a hearty breakfast, Rhiorsnan guardsmen ushered them into the Great Hall of Ewellinoth. Lil' Man and Chumsey led them, followed by Thurir and his pack. The floor and walls were made of white marble, with hundreds of huge crystal columns supporting an arched crystal ceiling that seemed to soar towards the sky. The sides were cluttered with gold and silver armor, bows and iron-tipped arrows, and swords of silver, gold, and crystal blades. Many courtiers stood along the side, dressed in colorful gowns, with tunics underneath made of white silk.

At the end of the Great Hall sat Kraneth, the Lord of Mistmere, on a large throne carved of crystal. He wore a black silk robe and held the royal scepter of sheen white stone which was as long as a wizard's staff. A crystal globe was secured to its top with shiny bands of gold. He was an old man with long grey hair, stooped over with age and dissipation. He was small in stature and was ailing and more than ever enfeebled. Behind him, to one side of the throne stood Glaeynd; to the other side stood her brother Goselthout. The three captains of the Rhiorsnan stood near Glaeynd in full battle armament. And within the shadows, behind the throne, was the thin pale figure of a man whose white face seemed to float within the darkness.

As they approached, Glaeynd smiled and gave a small wave to Lil' Man, while Kraneth stared at them with a strange, almost haunted look in his eyes. He leaned over and whispered something to Goselthout, who nodded, turned, and summoned the man from behind the throne. The man stepped from the shadows and walked slowly to one side of the throne. He wore a long black leather coat with brown fur trim. He appeared withdrawn from life, with hollow eyes, and a high forehead, and though the form of his face was unusual, nothing was striking in his appearance.

The man was Gurandurm Grimshade, Grand Vizier, the premier of ministers. He heralded from the north and was known as someone cold and unfeeling, clever, and cunning. Lil' Man and Chumsey were aware of his reputation, that of a despicable scoundrel, someone not averse to performing evil deeds to quench a lust for power.

"They draw near. What do you sense?" Kraneth asked Grimshade.

"My Lord, the Fenri royal and vermin cats bring news from the east," whispered Grimshade. "Nothing can be gained from their contemptible words. In such troubled times, they offer little hope; same as in ages past."

Now, the cats and Fenri stood before Kraneth. Their hearts raced in nervousness for they regarded him very steadfastly and with slight fear and awe. But Lil' Man and Chumsey were concerned. They saw that he was clearly in a declining state of health. He looked unwell and weak. His eyes were sunken and his skin was pale. He was taking in his breaths in great gulps and wheezing. He looked like a man who was about to die.

Kraneth kept his stare on the group. His expression betrayed his anger, exhaustion of deferred hope, and consuming hate. The grimness of his look - the hardening of his eyes, white-lipped, and pinching at the corners of his mouth - made it apparent that the encounter would be at best difficult.

"I fear this may not go well," whispered Lil' Man to Chumsey.

"Many of your fears have been quite valuable to you," said Chumsey.

The irritated old man cleared his throat.

"Look what we have here," he said loudly with just a hint of a choke in his old voice. "Two little kitties from Katzhu Pu and a Fenri pack from the Rakl. To what do we owe this honor? Is this the best the Edainar or the Guilds can do at such a grim time?"

Grimshade smirked at the sarcasm.

The cats thought Kraneth was under the influence of his advisor. But on this day, they knew such thoughts did not matter. Their success lay with convincing him and perhaps Glaeynd of the struggles ahead.

Lil' Man gave a bow.

"My Lord," he said. "We are honored to be in your presence and most grateful for the hospitality you have shown us. We are here having ventured from the Drueger. We bring dire news. We have witnessed thousands upon thousands of brood gathering at Gortha-Losh and they are joined by Fenri. They set their sights on the west."

"And my Lord," said Chumsey, "Ug' Cthuth has been rebuilt and a second tower of doom born in the blackness, home to a hive of ajatars and Dark Riders. We have witnessed this through the harsh rains of the Crag."

Kraneth smiled and then gave a hideous laugh.

"Ah, so the great Balor Guild of Katzhu Pu speaks," he said. "You must think me feeble, eh? You must think me daft, eh? But I remember you, both of you." He pointed to the cats, his hand shaking uncontrollably. "Oban Pan and the other one called Chum Sey. You think me a fool. Do you think I do not know that a darkness comes from the east? Do you think me blind to the dark clouds that thunder in the sky? Do you think me deaf to the wretched cries of ajatars overhead?" He leaned back into his crystal throne. "Such fools you be. I have seen it all before. Do you not remember that time? Do you not remember the dark clouds and storms? The lightning? The thunder? The rain? The wind? The lies? The secrets? The pain? The misery? Oh, you may not remember, but I remember it well, about the time when all became ill."

Lil' Man had a terrible feeling about where this was going: Kraneth was indeed old, belligerent, and frail, but his memory of the past, a haunting nightmare of betrayal, was sharp.

"Yes, we remember my Lord," he said.

"Good! Then you remember when the Edainar abandoned my city. You remember the bravery of my Rhiorsnan as they held the brood just beyond the outer walls of my city. For season upon season, my beautiful Mistmere was under siege. We struggled, and we fought, protected by the Old Hills. But tell me, where was the great Carrick? Where were the great warriors of the Balor Guild? Where was the great Elven army? Where was the army of the Axe? I will tell you where they were - they were elsewhere - they were in the Ahlgren and the Eldor, fighting battles in open fields, all the while my Mistmere slowly bled. Generations of my people were lost to a great cataclysm of ignorance and wickedness."

He paused to catch his breath, leaned forward then continued in a contemptuous tone.

"Oh, and let us not forget the gifts of the wizards," he said. "Shall I tell you of the glorious gifts bestowed upon us by the Edainar? Do you wish to know, eh? Allow me to enlighten you then. The revered wizards, with all their wondrous magic, gave us nothing but war, war brought about by Dark Wizards, those from their own Order, those who revolted. Ignorance and wickedness, I say! And answer this question, my dear kitties: do you know what was taken from my beloved Mistmere? Do you, eh? Let me enlighten you with yet another answer – thousands of young sons and daughters, maimed or dead, and lands once verdant with fruit burned barren by battle. You see because of such ignorance and wickedness, I have no use for the Edainar, or the Guild Lords of Katzhu Pu, the Ra Cath, or the Elves, or those tiny ones who dwell in Mortha, or even the great Carrick for that matter. They are all useless to me, traitors, thieves of the worst kind. And I, I will never forgive them."

"Those were difficult times for all . . . difficult decisions were made," said Chumsey. "Surely, my Lord does not mean what he says."

Kraneth lifted his scepter and slammed it against the marble floor. The echo of the blow reverberated through the hall and beyond.

"Vermin!" he shouted. "Do not tell me the meaning of my words! You have no idea of our suffering and struggles!"

"Father!" cried out Glaeynd. "You speak of the past. Times have changed."

"Hush girl," he reprimanded. "You know not of what you speak. Be silent!"

"Listen to your father!" Goselthout told her, a meanness to his voice. "You're ignorant in such matters!"

She was surprised by her brother's and father's words. Emotions came to her in a torrent, and she began to cry. This further infuriated Kraneth.

"Hold your tears!" he told her. "The Lead of the Rhiorsnan must show strength, not the tears of a child."

The Lord's words cut deep, wounding Glaeynd, and Lil' Man could see a look of horror on her face.

"My Lord, please listen to reason," said Lil' Man looking to bring Kraneth's focus from Glaeynd and back to their mission. "We are here to warn you of the threat. It grows and can be upon your city in days. You must send word to Katzhu Pu for help."

"Help?" roared Kraneth, his words echoing through the hall. "The vermin speaks of help but does not know the meaning of the word. He warns of a threat I know all too well. Do not make empty promises of help, vermin." He stared down at them with eyes of rage. "I had asked for help in the past and received none. Your friends have no interest in coming to our aid. They have not done so in the past; they will not do so now. So, let me tell you this – I will do what is necessary to protect my city, as I have always done. I do not need the Edainar or the Guild Lords or the Elves! And I surely do not need you or the Fenri. Your offer of help is meaningless to me, and your undertaking today a failure."

Thurir was about to speak but Chumsey interrupted him.

"Quiet," he hissed. "Don't speak."

Thurir kept silent, now having thought better of getting involved.

The hall fell silent as all eyes turned to the cats and Fenri wolves, who were disturbed by Kraneth's comments. Because Lil' Man couldn't persuade Kraneth to change his mind, he decided to end the discussion.

"My Lord," he said. "You have been most gracious. We shall not take any more of your time. We express our sincere gratitude for all your favors. May we ask permission to take leave of your lordship?"

Grimshade leaned over and whispered something in Kraneth's ear.

"Yes . . . yes," the Lord said softly to his vizier with a nod. He then turned to Lil' Man with a devious smile. "You may take your leave and you are welcome to stay the night if you wish. Consider this a last good-faith gesture to the old ways. But heed this warning my fair kitty: when the sun rises in the morn you are to be beyond the Old Hills, far from my Rhiorsnan's aim. I want you to be a faint memory in my mind."

Lil' Man bowed.

"Yes, my Lord," he said.

"One more thing," said Kraneth.

"Yes, my Lord."

"Tell your Guild Lords and the sorcerers of the Edainar and those of the other races, that they and their kind are no longer welcomed in my city."

With the Lord's words, the group gave one final, gracious bow and left the hall.

As they walked the hallways and returned to their chamber Thurir was frustrated.

"Perhaps if I had spoken," he said.

Lil' Man looked up at him with a look of deep sadness and despair, raw and bare.

"Mistmere is lost," he gently said with disappointment in his orange eyes. "There was nothing more to say."

"Perhaps, I could have convinced the old man," insisted Thurir. "If he knew of the treason . . . the struggle of my people . . ."

Chumsey was dejected.

"A waste of time I am afraid," he told Thurir. "He does not care about the Fenri. He does not care about anyone or anything. The old man is bitter and to a certain extent, he has every reason to be so. There is some truth in his words, but his anger has blinded him of reason."

"Grimshade," said Thurir angrily. "There is something about him. I do not trust him. The Lord is under the wicked man's spell."

Chumsey shook his head.

"Grimshade is many things but is untrained in the art of spell making. No, Grimshade simply feeds Kraneth's hunger for despair and bitterness. Alone, he would see his folly, but Grimshade weaves a pattern of anger and frustration before the Lord, daily reminders of the past. It consumes and captivates him; he retreats deeper into his anger, a prison of emotions he cannot escape. I am afraid the old man will drown in a sea of isolation. No, Grimshade wields no magic, just the power of words."

The cat's words did not please Thurir. He had hoped to convince Kraneth to join the forces of good in what surely would be war. But he also had a selfish reason for coming to Mistmere – to persuade Kraneth to help him retake the Rakl. Now his hopes were dashed. He felt helpless.

Time and distance are against me, he thought.

But in the bitterness of his disappointment Thurir took solace in his fellowship with his two feline friends.

They understood his loss and his rage. He had strength through his friends.

When they returned to their chamber there was much to discuss. They were troubled that Kraneth did not heed their warning. But there was little to debate. They knew they would need to leave first thing in the morning, so as not to provoke the Lord.

They began to gather what few things they could for their departure. Thurir held discussions with his pack. Many wished to return to the original plan, to venture back east to Ragmorok and attempt to retake the Rakl. Others wanted to head south to join forces with the armies of men, as it was thought that if Carrick were to lead them in battle and witness their bravery, perhaps he would agree to take his great army to Ragmorok and wage war against the traitors. For Lil' Man and Chumsey, the next step in their journey was obvious – to continue west and to Katzhu Pu where they could take counsel with the Guild Lords. But, in the end, everyone agreed that, given the circumstances, it was best to travel west to the sacred citadel of Katzhu Pu and be thankful for one more good meal and a comfortable night's rest in the Great Hall.

* * *

The sun shined brightly through a high-barred window in the morning. The warmth tickled at the girls and they slowly opened their eyes. They allowed themselves to lie indulgently in bed, listening to the joyful noises of birds outside in the courtyard. After a few moments, they looked around their room and saw Big Grey sitting in the doorway. He was staring at them with large eyes.

"Come now," he said. "We do not have much time. Many things require our attention today. Go ahead and get dressed."

Clothing ready for that day was neatly laid out at the end of the bed. For Molly, there was a red velvet dress that was the shade of a red rose. It reminded her of the Professor and his gardens. For Elizabeth, there was a blue dress decorated with white lace. There was also a blue ribbon for her hair. Both dresses bore the Mark of the Tree, in silver threads which sparkled in the early morning light. The girls were excited and quickly changed into their new clothes.

The cat looked at the girls.

"Lovely," he said, "both of you, simply lovely, and very fitting for such royalty."

"Do you really think so?" asked Molly.

"Yes, really, do you think so?" asked Elizabeth.

"Indeed, yes," he said. "You are both beautiful. The Professor would be so proud."

They left the chamber, quietly closing the door behind them, and walked down the long hall to the dining room. Upon entering the room, the girls saw many of their new friends. Sitting at the large wooden table were Dithil, Entur Donduin, and Calen Ancorbow. Fairfax was standing near the great fireplace with Brows and Halbierd. Closest to the door, Dalgaes and Tinnfierl stood at one of the tall windows gazing out to the Garden Courtyard.

Everyone was deep in conversation and did not notice them as they entered the dining room. Molly was about to greet Dalgaes and Tinnfierl but froze in amazement as something caught the corner of her eye.

"My word!" she said. "Elizabeth, come quickly!"

The girls stood alongside Dalgaes and his faithful archer, their hands pressed against the window, staring out.

"Can you imagine?" gasped Molly. "I've never seen such a thing."

"It's unbelievable," whispered Elizabeth.

In the courtyard was a most incredible sight, a massive red ajatar nestled beneath the treetops. It lay curled up, asleep, its leathery wings folded over its back and tucked around, its long sturdy tail curled around to its head. Its scales formed complicated and extravagant spirals of various tints of red, although some were worn, and in places turning a dark red. As it softly breathed, small red flames and soot flared from its nostrils. The ajatar was a beautiful creature.

Dalgaes looked down at the girls and smiled.

"My Queen, the creature that you see is a good friend," he said.

"He's so magnificent. Does he have a name?" asked Molly.

"Yes. He is called Moondancer. He is, unfortunately, the last of his kind."

"What do you by that?"

"There are two kinds of ajatars in the Harrow: black and red. The black are the Lok Tumu. They are evil in nature. The red are the En' Carad. They are of the good and righteous. Ages of war and onslaught by En' Carad's malevolent Lok Tumu brothers led to their elimination. They still pursue our friend to this day. But he's stronger, much stronger than they are."

Molly was saddened by the tale. But as she looked at the red ajatar in wonder, she smiled. The Lia Fail began to warm. She felt a connection, and she sensed herself drawing closer to the essence of his soul.

She reached out to him with her thoughts. He opened an eye and looked at her only for a moment then closed it.

There is strength in him, the integrity of purpose that has come with years of struggle. He is such a wonderful creature and even though I have never seen an ajatar before I feel I know him, as a good friend. There is a connection between us. But what is it?

She thought back and remembered the conversation Big Grey and Mr. Farlerstock had about ajatars. It was when they first came from under the tree.

"Mr. Farlerstock talked about how he heard of ajatars in the sky," she said. "Now I know what they look like. Where we come from it is very similar to what we call a dragon."

"Ah yes, mythical creatures the Professor spoke of," said Dalgaes. "One thing you should know, Moondancer has a very special power."

"What is it?"

"In time, it will be revealed to you. But you must wait for it and be patient. Do you both understand?"

They nodded.

"Can we go outside and get closer?" asked Elizabeth.

"Why of course," said Dalgaes. "Moondancer is a friendly ajatar, or as you say, dragon. I think he would very much like to meet you."

The girls bolted from the dining room and ran through the stone archway to the Garden Courtyard, stopping just in front of the red ajatar. The air stank of ashes and smoke, and they could feel the heat radiating from him, like the warmth of a roaring fire. As they crept closer, the body was like that of a large serpent, the layers of shimmering red scales seemed sharp at the edges like knives. His eyes were closed; his head resting peacefully on its front talons.

They could hear him take a deep breath, soot puffing from his nostrils, blackening the ground.

A smile formed on his, his eyes still closed.

"What is this," he said in a rich voice. "Is it the smell of human children?"

The girls got scared when he looked at them from the corner of his eye. They took a few steps back.

"Why yes," came the rich voice again. "My sense of smell was correct . . . human children it is . . . ah, and a Queen and Princess at that."

Slowly, he stood on all four legs, stretched, and yawned. He was a tall creature, his head soaring above the treetops. Gradually, he brought his two wings that had been stretched back and lifted them high into the sky. He extended them outward, blocking out the morning sun until he gently folded them back again. He let out a snort that sprayed ashes into the air, followed by a soft sigh that lightly shook the ground. Those that were in the dining room made their way outside to join the girls.

"How did you know I'm Queen?" asked Molly.

The ajatar laughed.

"In my mind, I see many possible paths to travel, all with differing degrees of difficulty. But even though I have this sight, I am not certain of much of what I see, and there are a lot of things in the shadows about which I have no knowledge. Because of this, total assurance of what my sight tells me is out of the question. There is so much disorder, and order only emerges from its midst, after some time. But with you it is different. When I look upon you there is no chaos. I see only order. So, you must be the Queen."

She was not sure what to think, but as the Lia Fail continued to warm, she could sense a deep commitment in him. Here was a creature who could be trusted, a helpful soul, who would lay down his life for her, and that meant something. He was more than just a large beast. He was a living, feeling, thinking creature, worthy of her trust and respect.

"My name is Molly, and this is my sister Elizabeth," she told him with a smile. "We are pleased to make your acquaintance."

"Welcome, my Queen. I am called Moondancer and am at your beck and call."

"Why are you called Moondancer?" she asked.

"I was born on the day the Shyjael Tyl is closest to our world. On that day, as my mother gave birth to me, she gazed up at it. She told me its light danced across her face and cast a mystical glow on her scales. That is how I the name came to her, using the common tongue."

"It is a beautiful name, and you're exquisite," she said. "I have never met an ajatar before." She hesitated then asked, "Can I touch you?"

He gave a nod.

"Why of course. I would be honored. But please be careful of my scales. The ends are sharp as swords."

Molly came forward and cautiously extended a hand. He dropped his head in response. She reached out and carefully touched him, taking care to avoid the rough, sharp ends of his scales. Elizabeth also reached out and touched him.

He grinned at the girls, but his expression quickly changed when he saw a young man with Hadram and a guardsman at the doorway. The young man was unfamiliar to him. He brought his head gently around to get a closer look at him, his movements forcing the girls to switch their attention to the doorway.

Hadram announced the two men.

"My lords, I present Galsham, master guard to the Keep, and Elban Miragrin from Portmoor," he said.

Elban Miragrin looked haggard and weary, as though it had been too long since he had slept last. He was breathing heavily, and he seemed frightened. His eyes were sunken, and his expression grim. But as he stood at the doorway he was amazed at what he saw - wizards, elves, men, a bobbin and dwarf, a cat, two human children, and an enormous red ajatar.

An ajatar! he thought. *A red one at that!*

Never had he seen such a majestic and formidable-looking beast. He tried to clear his head.

"Announce yourself, young man," said Fairfax. "What brings you here?"

"I am Elban Miragrin. I've journeyed long from Portmoor," he rambled, exhausted and out of breath, "from Portmoor . . . for days and nights . . . on my master's horse . . . the one called Saraanth . . ."

Fairfax raised his hands, trying to calm Miragrin down.

"Peace be with you, young man. You are among friends here," he said. "You have nothing to fear here - no concerns or frets. But I do wish to ask. The horse you speak of — you called him Saraanth. Is this the same Saraanth who served as Master Skag Harwell's trusted steed?"

"Yes, the same," said Miragrin still trying to catch his breath. "My Master instructed me to come here and inform you of what approaches from the sea. He told me to ride day and night without rest. He told me he would care for my family . . ."

"What's this?" interrupted a concerned Brows. "You said something approaches. What approaches?"

"Hundreds of black ships . . . too many to count . . . many leagues out to sea," said Miragrin.

Everyone was caught off guard by this and their expressions went blank. Fairfax, Brows, and Big Grey silently looked at each other. Each remembered their time at The Cauldron and Scroll when the Professor appeared in a wood carving and spoke of Portmoor. They told Halbierd of this the night before, at the end of their meeting. Now they feared with good reason that something horrible might have happened. They were upset that they had not given more thought to the Professor's cryptic warning.

Moondancer lowered and shook his head in resignation.

"I was at Portmoor last night," he said. "I do not wish to speak of what I saw with the young man and human children here. There is a time and place . . ."

Fairfax turned to Miragrin and the girls with a hardened eye, then to Moondancer.

"There is no better time or place than now and here," he said. "Listen to me. At times like these, there can be no secrets. We must show courage, for courage is the understanding of the truth of life. Such courage gives us strength, and it is this strength that replenishes the soul. My friend, tell us what you saw."

Fairfax looked at Miragrin and the girls, each holding a stare on Moondancer. He could feel strength in them.

"Please, go on. Tell us what you saw," said Fairfax.

Moondancer wavered and said, "This is why I came to you today. Evil has taken hold of that place. I am afraid it is lost. It is now a place of ruin and death, overrun with orcs and other brood."

A sickening silence draped about them.

Fairfax closed his eyes in deep sadness as Miragrin's stare quickly turned to a look of bewilderment. The young man felt his strength fleeting away. He was stricken by a trembling terror, a concern for the safety of his family and his friend Harwell. But he was overtaken with emotion by what he had heard. His eyes bulged, and his chest heaved.

"Noooooooo!" he shouted. "No! This can't be!"

Fairfax walked over to him and threw his arms around him in a tight hug.

Miragrin burst into tears, fighting to break free from the wizard's grip.

"Let me go!" he shouted. "Let me go! I must ride Saraanth! I must go back to my family!"

"There . . . there," said Fairfax unrelenting in his hold. "Calm yourself. Returning would be foolish. If Master Harwell gave you his word, as you said he did, that he would see to your family's care, then you have nothing to worry about." The wizard took Miragrin by his shoulders and held him at arm's length. "Most likely, your master gave his life protecting your family. Young Miragrin, if Master Harwell told you he would protect your family, then I know they are safe. You must believe me. I know Master Harwell. He would give his very life to protect your family."

Miragrin sensed sincerity in the wizard's voice and looked soulfully into his eyes.

"I believe you," he said now trying to restrain his emotions. "He was like a father to me. But still, I must go to them. Don't you understand?"

"Yes, I do understand, and you will go to them. Do you know how Master Harwell may have protected your family?"

"He said he would take them to his home, east of the city," said Miragrin, his voice cracking as his eyes filled with tears.

Fairfax lifted a hand and placed a light, calming spell over Miragrin.

"You will see to their safe return when the time is right, and not alone," he told him in a whisper. "Of this, I promise. You will go with friends who can help."

Miragrin nodded and rested his head on Fairfax's chest. The wizard motioned for Hadram and Galsham. They took Miragrin and walked him from the Garden Courtyard and into the Keep. He needed warmth and food, and time to rest. Most of all he needed time to think.

An overwhelming pall of gloom and despair settled over everyone as Miragrin left. For many, there was a feeling of depression and isolation, and for others, hopelessness followed by anger. They well understood the gravity of the situation - evil now attacked from both the east and west - a darkness from the east, the brood now with a stronghold to the west. Deep silence reigned over them. The girls did not exactly know what the young man's news meant, but they could tell that his words were discouraging. Both felt saddened by the emotional tale and Molly wanted to help in some way, but what could she do?

Moondancer raised its head.

"I am sorry my friends," he said softly. "I did not know about the young man or his family. If I had known, perhaps, I could have helped. For now, you must know that Portmoor is not safe. It is a place of evil and darkness, barren, a place where, except for brood, life is lacking. If I were you, I would leave well enough alone, and stay clear of that place. But something tells me you will not follow my advice."

"I have never known the great red ajatar to run from evil," said Fairfax.

"I do not run from anything, good wizard," bristled Moondancer. "I have seen great evil and stared it down. But much darkness stirs across the land. I fear the forces of good are ill-prepared."

"My friend, when the forces of good find their backs against the wall, they can be most formidable."

Big Grey turned his thoughts to the young Miragrin.

"We must remember, he is family to our good friend Norba Gringshek, proprietor of The Cauldron and Scroll," said the cat. "I do not think we have any choice but to help him find his family and safely deliver them from Portmoor."

Gringshek!

Molly remembered the name and the kind innkeeper. She looked at her sister and both now felt bad for him. He had shown them great hospitality, kindness, and warmth.

Fairfax rubbed his chin in thought.

"Yes. We must help him," he said. "There is no choice here." Everyone nodded in agreement. He looked at Moondancer. "I do not mean to impose, but would you help us, my friend?"

"It is very disheartening when I am right," said Moondancer in an unfortunate tone of voice. "Rarely do you heed my advice. It is against my better judgment, but I will help to get the young man and others there and back again. It will not be easy."

Fairfax patted Moondancer on the cheek.

"Thank you, my friend," he said. "That is a very kind offer. One we'll gladly accept."

They returned to the dining room for breakfast while Moondancer remained outside. As they ate there was talk of how best to mount a search for Miragrin's family, and if Molly's plan of the previous day made sense considering the news of Portmoor's destruction. There were suggestions of battle plans and how to engage the enemy, while some wondered if Carrick had yet joined with his army. They talked of war as if it were so familiar, and indeed it was, for war had gripped them so closely for such a long time; it had bloodied every field; it had marked every door; it had touched every family. The more they talked, the more ideas they had and the more confident they became. After all, they had Erol Carrick who had defeated the brood on battlefield after battlefield, and now the races would begin to gather their forces to face the enemy. They had the Lia Fail and someone who, they believed, was possibly capable of wielding its power. For, as Fairfax told them, "The Queen is our only hope. The root of the evil, that which dwells in the second tower must be destroyed."

When breakfast ended many decisions were made. A winged messenger would be sent to the Thorndell in hopes of informing Carrick of Portmoor's demise. Brows, Big Grey, Donduin, and Ancorbow, would take Molly and Elizabeth, along with the orc Ug'ghi Otha and several Keep guardsmen, and travel to Katzhu Pu. There they would take counsel with the Guild Lords. Dithil and Fairfax would take

Elban Miragrin back to Portmoor to search for his family, and hopefully, bring them to Blackstone Keep. They would ride Moondancer in the blackness of night. Once the young man's family was safely brought to the Keep, Dithil and Fairfax would join with the others on the way to Katzhu Pu. Dalgaes and Tinnfierl would return to Tir Nan Og and muster the elf army.

"And where is Mr. I'Kinillel?" asked Molly. "I've not seen him today."

"My Queen, he has already gone," said Ancorbow. "He left last night and returns to the Eldor. He'll lead their army and join the battle."

"Aye, and don't forget the mighty dwarf army," said Dithil proudly. "It heads south to the Thorndell led by none other than Bombadorn Roundthaler."

Ancorbow gave the dwarf a strong slap across the back and exclaimed jubilantly, "With Roundthaler joined once again with the great Carrick, there can be no defeat!"

"Roundthaler," said Elizabeth. "Now, that's a funny name, isn't it?"

Before the group parted Molly asked to speak with Fairfax and Big Grey privately. She told them of her dream, of the mechanical voice that repeatedly said, *I have a message from another time.*

Fairfax hesitated when he heard those words. Emotions fled over his face: fear and sorrow. Finally, resignation settled there. He took a deep breath.

"It was only a matter of time," he said. "You have nothing to fear for you have the stone and many friends.

Know that you will have dreams that'll foreshadow the future. They may help to guide you. It is the stone's influence. But this dream, this dream about a messenger, I am unsure of its meaning. Whatever you do, do not accept the message. I fear no good can come from it. Do you understand?"

Big Grey gave a worrisome smile.

"You will hear many voices in the Harrow," he told Molly. "As long as you listen to the voices of your friends, you will be fine."

This is the first time they've expressed a hint of fear, she thought.

She clutched the stone and could its warmth in her hand. It gave her strength and confidence.

Somewhere, something incredible is waiting to be known.

She was drawn to the thought.

Professor, I am ready.

She smiled at them.

"Don't worry. I understand," she said in a resolute tone.

This pleased Fairfax. He gave her a gentle kiss on the forehead.

"You make such a splendid Queen," he told her.

The group soon parted and went their separate ways. Brows and Big Grey took the girls back to their chamber so they could pack extra clothes for the trip. On their way down the long hall, Molly thought about what had happened, about all the plans, and all the talk of war. Yet she remained strong in her conviction that the Professor sent her and her sister to the Harrow for a reason, that she could defeat the evil, and in doing so perhaps save thousands of lives. She took her sister by the hand.

Elizabeth looked up at Molly.

"Do you think we'll be back for dinner?" she asked.

Molly just shrugged her shoulders.

* * *

Lindisfarne was a small town in northern Ahlgren just south of the Strongdale Downs. It was a place where people listened to minstrels, watched children play in grassy fields, and gossiped at the local pub. News had spread quickly that Erol Carrick would pass through the town on his way to an army encampment just east of the town. Townsfolk had gathered along the streets awaiting Carrick's return, and soon peasants who had come in from the countryside joined them. Just as the morning dew began to glisten in the new day's sunlight, a young boy came dashing down the main street.

"He's come!" the boy shouted. "He's come!"

The boy pushed his way into the crowd which now stared in silent awe at the spectacle of Erol Carrick entering the town atop the huge black steed Warsinger, with Windthrasher, the great falcon, perched on his shoulder. As the horse continued down the street he did so as if moving to music, his large hooves pounding rhythmically against the cobblestones.

At the center of the town, Warsinger halted, and Carrick raised a hand in greeting while Windthrasher lifted his head and stretched out his great wings. For a moment, time seemed to stand still as all eyes gazed at the glorious sight of Carrick. Then there came a rousing cheer and applause from the crowd. Carrick reared Warsinger and lifted the swords Eligor and Ravenscar high into the morning sun.

"Look!" said the boy in amazement. "The fire swords! The fire swords!"

There was a flash of light and a crashing boom as Eligor and Ravenscar transformed into swords of fire, the white pulsating flames of which held to the shape of the steel blades. The crowd roared with approval but soon was quieted by a commotion down the street.

"Move aside! Move aside!" came a deep and raspy voice from the doorway of The Wandering Bawd Tavern. "All of you! Out of my way! Out of my way!"

The crowd began to part unevenly as a dwarf, stout and round, with long brown hair and a beard with streaks of grey, staggered through the crowd and burst onto the street. His face was worn with thick creases and scars, and he wore chain mail tied tightly about his waist with a golden belt. In one hand, he held a tall glass of barley ale from which he would take sips, while in the other, he dragged behind him a heavy axe that was more than his height along the cobbled street.

As he approached Carrick, Warsinger neighed loudly. With a word from Carrick, the horse steadied and bowed allowing Carrick to quickly dismount, the fire swords still ablaze.

A hush came over the crowd as the dwarf threw the drink aside, the glass shattering in bits along the street.

Using both hands he raised his mighty axe and swung it in a slow arc at Carrick. Carrick brought both fire swords aloft to meet the mighty axe. A booming sound exploded from the clash of metal and fire as white flames leaped into the sky, sparks showering the combatants. They both wrestled for advantage until Carrick mustered enough strength to push the dwarf backward. He stumbled and fell to the street dropping his axe. Carrick quickly gained the edge and hovered over the dwarf bringing Eligor and Ravenscar to but an inch of his neck.

"You're drunk," said Carrick scornfully.

"You'd refuse me a mere drink of ale while I await your grand entrance," said the dwarf, breathing heavily. "And you're late, as usual!"

Carrick brought the fire swords to his side, bringing both to one hand, before reaching down and offering the other to the dwarf. The dwarf took Carrick's hand who lifted him to his feet. Both smiled and Carrick hugged the dwarf.

"It is good to see you, my friend," Carrick told him.

"Aye, and you are a sight for sore eyes," said the dwarf.

The crowd erupted into applause and cheers.

"Roundthaler!" someone shouted.

"The great commander of the En' Naug!" shouted another.

"The greatest warrior who ever lived!" shouted someone else.

"Long live Roundthaler!" shouted another.

There were some in the crowd who did not know the dwarf, but there were those who knew Bombadorn Roundthaler well. He was one of few dwarves who frequented Ahlgren, a good friend of Carrick who many years ago commanded the dwarf army during the Shadow Wars, alongside the armies of Ahlgren and the Eldor. Roundthaler and Carrick were comrades, even though the conditions were not of their choosing. Theirs was a unique relationship, opposites in almost every belief and course of action, but they were, for each other, the perfect friend and confidant. They had lived, and lived still, by battle and war, soldiers suffering the drama of life and death played out on field after field. Together they had fought hunger, cold and utter despair, and an enemy as cunning as any predator. They were warriors in the service of good, who would compel adhesion to that which was righteous, at the point of the sword, and they asked for nothing more and expected nothing less.

Roundthaler gave a sharp whistle. A small, sturdy pony with a bright white mane galloped from a side street. He stepped forward and mounted the pony, its name Shimmerstar.

Carrick brought Warsinger alongside his friend and raised a hand to the cheering crowd.

"Peace to all," said Carrick, "and may the Maker bless you."

Erol Carrick and Bombadorn Roundthaler galloped out of the town and to the east. They soon crested a ridge just outside Lindisfarne and suddenly the place known as the Thorndell Fields appeared. It was a valley of most rugged scenic beauty, with outcroppings of jagged rock, patches of wildflowers, and tall golden grasses that danced in the wind. From this vantage point, both gazed across the fields and over a massive army encampment below.

Here gathered the great armies of Ahlgren and Mortha, row upon row of white tents stretching as far as the eye could see, the banners of the Tree and the Axe fluttering in the wind. The tents were clustered in three areas covering the whole of the north. At the lead and farthest to the east was the vanguard, composed of archers, longbowmen, and crossbowmen, patiently honing arrow tips and stocking their quivers. At the center were great wooden siege engines: catapults, battering rams, siege towers, and other devices of war. This was also the place where dark smoke billowed from hundreds of fire pits as blacksmiths forged tools and weapons. Surrounding the structures of battle were the infantry and armored cavalry, thousands of spear men, javelin men, and axe men, sharpening their weapons and polishing their armor. Light and agile cavalry formed the rearguard and closest to the ridge, their horses groomed as farriers set about trimming and shoeing.

"Time is at hand," Roundthaler told Carrick. "Soon we'll be ready."

But Carrick was silent. He looked to the valley's southern extremity where the soil was stony and the fields became barren, to the most hallowed burial ground in the Harrow. It was a solemn place, a scene of desolation, swept with sighs, washed with tears, and covered with graves. Very little of the effects of the battles of ages past were to be seen, other than the thousands of mounds now covered with rank weeds and short grasses. The Thorndell was a graveyard of bloodshed and sorrow. But now before him, a new army gathered, poised alongside one of skulls and bones.

"There will be time enough for battle and death," Carrick told his friend. And then he was off with Warsinger and Windthrasher, galloping down the ridge and to the graveyard below.

* * *

Before leaving Blackstone Keep for Tir Nan Og, Dalgaes sought out Big Grey and asked to meet with him as soon as possible. They decided on a meeting time and location because Big Grey first needed to finish some tasks. They met in the late afternoon, at the back of the Garden Courtyard, near the lake where the large waterfall spilled. Dalgaes was the first to arrive. He stood alone in his pristine white robes, his long black hair cascading over his shoulders, staring at the waterfall as it gushed into the lake. The air was sweet and clear, and birds sang their welcome as they perched in the trees. He was so absorbed in his thoughts that he did not hear the cat approaching. But he sensed his presence nonetheless and turned to discover him trudging along a stone path and to the lake.

The two friends walked a bit, each enchanted by the surrounding beauty. They marveled at how the mist sprayed upon the trees, forming diamond-shaped particles of light that reflected from the leaves, and how rainbows danced like prisms against the watery haze. Eventually, they found their way to a marble bench at the lake's edge beneath an arch of red roses, a cool shade of sweet fragrance that overlooked the misty scene.

"By the Maker," said Dalgaes, "is not this place wonderful?"

The cat rubbed up against his good friend's legs.

"Indeed," he said. "Do you remember the last time we met here?"

Dalgaes smiled.

"Yes. It was several years ago," he said. "A day much like today with the perfume of growing flowers pervading the air, their blooms glowing in the mist. Sadly, if I am not mistaken, we did not speak of such beauty. Rather, we spoke of war and battle."

The cat nodded.

"You have a fine memory," he said. "Tell me, my friend, what shall we speak of today? Shall we speak of war and battle again?"

"In a sense," said Dalgaes. He reached down and gently rubbed the top of the cat's head. The cat closed his eyes as a deep purr rumbled. "I must confide a secret with you, a secret of utmost importance. The Professor asked that I do so, and I promised him we would have this discussion. No one knows what I am about to tell you, save for the Professor and me, and others unknown to us. Now it is time to join with another."

"Just what is this secret you speak of?"

Dalgaes hesitated as he looked about to ensure they were alone. He leaned down.

"It is a secret of grave consequence, for it affects the cause of good and every single one of our lives," he whispered. "The Queen of Ahlgren cannot wield the stone alone. She requires the help of another, but she does not know this."

"I do not understand."

"Unbeknownst to her, the Lia Fail requires two to unleash its wrath. The one she is unaware of must first speak secret thought-words, thought-words that unlock the stone's power. Once this occurs, she can wield the stone's strength. As long as there are two, the stone's fury can be unleashed, and its power controlled."

The cat was surprised. He had not heard of this. It was common knowledge that the Lia Fail could only be used by a young girl, one of innocence and purity as chosen by the stone's Keeper. Now, before him was a secret never alluded to even by the whispers of those close to him. He thought for a moment. It started to become clear as to why prudence dictated that such a secret be so closely held.

"I was not aware of this," he said. "But there is logic to what you say. The need for two protects the Harrow. If two are required to use the stone's power, there is clarity in the situation. It is a check of sorts. And, if the stone were to fall under the control of someone with evil intentions, without the other, the stone would be rendered useless. But there is deception here, and where there is deception there must be control. How is the deception controlled?"

"Master Purr, you are correct. There is deception, but deception can sometimes be justified. The Queen of Ahlgren will believe that she alone has the power to wield the stone, but over time she will doubt her ability, for the stone brings about dreams of strangeness, dark dreams that can be maddening. In the beginning, she will attempt to use the stone's power, to test her ability with the stone, but she will fail. Doubt will creep on her like night shadows. She will become frustrated and angry. But all of this is required. It is part of her learning.

"You see, the one who possesses the secret thought-words must always remain near to the Queen of Ahlgren. This is necessary for it is he who quietly works with her, teaching her how to use the stone for good. She will experiment with its power. She will try to use it in all sorts of ways, trying to understand how to harness its fury. But it is the word-keeper who unlocks the stone's capabilities, but only when her experiments are principled and when the use of the stone's power is appropriate for the situation. With the word-keeper's proper guidance, she will understand that the stone can only be used for good purposes. The Maker has devised it as such.

"But my friend, there is more to all this. There are several stones, three that are known to us. Few know of this secret. Each stone is coded to the one who receives it from its Keeper, and as with the Lia Fail each stone requires one to unlock its power and a master to wield it. The stones seem to have their own signature, each knowing the kind of person that can wield it, and each having a unique spell to unlock its might."

"Do you know who has them? Do you know where they are?"

"Those who know of this secret are uncertain. The whereabouts of the stones and those who control the power became lost with the last war. We only know of the Lia Fail."

"Who knows of this?"

Dalgaes paused and stood. He again faced the lake, took a few steps forward, lowered his head, and from the corner of his eye and over his shoulder looked back at the cat.

"We have kept this knowledge hidden, and have done so purposely," he said. "Not even the Edainar knows of this. Some are concerned with the wizards, concerned that their magic could corrupt some in the Order, corrupt them to use the stones in terrible ways. Mind you, some in the Edainar may be aware of this knowledge. We do not know for sure. Typically, secrets beget secrets and lies beget lies. But if a stone were to ever fall into the hands of one with ruthless intentions, without the second one, without knowledge of the thought-words to unlock its power, the stone is useless. Master Purr, you must be the word-keeper to the Lia Fail. You must be its Caedaes."

"I have not heard that word before," said the cat. "What is a Caedaes?"

"It is the one who knows the spell, the word-keeper, the one who speaks the thought-words at the right moment, the thoughts that unlock the Lia Fail's power. It is the Caedaes who knows when it is appropriate to unlock the might of the Lia Fail. It is the Caedaes who trains the wielder of the stone, helping the wielder to understand what is good and evil, and when power is best used. It is the Caedaes who has insight into some of the Queen's thoughts and must fulfill his duty in perfect harmony with her. My dear friend, you are to be the one. You are to be the Caedaes to the Queen of Ahlgren."

Big Grey looked at Dalgaes. He saw concern in the Elf-King's eyes, born from the burden of his request.

The cat met his friend's concern.

"Do not worry," he said. "There is a modicum of deceit in all this, but I will do what is expected of me."

"Thank you," said Dalgaes. "I understand your worry. But deceit is sometimes a necessary component to the truth. I trust you will do as expected, as you have been a faithful servant to all that is good. I would have never dreamed to ask so much of you, but the time is at hand, and you are right for the task."

"Tell me what I must do," said the cat in a reassuring tone.

"The Caedaes must always be near to the Queen, watching over her, ready to use the thought-words when she does her part, but only when it is appropriate to do so. Only by using the sacred thought-words can the full power of the Lia Fail be unleashed. The Queen can control the stone in a rudimentary sense, but only the Caedaes can release the stone's might. As I have said, there will be times when she will try to use the stone, to test her abilities. Such times will provide you with the ability to listen to her thoughts and show her the path to what is good. You can never tell her the sacred words. The Queen is to always believe that she and she alone can unleash the power of the

Lia Fail. You are to never tell her or anyone of this. Not even the Guild Lords."

The cat felt some anger in Dalgaes.

Why did he specifically point out the Guild Lords? he thought.

"The Guild Lords?" he probed.

"Yes. Not even the Guild Lords," said Dalgaes. "There are some who do not trust them, the decisions they've made."

There is something there. But what?

Dalgaes had an intense look on his face.

"What is important to know," he said with a seriousness in his voice, "is that to divulge this secret would not only undermine our greatest advantage, but it would also endanger the Queen's well-being."

"How so?" said the cat, his heart pounding.

Darkness came over the Elf-King's face, as when the shadow of a cloud passes over a lake. He sat for a moment in silence.

"If a Queen of Ahlgren knew how to unlock and wield the stone," he said, "she would become obsessed with the power. Remember, unchecked power feeds on hatred. In time, it would consume her every waking moment and dominate her. There would be an ache in her heart, and she would welcome the pain. She would become a creature of great evil. Life would cease to have any meaning within her soulless prison, and she would use the stone to melt flesh from bone. Not even Carrick's army could stop her. There would be no right or wrong, only the will of one person, and she would dictate everything. She would control life itself."

"Why the Queen must never know the spell," muttered the cat.

"Yes, and why the Caedaes brings balance to the stone's power."

Big Grey saw that Dalgaes was so certain, beyond any touch of doubt, that what they were now discussing was the most important thing in the Harrow. The Lia Fail was a power that only a child could wield, but uncontrolled and in that same child's hand it could destroy the known world.

But what if the wrong Caedaes were selected? What if a Caedaes became corrupt? What if there was a conflict between the one who wields the stone and the Caedaes?

"You have questions," said the Dalgaes. "There are questions that sometimes go unanswered because to contemplate the answers can be most terrifying."

The cat nodded.

"My friend, your burden will be great and never lessened until the Lia Fail is no longer needed," said Dalgaes. "Know that where the Queen faces terror so too must the Caedaes."

Big Grey loved Molly, he loved the Harrow, and if needed he would gladly give his life to both. He accepted the task now imposed on him and without reservation.

"It is an honor," he said bravely. "But I do have one question I would like answered."

"Yes. What is it?"

"Who was Caedaes to Queen Aerin?"

Dalgaes smiled and stroked the cat's back.

"Why it was the Professor that unlocked the stone's might. He was the Caedaes and then its Keeper. Just as you will one day be the Keeper, to help pass the stone to the next Queen. You are in good company."

The two spent some time in silence; a sacred silence that no one disturbed. They watched as time slipped slowly away, alone with their thoughts, knowing that from this day forward, their journey would be long and difficult.

Big Grey decided not to press Dalgaes on his apparent dislike of the Guild Lords. That he was angry with them was clear enough, but the reasons for it were a mystery. He would have to ponder this at some later stage when he had time to himself. For now, there were too many other things to occupy him.

Time reveals all things.

Later and only briefly did they chat and at that time did Dalgaes give Big Grey the sacred thought-words. But all the while the cat worried about his unanswered questions.

* * *

Ewellinoth had many great hallways and within each, there were numerous dark nooks and crannies. Glaeynd knew them all. But there was one, a quiet place off a hallway near the Rhiorsnan's chambers, where she could take refuge, to sit and think over her troubles. It was her sanctuary of sorts, a place to hide from overpowering dreads. She would sit there, sometimes for hours, and stare into the gloom, the darkness, and the quiet.

So, there she sat, again, alone in the pitch black with sad thoughts, upset with her father and brother for how they treated her and her friends. What she had experienced was so disturbing to her that she could not bear to go over it again, but she did, in hopes of understanding what had happened. She was distraught with the way her father had spoken to her friends and shattered by his cutting words to her. It was a cruel rejection, and, in her sadness, she began to weep. Her sorrow quickly became anger, but she realized this to be a weakness.

I will gather the strength to stand this storm.

She had a certain persistence of will that allowed her to overcome weakness in times of difficulty and overcome apathy when there was a need for action. She was able to do this because she had a strong sense of purpose, a sense of what she wanted to achieve in her life, and a strong sense of who she was and where she came from. This sense of purpose, this determination to overcome difficulties, this loyalty, and the sense of who she was, were always there. But it took her time to find it. She had to first overcome her emotions and fears.

I will confront my father and brother.

She rose from her chair and wiped her tears. Just then she heard a faint sound from around the corner.

In several dim alcoves along the hallway, she could hear whispers and the unmistakable voice of Gurandurm Grimshade. His was a haunting voice, almost unnatural, strangely soothing, but at times harsh and piercing. Glaeynd peeked around the corner and saw him with Gultat Ramd and Conder Forge, two of the three Rhiorsnan captains.

I must be still, her instincts told her.

"The order is given by the Lord himself," whispered Grimshade in a devilish but calm tone. "After dinner, they will be provided nep. Wait until you receive word. When the word is given bring your forces from below and kill them as they sleep."

"What of the other captain? What of Twain Boggans?" asked Forge.

"Boggans remains loyal to Glaeynd. They are close," said Grimshade gently stroking the fur trim on his leather coat. "We have sent him away with his guard under orders of the Lord, on a reconnaissance mission to the east. We are sure that with all the evil that now gathers in those places he will face a most painful death. He will be of no trouble to us."

"Glaeynd, is she to know of this?"

"She is of no use anymore. Her fate is self-chosen," said Grimshade. "The Lord has deemed the cats and Fenri enemies of the sovereign and state. If she appears later, she will be told that her friends were conspiring against her father and that they were dealt with as all criminals are handled. But if she is in the chamber then she is one of them and will suffer their fate."

"What about the bodies?" asked Ramd.

"Dispose of them in the furnaces," declared Grimshade, calmly, without hesitation. "Let the winds have them."

He turned and withdrew into the shadows and in the direction of the Great Hall while the captains made their way to the Rhiorsnan chambers, towards Glaeynd.

She quickly brought herself up against the wall and slowly back into the shadows of the corner as the captains passed by. They did not notice her.

What is happening?

She was horrified. She could not escape the realization that something was wrong, and now she feared for her own life and the lives of her friends.

But Twain . . . my dear Twain remains.

Her thoughts wandered.

When the hallway was clear, she quietly made her way along the walls, from alcove to alcove.

I must reach my friends. I must help them, to find a way out!

She had to warn them of the danger that threatened.

But something bothered her, something Grimshade said, and she replayed his words in her mind.

Bring your forces from below . . . bring your forces from below . . . what did this mean?

She quietly slipped into the large chamber where her friends were still preparing for their departure. Few noticed her at first. She attempted to keep her nerves under control, but it was difficult. She casually glanced around the chamber with a small smile, but she was sweating and her hands trembled. She was nervous, and she was angry at herself for being nervous, as a thousand thoughts whirled and mixed in her head haphazardly.

What to do . . . What to do . . . I know . . . I must lead them from the city and to safety . . . They're in danger . . . I'm in danger . . . Father, why?

Chumsey approached her and stared up into her eyes.

"Are you alright?" he asked.

He startled her. She looked around for Lil' Man as she tried to soothe the turmoil in her mind.

"Lil' Man," she mumbled. "Please, I must speak with him."

He sensed her anguish and quickly brought Lil' Man and Thurir to her. Immediately, Lil' Man saw her nervousness and it drew him toward her.

"What is it Glaeynd?" he asked. "Tell me. Whatever is troubling you, perhaps we can help."

She hesitated in fear and disbelief.

"You are in danger," she said choking back tears. "I overheard Grimshade give the Rhiorsnan captains orders to . . . to . . . to . . ."

"To do what?" asked Lil' Man.

Her lips quivered and her eyes dropped before his.

"To . . . to . . . kill you all of you . . . after dinner . . . tonight," she said in a faint voice.

"I knew it!" roared Thurir. "So be it! Bring your mighty Rhiorsnan here! If it is death they crave, we will give it to them."

Chumsey shook his head.

"No, my friend," he said. "We are no match for their numbers. And in this room, we are but caged birds."

Glaeynd felt utterly frustrated and powerless as she looked over the chamber, dark stone walls lit by black iron wall sconces.

From below . . . what did it mean? From below . . . from below . . . how does one get into this chamber from below?

Then it came to her.

The catacombs! A secret passageway!

Her eyes darted from one flickering wall sconce to another.

The lights! Maybe they're the key!

But there were so many of them.

"The lights," she laughed, almost hysterically, wiping the tears away. "The lights! Yes, the lights! Why didn't I think of it earlier? Quickly! We've not much time!"

Lil' Man was confused.

"What are you talking about?" he asked.

She made her way through the Fenri to the nearest sconce and tugged down on its base. But it did not move; it was firmly secured to the wall.

"The sconces! They may open a secret passageway," she said moving to another sconce. "Every chamber has a secret passageway to the catacombs. Ewellinoth was constructed to provide such passage, escape if you will, but only to those who know the secret. The catacombs lead outside, past Mistmere's walls. I'm sure that's how the Rhiorsnan plan on making their surprise attack, from the catacombs below."

"Catacombs?" asked Chumsey.

She pulled down on the sconce, but it was firmly mounted to the wall.

"Yes," she said hurrying to the next one, "catacombs . . . the old city . . . you have forgotten your history lessons. Mistmere is built over the ruins of ages past. A section of the old city is still maintained beneath

Ewellinoth and other parts of Mistmere. Most of the passages have been sealed over time. But I think there must be a secret door somewhere in this room that will lead us there. I'm sure of it. From the catacombs, you can escape the city. I'll show you the way."

She pulled on it, but it did not move.

She ran around pulling down on each sconce, one after another, in hopes of triggering a secret tunnel to the catacombs. But as she approached the final one, she felt a wave of despair wash over her.

Maybe I was wrong! If I cannot find the secret passageway all will be lost.

She looked about the room one last time before placing her hands on the last sconce.

This must be the one!

She turned to it, closed her eyes, and pulled.

It was hinged!

The sconce swung downward. A section of the stone wall began to slide, and the room began to rumble. In her excitement, she held her breath.

A passage into what looked like a cave was revealed. The opening was dark and there was no way to determine how deep it might go. She smiled, happy that she could help her friends.

"Quickly now," she told them. "Gather the others and your provisions and let us be on our way."

CHAPTER 9
THE CATACOMBS

THEY WENT DOWN INTO the catacombs using a stone staircase. Glaeynd led the way walking with a flickering torch, followed by Lil' Man and Chumsey, with Thurir and his pack behind. Threading their way through narrow passages of rock and stone, they came to a junction. Glaeynd hesitated. She looked left then motioned to the others to follow her as she made her way in the opposite direction, down a long dark tunnel which led them further into the depths. Their pace quickened, the wet gravel of the floor crunching under their feet. All around them water dripped steadily from above, slowly forming dripstones above them and on the ground. In some places, the dripstones met creating large misshapen white columns that sparkled in the dim light.

As they continued down the dark passage, they came to a great stone archway that opened to a large chamber supported by several thick columns. The columns were square, rather than round, the walls were straight and smooth, and the roof vaulted high above their heads. Great stone balconies, one above another, tier over tier, projected out over the space. From this chamber there ran other passageways, and stone archways leading to other gloomy antechambers, forming a perfect labyrinth of rooms. They stopped as Glaeynd surveyed the chamber, her eyes darting from archway to archway.

"Which way is which?" she muttered to herself.

Quilted along the surface of the walls were heaps of bones, in some places more orderly than others, but there was a clear pattern to how they were arranged. Lower sections of the walls were made up of leg bones stacked one atop the other, followed by rows and rows of skulls, a row or two of more leg bones, then a final row of skulls topping it all off. There were no intact skeletons; the goal of the arrangement was maximum compactness.

"This is not a pleasant place. Is it now?" smirked Thurir. "There is an eerie coldness here as if it is haunted by those souls trapped in the walls. How did this place come to be?"

"As Mistmere evolved it needed to reclaim the large swaths of land used for graveyards," explained Glaeynd. "The remains of the departed were moved here, underground. I can assure you there are no ghosts down here."

Something in the damp air caught Chumsey. He lifted his nose. There was a faint scent he could not make out. He turned to Lil' Man.

"Do you smell it?" asked Chumsey.

Lil' Man looked about the chamber, his nostrils twitching.

"I do. Strange scent but I do not know what it could be."

Thurir lifted his nose to the dampness.

"I smell it too. What do you suppose it is?" he asked.

"Not sure but stay close," warned Chumsey. "Something is very wrong here."

Then a strange whirring noise followed by a dull thump shattered the silence. From behind, a Fenri fell dead. It was a moment of dread and horror. Everyone realized what had happened, but there was little time to react. The chamber now screamed with the noise of arrows hissing in flight, speeding through the air, splitting through Fenri chests. Glaeynd and the cats looked around and quickly discovered the lurking foe.

"Firbolgs!" shouted Lil' Man.

The deformed creatures with bent legs and hunched backs poured over the stone balconies, firing arrows from powerful crossbows. They were large, grotesque demons of human form, but with a snout full of evil teeth and with eyes slit like a lurking reptile.

The group dashed through the nearest archway and down a dark passageway.

"Protect the little ones!" roared Thurir.

Janru grabbed Lil' Man by the scruff and flung him onto his back. Talro did the same with Chumsey. Thurir rushed at Glaeynd, wrapped his big front legs around her, and tossed her onto his back in one motion. As he raced, she quickly grabbed his thick hairy neck to keep her balance.

She pointed to a passageway, and they tore their way into its darkness. Some of Thurir's pack turned to defend against the attack only to be met with carnage, their bodies were strewn across the floor. But this helped to slow the firbolgs as the evil beasts stopped to ravage the fallen Fenri bodies. But some kept their pursuit and in no time, they were gaining on the others.

"I don't know if this is the way out!" screamed Glaeynd.

Thurir looked back to see just how close the firbolgs were.

"No matter!" he thundered. "We will run twice as fast as our foul pursuers! I would have rather dealt with ghosts!"

Suddenly, a pale blue light shone into the corridor as ahead, an opening appeared through the darkness. Janru and Talro led the pack through the opening and into a clearing beyond Mistmere's enormous white walls. Under Thurir's orders, the pack turned to face its pursuers. The demons closely followed and were about to attack when far off to the north there was a howl and a flash of lightning that slashed from the sky to smite the firbolgs. The corpses were burnt beyond recognition and piled on top of one another, smoke burning from the mound. A few more firbolgs followed through the opening, but seeing the deaths of the others, they fled in fear. For Glaeynd there was nothing neither close to nor worse than the smell of burned flesh. Bile welled up inside her and rose in her throat.

With everyone now safe from the firbolgs, they took a short rest to catch their breath. They surveyed the area, a grassy plains expanse rimmed by the mountainous Old

Hills. They were west of the city and could see few options of easy passage.

That is when an old man in a hooded, tattered brown robe appeared from the mountains. He motioned to them.

"We do not have much time," he said. "Up the mountain, we will go. Your attackers may be easily frightened, but they will return with a vengeance."

Instinctively they followed his lead up the contours of the mountain in their climb. They soon discovered the sweet scent of a night wind that swept across pines and firs, while far below they could see the flickering city lights of Mistmere.

Glaeynd was torn by conflicting emotions as she gazed down on the beautiful city. She remembered her father and brother from another time, before the darkness and before Grimshade, then she thought of Mistmere's citizens and the horrors they would soon experience. While these thoughts haunted her, she recognized that a web of evil had ensnared her family and now, the entire city. She was aware that she would not be able to return.

Why? Father, why have you forsaken all that is good? She thought.

* * *

It was twilight when Fairfax retired to his chamber, high within one of the Blackstone's tallest turrets. He sat in a chair near a window with a view of the Garden Courtyard.

Under twilight's blue veil, he could hardly see the great waterfall, but he could hear it rushing and roaring down the mountainside. Above, a sliver of the broken moon cast fluttering shadows with wisps of thin clouds floating gently across the darkness. He closed his eyes as the moon gently arched into the evening sky; he intending to relax a little before heading on to Portmoor.

At peace, his breath slowed. In his mind's eye, he saw a sky that changed from blue to grey to black, with the lands moving under him as if he were flying, his soul soaring like a bird amid the clouds. His vision took him northward, soaring high above the Thornback, then east above the Old Hills and Mistmere and over the Snowwynne Barrens, and into the gloom of the Crag. Over the demon land, he descended, through earth and rock, down into a chasm which led to the underground furnaces of evil. There amidst the heat and toil of brood were great war machines forged of molten steel, with thousands of orcs gathered in column after column, marching up to the surface, readied for battle.

Deeper and deeper, his vision took him until he came to a large, cavernous place overlooking the forges. Here, it was cooler, and the rock was a bluish dark with hundreds of small waterfalls cascading over large boulders and outcroppings. On a lone precipice he saw the hooded master with his Uth' Egoreyr, and alongside was a Dark Rider and black ajatar. They stood proudly, looking down upon the evil work.

They must not feel my magical presence, he thought.

Swiftly he ascended and back through the chasm and out into the dank air. He lifted himself from the underground cavern and back to the surface. Higher and higher still he drifted into the air, northward until he could see the Rakl through the heavy grey clouds. It was a desolate place of black and grey rock, snow-capped and icy mountains that jutted up from the flatlands, its crest sharply defined against a bleak sky. Such was the home of the Fenri.

At the foot of the mountains, he was surprised by a horrific sight, for there loomed the bulk of a tower, huge and sullen in the dark mists. It stretched high into the blackness, a tapering shape, twisted and contorted, that vanished into the shadows. It was built with limited egress and had a simple black gate of iron. Sharpened angle-iron stakes surrounded its perimeter like teeth bared to the skies. Below were thousands of brood and Fenri bearing loads of stone toiling over twisted slopes of rubble. The sound of the overseers' whips, beastly orcs, and the savage cries and moans of those enslaved as they labored, pierced the night wind.

His eyes still closed; he circled high above the tower where a dark figure appeared. He could not initially see its face, only the sculpted silhouette of its long black robe. But as he came closer, he could make out the tall and slender form, pale and gaunt, with large round black eyes. This was the Dark Wizard, Varul Teardash.

He must not sense me.

But it was too late.

Teardash felt the magic. It was not the type of magic he held dearly, rather, it was the good type of magic, the kind he despised and feared.

"Who is calling me?" he shouted.

Fairfax quickly ascended but Teardash recognized his presence and responded with a ravenous howl and a startling burst of flame from his hands. The wizard continued his ascent, faster and faster still, but could not outrun the flame or the pain.

Then there came a faint voice calling to him from afar.

"Master Fairfax."

He stirred as the voice called again, this time louder.

"Master Fairfax!"

He felt a tug on his shoulder. He opened his eyes to find a concerned Ranagul Dithil staring up at him. The dwarf was holding a candle, by the light of which he could see his chamber.

Outside he could hear the waterfalls in the distance. He was shaken, a single trail of sweat dripping from his brow and into his left eye.

He was glad to see the dwarf.

"Master Fairfax it's time. We must go," said Dithil. "Are you well? It seems you were having quite the nightmare."

Fairfax took a deep breath.

"Oh, I am fine," he said. "I beheld visions from the east, visions dark and dreary. Indeed, my good friend, it was a nightmare."

He took his staff and struggled to lift himself from the chair. Dithil helped.

"Now's not the time to be concerned with such darkness," said the dwarf. "We promised to help the young man and it's time to do so."

"Yes. Thank you for wresting me from such darkness. We'll help young Miragrin. We must also warn others. Countless war machines spew forth from the Crag and a third tower rises in the east at the Rakl. I've seen this and more. Every moment is precious now."

* * *

Somewhat rested, Fairfax, Dithil, and Elban Miragrin prepared for their journey to Portmoor, each packing a small bag of provisions tied around their waists. From their chambers they went to the Garden Courtyard where Moondancer stood as tall as the trees, silhouetted against the great waterfalls. Once at the courtyard, Fairfax met with Hadram who, along with other courtiers, had arrived earlier to help with the departure. The two spoke for some time, Fairfax telling Hadram of his visions.

Miragrin was nervous. He had never flown on an ajatar but his nervousness was quickly replaced by a greater emotion, the anxiety to find his family. Fairfax reassured him that flying on an ajatar was of little concern, that is, so long as he held on tightly and closed his eyes at the right times.

While the two talked, Hadram and the other courtiers placed several large leather saddles onto Moondancer, strapping each tightly about the red ajatar's torso. Each rider was then boosted into a saddle, Fairfax first and at the head, followed by Miragrin and Dithil. As each settled into their saddle Hadram brought large leather straps about each, leashing each of them to their saddle and Moondancer.

Fairfax looked down at Hadram.

"Remember to inform Halbierd of my visions," he told him.

"I will," said Hadram.

Fairfax nodded then gave Moondancer a gentle pat on his long neck.

"Now, let us be off my dear friend!" he said.

Moondancer slowly lifted and stretched out his massive leathery wings, as the three braced themselves, tightly clutching the leather straps. He took a few mighty strides that shook the ground while bringing his enormous wings front then quickly back again, slightly folded inwards, a down-stroke that provided upward thrust and force. Another stride and down-stroke of his enormous wings and they were off, high above Blackstone Keep, circling higher into the night sky. They climbed higher and faster as he gained speed, his wings creating tremendous gusts of winds that swept about the riders.

"I'm feeling a bit sick!" Miragrin shouted to Fairfax.

"Remember to hold on tightly. When need be, close your eyes!" Fairfax shouted back.

Miragrin heeded the wizard's advice, clenching his eyes shut. Moondancer banked one wing, and turned in a lazy arc north, away from the Blackstone Ridge toward the Greysage forest east of Northsage Barrow. When it seemed as if Moondancer had leveled off his flight, Miragrin opened his eyes.

Moondancer was gliding now, lifted by cool evening winds coming off the Western Seas. It was a gentle flight that soothed Miragrin's nerves as he looked down upon the land far beneath him. All was dark except for the light that streamed from the pale moon. He could make out many of the landmarks; the Greysage with its tall pines; the cobbled Northway Road that followed the Aiden River; the town lights of Shadow Barrow to the north and Rivers Barrow to the south. The land seemed to stretch away endless and emptily to all horizons.

Moondancer made another gentle bank. They were now headed directly toward Portmoor. Desperately, Miragrin searched for city lights ahead but could only see blackness on the ground and a large grey cloud of death that hung in the sky. It was as Moondancer described. He slumped in his saddle; his worst fear realized.

High above the dead city of Portmoor, Moondancer flapped on leathery wings. His reptilian eyes surveyed the destruction below with a vision that detected brood and magic as easily as food. All that could be seen were ruins, skeletons of buildings in smoldering white ash, like something from another world.

Some distance away, Fairfax saw a legion of brood leaving Portmoor, traveling east to Rivers Barrow. Above the wicked minions flew a black ajatar guided by a Dark Rider.

"Uakor Turg," Fairfax told Moondancer in disgust. "The evil has summoned tomb brood to do its bidding. We must make haste to find young Miragrin's family and return to Blackstone."

He pointed to a place east of the city, a signal to Moondancer where to land. He then turned to Miragrin.

"Better close your eyes," he warned. "It will be a quick drop."

With that Moondancer descended rapidly and forcefully through the clouds, streaming over the ruins and ashes of what was once Portmoor.

Miragrin slowly opened one eye then the next, and suddenly was faced with a most horrid sight. A city once vibrant and teeming with life, a city he had left but a few days ago, was now reduced to rubble and ash. Moondancer banked sharply east and to the outskirts of the city, landing gently on the scorched crown of a hill, wings spread wide to break the flight. The stench of death's decay hung over the place, a smell that would forever remain in Miragrin's nostrils.

The three dismounted Moondancer.

"What could've done this?" asked Miragrin.

"Powerful black magic," said Fairfax solemnly. "A dark magic this land has not seen for some time. Quickly now, we must find your family."

They stood overlooking the eastern fringes of Portmoor. From the hill ran a road down and into the city of ruins. Miragrin searched intently for some remembered landmark, anything that would help point him to Skag Harwell's home. As he scoured the darkened landscape he saw a large tree, fallen, black and charred, perhaps a tree that had once been an oak. Nearby, the shattered remnants of a house stood bleak and bare.

"There!" said Miragrin pointing to the ruins. "That could be it."

"Hurry now," whispered Fairfax.

They went down the hill and to the ruins. There was a deathly stillness, unbroken save for a gentle breeze off the sea. Dithil thought that nothing could have survived whatever destroyed the city, but he kept this thought to himself.

Before passing the tree and entering the ruins Fairfax stopped Miragrin. He tightly gripped the young man's shoulders.

"Listen to me," he told him. "Whatever we find in this place you must be strong and courageous."

There was worry in Miragrin's eyes. Unmistakable pain and fear too. He understood what Fairfax said.

"Yes, I will. You have my promise."

Fairfax led them into the ruins using a bit of magic, a pale blue glow that emanated from his right hand. The smell of death, that pervaded Portmoor, seemed much stronger in the ruins. It was a pungent odor that now pulsated on each sickly breath of air. He slowly guided his light about the ruins, over the debris of wood and rock and dust, until it shone on two decapitated orc heads. They gasped at the grisly sight. Using his light, he followed the trail of blood-stained dust to a wooden bookcase where the corpses of two headless orcs and a black dog lay rotting. Dithil knelt and examined the wounds.

"The brood died at the hands of one of their own," said Dithil sickened by the sight. "The slashes are jagged, made by an orc's heldror."

Fairfax knew the word. The heldror was an orc's weapon of choice. It was a long steel sword fashioned with sharp jagged teeth on both sides. The teeth were curved and pointed to the sword's tip, engineered to rip into the flesh of an enemy most painfully. It was heavy, almost impossible for a man to wield, but in the hands of an orc, it was a painful and deadly weapon. For those fallen by a heldror, death was slow and excruciating.

He then shone the light on the bookcase. He sensed something unusual with it but could not quite make out what.

"Hmm . . . it seems out of place," he said.

He placed his hands on the bookcase, feeling around its edges.

With a gentle nudge, the bookcase slid open on an iron track to reveal a hidden door. Miragrin moved toward the hidden door, his heart pounding in his chest. He trembled, and his hands became moist.

Fairfax moved the light to the door's handle.

"Step aside," he told Miragrin.

He focused the light on the handle until it became a deep red.

The handle soon disappeared as if melting away. He motioned with his hand and the door opened revealing a staircase. Carefully he guided the blue light down the staircase.

Fairfax and Miragrin leaned to their left and peeked around the door into the darkness below. Fairfax moved the light, very slowly, around what appeared to be some sort of room. There was no movement, no sound, no sign of life. A deep sadness gripped Miragrin. Then, as the light moved to the farthermost corner of the room it came upon something, a hint of red. Fairfax steadied the light on the red object. He squinted his eyes, trying to determine what it was. The object suddenly shook with a shivering twitch and seemed to turn, revealing round eyes upon an angelic face staring back. He grinned with delight.

"Mora Gringshek," said Fairfax happily. "We have been looking for you!"

Miragrin rushed down into the room and hugged Mora, his children, and her mother. All were crying, tears streaming from their eyes. He was so happy to see his wife that he picked her up and swung her around.

"I don't believe it," whispered Dithil to Fairfax.

Fairfax looked upon the joyous family reunion with a smile, but his thoughts quickly turned to Skag Harwell and his sacrifice. It was this thought that now painfully swept over his heart, a thought that would never quite leave him.

"Even in the darkest situation, a miracle shines bright," he told Dithil, his throat still tightened as he thought of the death of his friend.

"What do you think happened here, with the orcs and the black dog?" asked Dithil.

Fairfax had a look on his face, and around his eyes, like he knew the answer to the dwarf's question, but he did not speak. Instead, he and Dithil rushed Miragrin's family up from their sanctuary and wrapped each child in blankets for the ride to Blackstone Keep.

Soon, they were on Moondancer and into the cold night sky and far away from the nightmare of Portmoor.

Later that evening, as Dithil and Fairfax entered the Keep and made their way to their chambers, Dithil repeated his question to the wizard.

"Surely, you must have an idea of what happened at Harwell's, with the orcs and the dog. Tell me what you think?" he pleaded.

There was a look of worry in Fairfax's eyes. Dithil saw it.

"We must send word to Carrick that brood advances from Portmoor," said Fairfax. "Then we must rest. Things are in motion and I am afraid a great struggle of many opposites is upon us."

* * *

The wagon ride was bumpy and jostled the girls around quite a bit, but Molly tried her best to stay as still as she could. During the ride, she thought about many things – about everyone she had met, about the orc, about her sister, about her plan, about what others had said. She knew that so much rested on her ability to befriend the orc and master and control the power of the Lia Fail.

Everything seemed so strange in the place and at times frightening, but she had friends to help her, and she thought that she would meet even others along the way, more friends that would help. Anything could be possible, she supposed, in such a strange place. But still, a feeling of dread gnawed at her.

What if I fail?

She felt a shiver run through her and felt as though she could hear everything around her, a sense of the unseen. She felt it, and it filled her with power but also anxiety. She had to keep her focus on the task at hand.

One thing at a time.

The wagon plodded along, and soon she began to grow weary of the up and down jarring. The sensation was almost too much for her to bear, and she grew a little nauseous. She looked at Elizabeth who was also tired of the jarring wagon movements.

"We've never been in a wagon before. How do you like our first wagon ride? Isn't this fun?" she asked sarcastically.

"Not really," said Elizabeth.

She smiled and nodded.

"We've had so many other firsts, since coming here," she said. "How many do you think?"

"I've lost count of how many new things we've seen or done!" said Elizabeth. "But I don't think I'll ever want to ride another wagon."

Brows who was steering the wagon, pulled along by two large black horses, laughed at what he heard.

"What is this? You do not like a good wagon ride?" he asked. "I cannot believe that. Where you are from, how do you get around?"

"Where we come from adults use cars," said Elizabeth.

"Do these . . . cars," he struggled with the word, ". . . have horses?"

"No, they don't," tittered Elizabeth. "You're a silly one, not knowing what cars are. They have motors and you must put gas in them to run."

"Ha," he laughed. "Like horses, I suppose, except with horses you put in some hay and oats, and off they go."

He snapped the reins and the wagon groaned and creaked, inching its way up to a steady speed.

Molly turned to look back at the others who were following. The caravan included four wagons, each different in color and design, but all having broad wheels made of hardwoods with thick iron rims. The girls traveled in the lead wagon, which was painted green with the Mark of the Tree on its sides. Brows and Big Grey accompanied them while Donduin and Ancorbow rode in a second wagon, larger and painted blue. A third wagon was brown and carried provisions for the trip and was used by the several guardsmen who followed on horseback. The last wagon was black with broad iron bars on the outside. It resembled a cage and carried the orc Ug'ghi Otha and three guardsmen who kept watch over him.

Since leaving Blackstone Keep, they followed the dusty Jhyl Vyr. Along the road were trees in clusters and clumps, and fields of tall grasses, filling in the spaces right up to where the colossal mountains of the Thornback swelled from the land. The long road led east then curved slightly north running through the Jhasi Var, a well-wooded mountain pass between the Thornback and the Old Hills.

From the Jhasi Var the road continued into the elven realm of Tir Nan Og, eventually coming to the city of Glathria before ending at the stronghold of Vys Toria at the Northern Seas. However, they would not travel that distance. Instead, they would leave the Jhyl Vyr behind, south of the small town called Hammer Fief, and travel east over a series of meandering paths, to Dagda, through the Tangle forest, and then to the spires of Katzhu Pu.

As they traveled, Brows and Big Grey told the girls of the race of felines, or En' Onna, and the city of Katzhu Pu and the Guild Lords. The girls learned that Katzhu Pu was a holy place for felines, an ancient city revered by the En' Onna because it was said to have been built over the ruins of the first feline settlement. It was also said that its great domed structure, the Kaer Taraedar, was constructed over the gravesite of the first Guild Lord, the Prime Heru, the cat known as Ra Carathor. The girls learned that the Guild Lords were much like the wizards of the Edainar, in that they were entrusted with the leadership of their race, the felines, also known as the Ra Cath.

"The Guild Lords are wise and ancient creatures. They are honored by all the races and believed to have special powers," Brows told the girls. "They are adored like divine beings and as symbols of radiance. Many will say that they can see the truth of a creature, the very essence of its being. But it is this same ability that brings fear to many in the Harrow, those who are not transparent and lack an inner voice.

"What's an inner voice?" asked Molly.

"It is that little voice inside of you that talks to you," he told her. "It tells you what you should do. It guides you and leads you down a path. Now, if you have a proper inner voice, the path will be peaceful. But there are some who have no inner voice, nothing to guide them down the path of peace. These are creatures of evil. They cannot see the difference between right and wrong."

"Oh, you mean like the orc," said Elizabeth.

"That's not fair," said Molly sternly. "You don't know what he's like at all. Do you?"

"Molls, I'm just saying what others are saying . . ."

Molly interrupted her.

". . . and it doesn't matter what others say," she said, resolve in her voice. "Does it? Maybe they don't understand him."

"Shhhhh," said Big Grey. "Hush. No arguments. We will meet with the Guild Lords. We will listen to their words, won't we, eh?"

After the cat's admonishment, the girls were quiet.

Time seemed to pass slowly. A cold wind began to swirl. Molly became tired and she withdrew into herself. She clutched the Lia Fail. It felt warm and throbbed in her hand. She closed her eyes, and a vision came to her. She saw herself traveling over a forsaken and barren land, dreadful, cold with a strong wind. She could feel the icy wind on her face, almost unbearable, and thought it strange.

I can't be dreaming. I'm not asleep. But I can see and feel things in my mind.

In her vision, others were traveling with her, bundled in heavy layers of clothes, their pace slow but strong and steady. The group of travelers slowed then came to a halt, for before them stood a tall, black tower, engulfed in flames and smoke. Molly was frightened. She could feel the Lia Fail warm and gently pulsating. She squirmed and opened her eyes.

My plan. Will my plan work? she thought.

As the night deepened, they made camp just off the Jhyl Vyr, in a field near a wooded area. For defensive purposes and shelter from the weather, the caravan formed into a circle. The horses were fed, wood was cut for a campfire, and food was prepared. Several guardsmen were positioned beyond the circle's perimeter, while others were hidden further out, on the lookout for intruders. They rotated their positions every few hours. Inside the camp were additional guardsmen, including three that always guarded the orc.

The night sky was filled with the flush of moonlight as a gentle and cool breeze descended, drifting, and ruffling the tops of the tallest trees. Brows built a campfire and the girls sat cross-legged on blankets near its warmth, with heavy blankets wrapped over them for additional warmth. Big Grey was curled in Molly's lap with a gentle purr that stirred, while Brows sat near, wrapped in a velvety brown blanket. Across from the fire, Donduin and Ancorbow busily engaged in reviewing maps of the Tangle. The fire lit its way into the night sky and the girls were reminded of times on rainy, cold nights when they would visit the Professor in his library, a cathedral of books with a roaring fireplace that made for a cozy setting.

Brows had made a pot of stew which was cooking over the fire. It was plain fare, some dried pieces of mutton with vegetables in a thick and savory broth. The smell was delicious and made Molly's mouth water, but she could only think of her plan and the Guild Lords.

She closed her eyes and withdrew deeper into herself. Another vision came to her, of great cats upon golden thrones in a large hall, each dressed in flowing robes of bright colors. She could hear the song of bagpipes that swelled and ebbed and ebbed and swelled. The cats looked at her and beckoned to her, but she could not move; she was rooted to the spot, unable to answer the summons. The great cats rose and stretched and slowly walked towards her, tails swinging, eyes flashing. She was frightened of them and wanted to run but could not.

My plan. Will it work? What will the Guild Lords think of my plan? What will they think of Ug'ghi Otha?

She heard a voice. It was Brows. She forced her eyes open, forced them to focus. She saw Brows stirring his stew.

"Tomorrow we should reach Hammer Fief by nightfall," he said. "If all goes well for the good wizard, he could meet up with us tomorrow. Then it will be one more day through the Tangle and then northeast to the golden city. About a three-day journey in all, I think."

He served large portions of the hearty stew in wooden bowls as the night sounds of the woodland began to sweep across the camp. The girls enjoyed his concoction, even though for their taste it was a bit spicy. They ate in silence by the warm fire. After their meal, Brows coaxed the fire with kindling, and placed a kettle of water over it; when the water began to simmer, he added some leaves and a few small berries. He poured some into cups for the girls.

"It is a tea from the camellia plant," he told them. "It only grows in the North Sage Barrow, on the coast. It'll help to warm you."

They took a sip of the tea. It was warm, fragrant, and sweet like nectar.

"It is very nice," said Molly. "Thank you."

"You are very welcome," he said as he lit his elf pipe. The woodsy scent filled the cool night air.

Everyone was lost for words as they stared into the fire. Molly found herself deep in thought again as she watched golden sparks snap free from the wood and float upward through the smoke into the sky.

Brows sensed something was troubling her. He looked at her, but she did not notice him. She just remained silent, staring into the flames, recounting the many conversations since arriving at the Harrow, and what the Professor had told her. Doubts continued to creep into her thoughts. Dreadful suspicions began to torture her, suspicions of what could happen if her plan failed. She closed her eyes to images of war, havoc, and terror.

If I'm not right, things could easily get out of control. But I have the stone. How will I use it? How do I make it work?

"Is something the matter?" Brows asked her.

But she was still caught up in her thoughts, that is until Elizabeth nudged her with an elbow.

"Molls, are you alright? Mr. Brows is talking to you."

"Oh, I'm fine," she said startled. "I'm sorry, Mr. Brows. What was that you were saying?"

Brows realized something was indeed bothering her. He could see that a burden was weighing on her. It was all too familiar to him.

He poked at the fire with a branch.

"Can't get it out of your head, eh?" he said.

Molly looked at him, puzzled.

"What do you mean?" she paused. "Can't get what out of my head?"

"Worries. You can't get them out of your head," he said. "They begin to consume your thoughts. When you close your eyes, you see things. You dream without sleep. The images are crisp in detail, your senses are heightened. You feel and smell in these waking dreams. It is as if you are there." He blew smoke rings into the air, watching them float upward and disappear into the darkened sky, the continued. "Doubts. Anxiety. They well up within you. It is the stone, the Lia Fail. It begins to burden you."

She was amazed.

"How did you know?" she asked.

"Know? How does one know anything for sure? Is the faint, determined scratching one hears beneath the bed a bug or the product of imagination? In the twilight in a forest, you think you see a man. But is it a man, or a tree stump that presents a peculiar appearance? How does one know anything? How does one know what is true, or for that matter not true? Let's just say that over the years I have come to know many things. I have seen patterns all around, and I remember their shape. That is what a historian does.

You are becoming one with the stone. I have seen it before, with others."

"What do you mean?"

He took his blanket and wrapped it around her. He rubbed her shoulders for warmth.

"The stone's becoming a part of you and you a part of it," he said. "And soon, soon, you will master its power."

She reached out to touch the blanket. It was so soft and immediately warmed her. She cuddled up to the old bobbin, her troubling thoughts slowly fluttering away.

"You have never felt bobbin wool, have you?" he asked.

She closed her eyes and gently shook her head in response.

"I thought not," he said with another puff of his pipe. "It is made of bobbin wool, and that's the softest material known in the Harrow. This blanket was woven at the hands of a skilled bobbin weaver. So, a cold night can feel like the warmest."

She smiled in the warmth as Elizabeth huddled near her, finding her way under the blanket. Even though they argued and at times disagreed, no matter what, they were sisters, and they still loved each other. There was a deep underlying affection between them, for each knew that regardless of the situation they would always be there for each other.

Brows took a couple more puffs from his pipe. Molly nuzzled into his neck, and he could tell she was drifting off.

"I have a tale for you, a tale known by young and old," said Brows with a trace of a smile on his lips. "It is about the origins of the Lia Fail. Would you like to hear it? Or would you rather sleep?"

Elizabeth became excited.

"Why yes," she said.

Molly lifted her heavy eyes and turned them upon him.

Maybe his tale will help me to understand our situation, she thought.

"Well, then . . . it was a long time ago, a very long time ago, and during the age when kings ruled the land. Deep in the mines of the Old Hills, the dwarves of Mortha had discovered a large stone. It was the size of a large boulder and was a bright red. The dwarves thought they had discovered the largest gem ever, and everyone thought it had to be worth all the wealth in the Harrow.

"The quarry master had never seen anything like it, and as you might expect he had seen plenty of rock in his time. Immediately he ordered his most gifted stonecutter to excavate the red stone from the mine. It was painstaking work as the stonecutter and his apprentices carefully went about removing the surrounding rock without damaging the large gem. It took hundreds of dwarves to move the rock from the mine. Eventually, they were able to bring it to the dwarf elders in the city of Volemill.

"I can tell you the elders had never seen such a sight. The stone was a brilliant red. It had remarkable clarity and a bright white spot in the middle. The color around the white spot was vivid and it changed its shape as you walked around the stone. Oh, and in the sun - why it just glistened, like a star! The elders were awed by its beauty and decreed it to be blessed by the Maker as Ondo En' Tir. They ordered it taken to the elves, to the ancient city of Eilthir.

"The dwarves set out to construct a great carriage of wood and metal. It was magnificent with intricate carvings and all gilded in gold. The stone was housed in the center of the carriage, encased in glass for all to see. Over thirty horses were needed to pull the carriage, and protecting the procession was a full regiment of Mortha's bravest warriors. Word spread about the stone. There was great fanfare and excitement as it made its way to Eilthir, and along the very same road, we now travel. There were minstrels and musicians who paraded alongside the carriage as it went from town to town. The procession grew and grew."

Brows took a few more puffs of his pipe; he continued his story.

"Ah, it was a glorious time to be alive. So many young and old, from all the races, came together in celebration. When the stone finally arrived at Eilthir the procession had grown to thousands. It wound its way through the grand streets of the elven city until it came to the Kaer Tari, the castle of the Elf-King. There, dwarf and elf worked together to lift the large stone. They placed it on a large gold pedestal in the Kaer Tari rotunda. For weeks, elven shamans debated the meaning of the stone, its origins, its purpose, as more and more from the Harrow came to Eilthir to join the celebration."

"Shamans?" asked Elizabeth.

"A shaman is a person who has heard the voice of the almighty," said Big Grey. "They are wise and possess a certain level of magic too."

"Almighty? You mean God?"

"Here, he is called the Maker. It is the Maker who created all life. It is the Maker who rules everything, the land, the sky, the sea. It is the Maker who arms the races with strength and the way to a secure path."

Brows smiled.

"The Maker created everything you see, and he is the one who gives it life," he said. "Life is what all should be directed towards. Life is what all should be dedicated to. It is the end of all the other things in life. But to continue with my tale - the shamans gave the stone a name . . ."

"The Lia Fail," said Elizabeth excitedly.

Brows chuckled.

"Well, not exactly," laughed Brows. "They called it the Fail stone which in the common tongue means *of the heavens.* As the shamans continued their debate the King of Ahlgren came to Eilthir with his family to see the great gem. He was of the race of man, the En' Edan, and from House Riorn. His name was Aelis.

"In his days there was great prosperity in the Harrow, and King Aelis was beloved throughout the land, as he was known to rule with great kindness. He bestowed great diligence and expense in making roads through many uninhabited parts of the land. In this manner, his kingdom was populated, and trade and commerce grew. When the

King arrived at Eilthir everyone who had gathered bowed, and the women curtseyed to him. He was welcomed by the Elf-King at the time, King Tasartir, the father of Dalgaes."

Molly was confused. Dalgaes looked no older than Fairfax or Brows.

"The father of Dalgaes?" she asked. "How long ago was this?"

Brows gave another hearty laugh, his thick bushy eyebrows seemed larger by the campfire's light.

"Oh, it was a very long time ago," he said. "My dear, elves can live up to three or four times longer than man or other creatures. But we can talk about the race of elves later. So, it was that King Tasartir welcomed King Aelis and his family. As I said, Aelis brought with him his family – his wife, Queen Aulona, and their two daughters, the oldest of which was Princess Arakarra. Because the King had no male heirs, Princess Arakarra, being the oldest of the King's daughters, would eventually rule as Queen.

"As the shamans continued their debate the children of Aelis played with the Elf-King's children. Throughout the day they played in the gardens and in the great halls of the Kaer Tari where beautiful flowers grew out of the walls. There were so many places for the children to explore and discover. One night, as they played, they found themselves in the rotunda alone with the stone. The guards on duty had no idea what to do with the children as they played. After all, they were royalty. Well, Princess Arakarra seemed drawn to the stone. She reached out to touch it and when she placed her tiny hand on it, it began to glow and became brighter and brighter. As it did, it warmed the rotunda and the ground began to tremble. No one knew what was happening, even the guards. The children stood and watched frozen in fear. Both Kings and the shamans rushed to the rotunda. As they gathered, they saw Princess Arakarra remove her hand from the stone. In that instant, it ceased to glow, and everything became calm. In this stillness, a small piece of the stone, a shard, fell from the gem and at the feet of the Princess. She stood there in amazement and looked down at the small piece."

"What did she do?" asked Elizabeth.

Brows turned her with a smile.

"What would you have done?" he asked her.

"I know exactly what I'd do," she said abruptly. "I'd pick it up."

"Oh, I see," Brows muttered as he chewed on his pipe stem. "Well, that is precisely what the Princess did. She picked up the shard and said something that history does not record. Almost immediately that small sliver of stone began to glow and shake. A great beam of light shot up from it and pierced through the rotunda's great marble dome. The dome began to crumble all around, and everyone scrambled for cover. When it was over, Arakarra stood alone, untouched, not a flake of dust on her.

"Oh, it had to be an incredible sight for sure - a tiny girl unharmed amongst great boulders of marble. It was as if she were protected by the Maker himself. Immediately the shamans began their study of the shard. They called it the Lia Fail, Lia meaning *little one*, and the elders of Volemill considered it blessed by the Maker as Ondo En' Tir, since it came from the larger stone. The shamans discovered that the Lia Fail could only be controlled by a young female of innocence and purity. It was given to King Aelis and from that day forward the Lia Fail became the inheritance of every Queen of Ahlgren.

"So it goes. Now you are Queen of Ahlgren, as it was given to you by the Professor, the Keeper, who received it from Aerin, the last Queen of House Riorn. Like Arakarra and those that came after her, you will learn to control its power."

He put his arm around Molly as the stone glowed.

"What of the larger stone?" she asked. "Where is it?"

"It remains with the elves, at Eilthir."

"Can we hear of more tales?"

He smiled and nodded.

As the night grew on, the woodland sounds hushed. The lights of the stars twinkled like fireflies and under the dark blanket of the night he spoke of histories of faraway lands and ages past, and of what he called Ay' Panul, or how the Harrow came to be. The girls sat staring into the fire listening to every word that fell from his lips.

When he had finished his tale sleep came creeping softly in on the girls. Donduin and Ancorbow gently lifted them and brought them to their wagon where they were tenderly tucked into bed. Big Grey also made his way to the wagon and nestled between them.

As Molly slept a dream came to her. It was a clear dream where the Professor was talking to her, repeating strange words over and over again.

Treachery wears many masks . . . treachery wears many masks . . . treachery wears many masks.

* * *

Bombadorn Roundthaler left his command tent to observe the encampment as the broken moon hung low in the night sky. Before him was a spectacle of dancing light against the darkness, hundreds of campfires scattered across the Thorndell, bright red embers glowing through the smoke. A look of worry was on his creviced face as he turned south. As he gazed at the thousands of grave mounds that loomed like ghostly shapes, he saw Carrick sitting by a solitary fire in gloomy silence. Behind the great man were Warsinger and Windthrasher, framed against the night by the glow of the flickering flames. It had been several hours since he and Carrick had arrived at the Thorndell, but Carrick remained in the field of grave mounds, tormented at one, all the while his massive army awaited him. An eerie pattern of red light and black cast dancing shadows upon Carrick, sending visions of sadness into Roundthaler's heart.

Roundthaler reached into his trousers and withdrew a pipe, short-stemmed and stout, its bowl carved in the shape of a dwarf wielding an axe. As he began to pack the pipe, a commander of a legion of men from South Eldor approached. His name was Theor Thaken. He was a young man of marked ability as a leader. The young Thaken, known as a boisterous warrior with shrewdness and talent on the battlefield, had quickly climbed through the ranks and was now commanding one of Etinia's largest armies.

"I don't understand. He's been at that one grave for hours," said Thaken. "My men have traveled far and long to fight at his lead. And I, I've waited my whole life for this day, to lead with the great Carrick. But he just sits there staring into a fire."

Roundthaler lit his pipe and took a few puffs.

"He pays his respect," spat the dwarf. "It is an act of honor lost on youth. Be patient Thaken. There is time enough to die."

The brazen young man smirked, almost dismissive of Roundthaler.

"Who's buried there that such a great man would leave his army waiting?"

Roundthaler firmly gripped his mighty axe and turned to Thaken.

"In this world, there are some questions that should never be asked," he said, his face flushed with anger.

Shaken by Roundthaler's stern words, Thaken quietly bowed and walked away.

* * *

As the night unfurled Carrick and his companions left the sacred grounds and quietly entered the encampment. There was no fanfare, or ballyhoo, nor sounds of trumpets or roll of drums. Legions upon legions of man and dwarf stood in silent awe, out of deep respect for him, because all believed the might of the Maker was with him, to free the land from the darkness. As he dismounted Warsinger a soft rumble of thunder was heard from the east, where the night sky burned an angry orange just beyond the Crag. A great wind began to blow as the warriors gathered around him.

"The furnaces of evil roar and the hammers descend through the night," heralded Roundthaler.

Carrick defiantly faced east, his grey locks streaming in the wind.

"Let their forges roar," he announced, "for we shall meet the enemy on the battlefield, under the banner of the Tree and Axe. May the Maker have mercy on this evil, because it shall be the only mercy it receives!"

The throngs raised their weapons in a thunderous cheer, a cheer, it was said, that shook the deepest and darkest holes of Urth' Goroth.

* * *

The great eagle, with the little yellow cricket nestled on its neck, flew east past the Old River and over the remains of Gortha-Losh, a city of tumbled structures and flickering campfires. Within its walls, a great army of brood began to form itself into several large squares. Towering wooden structures, and siege engines, were slowly rolled out from the city, and behind, the brood followed in an orderly advance spewing forth from the city gates. Column after column of brood marched with ferocity, pounding the ground in a rhythmic dirge, their spears, swords, and axes lifted high into the night sky. As the army marched, the swirling wind blew smoke and ashes from the city in their direction. But the brood maintained their advance behind the monstrous siege engines and began a howling chant that grew until it drowned out the wind. The brutish sounds of the march and chants spoke of pain and torment and the desire to bring both to the Harrow.

Amidst the countless columns and under the banner of the Tower rode an Urur Maw upon a muugaan, an evil creature that was more devil than a horse. The beast's tall body was black with reddish blotches, thick leathery skin stretched tightly over a muscular frame. It possessed a knobby curved neck, a mane of coarse black hair braided and off to one side, and a pair of fiercely red nostrils. It was fast and afraid of nothing and when it was turned upon an enemy it struck at full speed.

With a heldror in his hand, the Urur Maw spurred the beast and rode up through the columns at a canter. He started wailing loud enough to be heard over the chanting. From inside a black leather mask and helmet, his orange eyes flashed with wrath, casting a diabolical glare on the evil army. The brood army moved west in the dead of night, amidst the smell of Gortha-Losh.

The eagle circled then banked. Its direction now north, the enormous bird caught a breeze that lifted it high and above the Crag. The snow-capped summits soared as far as his eyes could see, harsh, unfriendly mountains piercing an orange sky.

The eagle banked a final time where a river of filth and sludge carved a pass through the mountains called the Dregec Kuul. It followed the river southeast and into the desolation of the Drueger where an even larger army massed along the river. Thousands upon thousands of legions, tight formations of heavily armored orc and other brood, while overhead circled Dark Riders upon black ajatars.

The eagle knew he was close to home, he could feel it.

He maintained his course through the gloom of smoke and death. Ahead, he and his companion could barely make out the two evil towers. They quickly came upon the glow of red embers, the furnaces, and forges of Ug' Cthuth that clanged and heaved forth armor and metal machines of war. They sailed past the tower and through the dark mists of the Ordraar when the second black tower slowly came into view.

Ripples of intense heat billowed up from the wasteland, smoke, and soot swirling in a fury with the winds. But through the churning fervor, he was unwavering in his flight as the sounds of Urth' Goroth's forges ringing through the night became clearer. He circled higher and higher until at last the mottled metal posts and grand fire from atop Urth' Goroth could be seen.

He was home at last.

He looked down and saw the Szard atop Urth' Goroth with Grimsor.

"Ah, there they are," came the Szard's deep voice. "I have so missed both of you. Come to me. Come to me."

Hearing his master's call, the eagle descended from the sky, with a noise of his wings that produced sounds resembling thunder. He perched bravely on the Szard's arm.

The black-robed master gently stroked the bird.

"My Azariel, tell me what you have seen?" he asked.

The bird was glad to see his master. He opened his wings wide and lowered his head in deference.

"The sorcerers know of you, my master," said Azariel. "One of them weaves a spell that penetrates the darkness. But it drains him and leaves him frail, and weak. The puny creatures of Mortha have captured an orc, but he's said to be harmless as it has the mind of an orc-child."

The Szard gently patted the yellow cricket's tiny head.

"And you, my Elspeth, what news do you bring?" he asked.

"They give the stone to a child, not of Ahlgren but treat her as Queen," she said. "The fools have hopes that she will lead them to victory. She asks to speak with the orc, and the sorcerers have granted her permission. She is family to the Professor and comes from under the tree. I believe their plans are of no consequence to my master."

The Szard was silent. He was not surprised by the news.

What choice did the Professor have but to send the stone back to the Harrow, along with a female child who could use it, he thought.

Regardless, he knew the Professor had most likely failed to appreciate or discern his plans of conquest, death, and destruction.

Whatever the Professor has planned will be too little and too late.

An overwhelming feeling of victory and accomplishment came over him as he pictured himself at the Aina Dur overlooking the whole of the Harrow, with all the races fallen to their knees crying in shame and mercy.

I will be honored and remembered by all as touched by the darkest of the dark.

He could almost taste the power, the knowledge that he had beaten them all. He would have everything he ever wanted. But then his thoughts turned to the present.

All but one piece of my plan is in place, and soon that last piece will be realized. There is little that can stop me.

"My Azariel and Elspeth," he said, "return to your forces and await my word. You have served your master well."

With that, the eagle and his accomplice took off and soared in a gentle arc northeast and over the Dregec Kuul.

The Szard turned to Grimsor. He reached up and placed a gloved hand on the Urur Maw's shoulder.

"It is time my friend," he said. "The mighty Uth' Egoreyr must join with his legions. Go now and take your army just beyond the Crag as planned. The time of great war is here, before us. Let your ferocity pervade the battlefield."

Grimsor took his leave. There was a moment of silence for the Szard, one which he savored. The swirling of the winds and dark clouds brought a sense of foreboding, and it filled his soul.

But there came a crackle and a hiss from the grand fire. The mysterious creature was present, and it slithered within the mighty flames.

"My dear, what of the orc?" it asked.

He remained silent. He stood in silence and blackness of soul, peering through the dense fog of doom and the distant flicker of the torches of the enormous army advancing along the Dregec Kuul on the horizon.

What moments these are!

He listened to what seemed to be a deeply deep wave of sound expanding from below, the pounding of his army of evil as it marched, throughout the murky darkness. He did not say anything or take a breath. He simply delighted in the evil he had set upon the land.

"What of the orc?" the question came once again.

"All of my creatures serve a purpose," he whispered.

CHAPTER 10
THE HERMIT AND THE TAR MALAL

HIGH ON THE MOUNTAIN, Glaeynd, and the others continued their ascent, following the old man's lead along a narrow rocky pathway that wound its way deeper into the Old Hills. Occasionally she would turn to gaze upon Mistmere, now far below, the city but a small gleaming light, a bare flicker that quivered in the darkness. Her thoughts would wander, and her emotions would churn like rough seas.

As they climbed higher the night air grew colder. The old man quickened his pace motioning the others to do the same as threatening black clouds crept across the sky from the east. A clap of thunder soon rumbled through the night, followed closely by rain and strong winds. The powerful winds drove the rain, becoming a vertical wall of water making it impossible to see forward. But they pressed on, keeping their eyes on the pathway, sloshing through the mud with one of them slipping now and again. In the distance there came a crackle and another streak of lightning, their surroundings flashing in and out of existence.

Tired and anxious, they arrived at a bend on the north side of a mountain, where they were greeted by an incredible sight. Towering before them was a stone structure built into the massive mouth of a cave. It soared as high as the mountain's peak and had four round towers, grand and lofty. The walls were made of large stones on the outside with inner spaces filled tightly with smaller stones and pebbles. There were windows of different sizes with several large ones near a great wooden door.

They followed the old man down a pathway to a sweeping promenade under a stone archway that led past a small oblong bailey and to a door. As they neared the door, from a window they could see what appeared to be a cat inside. It was thin, had white fur, a long neck, and large round red eyes. Rain on the window blurred their sight, but what they saw was unmistakably a feline. The cat stood motionless; its face uplifted to theirs.

"Do you see it?" Lil' Man asked Chumsey.

Chumsey peered through the window at the gangly white cat who stared back and gave a meow.

"I see it," said Chumsey. "Poor thing."

He knew white cats were outcasts of the Ra Cath, fragments cut off by the Guilds. They had to survive using their wits and lived in isolation or hiding.

"What do you make of it?" asked Lil' Man.

"I do not know but I have got a feeling we will find out soon enough."

"Quickly now," the old man told them, "to where it is safe and warm."

He pushed and held the large wooden door open. They felt a rush of warmth as they entered a magnificent hall the height and breadth of which could not be easily determined. They were in the mountain itself. It had been excavated, hollowed out, creating a cavernous place dimly lit with ghostly shadows. This was an ancient structure with rough stone walls supported by enormous round stone columns with round arches overhead. The air was full of the smell of the mountain, moist and cool, and there was the echo of a murmur of wind.

To one side of the hall were arched doorways extending the length of the vast chamber. On the other side was a raised stone dais where there sat a very long table and chairs. In the center sparked and roared a grand fireplace made of striated sections of stone in hues of green, red, black, and brown that stretched high into the darkness above.

They gathered near the door as the old man made his way into the hall. He turned to them and pushed back his hood revealing his face. There was a purity about him, wizened and radiant, his face crisscrossed with gentle ravines. His hair and beard were long and curly with streaks of light grey and pure white, and his cheeks were plump with a rose color to them.

He gave a warm smile.

For Lil' Man and Chumsey, there was familiarity with the old man's face. They had seen him before, or so they thought, but they could not remember where they had seen him or who he was. They looked at each other perplexed.

"Is this some sort of magic?" whispered Lil' Man to Chumsey. "I feel that I know him."

"Me too. But from where?" said Chumsey. He shook his head and shrugged his shoulders.

The cats sniffed the air. There was a faint trace of magic.

"Best to be very cautious," whispered Lil' Man.

"Come by the fire," the old man told everyone. "All of you now. Dry yourselves and be warm. Food will soon be on its way."

As he walked to the fireplace the skinny white cat ran out to him, carefully weaving its way through the legs of the taller Fenri until it strutted alongside him. The cat was sickly in appearance, its ribs showing, with a rather large head atop a long thin neck.

"Prrrrrrrrr," went the cat.

It arched its back rubbing up against the old man's leg, its tail straight up in the air.

"I do what I do and that's the best I can do," it said, merrily, as if happy to see the old man.

No matter how meaningless the cat's words were everyone sort of understood its meaning merely by its tone. There was something odd about it, its eyes, and how it spoke. It was a strange creature. Both Lil' Man and Chumsey kept an eye on it.

The old man bent down and petted the cat on its head and then along its side.

"Ah, Shaer," he sighed. "Yes, I am happy to be home. Did you miss me?"

The cat reached up with its front paws onto the old man's leg.

"Prrrrrrrr. I do what I do and that's the best I can do," said the cat again, this time slowly and softly, in a warm tone.

"And I missed you as well," said the old man.

The old man placed some wood on the fire. There was a rocking chair nearby, high-backed with curved spindles, hard and stiff. He sat down in the chair and as soon as he did, the white cat jumped into his lap and rubbed up against him. As he stroked the cat, it circled then settled and curled into his lap. It lifted its head and stared at the group with its odd bulging red eyes. They made him nervous, and he gave a throaty yowl.

"I do what I do and that's the best I can do," the cat told them, its words quick and tense.

"No, they are friends Shaer," said the old man. "Do not fret so. I have invited them here, out of the rain and cold."

His words were reassuring to the cat as it nestled its head against his leg and purred loudly.

But Thurir was troubled. He was in a strange place and he found the old man and cat very peculiar.

"Where are we? Who is the old man?" he whispered to Glaeynd.

"Our people call him Ghuukac, the mountain hermit," she whispered back. "He would come down from the mountains to trade furs for bread and fruit. I do not know of this place or him."

Overhearing the whispers, the old man smiled.

"Oh, but I know you Glaeynd, Lead of the Rhiorsnan, daughter of Kraneth, Lord of the Mists," he said as he stared at each one of them. "And I know you Thurir, Prince of the Fenri, son of Threch, great King of the Ra Draug. And I know every member of your pack, their names, and ancestry. And you Chum Sey El Ta and Oban Pan El Tar, great warriors of the Balor Guild. I know you as well."

Hearing the cats were of the Balor Guild, the bony white cat popped its head up from the old man's lap and stared at Lil' Man and Chumsey. There was disdain in its eyes.

"I do what I do and that's the best I can do," said the cat slowly and rather pointedly to Lil' Man and Chumsey, in an angry tone.

They stared back at the odd cat, watching for any sudden, aggressive moves. They did not care for the tone of its strange words.

"Now, now, there, Shaer," the old man explained to the white cat. "I told you they are friends."

Still staring at Lil' Man and Chumsey the white cat gave a snarl. The old man sensed an uneasiness with the group.

"Please understand my friend Shaer is unaccustomed to visitors," he told them with a smile. "He means you no harm. Please, please, come by the fire and warm yourselves. All is well."

Thurir growled deep in his throat.

"What's this treachery? Who can hear such whispers? How do you know our names? Who are you? What's this place? What magic do you wield?"

The old man calmly rocked in his chair.

"Be at peace my Fenri friend," he said. "The Harrow holds many dark secrets and treachery abounds these days. But do not fear me. I am not your enemy. I only ask that you treat me courteously, and at the same time cordially, and consider me a good friend. I have followed your journey and the journey of many others, those on the side of the good and the righteous. I have observed and when possible, I have helped many in ways unbeknownst to them. I am but a friend."

Thurir remained suspicious. He nervously paced, his eyes scanning the great room for any threatening movement, until they fell back upon the old man.

"What is this deceit, this fraud?" he said to the old man. "Yours are the words of a Dark Wizard. I have heard them before. They give one a sense of calm only to have it torn away by acts of rage. Old man, I see through your words. I know what you're up to."

The white cat raised its head and looked straight at Thurir, its red eyes flaming in rage.

"I do what I do and that's the best I can do," it said angrily.

At that the old man became serious. The line between his eyes seemed to deepen as he slowly turned from them and stared into the flames of the fire. He then closed his eyes and took a deep breath as if to compose himself. He began to slowly stroke the white cat.

"Shhhh . . . Shaer. Hush now, do not worry. They are young, they do not remember," he told the cat.

His words seemed to calm the cat who again rested its head within the old man's lap and purred.

"Tell us now! You're Dark Wizard!" shouted Thurir. "Tell us now before we have to kill you!"

The old man gave a smile.

"Dark Wizard? No. I am not accursed or corrupt, even though you choose to think so," he said softly. "I have watched you from afar as I have watched many things lo these countless years. I just needed time, time to heal . . . time to think . . . and I have waited . . . and waited . . . for the right time . . . and I believe that time has come."

Chumsey was intrigued by his words.

"Time? What time has come?" he asked.

The old man looked at the large orange cat.

"The time for atonement, a final reconciliation."

Thurir was agitated, thinking they were now ensnared in some trap. He ordered his pack into defensive positions about the large hall.

"The old man speaks in riddles," he said. "I for one do not trust those who play with words. I will only ask this once more: who are you and what is this place?"

The white cat raised its head and stared at Thurir, but this time it started to shake uncontrollably, its lips curled under in anger. The old man lifted his hands away from the cat as if he knew something was to happen.

Thurir met the white cat's stare without flinching when something strange occurred. The cat's bulging red eyes widened and began to glow. As the red glow grew stronger it exploded into an extremely bright ruddy tint, sending shock waves of light rippling through the cavernous hall. Everyone turned their heads from the brightness. They covered their eyes and gasped in horror as the explosion hit hurtling them backward.

For a brief moment, the cat spoke words that had meaning.

"He is Ras Amon and he will lead you to the golden city," said the cat in a deep, powerful, and unnatural voice that echoed through the place.

Then, just as suddenly as it appeared, the light vanished. The brightness had been so intense that everyone was momentarily blinded in the subdued light of the hall. As their vision adapted, they could see the white cat in the old man's lap. It gave a slight twitch and again nestled into his lap.

In fear, everyone took several steps back and away from the old man and his cat. Thurir's pack quickly regained their positions.

The white cat looked up at the old man.

"I do what I do and that's the best I can do," it said meekly.

"Yes, yes, there, there, now, I know my friend . . . I know," the old man told the cat. He then turned to them. "It's alright. My little friend here means no harm at all. No harm whatsoever. He is just very protective of me."

Thurir took a step forward but Lil' Man pushed him back.

He seems so familiar. The cat called him Ras Amon, thought Lil' Man. He cocked his head looking at the old man. *Is he Ras Amon? Could it be him? Could this old man be the Learned One?*

Ras Amon, the Learned One, was a great teacher of wizards and master of the evil Mauldragw Foulhand. So ingrained was the tale of Ras Amon and his death at the hands of his apprentice, that they could not believe what they had heard. It was widely known and written in histories that years ago the great teacher of wizards had been thrown into the great fissure of fire-on-high called Drar Druul, before the Shadow War.

"The called you Ras Amon," said Lil' Man. "But the Learned One is dead, killed by Foulhand. If this is your idea of some kind of trick, I do not find it amusing."

There was sadness in the old man's eyes.

"No. No tricks my Balor friend,' he sighed. "Indeed, this land breeds much distrust these days, and it is so disheartening." He looked down at the white cat and said, "Shaer, I am afraid they require proof. Should I show them, my friend?"

"Prrrrrrrr . . . I do what I do and that's the best I can do," said the white cat, unexcited and almost indifferent.

The old man reached back and pulled his long flowing hair from around his neck. In the dim light, they could see the Mark of the Tree, black and livid, burned into his neck. Rarely shown, this was the mark of a good wizard, and fade it would if the wizard turned to darkness.

Lil' Man's eyes widened in surprise.

"The sign of the Edainar," he said.

"By my own eyes. He is Ras Amon," gasped Chumsey.

"Ras Amon?" roared Thurir. "This could be a trick, a sorcerer's spell."

"No. This is not magic," muttered Chumsey under his breath, staring at the old man in disbelief. "He lives."

"The Mark of the Tree is only given to a good wizard," Lil' Man told Thurir. "It is an eternal test of goodness and purity of heart. It measures the worth of the soul and fades under the veil of evil. No Dark Wizard can replicate the Mark of the Tree. He is who he says he is."

With a gentle smile, the old man quietly announced, "I am he and this is my home. You are most welcomed here."

An uneasy stillness came to the great hall; the only sounds heard were the crackle of the fire and the white cat's purr. The old man rocked in his chair and stared into the fire, all the while petting the white cat. He started to hum an elvish folk song in cadence with the rhythm of his creaking chair. It was a simple melody and filled the chamber with gladness.

With caution, Chumsey and Lil' Man approached the old man and sniffed the air. The scent was pure with enchantment. They now realized it was this magic that destroyed the firbolgs as they escaped Mistmere's catacombs. Their earlier familiarity was now clear to them; he was indeed Ras Amon, the Learned One, older, and thinner than before, but the same man they had known.

"He is Ras Amon," Lil' Man told the others, "the great wizard, the Learned One."

Chumsey nodded in agreement, a smile coming to his face.

Lil' Man and Chumsey bowed before the old man, knowing instinctively they were in the presence of greatness. A warmth came over them. For the first time in a long time, they felt safe and secure as they stood in the stillness of a good wizard.

Thurir, however, did not know what to think. But he had come to trust Lil' Man and Chumsey. He thought that if this was indeed a good wizard, perhaps they had gained a strong ally.

So too did Glaeynd trust the two cats. But she could not help herself. Her thoughts drifted to her father and what had become of Mistmere.

Sensing Glaeynd's struggle Ras Amon looked at her, as if to catch, to hear her thoughts. He held her with his peaceful, deep, and serene eyes as if absorbing her pain.

"My sweet Glaeynd," he said, "do not be saddened this day. All things happen for a purpose. And while your father and brother may have made an alliance with the darkness, comfort your heart that such a tragedy can be overcome. A deep wound indeed leaves a scar, but it is also true that a scar is a sign of healing. The process of healing takes time, in some cases a lifetime. Resolution and restoration are ongoing. But understand that as the heart heals and clears, greater depths unfold and will guard your heart against bitterness. The healing process is yours and yours alone. You are only going to heal when you decide you want to."

His words brought tears to her eyes, and she hurried to wipe them away before the others saw them. She could not seem to get thoughts of her father out of her head, no matter how hard she tried. But still, she recognized the truth in what he said. These were her demons, and she had to deal with them.

"Thank you," she said.

He nodded with a smile of recognition.

"My dear child," he said, "rejoice that you are with beloved friends who will protect you from harm. Find comfort in their fellowship."

She returned his smile and felt herself relaxing.

He then stood cradling the white cat in his arms.

"But Learned One, it has been told that you were dead, killed at the hands of the Dark Wizard," said Lil' Man.

"No, not dead, at least for now," he chuckled. He pointed to the table. "But come now. You are hungry and tired. Behold! A feast awaits us."

The once plain and long wooden table was now covered with platters of roasted and stewed meats and all kinds of food piled high. Bright green sprites hovered around the table; small human-like creatures no bigger than a thumb with light transparent wings. They were exquisitely beautiful, almost angelic, and went about diligently setting down dishes, bowls, and cutlery. They proceeded to the table, everyone taking a seat.

"We shall fill our bellies and talk of what has happened," said Ras Amon. "Then we shall rest, for tomorrow we start our journey."

"A journey? To where?" asked Lil' Man.

"Why, to Katzhu Pu as my friend Shaer said. Was not that your intention?" said Ras Amon.

"Yes, of course." smiled Lil' Man. "But how did he know."

"Well, he is a special creature," said Ras Amon.

The cats looked at each other inquisitively, still uneasy with the white cat.

"Learned One, about the cat, he is not of a Guild, is he?" asked Chumsey.

"No, he is not. The Guilds would not have him, or any of his kind."

Then it came to Lil' Man.

The cat's appearance, his voice! he thought.

"Is he Tar Malal?" asked Lil' Man.

Ras Amon's look became serious, and the cheer vanished from his face.

"I know of you both. You are from under the tree," he said. "So, even though you are Ra Cath, your roots are from another place. Such roots are strong and they give you a different perspective."

They nodded.

Still cradling the white cat, Ras Amon sat in a chair at the head of the table and gently placed the white cat in his lap.

"Yes, he is Tar Malal. To him, this is a cold, unfamiliar world into which he has blundered. But the fact that he is Tar Malal should not matter to you. Should it now? What is important for you to know is that he is a good friend. His name is Shaer Thol, but I sometimes call him Vaeler which means *white imp* in the old tongue. I came to know him through his friend the Professor."

Lil' Man was surprised.

"The Professor?" he asked. "He knew of this Tar Malal?"

"He knew of this friend," Ras Amon said pointedly. "The word we use is *friend*."

Lil' Man accepted the rebuke.

Ras Amon cast a tender gaze upon his guests.

"The Professor told me of this friend," he said. "He asked that I check on him whenever I passed through the Tangle. Which I did. He was always so sweet and so kind. But on one journey to the golden city many years ago, when I came upon him, he was barely alive, beaten by his kind."

"Even in the Tangle, by another Tar Malal?" asked Lil' Man.

Ras Amon nodded.

"Sadly so," he said. "I knew what I had to do. I freed him from the forest. In time he left my side and went his own way. I must confess I worried about him all the time. I worried about him surviving in a world that thought him an outcast, even by other outcasts. But I knew he was strong of spirit, strong of mind, and with a sharp awareness of his surroundings. I also knew that the Professor saw something in our little friend here, something I did not see at first. But now I see what the Professor saw. It is our differences that make us great. I have always believed the Maker will judge us by how we treat those who are different."

"What is Tar Malal?" Thurir asked Chumsey as they began their feast.

"A Tar Malal is a feline who, shall we say," Chumsey paused looking for the right words, "is mostly intellectually different, but demonstrates an extraordinary ability or intelligence in one or two things. The Ra Cath believes their abilities cannot be controlled, so they are outcasts. They live all around us but are hidden, afraid they will be found. Most live in the Tangle where they are protected by the forest."

Ras Amon gazed at Thurir.

"The truth is," he told Thurir, "they were forced to confinement for the sole purpose of an eventual death filled with horror. They are considered the lowest of the Ra Cath."

He looked down at the white cat, still in his lap, purring. It was a loving look of respect and appreciation.

Saddened by what Ras Amon had said, Lil' Man could only shake his head.

"It is unfortunate, but the Learned One is correct," he said. "I cannot speak to why this occurred."

"Sometimes we drive a wedge between members of our kind," sighed Ras Amon. "Sometimes even between the other races."

"What is it you see in him Learned One?" asked Lil' Man.

"Courage," said Ras Amon. "Courage to live his life in the only way he knows how. Courage to accept us as we are. Courage to overlook our many shortcomings, even though many refuse to overlook his. He has been very dear to me. His courage has helped me to heal these many years. Tar Malal! Tar Malal! Such a scurrilous phrase, is it not? It is a foul oath uttered by the Ra Cath. They refuse to see him. I ask: who needs eyes to see when they are closed? If only they would open their eyes, they would understand him and they would know his very special ability."

"What is his ability?" asked Chumsey.

"He is a prophetic angel, meaning he can foretell the future and unravel mysteries," said Ras Amon. "That is his gift. Oh, his words may not make sense at times, but you can feel their meaning by his voice. But then, and every so often, his voice will change from it a great power. That is when he speaks with utter clarity forcing you to pay close attention."

"I do what I do and that's the best I can do," said Shaer Thol in a confirming tone and through a deep, rumbling purr.

Ras Amon gave a wave of his hand.

"Ah, enough with such talk, eh?" he said. "You are all hungry. Let us drink, eat, and share adventurous tales."

They began their feast, and as they indulged on assorted meats, several types of bread, and sipped on ale, their gaze was drawn to the majestic building around them. Talk flowed naturally as they told Ras Amon of their journey from the Crag and Mistmere. The two cats told of the gathering of brood and coming darkness from the dead lands of the east. Thurir described the terror that had fallen on his homeland, and of the Dark Wizard Varul Teardash, and the betrayal committed. He spoke of the great dark army, of the endless plains and the endless sky, and the dead city of Gortha-Losh.

Ras Amon listened intently to every word, nodding along the way for through his magic he had journeyed with them. When they had finished their tale, he began to tell his.

His tale was much different than what the histories told, and as the sprites brought out large bowls of chocolate pudding to the table, he told his tale to the end. His eyes were dim as he described his encounter with Foulhand at Drar Druul, the great mount fire-on-high, where the endless chambers of molten rock flowed like the waters of a red river, gushing forth from fissures and melting hard stone. He told them how for many long days, he searched for his apprentice. He desired to convince the young wizard to abandon the evil he had discovered in the vast fissures of fire and return to his studies. But when he found his apprentice, it was too late. The young wizard known as Mauldragw Brighthand, a person once filled with love, hope, and faith, was gone; and a different person, one instead consumed by evil, jealousy, hate, and manipulation, proudly stood over the smoke and fire of Drar Druul.

He told the story: "We stood on a precipice, peering out into the dense heat, and we sparred with words. But evil had a hold on him, and the young man lovingly embraced it. They were forever joined, and I could do nothing. At that moment, I knew he was no longer my apprentice, and nothing could be done to change him. So, I was the first to strike with a powerful magic, a magic that shook the great Drar Druul itself. But it did not move him. He laughed as he stood on the precipice, unharmed. It was a hideous laugh, halfway between that of a wild beast and a murderous maniac. It echoed through Drar Druul like the laughter of evil spirits. He said, 'You are a weak old man, and your magic is useless here,' He was correct. Drar Druul was sapping my strength, my magic, my soul. But it fed his evil spirit. He raised his hand and gave one last laugh. I will remember his last words to me for as long as I shall live. 'It is time for you to rest, old man' he said. Then he threw a red bolt of fire at me.

"I was too weak to shield myself from it. It sent me tumbling into the abyss, the fiery chasm of evil. I remember falling through the heat and fire, and I thought I would surely perish, that was until suddenly I landed on something soft. My robes were ablaze, and I could feel the flames tearing into my flesh. But a strange wind came and extinguished the flames. I could barely move. Intense pain flowed through me like rivers, pooling here, then moving on to pool there, then moving again to pool somewhere else. I remember lifting my right hand, and looking at it as the charred flesh fell off in shreds. Despair filled me. My life force was fading, and all turned black. When I awoke I was here, in this place."

He paused. He stroked the cat and forced a smile.

"It was a difficult time. For years I laid here, convalescing at the caring hands of the sprites you see, all the time knowing that a great war was raging. And I . . . I could do nothing about it. A deep depression came over me brought by the shame that my apprentice had wreaked an evil upon the land, an evil I had urged him to discover. The war and the blood of so many innocents were on my hands. Those were dark days, very dark days. I became angry, angry that I wasn't killed, angry that I was saved. My life meant nothing. I meant nothing. I should've died.

"I gradually regained my strength and slowly my magic was rebuilt and returned with greater force. I explored my new home and soon ventured from the mountain. It was then that my good friend Shaer Thol again joined with me. He had been searching for me and eventually found me. I learned from him that the forces of good had defeated the evil. But the shame still haunted me. I could not return to the Edainar since I had not restrained my apprentice. So, I decided to wander the land with Shaer by my side, on a mission of discovery. I took the greatest care to conceal my identity, just another faceless soul in this vast place. And with Shaer's help, I began to experience the excitement of learning again. Soon I found myself searching for that which is most elusive – the truth."

"I do what I do and that's the best I can do," said the white cat softly.

"Forgive me Learned One," said Lil' Man. "But what truth do you seek?"

"The truth about existence . . . why we are here . . . why things come to be . . . about the very essence of the Maker."

"Ha, a fool's errand," scoffed Thurir. "I will give you the truth you seek, wise one. It is this: all things are empty."

Ras Amon gave a hearty laugh.

"Ah, a Ra Draug philosopher-prince in our midst," he said. "And tell me, what do you mean by that my good friend? Why are all things empty?"

"I think you mock me, good wizard," said Thurir, his words barely coherent, for such was the food, fresh and tasty, and he continued gulping it down ravenously, eating rapidly and copiously. "I will tell you why all things are empty. It is a simple truth. In this place, when you are alive you barely eke out an existence, and when you are dead there is no existence at all. There you have it. There is but emptiness for those alive and those dead. So, you see my truth abounds."

The Fenri snickered at their leader's words, furtively glancing his way. All knew a Fenri's existence was indeed bleak, living on the bare wind-swept rock of the Rakl.

"Here, in this world, you accept less than what you dreamed of for yourself," said Thurir. "This is what I see. This is the truth of the Fenri. This is my truth, Learned One."

Ras Amon's eyes twinkled at Thurir.

"My Fenri friend, I do not mock you," he said. "What you speak of is much the same as the ancients called tu kai a' kai, in the ancient tongue, or *from nothing to nothing*. Your words are wise for you speak of your truth. I suppose my quest was foolish. Instead of seeking one truth, I should've looked for several."

Thurir raised a glass of ale to him.

"No problem at all Learned One," he said. "Let me know whenever you need my counsel. Tu kai a' kai."

The great hall echoed with laughter, applause, and stamping feet. Ras Amon gave a hearty laugh which startled Shaer Thol. He raised his head and peered over the table to see what the ruckus was all about. When he figured out it was over some good jesting, he settled back into Ras Amon's lap.

They continued with their meal and finished off several cases of ale and large bowls of pudding. They made small talk and complimented the sprites for their work in preparing and serving the meal.

As the evening drew on, everyone returned to the warmth of the fire. They talked of the morning and their journey to Katzhu Pu. Lil' Man and Chumsey said they thought it would take many days to reach the city from the mountains. But Ras Amon spoke of a pathway he had discovered during his travels, a way that would cut their journey in half. This pleased everyone and they came to rest huddled around the stone fireplace. Lil' Man and Chumsey curled up together in a nearby blanket. And though all felt safe and secure in the great hall, Thurir insisted on placing Fenri guards about the great hall in shifts.

Ras Amon returned to his rocking chair by the fireplace and with a blanket snuggled with Shaer Thol.

"Close your eyes and rest my friend," he whispered to the white cat, "for tomorrow boasts of a busy day."

The cat put his head under the blanket to shut out the light.

"I do what I do and that's the best I can do," he said half asleep.

* * *

Fairfax sat alone in his chamber that evening, in meditation without moving. He calmed his mind, settling it until nothing more adhered to it. Suddenly, there was a pounding on the door – louder and louder! He was not startled. He had sensed a presence at the wooden door and the pounding forced him to suspend his meditations. He slowly opened one eye and gazed at the door. Again, there was more pounding and now a voice was shouting from the other side. Fearing it was someone with dire news, he moved swiftly to open the door. Elban Miragrin stood there, alone.

The young man stepped inside the chamber and quickly closed the door behind him.

"I want to join the battle against this evil," he told Fairfax. "I've talked it over with Mora and she agrees."

Fairfax could see the savage determination in Miragrin's eyes, sharply piercing, raw and reckless.

"In many ways, you are still a boy," said Fairfax. "I doubt you have ever been in a fight before let alone a war. And wars, well, they are very different than skirmishes you may have seen at Portmoor. My young Miragrin, you are not trained in the art of warfare."

"Were the thousands that fought in past wars trained?" asked Miragrin.

Fairfax cocked one eyebrow up and almost with a snarl said, "No. That is why most died."

"You don't understand. I need to avenge his death, Harwell's death. He gave his life for my family. It's the least I can do to repay such a debt."

Fairfax stroked his beard

"So, I see," he said. "A death for a death. How noble. I do not see how that resolves anything. Remember, the one who seeks vengeance must dig two graves: one for his enemy and one for himself. Master Harwell would want you to be with your family at this difficult time. He knew the pain of war more than most."

Miragrin became frustrated with Fairfax, uncertain of the way ahead.

"No matter," he said. "If I cannot travel with you and fight against this evil, then I will take Saraanth and ride to join with Carrick on my own."

Fairfax turned from Miragrin, and stared out his chamber window, the great waterfalls rumbling in the background. He said nothing.

The rebelliousness and stubbornness of youth, he thought. *There is little I can do to change his mind.*

Miragrin could stand the silence no longer. He took a deep breath to calm himself.

"Please know I'll always be grateful for what you did for my family," he told Fairfax.

Miragrin left the room. Fairfax heard the door close. He did not go after him, instead, he lifted his eyes to the stars twinkling like so many points of flame above him. He smiled, a wild and wondering smile, for he knew he would see Miragrin again.

* * *

Drogur Vorn walked quietly within the Esku En' Urra amongst the slaves as they toiled. The large beast did not speak, nor did he whip or otherwise physically torture those lesser creatures; it was unnecessary, for it was his mere presence that tormented. As he loomed over the slaves and prisoners, he saw terror in their hollowed eyes, and this pleased him.

The slaves and prisoners were of varied races. Many were men who had been ensnared into slavery, those that lived in the northern reaches of the Drueger. But there were others, bobbins, and dwarves, and others still, those bred especially for this horror. These were the Ai di'thu, despised creatures, and minions of the brood who did not know of existence outside the huge fissure.

Within the Esku En' Urra life was not life at all. Slaves and prisoners were in horrible physical condition, appearing almost like living skeletons. Food rations were meager, warmed broth with small bits of meat, but sufficient for most to survive, enough to work the mighty forges. Those that became ill were allotted smaller rations. And when one became too ill or weak to work, they were killed and slaughtered. Under direct orders from Drogur Vorn, the dead were used as part of the meager rations.

"Tortured hunger, fainting from fatigue, in such conditions, the lesser rag has only one hope left - it wants to die," Vorn once told his master.

Of the Ai di'thu there was one who was favored by Vorn, and as such was given a name – Snerv Slog. Slog was a smallish creature, deformed, and showed a wide range of malformations from diseases to disorders of internal organs. His legs were very bowed, his back hunched over and his head twice the size of a man's head, hairless, and knobbed with dozens of brown nubs. And when he could, when the Szard was not about, he would follow Vorn and serve to his every need.

The little creature appeared from the shadows.

"Shall we see how the new ones are coming?" Vorn asked Slog.

"Yesssst!" the demented creature giggled. He ran and hobbled ahead.

The two came to the long stone wall at the back of the fissure, a place where brood demons were extricated from stone and mud. In one section of this defiled place, a different kind of brood was being bred by the Ra Orqu. Within the earthy slime, they could see the evil creatures twist and writhe. The demons had just started to form, with round heads, long legs, and arms. These were not creatures bred for battle; these were creatures bred for something much worse.

"The Gurtha Naur," the words fell from Vorn's lips.

* * *

Molly awakened in the morning to the soft chirping of small yellow birds. She lay there listening to the gentle sounds as the morning sun shone on her through a small window. While her sister and Big Grey slept, she quietly got up from her bed and opened the door of the wagon.

Something was wrong, terribly wrong!

She was not outside! The caravan was gone and there was a blackness where the Jhyl Vyr had once been. Everywhere there was blackness, even darker than night for there was no moon or stars.

She decided it best to turn around and go back to her wagon. When she did so, a white-hot light shone down from the sky illuminating what appeared to be a bare stage in a grand theater. She could make out rows and rows of shadowy seats, each one empty, and to either side, she could make out marble-clad walls with crystal chandeliers and winding staircases and splendid balconies.

This must be a dream, she thought.

At first, she was frightened and doubtful, and could not understand what was happening to her.

She felt the warmth of her skin and the warmth of the light.

If this is indeed a dream, it is so real.

She grasped the Lia Fail and could feel its warmth and how it pulsated, much like a heart.

I will let it guide me.

She decided to follow the light to the stage and as she did, she could see a young boy, about her age, with blonde hair and a slight frame, sitting on a box and holding his head in his hands. He was crying.

"Stop that!" a man's voice shouted from within the darkness. "Stop your crying!"

"Daddy," the boy whimpered.

"I said stop it at once! Be a man!"

The boy continued to cry and then sensing her presence looked up at her. He had a round face with soft skin, but his eyes were two black holes, empty. She covered her mouth, frightened, horrified.

"Help me," the boy whispered to her. "Help me."

She did not know what to do. She felt helpless.

"You disgust me," shouted the faceless voice. "How many times have I told you! When you don't do as you're told you suffer the consequences! Now stand up!"

The boy stood. He removed his shirt. There cracked the sound of a lash slicing through the air. She could not see anything strike the boy, but as the sound cut through the darkness, the boy winced in pain. Another lash came, and again, and again. Every stroke was accompanied by a deep lash mark on the boy's back and a weak and stifled cry of anguish from him.

She could not bear to see the suffering. She released the Lia Fail from her grasp and turned from the stage. She closed her eyes and found herself back in the wagon, in her bed with Elizabeth and Big Grey by her side, asleep.

It was still night.

She could hear the night sounds, the trees whispering in the wind, the chirping of crickets. From the small window, she could see the dark shadows of the trees dancing against the pale moonlit night sky. She stayed in bed, too terrified to sleep again, listening to the muted sounds and wondering what the dream meant.

CHAPTER 11
HAMMER FIEF

AS THE MORNING SUN poured into the wagon, Molly wondered if she was again dreaming. She could feel the warmth of the sun on her face and sensed the brightness. She slowly opened her eyes and rolled over, and saw her sister beginning to wake. She reached out and touched Elizabeth's hair, gently, feeling its texture, its weight, and the way the long strands curled at the end. She was half-convinced she wasn't dreaming, but to be sure she had a thought.

"Pinch me," she whispered to her sister.

Clearing the cobwebs from her mind, at first, Elizabeth hesitated but then happily obliged and pinched Molly's arm.

"Ouch," grimaced Molly. "You didn't have to do it so hard."

Elizabeth smiled and chuckled.

"You asked me to pinch you silly," she said.

"You didn't have to hurt me. I just wanted to know if I was dreaming again."

"Dreaming? Molls, we all have dreams."

"I know. But I had a dream last night that was so vivid. I could see and hear things, and I could feel things. It felt so real like I was there. And the bad part about it, I knew I was dreaming, but I was scared, scared that I wouldn't wake up."

"Was it a nightmare?" asked Elizabeth.

"Not at the beginning. I was in a big theatre and there was a boy on a stage and he was crying. His father was yelling at him. I couldn't see him, but he was there in the shadows. He had a large booming voice. It was terrifying. He began to punish the boy. I got scared and when I turned around, I was back here in bed. You and Big Grey were sleeping."

Elizabeth pointed to the Lia Fail dangling from Molly's neck.

"It's that thing," she said. "It's just like Mr. Brows told us last night. What did he say . . . something like . . . you're becoming one with it?"

Molly did not say anything, but she knew her sister was right. Her dreams were becoming more frequent and more vivid and complex with each passing day. The veil separating dream life from waking life was disappearing and it worried her.

"I'll speak with Big Grey and Mr. Brows first thing this morning," she said.

Elizabeth looked around the cabin.

"Speaking of Big Grey where is he?" she asked.

Molly saw the wagon door was ajar.

"Maybe he's outside," she said.

They quickly changed their clothes and left the wagon. Outside they could smell breakfast cooking over a campfire. They saw Big Grey, Brows, Ancorbow, and Donduin eating fried potatoes, eggs, and biscuits and talking about the day's journey. Thickly sliced ham hissed crisp in its fat and there were two big pots on the fire, one with coffee and the other with water for tea. The smells and sounds of breakfast beckoned to them, and the girls followed it.

Ancorbow stood and bowed before Molly.

"My Queen, good morning," he said.

The others also stood and bowed. Molly smiled.

"Good morning. Everything looks so yummy," she said.

The girls ate a hearty breakfast, and afterward, everyone sat quietly for a moment. The girls sipped lavender tea while the rest sipped on strong coffee. It was during this time that Molly told the others of her dream. She did not leave out a single detail for it was so real she could remember it as if it had just happened. She told them how real it all felt, how scared she was, how she did not want to see any more of the dream, that she just wanted to leave, and that when she turned away, she was back in the wagon as if nothing had happened.

"Your dreams become more real," said Brows. "so vivid that you wake uncertain of what is real and what is unreal. It is the stone's influence. It is heightening your senses, helping you to sense the world around you more clearly. But you will never quite grasp the full nature of it. You think you will know, but you will never be certain."

"But what about the boy I saw?" she asked.

"The stone is trying to tell you something."

"What is it trying to tell me?"

"I do not know," Brows grinned at her. "I am not Queen of Ahlgren. But what I do know, and as I told you before, you are beginning to control the stone's power. You thought me silly or mad when I told you that, eh?"

She was confused. She grasped the red stone pendant. It began to warm and gently thump in her hand.

"No. I never thought you silly or mad," she said. "But I don't understand. How did I control the stone during the dream last night?"

His smile grew, the kind of smile that lifts not only the corners of the mouth but reaches up to delight the eyes.

"You said you turned away from the dream because you were frightened, that you wanted to leave," he said. She nodded. "And when you did you were back in the wagon." She gave another nod. "You did not know it at the time, but my young lady, you controlled the Lia Fail. It sensed your thoughts, your wants, your wishes. It did as you desired."

Can this be true? she thought.

She took the Lia Fail in her hand. Its beating was calm and rhythmic, and it began to glow, softly at first then brighter, and it continued to warm in her hand. As it grew in warmth and brightness Molly thought to herself . . . *dimmer . . . dimmer . . . dimmer.* The red stone responded and began to cool, its brightness fading as too did the thumping.

She looked at Brows and smiled. He knew what she had done.

"See, I told you," he said. "You are a quick study, indeed."

"The Professor would be so proud," purred Big Grey.

"Yes, my Queen is learning," said Donduin. But there was hesitation in his voice, concern in his tone and expression.

She could sense that he had something on his mind, something he wanted to say, but that he felt tentative about broaching the subject. She sensed that his words were held back by some anxiety that he should not be the one to say them.

She looked at him with reassuring eyes and smiled warmly.

"Is there something you wish to say?" she asked.

"I'm not sure I should speak what's on my mind," he said.

"Go ahead, speak freely," she told him.

He hesitated, then took a deep breath.

"Last night," he said, "our good friend here only told part of the story. He didn't speak the whole truth. He didn't tell you that there is another shard."

Brows grumbled.

"I only spoke of what is known as the truth," he told the man. "A historian is not interested in legends or tall tales from northlanders. Such tales are not grounded in truth."

"Another Lia Fail?" asked Molly, her eyes focused on the man.

Donduin moved closer to the fire.

"Yes, indeed. There's another and possibly more," he said. "What the historian didn't tell you is that it's believed that more than one shard came from the mighty stone at the hands of Arakarra, perhaps three. It's said that a second shard was recovered and given by the Elf-King to King Aelis. In later years it was said to be fashioned into a ring and passed down to all the generations."

"I don't understand. How would it have survived the Night of Death, all that bloodshed?" asked Molly.

"As the tale goes," he said, "a young prince from House Riorn was stowed away by a chamber maiden along with the ring during the Night of Death. Many believe the young prince was taken to the Tangle and raised by a family of outcasts." Then he uttered with great difficulty, almost imperceptibly, "It's said the young prince grew to manhood in the forest never knowing of his heritage, until the time when the man who raised him, the one the prince called father, revealed the truth from his deathbed."

"Oh, nonsense, nonsense I tell you," said Brows in frustration. "Donduin speaks of legend. This ring he speaks of has never been found. Sadly, I am afraid House Riorn passed years ago."

Donduin looked taken aback, and the normally genial face became stern and solemn.

"Ask the historian if a child's body was ever found. Go ahead! Ask him!" he pleaded with her.

"Enough already!" bellowed Brows with terse lips. "You know the truth of it! You know what happened that night. The Queen does not need to hear all this." He turned to her with great sadness in his eyes. "It is true. The young prince he speaks of was never found and it is not known what became of him. The brood can do unspeakable things. It is best that we do not think of such horrors. As far as other shards, the Elf-King has always stated that there is only one, true, Lia Fail. This is all foolishness."

"What about the third stone?" she asked Donduin. "You said there may be as many as three stones. What about the third?"

"Many say the Elf-King kept the shard for safe-keeping," he said. "Others say that it was returned to the mountains. We don't know with any certainty."

Brows shook his head.

"More nonsense!" he said. "I tell you - utter nonsense! Legends and tales are not grounded in history - they exist out of time."

"Just remember one man's legend can be another man's truth," Donduin told Brows.

Big Grey sighed.

"Listen, we have long to travel," said the cat. "Let us agree to focus on what we know and what's before us."

Donduin gave a nod, with only a slight glance at Brows.

"It is agreed then," he said, "and for the good of the Harrow."

"Come now," said Calen Ancorbow. "We must be off if we're to reach Hammer Fief by nightfall."

The guardsmen started to break camp. They began by stowing their gear and hitching the horses to the wagons. Donduin dowsed the fire while the girls helped Brows clean and stow various pots and pans. But Molly stopped what she was doing. She felt the Lia Fail's warmth against her chest. She reached for it. Something was calling to her. At her feet, she saw a pot with leftover ham. She thought of the orc.

"Wait!" she said, picking up the pot. "Was Ug'ghi Otha given breakfast?"

Everyone was surprised by what she said. They stared at her as she started to walk over to the orc's wagon with the pot of leftover ham.

Brows called out to her. "What do you mean? What are you doing?"

"Was he given something to eat this morning?" she shouted back.

"Eat?" shouted an irritated Donduin. "Eat? Let him have all the bugs and maggots that infest his cage! No need to waste good food on that beast!"

She turned to Donduin, angered by his words, then looked past him.

"Someone bring me a plate! I'll give him our leftovers," she insisted. Donduin attempted to say something, but she interrupted by saying, "Please! Someone bring me a plate. Before we leave, we'll give him food."

Ancorbow found a plate and ran after her.

"Wait! I'll go with you," he said.

She nodded.

Watching Molly and Ancorbow walk to the black wagon, Donduin stood and shook his head, disgruntled and annoyed.

"I fear she is reckless," he told Brows, Big Grey, and Elizabeth.

Brows lit his pipe and lifted a few puffs into the morning air.

"Yet, she is kind, brave, and generous . . . as a Queen should be," he said. "She has a plan, don't you know."

Elizabeth was exasperated.

"It must be that stone the Professor gave her," she said.

The cat sat upright and sniffed the crisp air now scented by Brows and his pipe. He looked about rather grandly.

"The stone guides her, and she guides it," he said. "She is maturing and knows exactly what she is doing. I believe we will be fine."

"For our sake, let's hope so," said Donduin. "The fate of the Harrow is in her hands."

As she approached the black wagon, she could see that many of the broad iron bars were rusted while others were in good condition. Long lengths of steel chains and a tarnished padlock secured the cage doors, and there was a terrible smell, the stench of filth and urine.

She peered into the darkness of the cage. She saw movement. The orc had stirred, writhing in pain. She could see lash marks crisscrossed along his green torso, some of which were beginning to scar as others were infected. His hands and feet were still shackled in irons, and he was too weak to stand.

He struggled to get across the cage floor to her, heaving his body forward as hard as he could. She looked at him, his blue eyes wandering to hers. She saw that his lips were dry and cracked.

"Bring him some water," she instructed Ancorbow. "Quickly!"

But Ancorbow was steadfast.

"I'll not leave your side, my Queen," he said.

"Put the ham on the plate and give it to him, then go get some water," she said firmly. She was learning that firmness had its advantage. "I'll be fine. You've nothing to fear."

Ancorbow reluctantly did as he was told. He placed the ham on the plate and slipped it underneath the cage doors, where the orc rested his head. He then left to get the water.

Without the use of his hands, the orc thrust his head into the plate and ravenously ate the ham, tearing it into pieces with the greatest ease. His large sharp pointed teeth ripped into each piece, his lips aglow with the juices of the rich meat. When he had finished, he rolled on his back, exhausted, and struggled to catch his breath. He took a couple of deep breaths then twisted to his side facing Molly.

"Why are you so kind to me?" he asked.

She swallowed hard, looking past his hideous face, and staring into his soft blue eyes.

"I am kind because it is who I am," she said with a slight smile. "I am kind because like I said to you before, we have much in common. Our destinies are shaped for us, bound together by the stone. Lead me to your master and help me deliver the red stone to him. In exchange, there can be peace for this land. I know it. But you must help me."

She kept eye contact with him, smiling reassuringly.

While he stared solemnly into her eyes, he saw purity in her face, a mystery in her wide eyes. He was drawn to her, to her softly spoken words.

"I know not of peace," he said. "I only know of war, darkness, and anger."

He turned from her stare and gazed out into the morning sun. He liked its warmth, something unusual for an orc. Indeed, he was unusual even to his kind. This he knew.

He looked past her, surveying the surrounding terrain.

"We are along the Jhyl Vyr," he said. "The road leads to the golden city. You are going to meet with the Guild Lords."

She gently reached her hand into the cage, touching his cheek. His green leathery skin felt raw, thick, and dull, cold as death.

"Yes," she said. "You know your way around these lands."

"I have always wanted to see the golden city," he told her. "To my people, it is a place of great evil. But the descriptions of its grandeur seem wonderful to me. Can you imagine? A city made of pure gold, sparkling and glimmering, where all creatures live in harmony. It must be beautiful. I ask you: how could such a glorious place be evil?"

"I've been told that orcs are mean and nasty creatures who hurt people and things. But you are not like that at all. You are different. I mean you are not like other orcs."

He rolled back on his side and faced her.

"They would tell me that I was too sensible, that I had kind thoughts, that orcs never had kind thoughts. They would remind me that an orc pillages and massacres and must be obedient to its horde and master. They would tell me that I was worthless scum for wanting to explore and meet other creatures, the same creatures they considered vermin and food." He paused and gave a long sigh. "They would tell me that if I did not change, I would be hunted and killed, that I would die a most horrible death at the hands of the horde. My kind has never understood me."

A lone tear trickled down from his eye.

"I can't imagine," Molly whispered sadly, "what it must be like."

He stared at her as if he would understand something about her, something about himself. As their eyes met and held, he read something in hers, a message of sympathy and understanding, as if to say: "I wish I could do more to help."

For her part, she saw her reflection mirrored in his glistening blue eyes. She felt as if she was falling into them, disappearing, becoming someone else. She had never seen herself like this before. But sadness overcame her. His tale upset her. She began to cry, quickly turning from him to keep him from seeing her tears.

He sensed her sorrow and wanted very much to remove it but did not know how to.

"You must not be sad," he told her. "I do not wish to make you sad. Do not be sad for me. I am but an orc."

She drew a quick breath, trying mightily to hold back her tears.

"It's this place. It's how everyone here treats others. That's what makes me most sad. It should never matter whether you are orc, bobbin, or man. Maybe we can change things if we work together. Will you help me?"

He closed his eyes. He felt comfortable with her innocent and confiding manner, and he knew she understood him. He thought of how she believed that every living thing deserved respect, and it made him realize that maybe being different was not such a horrible thing after all. Fate had brought them together, and he knew that whatever he decided to do would affect his and her futures, as well as possibly the lives of others.

He decided.

"I will help you," he said, and then with a whisper, "my Queen."

She smiled at him.

My plan, she thought. *It is like a puzzle. Here is a piece.*

A sense of guilt came over her like a soft shadow, weakening her and drifting over her, revealing that she was now hiding behind a mask.

A mask hides the deceit in my actions. But such deceit is necessary to reach my goal. The dream . . . the dream of the Professor talking . . . treachery wears many masks.

She looked at him, again with a feeling of sadness.

Another mask. Sadness masks my guilt. But I cannot allow my emotions to lead me astray. My plan is for the good of this place.

She was sure he could help her, and she believed she could trust him. Although she was not afraid, she knew the others would be and she would have to deal with that.

They will have to trust in my judgment.

Ancorbow returned with a shallow wooden bowl of water and slid it underneath the cage doors.

"Thank you," she told Ancorbow. "Let's give him water to bathe and find a robe to fit him. He will ride with me at the front."

Ancorbow's eyes widened in shock.

"But . . ."

"You and Mr. Donduin may ride with me in the lead wagon as well," she said firmly. "This should put your mind at ease." She turned to Ug'ghi Otha with a comforting smile and told Ancorbow, "He's a friend to us."

The group finished preparing for departure. As they were about to start their journey Ug'ghi Otha came to the lead wagon, wrapped in a long, hooded robe made of a thick black canvas-like material. The hood concealed his face in shadow. He forced his gaze ahead. He sat near Molly and said few words as though unwilling to let any word go, but he was eloquent in those few that were spoken.

The wagon started with a jerk and the caravan returned to the Jhyl Vyr. The sky was cloudless and the sunshine gloriously bright. Ahead, the distant mountains were sharply defined in bright colors from the light of the sun. But a cloud hung over them. Donduin, Ancorbow, and the guardsmen did not like Ug'ghi Otha riding with Molly. Donduin told Big Grey that he was beginning to "tire of her surprises," and that "Fairfax would not be pleased."

The cat looked up at him, squinted in the sunlight, and reminded him that Fairfax had complete confidence in the Queen of Ahlgren. As for Elizabeth, well, she was getting used to her sister doing some silly things, and at first, even though she was a bit frightened of Ug'ghi Otha, she too became more comfortable with him as they talked.

* * *

Their journey soon led them but a league or so to a small, wooded area. There the caravan turned from the Jhyl Vyr and onto a short and narrow road that led through an open field of wildflowers and across a gentle hill. The birds sang merrily, and the wildflowers were taut in bloom, their scent carried on a breeze. A bend in the road and over another hill took them from the open field and to a grassy lane lined with white birches. Past the birches, the road led through a grove of tall pines and maples that provided a dense canopy above. Twisting vines and brambles were everywhere. Up the road, over a knoll, and across a rude bridge in a hollow beyond, they came upon the little town of Hammer Fief. It was the last town before the Tangle forest.

They pushed on. As they entered the town, dogs barked at them, drawing the attention of several townsfolk, all of whom wore ragged patchwork blankets, their faces masked in darkness. There was an old woman hardly able to walk, dragging pails of water; there was a man without legs huddled beneath a blanket talking to a hairless cat. When the cat saw the caravan and Big Grey it hissed and spat. Along the way were tall, emaciated men who were untidy, and disheveled, with long hair and unshaven faces, and dressed in tattered clothing. Brows called them Woodwose or Wild Men. Everywhere were pitiable little creatures of all kinds, deformed and shrunken, scarred and too weak to wail.

"Do not make eye contact," warned Brows.

"Why?" asked Molly.

"This is Hammer Fief," he told her, "a town of the displaced, where there is no difference between clean and unclean. It is a sordid place that belches forth despair and sorrow. It is a place where those fortunate to have escaped the Tangle live in hopelessness." He paused and looked at her. "Stare at it for too long and you become part of the misery."

The girls heeded his warning, keeping their eyes on the road ahead. But from the corners of their eyes, they gathered glimpses of the town. The sights were unlike any they had seen before. They were frightened and shocked by the strange and sickly figures and puzzled that such a place could exist in the Harrow. Big Grey nestled between the girls to hide from the townsfolk. He knew that members of the Guild were unwelcome in this place. Meanwhile, Donduin and Ancorbow looked over maps of the Tangle.

"Maps will do you no good," smirked Brows. "You are simply wasting your time."

"Historian, we know all about the Tangle," snapped Donduin. "These maps show the main pathways, those that don't change but are camouflaged."

Brows kept his eyes straight forward and, on the road, ahead. He took a few puffs of his pipe.

"Foolishness," he said. "All paths in the Tangle change. The forest moves."

"What's this forest? What do you mean that it moves?" asked Elizabeth.

"The Tangle is the home to outcasts, those who do not fit in," he said. "It is also a forest of magic. It was created many years ago by a lone conjuror to protect the outcasts, and it happens to be the only way to the golden city unless of course one is so adventurous to journey through the Old Hills." Brows looked at Elizabeth and gave a glint of a smile. "No wizard has yet to break the spell that protects the outcasts. And, when I said the trees move, they do, as do the pathways. Wait, you will see."

"You say it protects outcasts, but it sounds more like a prison to me," said Elizabeth.

"Perhaps one can look at it that way."

"But if it changes, how will we get through?" asked Molly.

"We will need a Tracker, an outcast who is familiar with the forest," he said. "They have got a keen sense of direction. We will find one here, in Hammer Fief."

"I do not know if I like this place," said Molly.

Brows gave a serious look.

"Well, I do not think it likes us either," he said.

* * *

Slowly, very slowly, Lil' Man awoke from a sound sleep to find Chumsey gently licking the top of his head. He could feel the warmth of his friend's pink tongue as it stroked his fur, this way, then that way, and he could hear a deep rumbling purr. He stretched and gave a yawn, and curled up again, his eyes still closed. He stirred, stretched, and gave another yawn. He curled up yet again, slowly waking, but not wanting to. Eventually, he opened his eyes and shook the grogginess from his head. He saw Chumsey sniffing at him. His friend then turned and started to clean himself, repeatedly licking his paw and scrubbing over his face.

"Good morning," he softly told his friend who continued to clean himself. "Are you that dirty?"

Chumsey stopped briefly, gave a chirp, and continued.

Lil' Man smiled and stared far above into the darkness that was the stone ceiling of the great mountain hall. He stood and hunched his back, his front paws stretching and pulling at the blanket. He yawned but when he looked up, became startled. The strange red eyes of the bony white cat were staring down at him. He froze.

"I do what I do and that's the best I can do," said the white cat rather hurriedly.

Lil' Man tilted his head. He could see the concern in the white cat's red eyes.

The white cat turned and raced away towards the great table where the others sat having breakfast.

"What does he want?" asked Chumsey.

"There is urgency in his tone. I think he wants us to hurry. We must have overslept."

Chumsey smiled.

"What's this? You understand him?" he asked.

Lil' Man gave a somewhat bewildered glance to his friend, then watched as the white cat jumped into Ras Amon's lap.

"Yes. I think I am beginning to understand him, in the way in which he has to be understood," he said. "It is strange. It is not what he says, it is how he says it, and the look in his eyes."

"Be careful my friend or you will be an outcast as well."

"Sometimes I think we are all outcasts."

Chumsey chuckled.

For the first time, Lil' Man was beginning to understand the outcast white cat. He seemed to have a sense of what kind of creature it was. Not being native to the Harrow he had only heard tales of outcasts: that they were creatures shunned with abhorrence, bereft of belongings or friends, solitary figures of perpetual darkness, denounced by the Guilds and the Edainar, and cursed by the almighty I' Ra Heru.

"Why are outcasts so forsaken in this land?" he asked his friend.

Chumsey jumped from the basket, gave a long stretch, and started for breakfast.

"I do not know," he said. "My Guild Mentor once told me that the life of an outcast is as of one dead. But I think your question is best asked of the Learned One.

Enough with that, we cannot change - hurry now! We are running late!"

* * *

After a hearty breakfast, they packed provisions, enough for at least a two-day journey, and then set off deep into the mountain. The white cat led the way followed by Ras Amon who held tightly to his crooked white staff of wood. Lil' Man, Chumsey, and Glaeynd walked alongside the wizard followed by Thurir whose pack formed a loosely knit defensive formation, a trailing half circle. A few Fenri lingered far to the sides with noses to the ground, and eyes watching the far distance for signs of movement.

They traveled far into the cavernous mountain hall, deep into the darkness, until they came upon a huge granite doorway leading to a hallway of stone that tunneled into the mountain for leagues. As they walked down the long hallway that curved in various directions, smaller hallways leading to vaulted rooms came into view. The light from great openings carved into the rock high above them cast eerie shadows within the expansive hallway. It soon became apparent to Lil' Man and Chumsey that they were traveling within the great mountains of the Old Hills, on a labyrinth of roads chiseled out of stone and rock.

They stopped and rested along the way, filling their leather canteens with water from great stone wells. They found hidden pantries stocked with dried food and blankets. Ras Amon explained that it was he who had stocked the pantries, along his many travels within the great mountains. He told of how he had traveled the stone roads and mysterious hallways for years, exploring and mapping them out in his mind.

"This place stretches for hundreds of leagues," he said sitting for a bit, "through the Old Hills, down into a great chasm, and then into the Thornback - hallway after hallway, room after room, and I, I have traveled it all. It is a colossal city beneath the mountains, a place where giants once lived."

"Trollock," said Lil' Man.

Ras Amon gave a wink.

"I believe so, small one," he said.

"Learned One, do they still live?" asked Chumsey.

Ras Amon took a deep breath, and lifted his arms, stretching his back.

"I do not know," he said. "In all my travels I have yet to see a living creature in this place. Come now, we must make our way swiftly to Katzhu Pu."

The two cats looked about the great hall. They wondered what the mountain city must have been like in the days of its glory, with its grand promenades, its wide column-lined ways, all thronging with giants. Noise, color, motion, rather than silence; a place teeming with life rather than an empty shell of vast stillness.

As they continued through the city carved, they came upon unbelievable sights. At one point, there was an enormous stone archway that led to a magnificent plaza. The plaza was unadorned, a paved expanse, a good thousand yards in all directions, with a circular grey stone platform in the center, where a fountain foamed and bubbled. Great stone facades surrounded the plaza - windows, doorways, and balconies overlooking the grand court. Around the plaza, there were great archways that led to roadways lined with courtyards with colorful mosaic tiles, stone terraces, and rock-hewn pools. They were amazed by how massive the city was, but also how beautiful it was — beyond anything they had ever seen.

Here, they rested for a moment. Some of the Fenri wandered cautiously about the great plaza in amazement while others drank from the fountain. Ras Amon sat at the edge of the fountain, looking into the pool with the white cat in his lap.

"Learned One," said Lil' Man clearing his throat as he approached the wizard. "I have been meaning to ask you a question. About outcasts, why are they shunned?"

The white cat looked up at him with his bulging red eyes,

"I do what I do and that's the best I can do," he said with a rumbling purr.

Ras Amon stood with the white cat in his arms. He smiled as he caressed the cat. He then reached down and stroked Lil' Man along his back.

"That a difficult question," he said. "You should not mind if the answer takes its time arriving."

He made his way through the great plaza traveling beneath a grand archway, deeper into the mountains. As he left the plaza, he tenderly placed the white cat on the ground who scampered off ahead of him, then quickly returned, rubbing up against his legs. The rest of the group began to follow him under the archway. Lil' Man stayed at the fountain and simply watched.

"Well, did you ask him?" said Chumsey.

Lil' Man's gaze remained fixed on Ras Amon and the white cat.

"Yes, I did," he said.

"And?"

"He told me I must wait for the answer."

Lil' Man bolted across the now empty plaza and through the grand archway.

Chumsey gave him a puzzled look and then followed after him.

* * *

The caravan made its way through Hammer Fief, finally resting in front of a dilapidated building on the outskirts of the small town. The two-story structure sat on a long slope below an oak-shaded wood, its paintwork flecking off, its shutters rotting off black hinges, while weeds and undergrowth spread in profusion. To the side were several horses tied to a rail with a troth of water nearby. A splintered wooden sign with the word Nagas scratched into it hung by a lone nail over a crooked doorway. Molly did not like the look of the place at all. She caught the bobbin's eyes which were fixed on her in amusement.

He hopped down from the wagon, grinning at her.

"Well, here we are," he said. "Does not look very inviting, does it now?"

"Not at all. What is this place?" she asked.

"It is an outpost, the last before we enter the Tangle," he said. "We will meet up with the good wizard here." He pointed down the road to a vast hazy forest outline that loomed along the horizon. "Oh, and that, my Queen, that is the forest – the Tangle."

She asked Ug'ghi Otha, "Have you ever been in the forest?"

"No. We were told to never enter the place," he said from within the darkness of his hooded robe. "In my tongue, it is called Drar Dhuugaan, a place of living death."

The girls stared into the forest's haze as it whirled and roiled, a white mist that ascended and descended about the heights of massive trees. They watched as the white mists swirled into streams that shimmered and surged about the trees, swirling in a frenzied dance. Then, ever so gently and quietly, the streams lifted the forest and positioned each tree and bush in a new place.

They could not believe their eyes. It was exactly as Brows had said - the forest moved and the earth along with it. It was then that they saw something very strange and horrifying – a man was attempting to crawl his way from the forest. He looked horrible, in tattered clothes, with wounds on his face and arms. They watched as the white mists settled and coiled around low-lying brush, fern, and the immense roots of the great trees, only to come up boiling again, swallowing, and dragging the man back into the forest. They could hear him scream and howl. Then they watched as the forest seemed to shiver in a white haze, fade, and reappear transformed and invigorated.

Molly was speechless.

"I don't believe it," gasped Elizabeth.

"What? That a forest could move?" said Brows. "What you see before you is the power of raw magic. It is the kind of magic the Harrow has not seen in some time. Mind you now, without a proper Tracker, it is dangerous and life-threatening. I have traveled through the Tangle countless times without incident and expect to do so once again. But each journey through the forest is tormenting. The constant change wears on you."

"How can anything live there?" asked Elizabeth. "Surely, they must be crushed by the moving trees."

"This magic has great precision. Many people and creatures call the Tangle home. They go unharmed because when the forest moves it does so ever so carefully. Not a single creature has ever been harmed." Brows paused and a serious look came to him as he continued. "Fear not the movement of the forest my friends, rather fear what secrets the forest holds. Now, everyone stay here while I see if our good friend has arrived."

Big Grey who continued to hide peeked up over Elizabeth's legs.

"Oh, we are here at Nagas. Do not worry. Fairfax will be with us," he said with a purr.

Molly reached over and gently caressed the cat as Brows made his way to the outpost's front door. Just as he entered the building, the ground thumped and rolled hard, and a dark puff of blackened ash rose skyward from behind the rickety structure. The girls thought it was an earthquake or that perhaps the magic that moved the forest was now upon them.

Suddenly, from behind the building at the height of its roof Moondancer appeared and snorted. Black ash blew from his nostrils, such strong blasts that the ground again thumped.

The red ajatar came around the building, the ground trembling with each step.

"Well, if it is not the Queen, Princess, and the Lawgiver," he bellowed. "It is so good to see you again."

The girls smiled and waved.

"Moondancer!" they shouted.

They were happy to see him.

He extended his large leathery wings and lowered his head closer to the lead wagon and the girls. But there was something in the air that he could neither forgive nor overlook. Cautiously, he flared his nostrils in the light breeze. He turned to the figure concealed in black next to Molly and sniffed at it.

"Hmm . . . but what is this?" he roared in disapproval. "It's the smell of I' Mortu, of orc, strong and unpleasant. How can this be? How can the Queen and Princess travel with such a vile creature?"

Ug'ghi Otha slowly raised his hooded head, unafraid. He looked at Moondancer then returned to staring at the road ahead.

"Be careful winged one," he growled. "Where I come from ajatars are the vile and despicable ones."

Moondancer flicked his barbed tongue at him.

"Ah, little beast. Horrible creatures orcs are but they make for a fine dessert," he snarled, snapping his jaws quickly. "If I were you, I would be very careful or I will eat you up like sweets!"

"Moondancer, he's a friend!" said Molly.

He kept his eyes on the orc.

"Friend? An orc? Hardly!" he said.

"He's a friend," she said. "Really, he's a friend."

He did not understand what was happening but when he looked at Molly, he saw a face he could trust, a face that would always be there. He raised his mighty head high above the trees and spread his wings

"If the Queen says you are a friend, then so be it," he growled. "But let me tell you this one thing orc - if you just look at the Queen or Princess, or any of their true friends in the wrong way, or say a wrong word, I will make quick work of you. Orc, mark this day! Mark my words!"

"So marked ajatar," said Ug'ghi Otha staring ahead, unfazed.

Moondancer stared down at Molly and smiled, revealing his sword-like teeth.

"My Queen, but may I ask, that you reconsider this alliance," he said. "Orc cannot be friends to the En' Edan."

Everyone was silent during the exchange. Gradually all eyes focused on the orc. Donduin and Ancorbow were pleased with Moondancer's words. Each hoped that perhaps he could change Molly's mind about the orc. But their hopes were dashed with a few simple words from Molly.

"He's a friend as you are," she told Moondancer. "Friends are those that accept you the way you are, they're those that are there when you need them. Please, believe in me."

Moondancer thought of her words, her gentle manner. He found her voice filled with a strange faith and a wonderful assurance. Maybe something was afoot, some sort of plan that he was not aware of what. Regardless, he knew there was nothing he could say that could change her mind. He gave a bow.

"I shall trust your judgment and good sense, for you are Queen," he said. He looked at the orc, with a warning stare. "But remember, trust is something that can be stolen by a thief."

Then Fairfax came from the building along with Brows, Dithil, and a strange man. The stranger was tall, heavily muscled, and stately in form and had a close-trimmed black beard rather than the full bush favored by most men in the Harrow. He was dressed in a long brownish cloak that fell straight like a robe and wore brown leather gloves. The man's black hair, which grew long onto his shoulders, shone with a curious reddish tinge to it.

They met up with Moondancer. Fairfax exchanged a few words with him, and in return, he gave a nod of his mighty head.

Fairfax turned to the girls and waved. They were glad to see their friend.

"I hope your journey went well," he said.

"Oh, yes," said Molly with a smile. "We're very happy to see you and Mr. Dithil. I hope Mr. Miragrin and his family are safe."

He returned her smile.

"Yes. Everyone is safe and at Blackstone," he said. "But unfortunately, evil has come to the west." He saw

Ug'ghi Otha sitting next to the girls. "Hmm . . . I see you have traveled with a companion. A new friend, perhaps?"

"Yes, a friend," she said.

He kept his eyes locked on hers. In his many meditations, he had, of course, understood what would come. But now he wanted to test her.

"Do you think it wise?" he asked.

"I remember something the Professor once said. He said, 'Wisdom, after all, is but trust in knowing which path to take.' My friend and I have much in common. We need to travel the same path, together."

She is maturing, he thought. *She is true to her plan.*

"Well, I see," he said. "We are all set then. We must be off. But first I would like to introduce you to a new friend. His name is Bran. He is from Dunhollow. His family name is Arundel. He is a Tracker and will help us navigate through the Tangle."

She held out her hand to the man.

"We're pleased to make your acquaintance, Mr. Bran," she said.

The man stepped forward, bowed, and taking her hand pressed it to his forehead. His eyes were penetrating, determined, and a sparkling dark black.

"My Queen, I am at your service," he said with a deep voice.

Now, more accustomed to such occurrences and her duties as Queen, she knew how to respond.

"We are thankful for your assistance, sir. You are most gracious."

She was intrigued by the man. She was curious about his past and sensed he possessed an indefinable power. She tried to reach out to him but could not. He was strange to her, something unknown.

What is he thinking? What are his plans?

She clutched the Lia Fail and gazed into his eyes. She found deep warmth and felt comfortable with him almost immediately. He was someone she could trust.

But Elizabeth was unhappy.

"Oh. I was hoping with Moondancer here we'd be able to fly to wherever it is we are going," she said.

Fairfax lifted a finger.

"That would be most grand," he said. "However, our good friend must fly south, to take counsel with others. Bran here will help us through the forest."

He lifted his hand and with a twitter of his fingers made sugar dust gently float about the girls. The dust sparkled in the sunlight. Molly lifted her head upwards and with her mouth open, went about catching the sugar dust on her tongue.

"Elizabeth, try it," she told her sister. "They're like sweet snowflakes."

Elizabeth joined in the fun, and they laughed as their wagon and the caravan was off, heading toward the misty white of the Tangle. The woods were leafy and there were dabbles of color about and the eerie white mist. Strangely, it seemed a peaceful place, but the girls knew that looks were often deceiving.

CHAPTER 12
THE TANGLE

BRAN OF DUNHOLLOW LED the caravan from Nagas and down the road to the Tangle forest, atop his horse that was named Wildflower. She was a beautiful horse - her coat was a sleek spotted grey, darker around the eyes and feet, her head small and perfectly formed, her ears perked forward at attention. For Molly, Wildflower was a horse quite unlike other horses she had seen in the Harrow. Her stand was decisive and strong, and her step would not raise dust when galloping, nor leave a trace of its steps behind. Molly was awestruck by the ripple of the smooth muscles as she walked, the curving of her powerful neck, and the burnished grey of her coat. She thought Wildflower was magnificent.

"Do you think Mr. Bran would let me ride Wildflower one day?" Molly asked Fairfax.

"Hmm . . . perhaps," he said. "You should ask him after our journey through the forest ends."

She nodded.

As they reached the mouth of the forest, Bran raised his hand and dismounted Wildflower. The caravan stopped and gathered at the front. Bran gave instructions to bring the wagons in a tight formation. He told the guardsmen to dismount their horses.

"Guide your horses slowly by foot, keeping close to the wagons," he told them. "For those who have not traveled through the forest, know it is important for us to stay together. The forest holds powerful and unpredictable magic. We will move slowly and move and stop on my mark. A raise of my hand will signal each. If anyone becomes separated from the group they will be lost forever, for we will not seek their rescue. It is a fate worse than death for the lost are destined to eternally wander the forest looking for a way out. One last thing, if we happen upon a Rambler let me deal with the creature. If the Maker is with us, we will be at the gates of Katzhu Pu by sunset."

This frightened Molly, and sensing this, Brows put his arms around her and told her not to worry.

"What's a Rambler?" she asked.

"It is a person not of the Tangle," he said looking straight ahead into the forest. "It is someone who has lost their way, usually a misguided traveler thinking he or she could navigate their way to Katzhu Pu. Yes, some do escape, but the vast majority live forever in the forest trying to find a way out of the changing labyrinth. They are a hopeless lot, and over time become crazed with madness and rave incessantly. They will try to attach themselves to anyone who they believe may free them from the forest. No good can ever come from helping a Rambler."

"Like the person we saw trying to escape the forest?" asked Elizabeth.

"That was no person. Once, in another life and time, perhaps, but now it is a Rambler, a creature without any sense or morals, a ravenous, slithering creature of the ground, maddened by their futile attempts to escape the forest. A Rambler is as close to the nothingness of death as any evil creature in the Harrow."

"Why doesn't Bran want the guardsmen to ride their horses?" asked Molly.

"Their horses are untrained for such a journey. He is concerned they would bolt when the forest moves, frightened by the magic, taking their rider along with them. They would forever be lost in the Tangle, never to be seen again. He knows best in these matters."

Bran mounted Wildflower and rode out some distance from the caravan. He stopped and raised his hand signaling the group to slowly move forward. The caravan nudged along a narrow dirt path for some time, while the forest closed in around them, and the air became cool. Soon there were no sounds. A breeze stirred some branches high above, and the slow, steady drizzle of leaves and flower petals turned into a shower for a moment. Vaguely, clouds could be seen drifting above the dense canopy when all became still.

Bran slowed his pace and turned to the caravan. He looked upon the forest and then up to the sky as if trying to establish a sense of direction. He raised his hand. Taking his cue, the caravan halted. Everyone looked around as a white mist, cool and cleansing, washed over everything, ascending, and whirling through the vegetation. From within the mists, large white streams of light churned, bright and blinding wrapping around the trees and brush. A frenzied dance of mist and light surrounded them as the ground began to tremble slowly at first, a rumble that grew steadily more powerful, until everything around them began to lift and move. The noise was deafening and the air heavy with dread as the girls clung to each other. To one side of the wagon, one of the guardsmen's horses reared up violently, twisting and wheeling in fear. The guardsman attempted to hold the horse steady, but it abruptly catapulted from the group and the guardsman became ensnarled in the lead.

"No! Let go!" shouted Bran to the guardsman. "Let go!"

But the guardsman could not.

The girls watched as the horse pulled the guardsman far into the white mist and light, beneath the uplifted tree roots and vegetation, until both were no longer visible. They closed their eyes in horror and looked away. The mists then began to slow their dance, descending from the treetops and swirling about the brush. All around, trees and rocks and flora came crashing down to the ground, shifted, and repositioned. When the sounds ended, they opened their eyes. The forest had changed; it looked different as did the sky above. Just ahead, the path now forked. One branch went to the left and disappeared around the bend of a hill that had not been there just a few moments before. The other branch continued further along to the right and from it another fork that branched down a slope and vanished.

Elizabeth put her hands to her mouth and let out a gasp that startled the others in the wagon.

"My word, we're lost for sure," she lamented. "This is like a nightmare."

Molly was unsure how to react to her sister, but she understood the fear.

Bran rode up alongside the girls in the lead wagon. He knew they were worried and wished to reassure them. He understood he needed to be extremely cautious about what he said and how he said it to avoid instilling further anxiety.

"My Queen," he said to Molly. "You will be safe with me. You have, my word. I was taught that one who conquers the fear of the unknown is master of their fate." He then turned and addressed everyone, shouting, "Do not stray off. The forest will move a hundred times if not more before we leave its grasp. Watch for my signal and stay close to the wagons. I do not wish to lose another to the forest."

Molly was still saddened by the loss of a guardsman. She looked up at Fairfax.

"What about your magic?" she asked. "Can't you use your magic to find him?" She looked down at her necklace. "Or maybe I can use the Lia Fail to find him."

Fairfax shook his head.

"I am afraid neither my magic nor your powers will work in this place," he told her. "The forest is a formidable force. It is old magic, conjured ages ago. It is far older than time itself."

"But Mr. Bran, can't we go after him before the forest moves again?" implored Molly.

"My Queen, please tell me, which way did he go?" he asked her.

She turned to her left where she thought the guardsman had been, but the forest seemed strange to her. She turned to her right and studied the forest that lay before her. Everything was so different now and she was unsure as to the direction the guardsman had been dragged by his horse. She was confused.

"I don't know," she said. "I thought it was that way, but then again perhaps it was over there, and then again maybe it was in that direction."

He shook his head.

"My Queen, I am so sorry," he said. She pointed. "Truly I am. But it would be foolish. The guardsman is lost forever in the changing forest. He and his horse are now Ramblers." His tone then became determined. "Time is against us. We must continue if we are to leave this place before nightfall."

With that, he turned around Wildflower and returned to the lead position, some distance ahead of the group. He then slowed her pace and raised his hand and the caravan continued. He guided them deeper into the forest, down the newly formed slope, as the girls compelled themselves to be calm.

* * *

As midday waned and having survived countless forest changes, they came about a hollow, a clearing in the forest, a gentle and beautiful space where the sunlight fell. All around them were soft rolling hills each covered with tall, dark trees and thick brush. The forest seemed to go on forever and Molly began to wonder if they would ever find their way out. Then something startled her. A girl was squatting on a huge tree stump in front of them.

She was young, with a lithe, active figure. Her face was round, and her blue eyes were clear, her skin fair, and her blonde hair a trifle curly. She wore a slender tight-fitting knee-length brown tunic, and black leggings, with a quiver of arrows, slung at her right side. In her left hand, she held a bow such as never before seen by Molly. It was long and black and looked to be carved of a bone from a huge creature.

Bran raised his hand and the caravan stopped. Slowly, he backed Wildflower up a dozen paces or so, turning her from side to side keeping his eyes fixed on the girl until he was at the lead wagon.

"Something is wrong," he said.

"What is it?" asked Fairfax.

"The girl — she is a Tracker, possessing great skill. Her name is An Van Au." His eyes darted about the mists that swirled about the trees. He was uncomfortable that they were stopped in a clearing. "She is of Dunhollow. We have known each other since childhood. I do not know why she is here or what she would want."

"Well, I suppose maybe you could ask her," said Brows.

But the man did not have the opportunity as the girl stood, a gentle breeze playing with her golden hair.

"Bran Arundel," she shouted. "It seems you have lost your edge. You have walked into a trap and had better yield gracefully."

In a blink of an eye, she had taken an arrow from her quiver, laid it upon the bowstring, and seemed to point it directly at Molly. Ug'ghi Otha jumped out from behind and wrapped himself around her.

Bran turned to the guardsman.

"Easy everyone," he said. "We will hold our ground."

Then there came the piercing sounds – whir and hiss – again and again, as arrows sang from the girl's bow in all directions, striking unknown targets. As each arrow hit its target there was the undeniable crunching sound of bodies thumping onto leaves. Twisted figures of fallen dead were scattered everywhere, to the left and right, each with an arrow squarely through the forehead.

Molly peeked out from the orc's black robe. The dead were hideous in appearance, with distorted faces, scarred and scabbed, their lips pulled back in a grimace, their teeth protruding and deformed. Each wore peculiar clothes made from skins, furs, twigs, and leaves. In their hands, each held a crudely made weapon.

Elizabeth had a disgusted look on her face as the stench of death filled the air.

"What are these horrible creatures?" she asked.

An Van Au jumped from the stump and made her way to the lead wagon.

"They are Ramblers," she said in a strong voice. "I was at the edge of the forest and saw several of them tracking you. Very strange. Ramblers are not known to work in groups." She turned to Bran. "I was concerned for my friend here."

She then placed two fingers in her mouth and filled the surroundings with a whistle of indescribable purity and power. A white horse galloped from the forest and with no effort, the girl sprang in one movement and swung herself into the saddle.

She looked around the forest, her eyes darting about as if seeking something. There was a strange gleam in her soft blue eyes.

"We do not have much time," she said. "The forest will soon change."

"Agreed," said Bran staring at her.

He raised his hand as all closed near to the wagons. He took the lead with An Van Au by his side.

Molly found the forest to be a world of deeper shadows, of sounds hushed and subdued, of aromas that were stale and stagnant, of light that seemed to come from an almost hidden source, of a sensation of being watched even when there was no one there. It was a place that was inviting and menacing at the same time.

She looked down at the Lia Fail. It lightly glowed red and instead of throbbing as it had in the past, there was a light hum to it. Then there came a gentle breeze to the air and with it a bit of sweetness.

Magic, she thought.

"Ramblers working together," said Brows to Fairfax. "In all my times here, I have never seen such a thing. Must be some form of powerful magic."

"Very powerful and malevolent magic to penetrate the Tangle," said Fairfax.

"The girl, do you think can she be trusted?" asked Brows.

Fairfax gazed at her on horseback, now far ahead of them with Bran. He studied her shrewdly. Somehow all this seemed right to him.

"Yes. She can be trusted."

* * *

After the incident at the hollow, the group encountered many Ramblers. They shuffled around with a crazed look about them, staring at the ground, mumbling, and at times laughing incessantly. With each step, their insanity seemed to be increasing. The girls were unnerved by them and were afraid that they would attack. As the group pressed on, there came a time when four Ramblers came at them. They looked less like the Ramblers they had previously seen and more like a chaotic pack of ravenous dogs. The girls did not know what to think, but they did know that they were protected. Quick snaps from An Van Au's bow and the Ramblers fell dead.

Maybe it was better for them to be dead, thought Molly. *But what a horrible thought to have.*

In time, the caravan came to an elevated point in the forest where there was a small opening surrounded by tall pines. As the caravan approached the opening, they could catch a glimpse of a golden valley below nestled amongst the mighty Old Hills. It was a breathtaking sight, and the girls were clearly enthralled, but more importantly, they were relieved to see the opening. The torturous forest changes were beginning to weigh heavily on them. They now understood how the Tangle easily corrupted those that dwelt in its trees and burrows. They were glad to be leaving it and its madness far behind. But Molly came to a sad realization.

"It just dawned on me," she told her sister. "I think the only way back will be through this forest."

Elizabeth sighed, tired and irritated. Just the thought of having to venture through the forest again was even more exhausting.

"This forest is a dreadful place," bristled Elizabeth.

"Do not worry," said Fairfax. "The forest's magic is less powerful on the return trip. Remember, the magic's purpose is to protect the city. Even so, we will still require the skills of a Tracker. Bran will again help us."

The girls were comforted by his words. Molly thought about what he had just said.

"It's as if the forest knows where you're going," she said. "Almost like it's a living thing."

He gave a hearty laugh.

"The Harrow is full of living things," he said. "One cannot escape that which is all around us."

As the caravan neared the forest opening, An Van Au raised her hand and the caravan stopped.

"We can rest here before traveling on," she told everyone. "If the forest changes, it will be far enough away from us." She pointed forward. "Up ahead is where the forest ends."

"No," said Molly abruptly. "I don't like this forest. We don't need to rest. We should leave this place."

Brows sighed.

"I could not agree more," he said. "If I am to stretch my legs, let it be far away from here."

An Van Au nodded. She raised her hand and the caravan continued through the small forest opening. Once beyond the Tangle, the group slowed in amazement. In front of them was the gilded city of Katzhu Pu with its golden edifices, nestled like a jewel amidst the vibrant green cradle of the Old Hills.

Molly had seen so many magnificent sights since beginning her journey, but none like this. She looked at the horizon, a mountain range dotted with snowcapped peaks. They were vast masses of stone and ice, and ruggedly beautiful. They were thickly covered with pine trees, poplars, oak, and evergreen hemlock; except where the rough bones of the mountains jutted out so boldly from the land. But her eyes quickly wandered to the city below. The late sun, from behind the forest's treetops, gave just a sparkle to the edges of the city's golden buildings.

"It's amazing!" she gasped. "A city of gold!"

Katzhu Pu's massive buildings and towering spires etched against the mountains, well protected by four great walls and four great tower battlements. The walls were lavishly decorated with symbols and carvings, and she could see that the streets were lined with columns and statues of gold, silver, marble, and ebony. In the center rose a domed structure of gold and mosaic. The gilded edifice was massive, hugging the citadel like an ageless monolith of faith and enduring security.

"The city is a monument to the glory of the past and the promise of the future," Fairfax told her. "It is built on the power of the Ra Cath faith."

She felt an overwhelming sense of wonder at the glorious view.

Then suddenly the golden city began to echo with the low-pitched, but surging chimes of bells. It was a call for the city's citizens to congregate.

"The Guild Lords bid us welcome," said Fairfax. "They know we approach."

The group slowly made its way along a stone path leading from the forest to the city's golden gates.

"When we get to the city, maybe I could ask Mr. Bran to ride Wildflower," Elizabeth said to Molly.

Molly shook her head.

"Something tells me from this point on,"she said, "we're not going to have time for such things."

* * *

The white cat gleefully turned a corner and ran down a long stone corridor.

"I do what I do and that's the best I can do!" he said.

Lil' Man and Chumsey slowed behind Ras Amon, peering down the stone expanse where they quickly realized it was a dead end. They could see the sallow cat arching his back, pacing back and forth, rubbing up against the stone wall at the end of the expanse.

"It seems we are at an impasse," Chumsey told Ras Amon.

The wizard smiled widely. Everyone watched as he walked down the long stone corridor moving into the shadows, steadied by his white staff. As he approached the end of the corridor, he gently stroked the top of the cat's head. He then lifted his arms and staff. White light streamed from his staff carving a doorway into the stone. The light was so bright that everyone had to turn their heads away. When it was over, they saw Ras Amon and the white cat standing outside on a ledge overlooking the Dagda valley and the golden citadel of Katzhu Pu.

Ras Amon beckoned to them with a wave of his staff. Ever so cautiously they walked down the stone corridor and joined him and the white cat on the ledge. Now outside, they were greeted with a spectacle the like of which they had ever seen. Katzhu Pu gleamed golden amidst a verdant valley, beautiful in its serenity. From where they stood and to the east and west the Old Hills cradled the valley; the mountaintops gold-rimmed in the setting sun. From the south stretched the Tangle forest; the tall pine trees looked like emerald green moss, its white haze and mists swirling amidst the flora like storm clouds. A gentle breeze swept from the valley and over the Old Hills. It brought the smell of pine but also the rolling sound of bells from the golden city.

"It seems the Guild Lords await our arrival," said Ras Amon.

The white cat rubbed up against his legs.

"I do what I do and that's the best I can do," he said nervously.

"I know . . . I know Shaer. You do not like the city. But you must be strong for me and our friends, eh?"

The cat began a slight purr.

The wizard and white cat started their descent down stone steps carved into the rock, zigzagging laboriously downward, twisting past tall trees and rock formations that encrusted tall cliffs. Carefully, the others followed. After rounding a bend, Glaeynd stopped and looked back up the stone pathway. To her surprise, the opening from the mountain had been closed, and the ledge and steps behind them were gone, disappearing completely beneath tumbled rock and brush.

Magic to avoid finding the mountain cities, she thought.

Turning back to follow the others, she looked down upon Katzhu Pu but her thoughts turned to her father and Mistmere, as they sooner or later always did.

Ras Amon stopped their descent. He looked back at her.

"There is no turning back," he told her. "We must move forward, always forward."

The red-orange of the waning sunlight sent shining ripples through the heavy waves of her long golden hair. She smiled at him but could not hide her sorrow. Her thoughts remained with her father and her beloved city of Mistmere.

"There is no point in looking for what once was," he said. "There is only one way to go now. Always moving forward."

There was a sparkle in his eyes. The others looked back at her. They understood.

She nodded and continued down the stone steps and the side of the mountain towards the golden city, the city where she had spent much of her youth.

* * *

Before entering the golden city, Ras Amon had everyone rest. While he sat on a rock cradling Shaer Thol, there was a light breeze, now brushing past, and he could feel the wind move his hair. He motioned to Lil' Man and Chumsey with a slight wave of his arm and watched as the two cats made their way through the others to join him. While he waited, he sat contemplating, doing what he could to take in the recent events and absorb them into what would soon occur. As he stroked the white cat who was purring, his mind was clearer than it had been for some time, so clear that he was prepared to address a matter he had delayed, a question that needed answering. He was now ready.

The two cats sat near him.

"Thank you for joining me," he told them. "I have been meaning to speak with both of you, on something that has lingered for a bit."

"What is it Learned One?" asked Lil' Man.

"The question you posed to me - the question about the Tar Malal."

Shaer Thol raised his head. The two cats were silent as the wizard looked down at the white cat and then off into the distance, to the golden spires of Katzhu Pu.

He continued: "You see, every creature is afraid of most aspects of life. We are afraid of disease, pain, old age, and all the sorrow that we know from the moment we are born. We are afraid of these things because they are always just around the corner. But we are afraid of something else, something that we do not know, that which we call death. We are afraid of death because it is also just around the corner, but also because we do not know what it brings. So, we are afraid of life, and we are afraid of death, and we are afraid of both because we understand neither. What we fail to understand, we fear. And, what we fear, we wish to avoid. This is your answer. It is a universal truth."

The two cats did not say anything or make any noise. They understood what the wizard had said. A moment passed when Lil' Man had a thought.

"How many universal truths are there?" he asked.

Ras Amon's gaze returned to the white cat and his two friends. He took a deep breath and smiled.

"Enough to fill the sky," he said. "Enough to fill the sky."

* * *

As Moondancer flew south, past the Cricklewood Forest to where the grassy plains of the Greenwood sloped up into the Strongdale Downs, he could see plumes of smoke from the west, in the direction of the Cairn; and far, far to the east, dark storm clouds amassed over the blackening Crag, bringing great shadows and beating rains over the Foghollow Barrens. He was fearful as a strong wind began to sweep over the lands, foretelling an ominous period. It soon became clear that his fears were justified for through the shadows of doom, he bore witness to a great army of evil marching west from Gortha-Losh.

I must quicken my pace, he thought. *Evil gathers on every front.*

With that, he thrust his great leathery wings onward, streaming through the clouds, in beautiful, blissful silence, all the time thinking of the news he would deliver to Erol Carrick.

The good wizard Fairfax brings news, of the desolation of Portmoor, of a tower at Ragmorok, and of treason by the Fenri at the hands of a Dark Wizard. And a great army of evil marches west from Gortha-Losh, towards the island city of Chyh-Mehm.

He rehearsed his words again and again, and he wondered what the revered Erol Carrick would do.

He has an immense force but faces tremendous odds, and now a war on several fronts, he thought. *A most difficult task even for the greatest of strategists.*

He was concerned. The upcoming war, like those before, could only produce terrible consequences for the Harrow. But as he began his descent through the clouds to the Thorndell Fields below, where the armies of the Tree and Axe spread for leagues upon the valley, the words of Fairfax rang through him . . . *When the forces of good find their backs against the wall, they can be most formidable.*

* * *

Perhaps of all the days in feline lore, the one most heralded, was when two groups each led by wizards came to take counsel with the Guild Lords on the same day, neither knowing of the other's arrival, one which traveled from the south through the Tangle and the other from the north through the peaks of the Old Hills. It would become known in the feline tongue as Vaelaer Sh' Talia, or *the day reached by many visitors*, and it marked a most momentous occasion. It meant, more than anything else, that something significant was about to happen. Rumors flew thick and fast as throngs of Katzhu Pu's cats crowded the narrow streets awaiting a chance to catch a glimpse of the visitors.

Before entering the city, it was decided that Fairfax would lead the caravan on foot followed by Bran and An Van Au. He led the caravan through the golden gates and into the city, following the twists and turns of the side streets and alleyways, shortcuts he knew well as he had visited the city often.

The girls looked about the large city. It was vast and endless with buildings built of solid gold, long straight streets, endless bridges, and incredible reaches of parkland. It was a sight unimaginable to them.

As they proceeded through the city, thousands upon thousands of cats lined the streets to watch as they passed. There were cats of every color, shape, and size, overflowing the sidewalks and onto the streets. Cats were leaning out of windows from buildings and others perched in windows and on rooftops. The girls could see some of the cats whispering to each other while others seemed to be gawking at them under what was now the deafening sound of the bells. This made them a bit uncomfortable, that was until some of the cats recognized Big Grey.

A shout came from a window. "It is he! He has returned! Look!"

"Lawgiver!" came another shout from the sidewalk. "We're so glad you're back."

"Welcome home!" another voice echoed.

Soon the crowds began to roar Big Grey's formal name over the bells.

"Sech Tur Midir El Tar! Sech Tur Midir El Tar! Sech Tur Midir El Tar!"

He sat upright in Molly's lap and acknowledged the crowd with a lift of his paw and a hint of a smile. There was great applause.

Molly remembered the greetings he received when they had traveled through Laurel Glen.

"It seems you're well known no matter where we go," she said.

Brows chomped on his pipe.

"Indeed, he is!" he said. "Some would say our friend here is a future Guild Lord."

"I will not hear of such talk," said Big Grey scolding Brows. "Mind yourself on this sacred ground. Do not speak of such things in this place. Heresy, it is and simply untrue."

Brows smiled and gave Molly a wink.

"Hmm . . . not what I have heard," he said.

The crowds of cats which continued to swell slowly started to part as the caravan approached the steps of the massive golden-domed structure called the Kaer Taraedar. The structure was immense, having grandness to its entrance. There were many golden steps leading to massive doors, and gold columns carved with precise twisted forms and inlaid with geometric mosaics. Looking down from the tall columns were several colossal golden statues of cats as if guarding the entrance. Flower petals, showy colored and bright, covered the golden steps on which sat two stout cats, motionless. They both were grey striped with white paws, and each was adorned with a red, white, and gold sash.

As the Kaer Taraedar's bells continued their rolling song, the throngs of cats pushed for a place closer.

"We must wait here," Fairfax told the girls. "We must wait until we are summoned by the cats you see on the steps. They're called the Thasaes for they speak as one."

As they waited, they saw that the crowds continued to grow, this time along the streets and alleyways opposite them. But something away from them started to attract more and more attention. Fairfax strained trying to look over the crowds of cats, to see who or what was drawing such attention. But he saw no one. Then the crowds began to slowly part.

"There! There!" said Brows. "Do you see them?"

"I do," whispered Fairfax.

He could see another group being led by an old man wearing a brown tattered robe. He had long white hair, and a beard, and was using a white, curled walking staff. He was carrying a white cat.

"Looks like there are two other cats, a girl, and what looks to be a pack of Fenri," said Brows. "Who do you suppose it is?"

Squinting, Fairfax tried as best he could to make out the features of the old man, but he was too far away. But as he drew closer, Fairfax thought he recognized him.

"It cannot be," whispered Fairfax in disbelief.

"Who is it?" pressed the bobbin. Who is it?"

"By the Maker . . . I believe it is Ras Amon," said Fairfax in astonishment.

Brows was speechless as he watched the old man approach. He too recognized him.

"The Maker is with us, my friend!" he burst out joyfully. "Thank the Maker! There's hope!"

"Ras Amon? I've heard that name before," said Molly.

"You have indeed, at Blackstone Keep," said an elated Brows. "Remember the story of the wizard who was killed at the hands of his student, in the discovery of an evil relic?"

"Yes, that's it," said Molly. "But he doesn't look dead."

Brows was smiling as he put away his pipe.

"No, he seems most alive," he said. "Thank the Maker he is! I am sure there is a very long story to be told, and in time we will know of it. He is a wizard of the Edainar, like our friend here. It is so good to see him and at a time when we can surely use his wisdom."

As the other group came closer, the girls recognized Lil' Man. They were happy to see their friend. They started to wave and call his name, but Big Grey stopped them.

"Hush now and be still," he told them. "There are formalities, protocols to be followed here. Shhhh . . . there will be time enough to speak with him. Remember you are a Queen and Princess of Ahlgren." He looked at Ug'ghi Otha and told Molly, "He should remain in the wagon. Donduin, Ancorbow, and Dithil can stay with him."

She wanted to argue this point but decided it was best to let it drop. She knew better than to argue with him. It worked out for the best as the orc agreed to the plan. So, they sat quietly, saying nothing, listening to the bells and watching the crowd and the others.

The crowd was joyous, watching the two groups approach one another, jubilant at the special treat that awaited them. Fairfax could not believe it was his old friend and hesitated at first until he was able to see the Mark of the Tree on his neck. He took a deep breath and ever so briefly reached out with his mind; he could sense the presence of good magic. There was no doubt now – in front of him stood Ras Amon, older and thinner, but it was the Learned One. He went to greet his old friend as Ras Amon gently placed Shaer Thol on the ground. The two embraced enthusiastically in the middle of the street, then stood back to inspect each other with critical eyes.

Fairfax smiled warmly. He was happy to see his old friend. They briefly conversed and he knelt to softly pet Shaer Thol. The lanky white cat seemed to take a liking to him, rubbing up against his legs, purring. He then stood and pointed his friend in the direction of the girls. Ras Amon looked at them and smiled. They returned his smile.

Molly saw that his eyes were clear and honest and that his face had a light of its own.

There is a pureness to him, goodness, something rare, she thought. *Just as with Fairfax.*

The cheers from the crowd grew louder and louder upon witnessing the reunion of the two old friends, and the streets seemed to swell with an even larger number of cats. Again, they embraced and spoke briefly, whispering in each other's ear, laughing, and thumping each other's back, as the cheers were still ringing. It had been too long since they had talked and both resolved to spend some time together, if possible, to correct that in the future. There was so much that needed to be told. All eyes were tearful as there was a great joy.

Suddenly the bells stopped ringing and the two cats who sat upon the steps, the Thasaes, each raised a white paw.

A peculiar silence overcame the crowd.

"The Guild Lords of Katzhu Pu have gathered," said the Thasaes, together, in one deep voice. "All who are now before us may enter this sacred place, all that is except the orc and the Tar Malal."

How did they know of Ug'ghi Otha? thought Molly. *And what is a Tar Malal?*

"Regarding the orc, he will remain in the wagon," shouted Big Grey. "He will be secured. It had already been decided."

Several cats appeared and surrounded the wagon, their faces streaked with red, black, and orange paint. They were of the Balor, the great warrior guild of the Ra Cath.

"The Lawgiver is recognized. It is agreed," said the Thasaes, speaking with one voice. They turned to Ras Amon. "What of the Tar Malal?"

A hushed nervousness came over the crowd as everyone looked to the Learned One who now held the sickly cat, gently stroking it.

"If you will not accept my friend, then I will not enter for I am of this creature, and he is of me," he told the Thasaes. "Inform the Guild Lords that at this time of great peril the Harrow must summon the abilities of all creatures."

A great murmuring and grumbling could be heard as the crowd was stunned by his unexpected response. They had come to know him and his feline companion, over the recent years and through their travels, not as a wizard or Tar Malal, but rather as friends.

All eyes fell upon the strange white cat when a feline voice, thinned by distance and a slight breeze, came from somewhere within the crowd.

"Let them in!"

The shout was soon going up from every throat.

"Let them in! Let them in! Let them in!"

These were passionate shouts; individual shouts that quickly became a collective call, erupting into a resounding chorus.

"Let them in! Let them in! Let them in!"

The Thasaes stood motionless. They looked at each other and then over the crowd. They lowered their paws.

There was a deep thump and clang as the monolithic golden doors slowly opened inwards.

"All may enter," said the Thasaes as one.

With that, the crowds cheered heartedly as both groups started up the steps led by the Thasaes, the two wizards, and the Tar Malal. Molly grabbed Elizabeth's hand and squeezed it hard. It was a gesture of love and her way of telling her sister that she needed her close by. Elizabeth nodded, her eyes revealing that she was there for her sister.

As the girls started up the steps, Lil' Man ran to Molly and rubbed up against her legs, and purred. She looked down at the small cat with a smile.

"I am glad you are here and well," she whispered.

Big Grey sniffed at Lil' Man.

"At least, you had the good sense to wash," he said with a smile.

"And to think I could have been enjoying myself back at the Crag," said Lil' Man, "But instead, I am here to enjoy your barbs."

Big Grey chuckled at Lil' Man shaking his head. Both were glad to see each other and to know that each was safe from harm.

"Big Grey, how did those cats at the steps know of Ug'ghi Otha?" Molly asked the cat. "And what is a Tar Malal?"

"The Thasaes have been given divine insight by the Guild Lords," he told her. "And as it regards the meaning of Tar Malal, you will soon find out."

As the group entered the Kaer Taraedar the place was filled with a brilliant light. The huge rotunda of the structure was magnificent, with a central nave and four side aisles. The aisles were divided into several sections by walls pierced with wide arches, ending on each side of the nave in massive piers. In front of these piers and at the corners of the nave were monolithic columns of gold. The rotunda was gorgeously decorated, too marvelous for words, with mosaics and polished gold, handsome and adorned. To the side, aisles were countless dark oak benches, and there were many towering golden statues depicting great feline warriors of the past. Above and circling about the monumental rotunda were two golden terraces with rows upon rows of benches. All around, tall panes of leaded glass stretching the full height of the structure allowed natural light to reach inside. At the far end were four large, gilded thrones engraved with cat designs, the arms of which were carved to resemble large paws.

As they approached the thrones, the bells began to chime again then peeled away softly as the crowds of cats entered the Kaer Taraedar, quietly, pushing and cramming for places from which to witness the coming event, until there was no space left. When all was quiet the Thasaes who now sat near the thrones turned to face the multitude. This of course meant that the Guild Lords would soon appear.

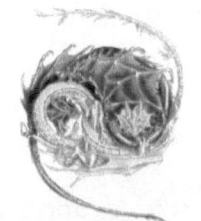

Chapter 13
The Guild Lords

THE UNMISTAKABLE SOUNDS OF bagpipes filled the breadth of the Kaer Taraedar with a melancholy symphony. The hard-edged, high-pitched tone was underscored with a solemn dirge sung in the old tongue by a multitude of feline voices. The sound of the pipes and voices was melodic and beautiful, yet it was eerily foreboding. The haunting sounds sent a chill through the air and set the hair on the back of Molly's neck on end. She shivered, but she was not sure why. She thought it best to not look around and kept her head down. As such, she did not see that four cats had appeared from four small doors on each side of the rotunda. They were the Guild Lords or Si Jhys. Each had a distinctive color and markings, were rather large, much larger than Big Grey, and they walked very slowly on the golden floor.

When Molly looked up, the four cats appeared able-bodied. She carefully studied each and discovered that they were old, ancient even. She remembered there would be four Guild Lords, one for each Guild: lawgivers, sages, healers, and warriors.

As the Guild Lords made their way to their thrones, Molly turned to Big Grey.

"How will I know which guild they represent?" she whispered.

"You will be able to tell by what they speak of," he whispered back.

When each had settled upon a throne, the bagpipes and dirge ended. The rotunda was silent, and all eyes were wide; everyone in the group stood before them without moving. Then one of the cats spoke in a low and slow tone. His voice was powerful, and it resonated through the rotunda like thunder.

"Welcome good wizard. We are happy to see you again, and we take it you are in good health," said the Belenus Guild Lord, the one who guided the healers. "We see you have brought many visitors with you, many of which are Cestal."

In the ancient feline tongue, Cestal was the word meaning *not of the same* and referred to creatures not of the Ra Cath, those that were not feline.

Fairfax stepped forward and bowed deeply before the Guild Lord. He cleared his throat.

"Yes, my Lord. I am feeling well," he said. "Those in our group who are Cestal are honored to be before you and in this magnificent and hallowed place. I would also say that some of us have received a most unexpected gift today." He turned to Ras Amon with a smile.

The Belenus Guild Lord paused and looked about the rotunda.

"We understand your surprise," he said. "Such gifts from the I' Ra Heru are wondrous and should never be forgotten or taken for granted." Fairfax nodded, casting down his eyes. The great cat continued: "We see those of the Ra Draug. Welcome cousins. We see those of the En' Edan and a Queen and Princess of Ahlgren. Such youthful exuberance in the Kaer Taraedar is indeed quite refreshing. It has been a long journey, but the Queen and Princess look well and fit for the task they will soon face."

"Yes, my Lord," said Fairfax. "They have traveled many leagues to take counsel here at the Kaer Taraedar."

He motioned to the group, and everyone gave a bow before the Guild Lord.

There was silence as each Guild Lord took time to gaze upon the girls. They stared at them as if trying to understand something about them as if they were trying to peer into their souls. The girls were uneasy in the silence, and even more uneasy with their stare. A peculiar sensation consumed them, a tingle on the skin, ever so lightly.

Molly believed she understood what was happening.

"It is a test," she whispered to her sister, "a test of our resolve. Do not be concerned. Be strong."

The uneasiness was soon broken as the supreme sage of wisdom, the Caridwen Guild Lord lifted a paw.

"The Professor has chosen well," he said, a voice as deep and reverberant as the Belenus Guild Lord. "We knew of this day. We have watched from afar."

He gave a charming smile.

The girls were relieved and carefully returned the smile.

"And we see two of the Balor Guild's finest have returned home," roared another Guild Lord with a powerful voice that shook the Kaer Taraedar. "We see Chum Sey El Ta and Oban Pan El Tar,"

He was the noble commander of the warrior guild, the Balor.

"The news you bring is known to us," he said. "Fear not, for you are most courageous, brave, and full of ardor! Act brave and you are brave!"

Chumsey and Lil' Man bowed deeply before him as great applause echoed through the rotunda.

The last of the Guild Lords raised a paw to quiet the applause. This was the Midir Guild Lord, the grand lawgiver. He looked at Big Grey.

"Welcome home, good Master Sec Tur El Tar," he bellowed. "We are so grateful that you are here. Your return to us is of great significance. We thank you in each moment because of your good presence in the lives of so many. There are many who trust their lives and their decisions to you. We are thankful for the great and abiding love you give to them."

Big Grey bowed.

"Thank you, my grace," he said.

The Midir Guild Lord then addressed the group.

"There are many Cestal in your company," he said. "Never has such a diverse gathering blessed the Kaer Taraedar, and never before have we been graced by the presence of two wizards of the Edainar."

There was applause.

He again raised a paw to quiet the crowd. He looked about the great hall and when all was silent, he turned his gaze to Ras Amon who stood cradling the sickly white cat. He held his look steadfastly upon Shaer Thol, a watchful eye.

"And, never has a Tar Malal entered this great hall, upon such sacred ground," he said. "Tell me, Learned One, what is to be gained by your insolence at the golden doors?"

A piercing hush came over the crowd. All eyes were on Ras Amon.

He thought for a moment and in the silence cleared his throat. He knew he had to be careful with both thought and words.

"My Lord, with the deepest respect," he said firmly, still caressing the scraggy white cat. "I have given this great thought. Even in your infinite wisdom, surely you do not deny that each of the Harrow's creatures brings a uniqueness born of the hands of our Maker. Purity of heart and soul is all our Maker has ever required of his creations. If there is one thing we have all been taught, it is that purity of body has never been a requisite in our Maker's eyes. Did not the I' Ra Heru speak of the obligation to others as the purpose of life?"

"My dear wizard, you do not understand," said the supreme lawgiver, calmly and logically, his eyes intent on Ras Amon. "We do not challenge our I' Ra Heru's teachings, nor do we attempt to give purpose to his judgment. In all his glory, he set upon the Harrow life eternal in such some manner whereby countless possibilities may occur. After all, life itself is but an iteration of that which has come before it and that which will follow. Variations are to be expected and acknowledged. But what you fail to understand is that for life to be sustained it must be structured, and governed by rules. It is such structure, such rules that provide safety and security. Your insolence violated our rules here, our law. If society is to endure it must do so under such principles. Would you not agree, Learned One?"

There was silence as everyone in the Kaer Taraedar anxiously awaited Ras Amon's response. Fairfax was worried that his friend could say something to anger the Guild Lords.

Be careful, thought Fairfax. *Now is not the time to put all at risk with rash words. Choose your words wisely.*

Ras Amon knew what had to be said. He gave a gentle bow.

"My Lord, please accept my offering of remorse," he said, humbly, avoiding direct eye contact with the Guild Lord. "I did not mean to be so abrupt. My intention was simply to represent the views of many and to express the importance of solidarity at this most urgent time." He slowly raised his eyes to the great cat. "My Lord, you said variations are to be acknowledged. Are they also to be embraced? Are there not times when the rule of law should be deferred for the greater of the whole?"

A murmur came over the crowd and then silence again. All eyes turned to the Midir Guild Lord who sat motionless, thinking the matter out.

But it was the Caridwen Guild Lord who spoke.

"Perhaps the Tar Malal has a role to play in what is to come," said the great sage, as if knowing something the others did not. "If he does then the conditions we hold must be set aside, for he can only play his part if this were to occur."

With a movement of decision, the Midir Guild Lord looked to the other Guild Lords. He then turned to Shaer Thol.

"I do what I do and that's the best I can do," the Midir Guild Lord said to the white cat.

Surprised, Shaer Thol looked up at the Guild Lord then turned to Ras Amon who was smiling down at him.

"It is fine, my friend," he told him. "It is fine. You can speak here."

The white cat with his bulging red eyes gave a shiver. He again looked at the Midir Guild Lord.

"I do what I do and that's the best I can do," he said to him in an accommodating tone.

The Guild Lord smiled and with a slight tilt of his head, gave a slow blink. Shaer Thol nodded. He understood.

The Guild Lord looked beyond Ras Amon and Shaer Thol and to the great gathering.

"Let it be known that on this day it is decided: the outcast shall be outcast no more," he declared.

There came cautious applause of pleasure and sympathy. The multitude was relieved that all had been forgiven. Fairfax smiled for he too was relieved, relaxing out of the tenseness.

The Guild Lord lifted a paw, quieting the crowd.

"Let it be known," he thundered, "that the Edainar respects the rule of law, and on this day of great importance, all will be as one!"

There was great applause.

Molly fixed her gaze on the strange white cat. She sensed strong magic in him. It was the same sensation she had when she first met Halbierd, only stronger.

I understand now, what a Tar Malal is, thought Molly. *They are outcasts of the Ra Cath. But there is powerful magic in him. This is perhaps what they fear.*

Then the Balor Guild Lord stepped forward. The rotunda grew silent. He was instinctively sensitive to the mood of a crowd. He continued to pause, almost excruciatingly so, with his front legs tightly folded, then started to speak.

"Let us be ready to take the battlefield together whenever danger calls," he said softly, uncoiling his front legs. His voice started to rise. "Let us not be afraid to die on the battlefield, let us be ready to die in defense of our freedom, for our future, and the lives of our children, and their children. Let us be united and strengthen the hands of each other by promoting a general union among us all." Then he roared, "What say you Katzhu Pu?"

There came thunderous applause from the crowd and responsive mirth. A chant of Eindraer! rang out confident, majestic, from within the rotunda and from outside, from the crowded streets and rooftops of the city. Repeatedly, with a thumping harmony - Eindraer! Eindraer! Eindraer! Rang over Katzhu Pu. The chant was loud enough to shake the Kaer Taraedar, more than loud enough.

Molly thought the chant strange, although she could not deny its raucous charm.

"What are they saying?" she asked Big Grey.

"They are signifying their acceptance," he said.

The crowd continued - Eindraer! Eindraer! Eindraer! Eindraer! The Guild Lords sat silently, allowing the chants to slowly fade till no sound whatever could be heard in the rotunda or on the city streets.

It was then when the Caridwen Guild Lord stared down at the girls.

"Come forth," he bellowed to them.

They hesitated. Fairfax softly patted their heads.

"Go ahead," he told them. "No harm will come to you."

He gently pushed them forward.

They cautiously approached the cat. As they got closer to him they could see he was truly an ancient creature. They could see his fur was black and grey with white sprinkled throughout, that he breathed deeply, and that his eyes slowly closed and opened.

"Do you love your uncle?" he asked.

There was a tenderness to his voice, purity, and ease of phrasing.

Molly did not hesitate.

"Why of course we do, sir. We love him dearly."

"That is good. Love is very special and for each of us, it is unique. It is a wonderful gift that should not be taken lightly, nor should it ever be taken for granted. Love is a special grace, a gift that will protect you, and it is more powerful than any weapon. Do you understand, my children?"

They nodded.

"Wonderful. This is how it should be," he said. He looked at the others. "Step forth good friends of the Edainar, our Fenri cousins, and those from Dunhollow."

The others made their way to where the girls stood.

"We know that darkness spreads across the east," he said to them. "We are aware of the Queen's plan that the Lia Fail shall go to the east." He shook his head. "Unfortunately, there is a sense of emptiness in life when there are few options and great responsibilities."

The Balor Guild Lord spoke, "However, when only one outcome is possible, such emptiness is readily overcome. Such a situation provides purpose to life. There is a sense of direction, of destination, and of what the future will bring. One can maintain a sense of hope and inspiration, knowing that one will succeed only by achieving one's goals." He then directed his words to Ras Amon. "Wizard, you also bring news from the east that darkness rouses powerful and grows each day."

"Yes, my Lord," said the Learned One. "There is treachery about. The Rakl has fallen and Mistmere is within an evil grasp. But the others can better speak to what has occurred."

He turned to Glaeynd. Her eyes told him she was nervous to speak. She felt that she should say something eloquent, something that would convey deep thought, but all she could manage was what she felt.

"My Mistmere is ruled by the demon clutches of a darkness unknown to me," she said. "My city cries out for help."

Unlike Glaeynd, Thurir did not hesitate to speak.

"Evil lurks over my lands," he said. "It took us by storm and my father . . . my father . . . well, I know not of where he is or even if he is still alive. What is to be done? How will the mighty Ra Cath help us?"

"And you, Fairfax?" asked the Balor Guild Lord. "What have you seen?"

"A vision came to me, a vision of horror and death," he said. "Darkness has awakened, and its mind turns to the conquest of all lands."

"We hear the cries of the helpless, the lamentations of war and death," said the Caridwen Guild Lord. "But restoration takes time. Have trust that there are plans. This evil has a strong hold on the land. It is an unrelenting desire for absolute power." He paused and stared at the girls, particularly Molly. He addressed her directly. "My Queen, the responsibility to rid the land of this evil is yours alone, for only you can free the Harrow of its grief. There can be but one ending to what befalls us now. Are you prepared for this burden?"

A burst of thoughts flooded her, too many to sort through. Still, as she looked into the Guild Lord's eyes, she felt more mature for her age than ever before, and she no longer considered herself a child. It was an odd notion because it did not come with any warning or instructions, only the firm awareness that this was what it was. It was strange. It did not feel anything like she had expected. But it was a pleasant notion, accompanied by a sensation of being in touch with who she was and who she was not. She was no longer a child in this place called the Harrow. She was instead the Queen of Ahlgren.

She was determined to let the Guild Lord know of her newfound self-awareness.

"Yes sir," she said confidently. "I have come to realize that there was a reason why my uncle wanted my sister and me to come here and a reason why he gave me this."

She held the Lia Fail firmly in her hand.

The Caridwen Guild Lord grinned broadly at her.

"Good! Your understanding is complete," he said. "But all is not as it should be. We know that you travel with a creature of the En' Rauko. He is distorted to us. His presence blocks our abilities to fully sense future pathways. This is of grave concern to us. So too are the complexities of your situation and your plans. Always be aware that you will have the aid of trusted friends. A small group will travel with you to the Crag. The man from Dunhollow will lead the company. He also possesses something of grand importance." He motioned to Bran with a paw. "Come forward and remove your gloves, good sir."

Bran did as was asked. When he removed his brown leather gloves, a glint of red turned into a crimson tide that filled the Kaer Taraedar. It was a breathtaking blaze of bright light from a simple ring, the stone of which was a brilliant red.

"By the Maker, I do not believe it," said Brows in disbelief. "It is the ring, the ring of King Aelis. Donduin was correct after all."

Ras Amon and Fairfax were astonished at the revelation. They smiled at each other, knowing they now had a second, formidable weapon at their disposal.

The crowd became quiet and still, listening with rapt attention.

"That which was lost has been found," proclaimed the Caridwen Guild Lord.

A mighty cheer arose from the crowd, swelling quickly to a roar.

"My dear young man, you possess a shard of the Fail stone," the Caridwen Guild Lord told Bran. "You are of the family Arundel, from the lost line of Dalrick, of House Riorn. It is as we thought."

"You are most wise my Lord," said Bran, standing before the Guild Lords confident and poised. "Long have I known of this, from my father, who told me of the story as he took his last breath. I have long accepted this destiny, waiting for this time, and now it is here." He turned to the multitudes lifting his fist high into the air, the red from the ring blazing through the rotunda. "The death of my ancestors I shall revenge, aye, if I shall suffer death thousands of times over for it," he exalted. "As I stand before you, I promise to all, the evil now before the Harrow shall fall whatever the cost!"

The crowd erupted in applause. It began quietly from a few voices, then got louder as more joined in until the rotunda shook with frenzy.

"Cyri Tas! Cyri Tas! Cyri Tas!" shouted the crowd, which in the feline tongue is *victory now!* "Cyri Tas! Cyri Tas! Cyri Tas! Cyri Tas! Cyri Tas! Cyri Tas!"

But through the craze, a sense of concern, of urgency came to Big Grey. He thought back to Dalgaes and their meeting at Blackstone's Garden Courtyard.

Caedaes, one with the spell, thought the cat. *Who is the man's Caedaes?*

He searched the rotunda when for an unknown reason he was drawn to gaze upon An Van Au. He scrutinized her face, staring into her blue eyes, fine and clear like drops of rain, trying to decide if it was her and if she was trustworthy or not. Eerily, as if she knew what he was thinking, she met his stare with an unwavering gaze, looking past the cat's light green eyes for a glimpse of the soul beneath.

Is it her? he thought. *Is she Caedaes to the second known stone?*

Her eyes narrowed.

Yes, it is I, Lawgiver, her thoughts whispered to him.

He returned the look and gave a slight nod.

The Caridwen Guild Lord raised a paw and quieted the crowd. Everyone was astonished over the sight of the second shard ablaze. Molly remembered the story told by Donduin, about a second shard fashioned as a ring. She was uncertain as to what it all meant. But one thing was certain: she would make sure that Brows informed Donduin that in fact, he was right about the ring.

Bran put his gloves back on. He bowed before the Guild Lords, then stood tall like a tree in silence.

The crowd quieted.

"The forces of good are strong this day," said the Caridwen Guild Lord. "Irrevocable events are now set in motion. Plans are required against the sinful empire and its desire to take hold of the future. Both shards from the Fail Stone shall travel east. The good wizard shall take a force to the Rakl to restore the realm for our cousins, the Ra Draug. The Learned One shall travel west. It is as it should be."

But Fairfax was surprised by what he heard.

"My Lord, and with all humility, should not I or the Learned One accompany the Queen to the Crag?" he asked.

"My dear wizard, you know as well as I that magic senses magic," the Guild Lord told Fairfax. "A wizard's magic surrounds him like an aura. It is easily noticed by those sensitive to such things. On the other hand, the Fail shards are small, their power barely noticeable until unleashed. If the Fail shards are unused, until such time when it is necessary to wield their power, they will travel unnoticed. You must do as has been directed. We have seen many futures, although clouded. Our direction provides the best hope for all. But there is one more thing. Know that it will be wise for you to first visit the Paragon at Mortha Vale. There is a gift he should present to you upon your asking."

Gift? thought Fairfax. *What could it be?*

Ras Amon was also concerned.

"My Lord, why must I travel west?" he asked. "Would it not be wise to combine our forces somehow?"

"Learned One, we have seen visions and dreamed dreams," said the Guild Lord. "To forget them or to refuse to act upon them would be treachery to the Harrow. We have felt an evil presence growing to the west, south of Portmoor. The Aina Dur will soon be defiled as great darkness rises. It is your destiny to face the past. You must travel there. Along the way, you will gather with some of Carrick's men. The Aina Dur must be preserved at all costs."

A hush came over the great rotunda that was intense and solemn. It was a silence like that of death. Everyone present thought of the evil and shivered, chilled to the bone. Molly had a similar reaction, remembering the beauty of the Aina Dur and the surrounding lands when they first came from under the tree. Now, images of death and destruction came screaming to her. For Fairfax, the situation was indeed calamitous and extreme, and the Guild Lord's statement only raised the urgency of the matter.

Fairfax broke the silence.

"My Lords, our resolve will remain strong, and we will be united in purpose," he said, "as we have done before when called to respond to a threat to our way of life. We shall not underestimate the risks, dangers, and uncertainty we face. We face a real enemy in this world, an enemy who seeks our death or destruction. But what of Carrick? What have you seen?"

"Ah, the Great Carrick!" thundered the Balor Guild Lord. "He will be compelled to meet a dark army to the east. War will rage on several fronts, for you see a great process of transformation is before us."

"We have seen all this and more," said the Caridwen Guild Lord. He paused as calmness awaited his next words that came in a subdued whisper, "We have seen the White Knight on the battlefield."

The crowd gasped.

"The White Knight?" said Fairfax. "What does this mean?"

The Caridwen Guild Lord hesitated and shook his head.

"We are uncertain," he said. "We only see fleeting images of the future. We do not know what is in the I' Ra Heru's heart."

"The Maker brings us the White Knight, who is descended from a spirit king," said Ras Amon solemnly. "It is said he shall do many great deeds, and he shall see the wisdom of all the Maker has done. If the Maker brings us the White Knight, surely we are indeed in the most difficult of times."

Hearing all the talk of plans, Glacynd had become impatient. No mention was made of Mistmere. Even with Ras Amon's guidance, her thoughts turned to her father and Mistmere and their struggles. Many emotions welled up in her, but the strongest was an unwillingness to endure any more talk that did not include Mistmere. Where before she hesitated to speak, now she would be heard. She would no longer remain silent.

"Wait!" she shouted angrily. "I have heard the stories of spirit kings and the White Knight. But talk of them does nothing to help Mistmere. Tell me . . . what of my father and his city?"

The Guild Lords were silent at the outburst. Such a tone was frowned upon in the Kaer Taraedar, an indiscretion within the holy place. But everyone understood her emotions.

"Ah yes, the daughter of Kraneth, Lord of Mistmere speaks," said the Caridwen cat. "Be calm and you will understand these hard words. Know that no good can come to covering the truth at such times. My dear, your city is gone for now. It is under an evil spell, and it will be used to launch a most wicked army. Larger battles must now be waged before the city can be liberated. But know that there are some, those loyal to you and your father, with whom you may yet meet up with."

She stood silent at the Guild Lord's words, words that fed the source of her greatest fear. The others could feel how the cat's truth rushed over her. They could feel the shock break upon her, the sudden clarity of it all. Her body shuddered. She had lost everything that mattered to her: her father, family, and the city she so loved. Lil' Man quietly moved to her and gave a gentle rub to her legs.

"It will be fine. You will see," he whispered.

The Caridwen Guild Lord looked upon Thurir.

"And cousin," he said, "are you pleased with the plan? It is with great hope that the Rakl should return untainted to our Ra Draug brethren."

Thurir bowed in affirmation. He was pleased that he would soon return to his kingdom to again establish the sovereignty of the Ra Draug. He was aware of the added responsibility of lordship and leadership that perhaps awaited him, and more troubling, the fight to regain the throne, perhaps against his brother.

If I were to battle my brother and be victorious, how would the stain of my brother's killing be cleansed? he thought.

The Caridwen Guild Lord heard Thurir's thoughts.

"The high tide of time washes away the memories of some moments," he told him.

Thurir bowed in affirmation.

Fairfax and Ras Amon understood the situation was frightful. The reality of it all came to them with terrible clarity. Engaged in a war on many fronts, with overwhelming groups of converging enemies, they knew that the forces of good would have to maneuver quickly. But there was one force, one great instrument of good that had not been discussed.

Looking at the Balor Guild Lord, Fairfax stroked his long beard. He thought of a most important question. He hesitated at first then decided to speak.

"Will the Guild Lords summon the forces of the Kyr Thysaer?" asked Fairfax.

His words brought a hush to the rotunda as the crowd awaited a response. The Guild Lords slowly looked at each other when abruptly the Balor Guild Lord jumped from his throne.

"Well, of course!" shouted the Balor cat. "What would war be without the great warriors of the Ra Cath?"

A great thunderous cheer rose from the rotunda and from all that had gathered outside on the streets. The sound was deafening and shook the Kaer Taraedar.

The Balor Guild Lord raised his head and gave a mighty roar. To the girls, it sounded like a lion, or maybe an angry bear. They jumped and looked up, startled.

"My friends, we are done here," he told the group over the cheering masses. "Quickly, make haste and retreat to the golden steps so you may witness what few Cestal have ever seen – the coming together of the Kyr Thysaer."

Looking around her, Molly felt a surge of anticipation. They began to push their way through the crowd and to the golden steps.

"Hurry . . . hurry . . . you mustn't miss it!" one cat gleefully told them.

"Quickly now Cestal . . . see what the I' Ra Heru brings to our enemies!" said another.

"Oh, it'll be the most amazing sight ever witnessed. You'll see . . . you'll see . . ." said yet another.

As they made their way through the crowd, the Balor Guild Lord stood on his hind legs before the Kaer Taraedar's multitudes. He closed his eyes and raised his front paws high into the air.

"Let it be known," he proclaimed in a crashing voice, "that on this day I call on the mighty Balor - to run! Kyr Thysaer! Val Shas! Kyr Thysaer! Val Shas! Dream about the moment we are one!"

At those words, the rotunda erupted in celebration. Applause resounded and a chant started, a chant that turned into a spreading, growing roar.

"Kyr Thysaer! Val Shas! Kyr Thysaer! Val Shas! Kyr Thysaer! Val Shas!"

Louder and louder, the words became more passionate, following the group as they made their way through the mass of cats to the top of the golden steps.

"Kyr Thysaer! Val Shas! Kyr Thysaer! Val Shas! Kyr Thysaer! Val Shas!"

Outside, the throngs of cats were immense and still growing. The wagons had been moved aside and the street had been cleared. As the chant grew louder, the cats became even more enthusiastic. They knew the Kyr Thysaer would form.

"Kyr Thysaer! Val Shas! Kyr Thysaer! Val Shas! Kyr Thysaer! Val Shas!"

Molly squeezed her sister's hand in fear.

"What's happening?" she asked Brows.

"My Queen, you will soon see the mightiest of all forces," he said, "perhaps the greatest force known to all worlds. It is something not even the Professor has seen, the moment when all become as one, when the great cat clowder is formed."

"Clowder?" she shouted over the noise. "I've not heard of that word. What's a clowder?"

"Just watch," he shouted back.

The girls held on to each other as the great chant rose all around the Kaer Taraedar and through the streets of Katzhu Pu.

Drums began to beat - louder and louder still.

"Kyr Thysaer! Val Shas! Kyr Thysaer! Val Shas! Kyr Thysaer! Val Shas!"

Cats scurried about. Some were standing and cheering, jumping on each other, whirling in a dervish dance to the sound of the drums, while others, those of the Balor Guild began to gather in the street. Thousands upon thousands gathered, a horde of cats taking formation. The great warrior cats had war paint on their faces and bodies. Streaks of red, black, and orange made them look like demons rising from the depths of darkness. The scene was one of hysteria.

The drums started to roll even louder and the ground rumbled.

Dum – dadumdum – dadada – dum – dadumdum – dadada – dum – dadumdum – dadada – dum – dadumdum – dadada.

Over and over again the drums roared, and bagpipes began to wail, while masses of Balor cats continued to collect in the street like swarms of bees. The gathering cats started to tightly pack together. They began a slow march, lifting their paws high to the thunderous beat of the drums, their eyes afire with excitement.

Dum – dadumdum – dadada – dum – dadumdum – dadada – dum – dadumdum – dadada – dum – dadumdum – dadada.

The march of the cats kept up steadily as more and more of the Balor cats joined what was becoming a massive torrent of felines.

Then the girls saw Lil' Man and Chumsey jump into the swarm, quickly becoming lost in the mass of fur which now appeared as fire. Looking on, they could no longer tell individual cats apart in the mass of felines that now swelled before them.

Dum – dadumdum – dadada – dum – dadumdum – dadada – dum – dadumdum – dadada – dum – dadumdum – dadada.

Faster and faster the drums rolled as the last of the Balor cats joined the massive heaving beast of flame, the Kyr Thysaer.

Suddenly, a crescendo of drums and bagpipes blared releasing the beast. Faster than one could imagine, the throng of Balor cats now as one sped through the streets and from Katzhu Pu. Those cats that remained continued their frenzied whirling dance to the drumbeat, cheering and applauding.

"Where are they going?" Molly asked Big Grey.

"They will travel south to the Thorndell Fields to join with Erol Carrick's forces," he said. "It is a journey that would take us several days, but the Kyr Thysaer will run day and night and most likely arrive in a day or so. They travel at great speed. Nothing will slow them, nor will they stop. Just hearing the drums gives my heart a rush and I still myself at the sight of the Kyr Thysaer's strength."

"But won't they'll trample on things along the way!" said Elizabeth.

"Not to worry," purred the cat. "The sound of the drums is a notice of caution and there are many Balor cats that run ahead of the Kyr Thysaer. They will warn those who may be in the way."

"What about the forest? How will they get through the forest?"

The cat gave a mischievous smile.

"Magic stops for the Kyr Thysaer," he said.

They stood in silence atop the golden steps for what seemed like forever, their eyes fixed upon the massive Kyr Thysaer as the tide of felines endlessly surged past them, studying what was easily the most intimidating site ever witnessed. Donduin joined them and without a prompt from Molly, Brows told him of Bran and the ring. At this, Donduin laughed and slapped the bobbin on the back. Both were joyous and reveled in the sight now before them. For Ug'ghi Otha who was watching from the wagon, the sight of the Kyr Thysaer was unbelievable. Never had he seen such wonder and he gasped in amazement. Even Thurir and his pack were without words. They had heard tales of the Kyr Thysaer, stories about the fierce Balor cats, but they could not have imagined such power. Molly looked up at Bran who now stood alongside her, his arms crossed, his stance proud and fearless. What she thought was tied to what she felt and what moved through her heart.

The Balor Lord's words resounded through her mind.

Dream about the moment we are one!

She now understood the meaning of the word clowder.

***

They would spend the night under the hospitality of the Guild Lords. The girls, and of course Big Grey, would share a majestic room overlooking the golden city. The others would have private rooms which too were gloriously adorned, that is except for the orc who would remain outside in the wagon and under close guard. In the morning, as planned, they would meet as a group and make their final preparations.

As the girls and Big Grey walked a long hallway to their room, Big Grey stopped and appeared to be in deep thought.

"What are you thinking about?" asked Molly.

"I had a thought. While we are here, I would like to visit a special place, a place that is important to cats," he said. "I'd like you to come with me."

"Of course. Will we be long?" asked Molly.

"It will only take as long as you wish," he purred.

She found his answer a bit odd, and this excited her curiosity. His manner seemed genuine. So, the girls followed him. They were silent as they walked, passing through several doorways, and down what seemed a labyrinth of hallways until they came to a golden stairway that descended into a bright light.

"This is the place. It is a most sacred place to the Ra Cath," said the cat. "It is the tomb of Ra Carathor, the Prime Heru, the first of the great felines of the Ra Cath. I will pass first and then you two will follow. But first, you will need to face the Guardian. Tell the Guardian your name and answer his question truthfully. He will respond with wise words, words you should remember, and never tell anyone. Then he will allow you to pass, as long as you are truthful."

Molly was puzzled.

"What? Guardian?"

The cat looked up at the girls.

"Trust in me and don't worry," he said.

They slowly descended the golden stairs to a massive entranceway that was solid gold and composed of two large spiral half arches each sitting on a tall column. Along the spiral arches glowed hundreds of glyphs. As the arches rounded upward they came to a large golden carving of a large feline face.

They approached the arches and could see that the brightness came from a large room beyond the entranceway. The intensity was almost blinding but the girls' eyes seemed to adjust.

Big Grey turned to the girls.

"Remember my instructions," he told them.

He then walked through the entranceway and into the brightness.

The girls were next. As they approached the arches, the light grew brighter and they heard a rumbling hum. They stopped. The feline face carved within the top of the golden entranceway caught Molly's eye. It moved up and down and from side to side and glared at them.

The Guardian, thought Molly.

They remembered the cat's instructions.

Elizabeth took a deep breath.

"I'll go first," she said.

Molly nodded and watched as her sister stepped closer to the entranceway. It appeared as if she was talking to the Guardian, but Molly could not hear any sound over the hum. Elizabeth looked back to Molly and then was gone, through the entranceway.

Molly approached the entranceway. The rumbling hum seemed to dissipate.

The golden feline face stretched out to her.

"Speak your name, human child?" came the Guardian's voice. It was deep and commanding.

"I am Molly, niece to the Professor, Queen of Ahlgren," she said. Her words were firm despite her nervousness.

"What do you fear?" asked the Guardian.

She hesitated. She had never been asked this question before.

Quickly! What do I fear? I must be truthful. What do I fear? What is it?

She could sense the Lia Fail warm and gently throb. Then the answer came to her.

"I don't know."

"Molly, niece to the Professor, Queen of Ahlgren, you may enter this sacred of sacred places," said the Guardian. It paused briefly, "Search for the voice that is silent."

The brightness dimmed and she walked through the entranceway.

Before she could look about the tomb Big Grey was at her feet.

"Do not speak of the Guardian's words, ever," he reminded her and abruptly walked away.

Search for the voice that is silent.

She looked about the golden vastness before her. She felt an emotion that she had never experienced before wash over her senses. There was something different about this place. Her conscious mind seemed to ebb away leaving her with a profound silence. The silent splendor of the moment entranced her. Her eyes took in intricate carvings on gold screens that hung from the walls; every detail seemed to come alive. In the center of the room was a glass structure, a sarcophagus, raised upon a dais of gold, and alongside it stood Big Grey and Elizabeth. There were many other cats in the room too, sitting or lying down, seemingly in quiet reflection or prayer.

Big Grey cast a sidelong glance at her. She made her approach to join them slowly and quietly, so as not to disturb the other cats.

Within the glass sarcophagus, she saw a very large cat. It had the appearance of a lion, but its shoulders were wider. The cat was placed on its side. Its eyes were closed. It was muscular, with long, velvety fur and three hues blended in - a flaming, burnished orange, black, and white. The cat's face was beautiful, strong but at the same time gentle.

There is a greatness to him, she thought.

She became entirely absorbed in a most profound calmness and reverence. She closed her eyes, and a vision came to her, of a little butterfly with a ripped wing. It landed on her shoulder. She went to touch it, but it flew away. She was not exactly sure what it meant, but it made her happy. The vision felt like it was supposed to mean something.

She opened her eyes and gazed upon the great cat.

The butterfly. It is your soul. You came to see me, to show me that everything will be fine, that I am growing in life, much like the butterfly does.

Just then, a strange voice was heard.

"You saw the butterfly?" said the voice.

Another cat had joined them. He was large, an imposing figure, almost twice the size of Big Grey. His fur was brown with streaks of black, and his ears were erect and pointed. His eyes were yellow, but more than just yellow - they were a vibrant golden yellow, and they shimmered, looking otherworldly. He was staring at her.

"Why yes. How did you know?" she said returning the cat's look.

"I know because I was there with you. We came together at that moment in time."

He turned and left the tomb without another word. The other cats, those that remained in the golden chamber, stood and bowed as he passed by.

"Who was that?" she asked Big Grey.

"He is Ra Correus, the Sil' Heru, or Great Leader of the Ra Cath."

She stood frozen for a moment, unable to take her eyes from the great cat as he left. She was drawn into his fleeting presence, feeling an instant connection to him on a level she could not fathom, much less explain. It was an extraordinary effect on her senses.

"I had a vision and he saw it with me. I don't understand," she told Big Grey.

"You do not have to understand," he said. "You just have to believe."

When they left the great place, they walked in silence through the hallways; no words had to be spoken. That night, Molly slept restful and deep for the first time since coming to the Harrow.

***

Before retiring to their rooms, Fairfax and Ras Amon spent time in a small library off the rotunda. The library was a glorious place, adorned with oak cabinets and shelving, with an exquisite woven carpet of red and gold. It was a place filled to the brim with books that just about reached the already high ceiling. The books were neatly arranged and all in order. In the center of the room was a golden fireplace where a fire crackled cheerfully. It was a welcoming sight to all who entered.

They sat near the warm fire in chairs behind a low table. The Learned One cradled Shaer Thol in his lap, gently stroking the gangly cat, who half-closed his red eyes with a gentle and soft purr. They made small talk and then discussed the day's events. They started to reminisce about their youth, about times in which they had behaved in willed and irresponsible ways. They talked and laughed, and then their conversation turned to themselves and more recent times.

Ras Amon recounted his tale with Foulhand at Drar Druul. He spoke of his healing, his depression, his friendship with Shaer Thol, his many travels, and his deep desire for atonement. He could see the gleam in his friend's eyes as he listened intently, picturing the events as spoken, sympathetic in the tales told.

Fairfax then shared his stories, of battles long fought against the brood, of great heroism, honor, and loyalty. He spoke of anecdotes and sometimes histories. It was an oration that missed no shade of expression, no reach of grasp. When the conversation had slowed and there was a bit of silence, he decided to ask a question that troubled him.

"Why did you not return to Blackstone?"

"Would the Dominar have me?" said Ras Amon shaking his head.

"The Dominar is many things. He is stubborn and deliberate in thought. At times he can be controlling to a fault. But he is no fool, my friend. He would have embraced the Learned One."

Ras Amon sat there staring into the flames, his mood quickly turning to agitation.

"Learned One? Learned One?" he said in a terse manner. "Did you say Learned One? Are you referring to the same person who couldn't control his apprentice? The same person who wreaked evil upon this place, an evil so voracious that it once again demands to be fed? The same person who for years wallowed in an ocean of blood knowing that it was he and he alone who had unleashed death? The same person who was so enfeebled he could barely touch his staff, while thousands of innocents died. Is this the Learned One you speak of?"

Fairfax felt the anger and sadness sweeping through his friend, the kind of emotions he could not begin to understand. This was a side of him he had not experienced; the intensity and speed of the emotions worried him.

For Ras Amon, these were emotions hidden within the darkness of his mind, firmly rooted in his soul. These were melancholy emotions, a torment born of guilt that gave rise to fury. They were of a deep, authentic, all-encompassing sadness that even he had difficulties dealing with.

Fairfax reached out and firmly grasped his friend's arm.

"I do not wish to anger you or raise memories that are haunting," he said. "It is not my intent. I do not wish to so burden you with such pain."

Ras Amon turned to Fairfax with tearful eyes.

"Pain! You know nothing of the pain I feel?" he said. "It is so cutting that your beloved Learned One has committed Amin Tarn more times than he wishes to remember."

Fairfax quickly looked away from his friend and stared at the fire. Amin Tarn carried a horrific emotional weight, for it was the forbidden act of a wizard spelling himself. It was an elixir, an addiction, to those wizards of weak mind and spirit, that if uncontrolled would drive a wizard mad in an illness that could never be alleviated. Wizards who became addicted to their spells were banished to the darkest of Blackstone's dungeons, never again to see the light of day.

He turned back to his friend.

"We shall not speak of this again," he told him. "All that matters now is that you are here. Soon, you will face the one who has brought you so much agony."

"You speak of vengeance," said Ras Amon. "You do not understand. But then again, how could you. I have no interest in vengeance. For vengeance is but madness, a walk in rain and darkness." He looked at Fairfax with a determined stare, almost ruthless in its exactness. "I will again meet my apprentice as you have said and I will destroy him, but in doing so I will destroy myself. We will go into the blackness as one."

Fairfax looked away. A profound sadness came over him as his stare returned to the fire. Time had changed his friend and sadly, it seemed there was nothing he could do. The two sat together, silent for most of the night, looking to the flames for answers. But none came.

* * *

The drums and bagpipes of Katzhu Pu sounded a distant echo throughout the land. It was the echo of war, and the steady thunder told the land that the Kyr Thysaer had been released. Across the Harrow, fields, and streets were emptied as townsfolk shuttered windows and bolted doors. Entire households gathered at windows, waiting, watching for the Kyr Thysaer. For most, it would not come, but for some, it would charge by in a thunderous wave, slithering to the distant thumping of the golden citadel's sounds.

The Kyr Thysaer was through the Tangle and across the North Downs in no time, heading south to Greenvale. The lead Balor cats would lead the ferocious Kyr Thysaer beast from Greenvale along the Greenway and then south, cutting a swath through the Strongdale Downs, past Lindisfarne, and to the Thorndell Fields.

The beat of the drums and bagpipes could be heard in the wind, deep throbs of sound that reached far and wide, over mountains and rivers, over dales and hills. It was a sound that called forth hope and courage from the hearts of the thousands who were preparing to lay down their lives in war. It was the sound of pride and purpose and the promise of victory.

Far from the golden citadel, Roundthaler, Carrick, and Moondancer stood on a hill overlooking the enormous armies of Ahlgren and Mortha. They could hear the sounds.

"Drums from the north. It can only mean one thing," said Roundthaler.

"Hmm . . . it is rare when drums are heard from the north," snorted Moondancer.

But Carrick stood silent, deep in thought. Moondancer had told him the news of the destruction of Portmoor and the treason at the Rakl. The inevitability of what was now occurring confronted him like a specter that would not leave him, and it filled his every thought.

There will be war on many fronts, he thought. *It will consume the Harrow.*

Along the horizon to the south, he could see dust clouds spiraling ever upward, signaling the march of the massive army. It was the army of men from the Eldor, led by I'Kinillel. For two days and two nights, the great army plodded wearily on the dust-choked roads. They moved at a steady pace. They knew it would not be easy, having expected little else when they set out, but they were trained for it and expected to be ready for they were marching to war.

To the east, he saw dark clouds growing denser, and with them came a squall of wind, while to the west, new darkness foreshadowed the sorrow to come. It crept its way across the lands like an animal stalking its prey.

Roundthaler slapped Carrick on the back.

"Argh, are you not listening, my friend?" he said. "Can you not hear the drums? The Guild has called the Kyr Thysaer! The battle is soon on its way!"

Carrick quietly maintained his stare at the horizon.

"I hear, I hear, good friend," he relented. "The whole of the Harrow hears the drums. The brood hears them as well."

"Ha! Let the evil minions know their fate!" thundered Roundthaler. "Soon the banners of the Claw and the Fist will join us! Aye, this will surely be a most glorious fight!"

Carrick clutched the small leather pouch containing Gallia's vial. It seemed to speak to him, of impending doom to the west. He knew what was needed.

"Dispatch Theor Thaken and his legion to the west," he ordered Roundthaler. "The brood will make its way to the Aina Dur. The tree will be under siege and the worms will befoul the library. Tell Thaken that the tree must be secured."

"Is this wise?" asked Roundthaler. "Thaken is brash and his men fierce. We could use his legion against the brood that marches from the east."

Carrick was firm and emotionless.

"Thaken will either secure the Aina Dur or he will fail," he said. "If he fails, he may slow the brood that gathers in the west and at least give us some much-needed time. I am in no mood to debate strategy. I have given an order. Go and tell him now."

Roundthaler was displeased with Carrick's frame of mind. He grumbled and walked away, waving his friend off with a caustic laugh.

"My good friend, I will follow you to the ends of this world," he said, his words slowly surrendering to the thumping of the drums. "But by all that is good do not hasten our demise by your foul mood."

He gave a stern glance over his shoulder to Carrick who was expressionless.

Moondancer looked down at Carrick.

"Someone once told me," he sighed, "that battles are won and lost before a warrior steps foot on the battlefield. I remember when you spoke those words. My friend, I fear you are much too distant."

He turned and walked away leaving Carrick alone.

The glow on the hills turned to gold as the sun began to set. The tall, white-bearded and stately Carrick stood unmoved, staring out across the fields, squeezing the leather pouch. He remembered the forest of hemlocks and pines; he remembered the forest muse Gallia; he remembered her haunting words.

Fear death, she told him, *the lost opportunity to say goodbye.*

* * *

It had been a long march for the massive dark army, through the Dregec Kuul Pass and just beyond the Ug' Foul marshes when it emerged from the Crag led by the Uth' Egoreyr. The sound of the brood beating their swords on their shields was deafening, and the ground trembled beneath the tread of the countless columns of evil warriors. They had paused for only a moment to sniff the air and take in the scene before them, and then they had continued their march, knowing that the armies of the good and righteous would have to be dealt with. The air would soon be thick with the stench of blood and death, and the screams of the dying would echo dully across the land.

Several Uakor Turg, Dark Riders, swooped down from the sky riding fiendish black ajatars, filling the air with a foul stink. The evil swarm slowly marched forward when in the distance the thumping of Katzhu Pu's drums could be heard. At first, the muffled drumbeat went unnoticed by the throngs of brood, until the force neared the open Snowwynne Barrens where the wind swirled, seizing the sound and lifting it high like a storm. It rose and intensified, spreading on the wings of the coil, filling the barrens with a mournful melody as the gale gave it strength. Soon the thumping of the drums became mixed with the skirling of bagpipes and rhythmic chants. The monolithic black army froze, stunned into silence. It began to recoil in surprise and fear.

But Grimsor would have none of it. The tall Urur Maw stood unflinching with orange eyes staring with great bloodlust.

"Weak scum! Maintain your march!" he shouted, his voice rising to a yowl above the thumping of the drums. "You whimper at a mere sound in the wind! March fools! March!"

The brood began to slowly move forward, but only at the stinging lashes of whips from Urur Maws and the screams of the Uakor Turg. Then there came a shout from the ranks that they all could hear.

"But master . . . the drums . . . the cats have been summoned!"

Grimsor raised his hand stopping the army. Deadly silence came over the brood. They were frightened. There was only one penalty for disobedience or neglect of duty: death.

Grimsor gazed over the ranks of his hellish force, his stare eventually falling upon a large, misshapen troll. He was as big as a small tree and covered in fur with a pointed snout like a beak. His large eyes were round, and his mouth full of sharp teeth, ready to tear off a person's arm at the first chance. But now he only cringed in fear at Grimsor.

Grimsor approached the troll and howled. His menacing body seethed in anger as he towered over the troll, who cowered with a whimper.

"You there! Why don't you open your mouth for us again?" he asked, gritting his teeth. "I'm sure you've something more to say. Don't you now, eh."

The troll was mortified. He clenched his lips, shaking his head as if he had nothing else to say.

"What's the matter? Cat got your tongue?" asked Grimsor with a devious smile.

The troll trembled.

"No . . . no . . . not at all," he said.

Grimsor turned away.

"What was I thinking," he laughed.

The troll took a deep breath and relaxed. He thought the nightmare was over. But he was wrong. Grimsor swung around and with his bare hands ripped off his lower jaw, tearing his tongue from his mouth and crushing his head. He collapsed in a pool of dark, red blood. His twisted body twitched convulsively for a moment, and then he laid still.

Grimsor looked at the tongue in his blood-soaked hand. It felt cold and moist. He lifted it high into the stench-filled air for all to see.

"What's this?! No cat has your tongue. I do!" he shouted. "Anyone else has something to say?"

He then flippantly cast the tongue aside.

The brood cringed in horrified silence. They knew well of Grimsor's treachery. They had heard the tales of his cruelty. They had seen him destroy whole ranks of brood with his mighty hands. No one wanted to be on the receiving end of this fury.

In the distance, the thumping sounds of Katzhu Pu's drums could still be heard while overhead the screams of the black ajatars seemed to grow terser and shriller. The brood once again started its slow march, beginning to traverse the open grassland, bush, and thorn patches of the Snowwynne Barrens.

* * *

The evening was unseasonably cold. Dusk had fallen and the broken moon shone very brightly. The eyes of Qinn Farlerstock's old house were aglow with the warmth of a fire in an old stone hearth. He had finished stacking wood for the next day when a strange sound came from somewhere. It wasn't the sound of voices, nor the sound exactly of restless movements. No. It was a sound like the sighing of the wind in a wood of brambles. At first, he thought nothing of it, but he still looked about the darkness anxiously, listening for any noises that didn't belong. He remembered tales told by townsfolk, of a band of marauding black demons from Portmoor, servants of evil, malformed creatures who snatched souls and fled away before the sunrise. He listened to the noises of the night for a long time, carefully, to the fall of a leaf, a soft breeze, and the hooting of an owl. He shivered in the night air. With all calm and still he withdrew to the warmth of his house.

As he bolted the door behind him a wind began to blow dark clouds across the sky. It gathered strength, picking up leaves and rushing through the trees and tangled thicket with a deep sigh. The thicket seemed to come alive as buried deep within its dark shadows came the piercing flash of orange eyes. They were eyes of rage, hatred, of fear that grew more and more intense with the wind.

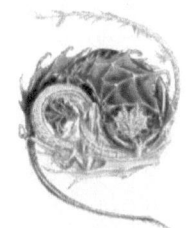

CHAPTER 14
SGURK BENTGIBBER

A NEW DAY CAME to life. As a pallid sun rose and shone through dark clouds, Qinn Farlerstock left his house and headed toward the woodpile. He stopped for a moment. There was something different about this new day. The morning air was musty and stale, and the winds howled and raged incessantly.

No matter, he thought. *My work is never done.*

He began loading wood timbers in his canvas satchel, carefully stacking them. When it was full he lifted it and slipped the straps over his shoulders. He took a deep breath before starting his journey up the hill.

I'm getting much too old for this, he thought.

He looked up the grassy hill to the Aina Dur. The tree was leafy and full of color and was peaceful and wholesome. He smiled. This place was his home, where all his earliest memories could be found, the earliest memories of his life. This was where he belonged.

He took a few steps when he felt a sharp rush of heat pierce through him. It was a strange sensation and something he had never felt before. It stopped him. The heat grew in intensity and soon overcame him. He looked down to his left. There, protruding from his body, was the end of a sword with jagged teeth on both sides. It was an orc's heldror. His eyes widened in pain as the rusted steel blade was yanked from his body in a powerful tug and a jarring motion. He felt it ripping through his flesh and biting bone.

The heat became scorching and he fell to his knees. He could feel his heart pounding heavily and it was becoming difficult to breathe. Weakened, he fell face forward to the ground, as he felt his life force slowly draining away.

A few moments passed - the last of his life.

He closed his eyes to the lasting image of the sacred tree, and to the last words he would ever hear, words that echoed from behind.

"Your services are no longer needed, Firekeeper."

He then fell into the darkness of forever.

Dracor and his brood trampled over Farlerstock's body and charged up the grassy hill. A Dark Rider circled above while to the north, vast columns of smoke rose from burning villages. The brutality revealed itself through animalistic, wasting, rotting smells - the decaying of flesh, the stench of death. As the brood reached the Aina Dur Dracor bowed to the ground. He touched his head and his heart to show great reverence to his master. A triumphant look came to him, for this new day would bring victory.

* * *

Molly awoke from her dreams, breathless, and confused. She took a glance around; she could not tell where her dreams ended and reality began. She closed her eyes and felt the Lia Fail's warmth on her chest. Her body felt normal, and she felt safe in her bed.

I have returned from my dreams, she thought. *But they are becoming too real.*

In her dreams, the feelings she felt, everything that she saw, touched, tasted, and smelled was as vivid as it was in real life. This frightened her. What troubled her was not the actual events in her dreams, but the fact that they were becoming more familiar. It was as if her dreams had grown tired of hiding from her and were now letting go of their secrets. The boy on the stage, the messenger from another time, the Professor's words, images of war and death - all haunted her while she slept and while she was awake. She decided that she would not tell her sister or the others about her dreams. She did not want to worry them.

Rising to the early morning, she gave a long yawn and stretched. She was tired. It was becoming more and more difficult to sleep.

I would love to sleep in, just for one day, without dreams.

She hurriedly dressed and did it quietly, letting her sister and Big Grey sleep. She looked out a window from their room in the grand Kaer Taraedar, through the branches of trees and the soft green foliage, where she saw a piece of sky that was becoming brighter. She knew that the morning always brought Elizabeth a sense of wonder, an enthusiasm that the new day would bring new travels and adventures. But for her, the morning brought a different feeling, a feeling of relief, that she was no longer dreaming. Images from her dreams remained with her, in her mind, vibrant and full of detail, images that she always tried to erase but could not.

She clasped the Lia Fail in her small hand, the warmth coursing through her.

The stone . . . it is more a curse than a blessing.

She sighed. She knew that with the stone's guidance and patience, she would be able to conquer her dreams and that they would finally make sense to her.

But when?

She remembered what Brows had told her when they made their way to Hammer Fief, that she could control the stone. She looked down at it as it pulsated in her palm.

I need to know how to control it. But how?

There was an arched doorway leading from their room to a small garden courtyard. She turned to make sure her sister and the cat were still asleep. She slowly opened the door, just a bit, holding her breath, hoping not to make a sound. When she heard no sound, she opened the door the rest of the way and quietly entered the courtyard.

The morning air was cold, clean, and sharp. She looked around the courtyard. It was a peaceful place with small trees, stone pavers with patches of grass, beds of orange and red flowers, and in the center, water bubbled from a decorative bronze spout. The fresh smell of trees with a touch of sweetness from the flowers wrapped around her.

If I am to learn how to use the stone, I must do so alone.

She looked around one more time just to make sure no one was there and that no one was peering into the courtyard from inside the Kaer Taraedar. She had enough of being surrounded by people, at least for now.

I am alone. Let's see if I can control the stone. What to do? Where to begin?

She turned to a nearby flower bed and stared at a beautiful red rose. She closed her eyes and tightened her grip on the stone, reaching out for the rose with her other hand. She wanted to burn the flower and, in her mind, conjured visions of flames within flames spewing high into the air. The courtyard became eerily quiet. Her heart raced. She could feel the melting heat as her visions began to fuel anger and hatred. Dark emotions started to consume her. It was a strange path. But she continued to try to burn the rose. When she felt she was successful she opened her eyes. The flower remained, unharmed. She had failed.

She was discouraged but determined to try again.

Maybe I need to think differently.

She focused her attention on the bronze spout. She clenched the stone with one hand and with her other hand reached out to the spout. She closed her eyes and thought of a forest with a small creek running through it, the water flowing clear over stones. She thought of the stones and of creating a stone wall to halt the flow of water.

The Lia Fail seemed to respond to her thoughts. It became warm to her touch and throbbed with great strength as her thoughts focused on the stone wall. She imagined the stones being lifted and delicately laid one atop another, one by one, until the water receded.

She stopped and opened her eyes. To her amazement, the bronze spout remained but no water bubbled.

Think differently . . .

She closed her eyes again but this time she wanted to remove the stone wall. She imagined removing each stone. She imagined lifting the first stone and placing it aside, then the second, then the third, and so on. She opened her eyes and saw the water flowing from the bronze spout.

She smiled.

I am beginning to understand how to use the stone.

When she opened the door to leave the courtyard, she was startled to see Big Grey sitting in the doorway. She gasped in surprise.

"I did not mean to startle you," said the cat. "What were you doing alone in the courtyard? Are you feeling well?"

"Oh, yes, I am feeling quite well, thank you," she said. "I just wanted to get some fresh morning air. It is so beautiful here. Isn't it?"

She briskly walked past him not wanting any further discussion.

"Molly," he called out. She turned to look at him. "The stone can only be used for good. Always remember that."

His presence amid the silence seemed to shake the air around her. It was overwhelming. There was a link to him at that very moment; she felt it. But then the connection vanished like a flash of lightning.

Strange.

She nodded her understanding to him and walked away.

* * *

Brows and Big Grey escorted the girls to breakfast. They were quiet and deep in thought as they walked. Molly was having trouble keeping track of all that had happened the day before. She still held to her plan of bringing the Lia Fail to the evil with the help of the orc. But now there was the secret of another Fail stone, Bran's ring, and the link between his ancestors and former rulers. Then there was the mystery of the White Knight. There was so much to understand, and she knew that the best she could do was ask questions, learn from the answers, and do her best to continue piecing together the pieces of this puzzle.

"Who is this White Knight?" she asked Brows.

"In the annals of our history not much is known about the White Knight," he said. "What has been written is that he is thought to have been born of flesh and bone and was joined with the Anar Ere, the great messengers, the spirit kings of the Maker. He is sometimes called Nim Dagora. It is written that he came into being well before the time of kings, during the time of great upheaval. Sacred writings say he fought to cleanse the land of demons and helped to bring a time of peace. But not much is known other than it is said the White Knight only appears at times of great difficulty, and when all has been resolved he mysteriously vanishes. He's not appeared in recent times."

"So, he will help us?" asked Elizabeth.

"I believe he will," interjected Big Grey. "But we will not know when he will appear or even if he appears at all. I think we should follow the path before us, regardless of the good spirit. There is much that needs to be done. Let us get some breakfast."

The girls smiled. They were hungry.

They met the rest of the group in a large antechamber off the Kaer Taraedar rotunda. Their breakfast was a simple meal, consisting of tea, oatmeal cake, fried meats, and potatoes. There was much talk about the meeting with the Guild Lords and what was said.

All was beautiful and calm until Fairfax who was speaking to Ras Amon suddenly winched in pain. His eyes closed and he began to shake, his face contorted in anguish.

Ras Amon was very concerned as those nearby crowded around.

"What is wrong, my friend?" he asked Fairfax.

Fairfax sat trembling, his eyes wide open in a pain-filled shock. He heard the words of his friend and the commotion around him, but he could not speak. A force had taken control of him. Terrible visions flashed in his mind – of a lifeless Qinn Farlerstock, of dark creatures laying waste to the library under the Aina Dur. He fought to regain control but could not.

"What's wrong with him?" shouted Molly. "We have to do something!"

"I believe it is a time rip," said Ras Amon. "Sometimes wizards are torn from one moment to another, the past or the future. It is our sensitivity to the magic that allows for this. But such times are rare. We must try to get him back or he'll be discovered by those in his visions."

Maybe this explains my dreams, thought Molly. *Am I becoming a wizard?*

Ras Amon closed his eyes and placed his hands on the head of Fairfax.

"I am here for you, my friend," he said. "I am here for you. Come to me."

Fairfax could see Ras Amon in his mind, a vision of him within gruesome images of death and destruction. He struggled to move, to stretch out his hands to his friend, to make a sound, to scream for help, but he was frozen.

He watched in growing horror as dark creatures desecrated the library under the Aina Dur. He saw the demons stomping out the fire in the fireplace and tearing at the door secured with timbers. They ripped the timbers from the door's casing one by one, and then in a fit of rage, the largest of the creatures rammed its massive fist through the door, shattering it and scattering wood shards throughout the library. The beasts howled in an evil madness.

But then the brood fell silent. They backed away from the door in fright, for they could see something but could not make out what it was.

Slowly, two huge and round white eyes, bloodshot and terrifying, emerged from the shadows. The stench of decay mingled with the smell of sodden earth, and the brood could hear a faint gurgling sound, the sound of desperation, of someone gasping for breath.

The lurking creature crept from the shadows, crawling on all fours, making disgusting sounds as gobs of drool slithered off his chin. It was a slimy, warty beast, twisted and hairless. It had the appearance of a bobbin but was more devil than bobbin. As it crept forward, it looked at the brood. It saw Dracor and raising a hand uttered words in the old tongue. Magic flowed from the vile creature, an invisible force that enveloped and strangled Dracor. He collapsed to the ground, clawing at his neck as if trying to break free from the grasp of invisible hands suffocating him.

Dracor struggled to speak.

"But . . . Master Bentgibber . . . I've come to . . . give you freedom," he said.

The creature gave a tilt of his head. He clenched his brown and black teeth.

"Freedom?" he gurgled. "There's no such thing in this hollow place. Freedom is a fantasy and a fraud."

The creature watched as Dracor suffered.

"Your pain sustains me," he said squeezing out the words with a despicable smile.

Dracor's muscles began to stiffen and with a final gasp, he had breathed his last breath.

The abomination crawled about Dracor's body, sniffing at it. He reached into a pocket of the Urur Maw's clothing and pulled out the glass jar containing the strands of golden hair. He then gave a most hideous cackle of laughter.

The other brood shrank in fear.

Fairfax was horrified at the vision. He struggled to stop it. He could hear his friend's voice, this time getting stronger.

"Fairfax, can you hear me?" pleaded Ras Amon. "Please come to me. I beg you . . . come to me."

"Help him! Help him!" shouted Molly. "Is he going to be okay?"

Fairfax heard Molly's voice.

He fought feverishly to escape the dark visions within the time rip, visions that were tearing their way into him. He knew that if he did not get himself out of the darkness soon, his magic would expose him to the demons.

He began to calm himself, trying to relax his thoughts. He concentrated on his friend's voice. It seemed to come from a long way off, almost as if it was coming through a tunnel. The sound of it started to give him strength and then he saw Ras Amon's hand reaching for him. Seeing the hand, he grabbed it.

"Old friend, I am here for you," said Ras Amon pulling Fairfax from the darkness.

Fairfax squeezed his eyes shut and shook his head. His chest heaved. He was exhausted, completely drained.

"It is Sgurk Bentgibber," he said attempting to catch his breath. "He has been released . . . Bentgibber . . . the Aina Dur . . . the tree is lost . . ."

"It is as the Guild Lords have said," whispered Ras Amon. "But tell us - is there more? What else did you see?"

Fairfax was breathing heavily.

"Hair . . . golden hair in a jar . . ." he said.

Ras Amon pondered then gave a heavy sigh.

"Hair from Foulhand! They free the demon librarian," he said.

"Yes, to resurrect the Cursed One," said Fairfax.

With those ominous words all became still and quiet, the mood dark and dismal. Fairfax shook his head in disbelief, almost tearfully so. Fear filled the room. Everyone had heard the name Sgurk Bentgibber, and those that knew the name also knew how it acquired its evil connotation. But the girls had not heard the name before and were curious about it.

"Who's this?" said Elizabeth hesitating because she could not pronounce the name. She became frustrated. "Who's this, whatever it is you call him?"

All eyes turned to the one in the group who knew the name very well, the one who could speak to the history of the demon.

"He was once my good friend," said Brows, his tone remorseful as if he regretted even knowing the creature. "Sgurk Bentgibber was once a bobbin. We grew up together and as children, we played in the lavender fields just north of Rivers Barrow. We discovered that we each had a fondness for history and over time we found ourselves working together, deciphering the old tongue, the histories written in ancient times. Oh, I remember - it was such a glorious age. I became a historian while he was a master librarian. We lived for the euphoria of research and discovery as we turned each page of the ancient texts. He was a dear friend and I loved him like a brother."

He paused, his mood becoming darker, a sneer forming on his face.

"But a change came over him," continued Brows. "The library became dark, and without light understanding becomes lost. My friend became fascinated with the dark arts, researching those passages from the ancient texts that were forbidden. Over time it consumed him like an addiction. He became twisted and evil. Self-interest was the only motive that swayed his mind. He turned friend to foe, and flattery became betrayal, promoting his selfish ends. He became lost in a sea of dangers and horrors. Alas, I could not help him."

Molly thought back to when she and Elizabeth first entered the library.

"It was him. Wasn't it?" she asked Big Grey. "It was him making the sounds from behind that door under the tree. Wasn't it?"

The cat nodded.

"I was there when the Edainar secured him in his crypt, never again to see the light of day," said Brows, saddened. "It has been so many years. We had all hoped he would leave us, that he would follow the path away from the Aina Dur, to another place, another time. But it seems he was just waiting."

"Well, can't we just put him back," said Molly. "Can't we do that?"

"I am afraid that is easier said than done, little one," said Big Grey. "He is as powerful as any Dark Wizard and perhaps more so."

"The Lawgiver is correct," said Brows. "It took the entire strength of the Edainar just to secure him once before. Under these tragic times, I do not know what can be done."

"But he has been away from the ancient texts," said Ras Amon. "His powers may be weakened."

Having regained some of his strength Fairfax stood. He wobbled a bit on his staff.

"We must not underestimate his powers," he told Ras Amon. "My friend, it makes sense now - why you must travel west to the Aina Dur. Surely, the darkness will try to resurrect Foulhand. You must face your student, as has been foreseen by the Guild Lords. It is your destiny."

The Learned One embraced Fairfax. He understood what his friend had told him. He looked around the room until his eyes rested on Shaer Thol, the tiny white cat, his friend. The Tar Malal's red bulging eyes showed confidence, an excitement that he had never seen in them. This brought a smile to him, and a sense of relief flooded him. The cat ran to him jumping into his arms. He gently cradled the cat and thought about the days ahead. He knew what he had to say to his tiny friend, for his sake.

"I know you wish to come with me, but you cannot," he told Shaer Thol with a tearful voice. "I must undo what I have done, or I will have no rest. This is something I must do alone. I cannot endanger you, nor can I ask you to accompany me on such a grievous journey. You must travel with the others. They will provide for you. The Lawgiver will be your companion."

He looked at Big Grey who nodded.

"He will be most welcomed," said the cat.

Shaer Thol purred. He brushed his face against Ras Amon's cheek.

"I do what I do and that's the best I can do," he said.

Fairfax looked at Ras Amon with grateful eyes. He knew the struggles his friend would endure. There would be hardships and sacrifices; there would be pain and sorrow. And he knew, in the end, death would come for his friend. For now, for the moment, they were together. He could feel their friendship; it was like a warm blanket wrapped around him, and it made him smile.

But Fairfax knew that the path forward would be difficult for the others as well. Evil had erupted in their midst, and there was no way to know what the fiendishness had planned for them. He was not sure how the others would respond in the face of such stark evil, but he was hopeful that they would fight back with everything they had.

"Each of us has a difficult road ahead," he told the others. "This will be no easy task, and I am afraid much of the time we will languish in uncertainty. But know that for us to be victorious we will need to draw upon our friends. The strength of our friendship binds us, and no evil can ever tear it apart. Let us not forget that the Guild Lords have given us direction. I think it is best if we hasten our departure. I am afraid too much time has already been lost."

Everyone agreed and the group left the antechamber and crossed a hallway that led to the courtyard behind the Kaer Taraedar. There they quickly divided themselves into three smaller groups, each arranged to set off on separate journeys. To the west, Ras Amon would travel alone. Fairfax, Thurir, and his pack, along with Glaeynd would journey to the Rakl. The girls would travel east, accompanied by Bran Arundel, Brows, Big Grey, Shaer Thol, An Van Au, Calen Ancorbow, and the orc Ug'ghi Otha. Ranagul Dithil and Entur Donduin would ride south to join Carrick's armies. They would tell Carrick of all that had been spoken, and the White Knight.

There were further discussions and arrangements made. Brows unfolded several maps before the group. They looked over them, turning them around to view them at all conceivable angles, with each group charting their journey. They would try to avoid traveling those roads and pathways most often used, and this meant the most direct route would not always be the most favored. Each group would need to travel secretly, for evil was hunting throughout the land.

When all was decided, Fairfax stated he would take his group through the North Downs and to Volemill. He said he had some business to attend to with his friend, the Paragon. From there, they would venture north deep into the Old Hills emerging into the North Eldor where they would continue to the Rakl. Bran planned a course south through the North Downs to Tollford Farthing, and then north following the Old River to the Snowwynne Barrens and then to the Crag. Lastly, Ras Amon would journey through the Cricklewood Forest in hopes of meeting up with some of Carrick's men, as the Caridwen Guild Lord foretold.

As they prepared to depart that morning, the start of a task beyond the realms of what anyone expected, sadness gripped the girls' hearts for they were leaving many of their friends and feared they would never see them again. They rushed forward and hugged Fairfax. They looked up at him with misted eyes.

He could sense their fright and anxiety. A gleam came to his eyes. He bent down and gathered them in front of him. He pointed to members of their group.

"There are friends all about you, look here and here, and here," he told them, pointing to the others in the group. "So, wipe those tears away. You have nothing to worry about when you are surrounded by friends. And do not worry. We will meet again. When and where, I do not know, but be sure, be sure, that we shall meet again. Of this, I promise."

Everyone was smiling at the girls and this made them feel better. They found it touching that anyone in this strange land should feel the way Fairfax felt about them, and this reassured them.

"Ah, but there is something very special, for each of you," Fairfax said with a great smile.

Two ponies came trotting into the courtyard followed by a little old gentleman who was much shorter than the girls. Each pony was pure white with a flowing golden mane and big feathery wings tucked back.

The girls lit up with enjoyment.

"For us?" asked Molly.

"Yes," said Fairfax. "They are elven ponies given to you by Dalgaes."

"The Elf-King?"

He nodded.

"Can they fly?" asked Elizabeth.

Fairfax laughed.

"Well, of course. All elven ponies can fly," he said. "After all, what are wings used for?"

"But we've never ridden a pony let alone one that can fly," said Molly.

"Now do not you worry. Riding an elven pony requires no experience at all. You'll see."

The little old gentleman approached the girls. He wore dark green leather boots and a charcoal grey tunic and had long grey hair that was tied back. As he neared the girls he bowed deeply.

"My Queen and Princess," he said, "I am Vyletaraes, horsemaster to Dalgeas. The great Elven King sent me here to present you with two gifts. For the Queen, he presents Adhara; for the Princess, he presents Shaula. Each is at your service."

Molly was amazed at the ponies.

"We are grateful for this gift and grateful for the generous spirit of King Dalgaes," she told the horsemaster.

The girls gently approached the ponies who fidgeted a little. While Molly patted Adhara on the forehead, Elizabeth put one hand on Shaula's mane. Soon they were seated atop their pony with wings tucked away to the side, and trotting about.

Horses, completely equipped for the journey, were brought out to the courtyard. As some of the others departed, they knew this meant their lives were about to change forever. But they also knew that they were not alone. They had been chosen to be a part of something larger than themselves, something that would change the Harrow.

Watching the girls on their ponies, Fairfax turned to Big Grey and Brows.

"You travel with two shards," he told them. "I do not know how they can be used or if they can be used at all. Only time will tell. Be careful." He then glanced at Ug'ghi Otha who was making his travel preparations. "Keep the knowledge of the second shard from the orc. Tell the others of this and the girls as well. I do not believe the Professor anticipated his presence in all this."

"Should not Carrick know of Bran's ring?" asked Brows.

"I have instructed Dithil and Donduin to tell him of that," said Fairfax.

Brows and the cat nodded.

When the girls finished riding their ponies, they joined their group. Everyone quietly rode through Katzhu Pu, the sky paling overhead, and the broken moon casting shadows about. They left the gilded city to the throbbing drumbeats. Once outside they said their farewells and each group went their separate ways.

* * *

Frozen in fear, the brood had all they could do to hold their places as Sgurk Bentgibber slithered over Dracor's body, still sniffing, searching for something else. In one hand he held the precious strands of golden hair while he used his other hand to feel about the dead Urur Maw's chest. A moment or two passed, when suddenly he flung his head up, and with eyes glaring began a most hideous laughter. He raised a hand with a clenched fist high into the air and then with brutal force brought it down ripping into Dracor's chest. The brood quivered with dread.

Bentgibber began to forcibly tear apart flesh and bone, pushing and tearing his way through muscle and internal organs, until he found what he sought. It was then when a most crazed smile came to his hideously deformed face. From the defiled body, he brought forth Dracor's once beating heart. He held the heart in his blood-soaked hands and began to gently rub it. He clenched his teeth and with the crazed smile still on his lips, placed the golden strands of hair onto the hollow muscular organ.

A shuddering sound in his throat began to rise. It was rhythmic in its manner and rose and fell on a definite beat, its pitch high and quivering. The pattern soon became words in the old tongue, incantations from before time, chants so old they even made the brood's skin skitter with cold. He placed the heart back into Dracor's chest. Then, a stream of light and vapor began to swirl about the corpse, faster and faster until the body seemed to glow an intense white. As he continued his incantations, the body began to transform into something quite different, into a man, the form of which was long and slender. The man's skin was smooth and pale, his hair long and golden, flowing past square shoulders, and he was shrouded in a deep red robe.

The brood recoiled in alarm, horror-stricken.

"The Cursed One . . . the Death Reaper . . . Dark Wizard . . . . Mauldragw Foulhand," they muttered in disbelief, words echoing far and wide.

The man opened his eyes which were a deep black.

"Rise my master," said Bentgibber. "You are again with us."

Slowly the man rose to a sitting position. A devious smile came to him as he looked at his hands and body. There was a glare of agony and hatred on his face. A soft chuckle welled up from within.

"Very good. Very good indeed," he told Bentgibber. "You have done well."

"Master, the Aina Dur is ours," said Bentgibber, his tone obedient and affectionate. "The tree will begin to wither away like wind preying on the weak rock. It will rot and fall."

Foulhand took a hand and lightly caressed Bentgibber's trembling cheek.

"My dearest friend," he whispered. "It is so good to see you again. There is much work to be done."

* * *

More brood made their way from Poortmor to the Aina Dur. Upon their arrival, they were directed by Bentgibber and Foulhand to construct a great stone fortress and tower. Its foundation came from the vast ruin of rock and stone from what was once a great castle that lay just west of the Aina Dur. In time the massive tower pierced the heavens, with walls so high that as eagles flew over, they looked as if they were as small as sparrows.

The dark tower endured against the sky, a brooding presence. It was like a fist of stone, thrust up into the clouds. Good beasts of the land, both large and small, tried to creep closer to the tower, to share in its protection against the wind and cold. But the tower did not accept them, and they withered and died before they could reach it. The tower stood in silence and stood unafraid and unchallenged in the face of the fury of the darkness, and its name rang over the land - Drar Dukhaar.

Brood toiled day and night, as the dismal, dreary kingdom came to be cradled amidst the Carn's mountains. They were armed with long swords, daggers, and heldrors and walked along the walls of the fortress, calling out to each other night and day. Over the countryside, patrols of brood ravaged the land, raiding farms and torching villages. Everything was laid to waste.

And, from the tower's ramparts, the red-robed ruler kept guard over the desolate vista, quietly contemplating the lights of Carrick's massive army far off to the east, while in the distance a lone eagle drifted high above the clouds.

"What is it that the eagle sees, my lord?" asked Bentgibber.

Foulhand could barely understand the garbled words, but there was no mistaking a tone of excitement.

A word fell softly upon the Dark Wizard's lips.

"Death."

* * *

The lone eagle soared aloft, high into the air, easily and lightly. Its white head and large talons were majestic against the sky and clouds. The great bird flew across the mountains, plains, and river lands until its yellow eyes saw far, far away, the converging armies below. Banners of four armies waved full proudly in the wind, beckoning across the fields – the Fist representing the men of Eldor, the Claw representing the cats of the Balor Guild, the Axe representing the dwarves, and the Tree representing the men of Ahlgren. The neighing of war horses occasionally wafted through the air, as did the herald of marching warriors and the steady thump of the Kyr Thysaer's drumbeats.

As the eagle continued its ascent, it could see a shadow emerge from the east. It was a dark massive army of brood marching slowly from the Crag against the growing shrieks of Uakor Turg circling overhead. Higher yet the eagle rose until the land beneath it looked like a bowl turned upside down. From this viewpoint, the great eagle, the imposter Azariel, could see the demon towers of Ug' Cthuth and Urth' Goroth to the east, the northern death tower of the Rakl now called Ur' Morir, and a new tower, Drar Dukhaar to the west. The pieces of war were upon the land.

He dipped his wing in the direction of the moon and rode a downdraft away from the Old River and into the vast Old Hills, deep into its northern regions where the mountaintops touched the stars. Higher and higher he flew until he disappeared into a hollow place in the greatest mountain of them all, the one called Muul'duul Durra.

He flew deep into the great mountain following dark sinuous tunnels of rock and stone that turned, running into each other and off to the sides like a labyrinth. The tunnels twisted around the eagle crazily, shapelessly, until his journey ended at a huge chamber in the center of the mountain. He flew high into the chamber, to its higher most reaches, taking a place upon a stone ledge alongside the already perched yellow cricket, Elspeth.

The chamber was massive, soaring overhead at the full height of the mountain. Along its edges perched thousands upon thousands of winged creatures, both great and small. This was the En' Raama. The sound in the chamber was deafening, thunderous, tumultuous, as there was much talk about the meeting that would soon commence. Somewhere from within the nether reaches of the chamber, a horn blew twice. Lifting an imperious black wing, the imposter Azariel quieted the crowd.

He proceeded with his speech. At first, he spoke softly with syllables drawn out and his enunciation precise, then he tightened his voice, almost calculatingly. He condemned the race of man, the Guilds, and the Edainar for bringing war to the land, and for not providing winged creatures full representation in matters of governance. As he made his points, playing on the fears of the crowd, he would raise one of his mighty wings, and his voice became tighter and less warm. At several points in the speech, the exultant crowd interrupted in glorious cheers and support for his words. When the speech ended, a celebrated chant filled the chamber as he and Elspeth smiled.

But not all of the En' Raama agreed with the words spoken. Some would meet in secret places, weaving a web of plans to plot against the great eagle.

* * *

Alone in his dark chamber, upon the cold stone of his massive throne, his hand to chin, the Szard pondered the darkness.

Urth' Goroth had unleashed its evil. Soon, a scourge would envelop the land the likes of which had never been encountered. The day would gradually turn to night, thunder would rumble incessantly, and the wind would shriek like a wandering spirit. Destruction would sweep from north to south, east to west, and evil would lurk around every corner. On countless battlefields, those who were soulless would eradicate the right and the just. The stench of death would fill the air, overpowering, and amidst the feeling of heavy, hopeless futility one would rise as all-powerful. It would be he, the bringer of grief and death, the master of the great dark demon tower who would reign over all; for he and he alone would ultimately triumph. The wars of ages past had been devised for this one decisive moment.

Soon, my time will come.

The black-hooded figure sat motionless in sober meditation, and even though his face was ever-cloaked in darkness his expression was calm, intent. His eyes were fixed on the darkness of the room, and in this darkness images of a mighty empire built on treachery and held together by blood came to him. It was his empire and he would be its master.

I will show them. I will show them all.

He thought of those who had doubted him, those who would thwart his will, and he became angry. He pounded a fist on the cold stone. He took a deep breath and paused, and after calming himself, he reflected on the past, on what he had learned.

So many lessons I have learned. So many.

The cold of darkness pleased him. It seeped through his fine robes and reached deep into his bones and heart. Another deep breath and his thoughts turned to upcoming plans of war. He thought of Vorn and the freshly bred brood, cunning and fearless.

Yes, I have learned my lessons well and so too shall those who oppose me.

* * *

Snerv Slog sat in front of the wall and laughed wildly and loudly at the terror before him. From within the stone and earth creatures were growing, taking shape and form. These were evil creatures of pure malice and there was no escaping their treachery. They were the Gurtha Naur and would be charged with only one task, a task they would not give up. For within their soulless spirit, death was their release, something they sought and longed for, while also believing that death was necessary for others.

"Perfectionsssssss!" he cackled.

He knew it was a fear of death that prevented most demons from completing their mission, and this knowledge was what inspired Drogur Vorn and the Ra Orqu to craft the Gurtha Naur.

He remembered Vorn's words.

They will be impossible to stop. They will terrorize the adversary like no other. You cannot defeat those who do not fear death.

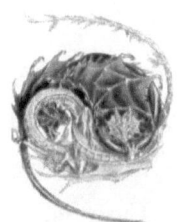

Chapter 15
The Draaklel' Daan Defile

MOLLY AND ELIZABETH'S GROUP rode slowly that day. Once through the Tangle and around a ridge of the Old Hills, they were traveling eastward over the North Downs. The journey took a few days and mostly they traveled through patches of trees — mighty oaks, ashes, and over rolling hills of tall green grasses and shrubbery. As they continued over the North Downs they had sunken deeper and deeper into the total peace of the countryside, the fields, woods, and forests heaving with life. In places, there were vast fields of towering sunflowers, vegetable farmlands, and vineyards that wreathed the hills. In other places, there were wide open fields of grasses, undisturbed, where yellow mists of butterflies fluttered about petals of colorful wildflowers and where bees drowsed busily.

But wherever they turned and amidst the beauty of the North Downs, danger lurked. The sky burned black, and thunder rumbled as evil slowly made its way west. Few words were said as they traveled; eyes ever wary of the coming storm. Along the way, Brows and Big Grey did as Fairfax had instructed. They quietly told everyone not to tell the orc about the second shard, the ring currently held by Bran of Dunhollow. Everyone understood, and no one questioned their judgment.

Eventually, there came a day that grew long into the grey of twilight and the group came upon a hill of thick grasses overlooking the shimmering lights of Thawnybire, a small village in the North Downs.

"This is as good a place as any to make camp for the night," said Bran. "Tomorrow we will continue, past Thawnybire and then on to Tollford Farthing. Our travels will become more difficult."

Under his direction, everyone went about their assigned duties. An Van Au and Calen Ancorbow reviewed security while Big Grey fetched wood. Brows cleared a patch of ground and when the cat returned with the wood, he made a roaring fire. The air was filled with the smell of burning leaves and wood and the sound of crackling flames. Everyone was grateful for the warmth and the warm hearty meat stew that Brows cooked. They sat around the fire eating, and they talked for a while, that is except for Ug'ghi Otha who kept to himself.

Molly ordered the orc's chains to be removed, but he was still far from being free. The journey was even darker for him, with some in the group looking at him with threatening and menacing eyes. But in the few short days that they had traveled, he had earned Molly's trust as part of her plan. He had also convinced a few that he was not pure evil and that he could lead them to the Drueger and his master. But while some in the group believed he had fallen for the deceit, that his mission was to provide safe passage to the east, some were ever suspicious of his intentions, and that perhaps he was playing along because it was his evil master's will. Calen Ancorbow was especially distrustful of him and kept a watchful eye on him.

After some tea, it was time for sleep. Bran, Ancorbow, and An Van Au took turns on watch while the rest slept. The girls slept in the largest wagon along with Big Grey and Shaer Thol. They nestled upon pillows of green moss and were covered by the warmth of the wool blanket given to them by Brows. In a corner, the two cats curled near each other. Across the space, on a small wooden table, sat a lantern. Its flame was lowered, providing a soft yellow glow.

Soon everyone fell asleep, but not Molly. She disliked the night. Lying in the dark, she clenched her eyes shut and waited for her dreams to come to her. They had become an enemy. Whereas she used to look forward to sleeping because she knew her dreams would be sweet, she now dreaded it since it seemed like a punishment, almost a necessary evil. She was afraid of the dreams sleep would bring, of what the dreams would tell her. But she had to overcome her fear. She knew that the only dreams she would have in this place, as frightening as they had become, were of the future, of whatever was waiting for her. She had no choice but to face her dreams, learn from them, and determine a path to be followed.

She took a deep breath and closed her eyes and quickly found herself in a dream of dark mist. Below where she stood, she saw rows and rows of empty shadowy seats. The walls were marble-clad with crystal chandeliers dancing from above. Along the sides, she could make out winding staircases and splendid balconies.

I know this place, she thought. *I am familiar with it. It is the dark theater, the same as in my past dreams.*

Past the rows and rows of empty seats, she could see the dark stage and the same little boy standing alone, round face with soft skin, his eyes empty, gaping black holes. She looked at him convinced he could not see her within the darkness. This time she was not frightened. She was more curious, determined to understand this dream, to learn something.

Who is he? What is the dream trying to tell me?

As if hearing her thoughts, the little boy looked up at the rows of empty seats, his eyes darting about as if he were searching for someone. His gaze, his black holes for eyes found Molly. Her face fell.

"I see you," he said in an impish voice. "What's your name? Why are you here? You shouldn't be here! Leave now!"

Fear consumed her. She kept still and did not make a sound. She looked around for a doorway or any other opening, a place where she could quickly slip and hide. But there was none. She became more anxious when the boy and the dark surroundings began to shimmer into a white mist and then slowly to the soft yellow glow of her wagon.

The lantern's flame.

The dream was ending, and reality was returning.

But something was wrong. She could feel a drip-drip of wetness on her face and there was a putrid smell, a smell that made her sick to her stomach.

As the yellow glow began to fade a most horrifying sight formed - a creature was hovering over her! He was a vile demon staring down at her with a devilish smile, his green tongue licking over jagged teeth. She felt his hot breath and the warmth of his drool as it dripped from his mouth and slimed onto her face. Her heart began to race but she could not scream. She was too terrified.

An orc!

"Me cutie wakes from hers dreams," whispered the orc in a guttural tone. "Sweets dreams me thinks. Sweets dreams for the little ones."

Her eyes widened in fear as panic seized her. All sorts of vague horrors sprang unbidden into her mind.

He placed a grimy finger over her soft lips.

"Shhh . . . now be quiet me cutie. No needs to wakes the others. Death will comes to you soon enough," he said, then continued, looking at Elizabeth fast asleep, continued, "and to the other one over theres. Me promises."

Her breathing became more rapid, more intense. She wanted to reach out and push him away, but fear had drained her strength. A feeling of despair came over her, the hopelessness that she had failed. She resigned herself to his mercy. She closed her eyes.

Then she heard a series of thumps and the utterances of muttered curses. She opened her eyes with a squint. Ug'ghi Otha had wrestled the orc to the floor, his powerful arms around her assailant's neck.

Elizabeth awakened.

"Help!" she shrieked. "Help!"

The cats stirred from their sleep while the two orcs struggled mightily. Others entered the wagon to the sickening scene.

Ug'ghi Otha tightened his grip around the other orc's neck.

"You are not to be here," he told the orc, overpowering him.

The orc could not maneuver and submitted. With what little strength he had left, he strained to see the face of whoever had subdued him. From the corner of his eyes, he made out some of Ug'ghi Otha's face and then saw the blue eyes.

The orc was astonished.

"It's you . . ." he said. He started to say something, but Ug'ghi Otha snapped his neck cleanly, like a twig breaking.

There was a final look of anguish on the orc's twisted face, a look of surprise and confusion as he went limp like a rag doll. Still with a tight grip on him, Ug'ghi Otha dragged the lifeless body from the wagon. He then returned.

Everyone rushed to Molly. Elizabeth hugged her and asked her if she was alright. Molly wiped tears of fear from her eyes. She was glad to feel her sister's embrace and she felt the warmth of the Lia Fail as it started to throb. There was a commotion all around her as Bran gave orders arranging for stronger security.

"You are a very brave young lady," Big Grey told her.

"I suppose Purr, but it was Ug'ghi Otha who saved my life."

The cat turned to the orc.

"How did you get to the wagon so quickly?" he asked.

"I could not sleep," explained Ug'ghi Otha, "and decided to get some night air. I saw the Queen's wagon door open. I thought that peculiar. So, I went to look in on her. As I approached the wagon, I heard some noise. When I entered the wagon, I saw the orc hovering over her. I was seized by rage. I did what I thought best." He looked at Molly. "You are my Queen. I am in your service."

She smiled.

"Thank you," she said. "We must complete our journey, to meet with your master." Prompted by the warmth of the stone, she turned to the others. "We must all work together to make this a better place."

Ug'ghi Otha did not speak, did not gesture. He simply left the wagon.

Brows stroked Molly's hair, and using a cloth, wiped the slime from her face. She closed her eyes and curled up against him.

"There . . . there . . . now . . . Master Purr is right," he said. "You are very brave, fitting for a Queen. On this day, our good friend the orc has proven his worth." He looked around the wagon, angry eyes now focused on Ancorbow. "We must sharpen our defenses," he told the man. "This was all too easy. And we must have eyes on the orc."

"We've only so many eyes," snapped Ancorbow.

He approached Molly and knelt to one knee.

"I have failed you, my Queen," he said.

"You have not failed me," she said. "It is I who have failed you by putting you in harm's way."

Bran gave a steadfast stare.

"My Queen, I can assure you this will not happen again," he said. "But the orc's heroism is all too convenient for my tastes. I don't trust him, nor must you!"

"But he saved my life," she said, snuggling into Brows. "That is all I need to know. That is all anyone needs to know."

Even though her words did not say as much, doubt of Ug'ghi Otha's intentions crept its way into her mind. She thought of the other orc, his last words repeating in her mind.

It's you . . . it's you . . . . it's you . . .

Then she thought, *Did the other orc recognize him? Did he know him?*

In her mind she saw Ug'ghi Otha, standing off to the side, silent, his eyes fixed on her.

Was this incident part of an evil deception on his part? Or, on the part of his master? No matter. He is needed.

She slid her hand over the pendant fingering the stone that continued to warm with her touch.

I have the Lia Fail and there is a second shard.

Things settled down, but it was difficult for her to go back to sleep after that. She had escaped one nightmare but fell into another. Her heart still thumped hard and her nerves tingled. From time to time she dropped into a light doze only to catch herself. She finally managed an hour or so of sleep and woke just before dawn to find that in all the commotion Shaer Thol had left.

* * *

As the morning sun peeked over the yawning horizon, a little boy, with light hair and a freckled face gave a stretch and rubbed his eyes. The sun felt good, and a shiver ran across his shoulders as the warmth penetrated. He wished he could have slept a bit longer, but the sun's brightness would not allow it.

He put on his brown trousers and a long-sleeved, green tunic with its elbows darned. His garb was too short for him, but his parents had little coin for anything else. Life was very hard, and he was always grateful for what he had.

He started the day early, as he did every day, to complete his chores, the first of which was fetching water for the family. This was his favorite chore if there could be such a thing. He did not love the chore so much as he enjoyed walking to the river and dawdling for a few moments, skipping stones across the calm surface.

He quietly slipped out of the house while his parents slept. He took a deep breath of the crisp morning air, grabbed two large wooden buckets, and started his long walk through the village and open fields, then down the mountain and to the river. The empty buckets were heavy and the rope handles rubbed his palms raw.

Along the way, he would stop to view the unspoiled and peaceful landscape, woodland, and marshlands where the river cut its way in giant bows and twisted turns through a mountain outcrop north of the Old Hills. This was his home, the Draaklel' Daan Defile, deep and overshadowed by trees. It was an unforgiving land where rocks reared like weeds and where uncaring winds blew hard and unyielding.

He was born and raised here, and though he often thought of what it would be like to live in a city, he was glad that in this place he would be given a chance to grow into a man. He wanted to show what he could do, and what he had learned, and he wanted to make his parents proud. He thought it was a good beginning, and hopefully would lead to a good end.

On this sunny morning, as he looked over the calm river, he could see dark creatures mulling about the mountains, positioning themselves amongst the rocks and ledges. He had never seen them, until but a few days ago when they first appeared. They were very strange. They had red glowing eyes and made strange clicking sounds like metal on metal. He called them clickers and even though he seemed to pay no attention to them, they surely kept a keen eye on him as he played.

When he first saw them, he told his father. But his father only chuckled at him, saying, "Your imagination sometimes gets the better of you."

He knew his father was wrong, that he was not imagining them. But at the same time, he did not want to think that something terrible could be happening. He wanted to believe his father. He wanted to be brave. So, he tried to ignore what his eyes told him.

If father won't take them seriously, why should I, he thought. *After all, they do seem harmless.*

The creatures kept watchful eyes on him, as they had in prior days. But something seemed odd this morning. They looked to be preoccupied in searching the shadows of the mountaintops for places to hide, places with a clear view of the land below, more so than in previous days. They started to make their way down from the mountains and to the river. There were so many of them, it was as if a cloud was passing overhead, its dark shadow slowly creeping down the mountainside. The clicking sound was deafening. Then the place grew quiet, and the mysterious, dark creatures disappeared, hidden within the shadows of the defile's rock ledges.

A sense of uneasiness filled him. He wondered what was happening and looked about the river. Everything was calm and tranquil. He did not know what to make of it all. He bent to pick up a smooth flattened stone when he felt a presence, someone near him. He looked about. There was no one.

He took a deep sigh.

Maybe father is right. Maybe it's just my imagination.

He threw the stone out into the river, watching it skip and dance – skip, skip, skip . . . eight times it flecked over the river until finally disappearing into the water. Just as he was about to choose another stone, a noise from behind startled him. He turned to see a tall, fair-skinned man with long black hair dressed in pure white.

"What is your name, my child?" asked the man.

"I am called Mas Tajae," he said apprehensively, eyeing the stranger. "What is your name, good sir?"

"I am called Dalgaes. I am from Tir Nan Og," said the man. "It is a place far, far from here. I am different from those who live here in your homeland. I am an elf, and I am King to all my subjects, those of the En' Edhel."

He was awestruck by the tall, white-figured man. He had never encountered an elf, let alone a King. So much was happening; so much was changing. He became nervous.

"Are you real? Is this my imagination?" he said.

Dalgaes could sense uneasiness in the boy.

"Mas Tajae, I am real," he said. "Do not fear me for I am here to help. This place is not safe for you and your family."

"My Lord," came a voice, "we must hurry."

Another elf appeared from behind. He was slim with auburn hair and also dressed in white. In one hand he carried a bow made of dark wood and ivory, and strapped to his back was a quiver of arrows. Two winged horses stood nearby, their size intimidating and even overpowering; pure white skin stretched over massive muscles, with mane and tail as gold as the sun.

Clickers. Elves. Winged horses. So many strange things, he thought.

His nervousness now turned to fear.

"Mas Tajae, I know you are scared by everything you see," said Dalgaes. "But you must trust me. This is my good friend, and he too is an elf. His name is Tinnfierl. Come now. We will take you and your family to safety and away from those on the mountains."

The frightened boy looked across the river. He could see hundreds of the dark creatures slowly making their way across the waters. Their eyes were blazing red coals, narrowed to slits. They waved long, curved swords that gleamed blood-red in the morning sun, and others had large bows and arrows. The beasts howled a horrifying scream of guttural, unintelligible words and metallic clatter. He turned to Dalgaes, a look of terror in his eyes.

"The clickers!" he screamed.

"My Lord, quickly! We do not have much time," implored Tinnfierl.

The boy then heard a sound he had never heard before, of air and wind swirling apart, a hissing and thunking as clouds of arrows flew through the sky and fell like fierce thunder. He saw the tips of the arrows clash with each other and emit sparks into the air.

Dalgaes quickly swept the boy from his feet in one motion. Along with Tinnfierl they mounted their winged horses and were off high into the blue sky.

As they soared above the expansive landscape, the boy could feel adrenaline filling him with excitement. Far below, he saw the dark creatures swarming over the mountains on both sides of the defile like flies on a carcass.

There are so many, he thought.

He hung on tight to the horse's long mane, and then its neck as the winged horse banked sharply east. He saw the fleeting shapes of the wretched dark creatures as they burned and pillaged his village. Dark smoke wallowed from the fires, and with it the dreadful stench of death.

He became fearful for his family.

Mother? Father?

He frantically searched for his family's house below but was confused, his sense of direction lost. Again, the winged horse made a sharp bank, this time westward, and as they swiftly ascended farther up the mountain he could make out his family's small house below. Through the tall pines, he could see it engulfed in flames, and to the side, a small gang of the evil brutes desecrating the charred bodies of his parents.

His eyes opened wide and stared unseeingly at the scene below. A moment of terror gripped him.

"No!" he cried out. "Mother! Father!"

In a breath, Tinnfierl lifted his mighty bow and released arrow after arrow down upon the demons. With a sickening sound, each arrow buried itself deeply into their bodies, their dead sacks of flesh slamming into the ground.

But it was of little solace to him, as a feeling of horror, heavy depression, and doom overcame him. He began to cry realizing he was now alone in the world.

Dalgaes embraced the boy.

"Be strong Mas Tajae. Be strong for your parents. We will protect you."

The winged horses soared high above the northern peaks of the defile, banked westward, and then began a sharp descent. Through his tears, he could see a great army of white under the banner of a White Star at the north entrance of the defile. It massed the breadth of the land for leagues, from the defile entrance north to the ancient ruins of the port city Huur Shec. As far as he could see, columns upon columns, thousands upon thousands of archers, cavalry, and those mounted on winged horses called the Vilyarok marched. The grand army was white-clad in armor, heavily armed, and perfectly in formation. He had never seen so many gathered in one place.

The winged horses softly glided down through the air and landed safely at the front of the enormous white army. They were met by a female elf of a slender frame with flowing black hair wearing a golden robe.

Dalgaes gently carried the sobbing boy to her.

"Mas Tajae, you are amongst friends," the Elf-King told him. "This is Aerdeil. She will care for you."

The boy knew he would never see his parents again, his eyes glassy and round in the sunlight.

"Why . . . why . . . did the clickers kill my parents," he whimpered. "Why would they do such a thing?"

A tear came to Dalgaes as he cupped the boy's soft face in his hand.

"There are some who act in ways because they are evil," he told the boy, "and evil only knows darkness and death. But do not fret Mas Tajae for you are now of the family of the En' Edhel."

Dalgaes handed him to Aerdeil who lovingly cradled him and pressed him to her bosom. He flung his arms around her. He could see her face, could feel her breath, could feel her warmth. He closed his eyes in a feeling of deep sorrow, feeling her arms around him, pulling him close. She gave him a gentle kiss on his forehead and then took him away.

A tall, young male elf, much like Dalgaes and Tinnfierl, approached. He was light-complexioned and lean, but with a hardened look about him. He was Jhaer Tystalaes, or *High General*, and his name was Col Shas. He was the son of the renowned Bur Shas, who had also been Jhaer Tystalaes, and confidant to Dalgaes and Erol Carrick. His father was an elite elven warrior who led armies through battle after battle. But warriors rarely know peace, and Bur Shas was no exception. He had been wounded several times in battle, and his body began to fail him. But he continued to fight. In his last battle, he was caught off guard by an orc's spear in South Eldor. It pierced his heart and became lodged in his lung. He stood for a brief moment in anguish before collapsing to the ground at the feet of his attacker, Drogur Vorn.

"The struggles of war take their toll," he once told Dalgaes, "and sometimes a warrior's only relief is death."

Now, Dalgaes smiled at Col Shas. The Elf-King saw the likeness of his father in him, along with a cold determination to do whatever was necessary to be victorious on the battlefield.

"My liege," said Col Shas. "A boy? Only one is saved? What of the others?"

"The brood moves quickly," said Dalgaes. "I am afraid we were too late. The defile seethes with evil."

"Where did they come from?" asked Col Shas.

"The seeds of evil were sowed, lo many years ago," said Dalgaes. "Your father knew this place and its riches. In times long gone, this place was a bustling trade route that connected the northern sea and the port city of Huur Shec to the Eldor. Elven wool, gold, turquoise, and ponies were traded for wheat, barley, rice, and sugar. It developed its own unique culture, one that fostered commerce and prosperity, especially in Huur Shec. The city grew rich and powerful from trading with surrounding towns and villages and engaging in commerce with merchants from the Eldor.

"But the times of peaceful trade were interrupted when the darkness waged war against the Harrow. Those of this region fled as overwhelming black forces ravaged the land, strangling trade. Huur Shec became a shell of what it once was. Eventually, the forces of good led by Carrick arrived and liberated the land, but it would never be the same. Few returned. Those that remained lived off the land as best they could, a simple and hard life. And now we are here once again to battle the darkness. My friends, time cycles, repeating over and over again. Hopefully, this time we shall get it right."

Col Shas looked at the defile's entrance, jagged rock on either side thrust straight up into the sky. There was an air of confidence about him.

"Time may indeed cycle, but on this day, we have numbers on our side," he said. "We can surge into the defile and easily overwhelm them, moving our forces along both sides."

Dalgaes nodded as he looked into the defile.

"Agreed. But not everything is solved with brute strength alone," he said. "Sometimes the best path to success is to review all the options one has."

Col Shas understood. He gave a deep sigh. Something had been bothering him. He had something else he wanted to say. He had been saving it up, reining in his emotions, waiting to find just the right words. Now he wanted to plunge forward.

"My King, if I may and with all due respect," he said, hesitation in his voice.

Dalgaes sensed reluctance in his Jhaer Tystalaes. He looked at him.

"What is it?" he said. "Speak your mind."

"We would not be facing this evil if we had traveled from the west, taking the Jhyl Vyr and Greenway, as I had suggested. We are far from Carrick and the Thorndell and any support he could provide. Why are we here in this forsaken place?"

"My friend, I understand your frustration. I have sensed your concern along our journey, and I have avoided explaining our strategy. It is time that I inform you of my plan. Yes, we could have taken the route you suggested, and yes, by now we would have joined with Carrick. But to what end? The northern lands of the Eldor would have been defenseless against the darkness. The White Star must secure much of the north, that which is west of the Old River. We will join with Carrick, not at the Thorndell but the citadel city of Chyh-Mehm."

He paused in reflective thought. He placed his hand on the forearm of Col Shas with a tightening grip.

"My friend, this war shall be different than those wars of long ago, those fought by your father. Carrick needs our help and the races of the Harrow depend on our forces. Soon, our world will become a world of victims and executioners, but through the mayhem and along the way we may meet with those who could help our effort. Trust me. Please, trust me."

Col Shas saw the resolve in the Elf-King's eyes and felt his strong grip. A chill rose inside him. He slowly closed his eyes and nodded.

Dalgaes took a deep sigh.

"So, here stands the great army of the White Star," he said, "at the threshold of the first of many battles. The mighty deeds of the Maker shall guide us as we crush the enemy. We shall put the flight to all those who despise righteousness and humiliate those who hate that which is good."

"You have my undying loyalty, my King," said Col Shas. "Let us wreak devastation on those who would wreak devastation on us!"

Dalgaes, Col Shas, and Tinnfierl set out their plans for the defile. As the brood was positioned within the jagged inner heights, they would send four wings of the Vilyarok, two on each side high above the outer ledges of the mountains. The brood would be forced to defend their positions by turning away from the defile. The Vilyarok would make several passes, and then another four wings would be sent into the defile itself, along the inner edges of the mountains, two wings on either side. This would pinch the brood, forcing them to defend in two directions. The second wave would be used to thin their numbers. After several passes, the great White Star would then march into the defile led by the full might of the Vilyarok.

When all was readied, Dalgaes gave the order.

"Sound the horns!" he shouted. "Let the whole of the darkness know the White Star is ready for battle, and that their punishment shall be severe! He who controls the skies conquers all!"

Tinnfierl joined the massive columns of archers while Col Shas relayed the order by giving a series of hand signals. Within moments blasts of horns could be heard echoing over the land and through the defile. The battle for the Draaklel' Daan had started.

* * *

The great elven army stirred under the sound of the battle horns. Hundreds of winged horses mounted with archers flew overhead in slow circles around in a rhythmic pattern, like a large white cloud against the sky, moving above the outer edges of the defile. The riders could see the brood horde, and as they flew lower, they could make out individual heads and bodies, some small, some huge. They shot arrows down on them, the arrows streaming through the ranks of the demons, hitting most of them. Cries of the brutes in pain rang through the defile.

The noise of the horns and wings of the Vilyarok was deafening. The second wave was soon released and the sky was filled with streaks of white. They burst over the mountaintops, soaring on a downdraft to skim the length of the defile's rocky walls. The evil creatures turned to defend their positions. But like a gathering thunderstorm, arrows continued to rain down on the demons with increasing strength, piercing through hands, throats, and skulls. The beasts whirled and let fly arrows in return, but the

Vilyarok's onslaught was ceaseless. The battle horns continued and mingled with panicked shrieks from the brood as both waves of Vilyarok passed overhead again and again. What brood remained began to fall back away from the mountaintops and into the defile. Blood spread across the defile and flowed into the river below.

Col Shas then gave the order, and the massive army began its march into the defile, with Dalgaes at the lead. Column after column made its way through the passage, following the river, trampling in the high, damp grass on the banks. Above, the Vilyarok now flew as guardians, maintaining a formation that stretched for leagues.

As the army marched through the defile, Dalgaes could sense a change. The warmth of the day was gone, and a chill came to the air. The sky, however, instead of being clear and bright, as in former calms, was now overspread with menacing clouds, swirling and ominous, billowing overhead. The heavy threatening clouds with their deep violent coloring approached the army with great speed and at the forefront was a deep black cloud. A strong wind swirled bringing a horrid stench.

Despair immediately gripped Dalgaes. He knew what the stench and cloud would bring. Quickly, he signaled Col Shas to release more Vilyarok into the sky and ready the archers.

Shouts rang through the Draaklel' Daan.

"Uakor Turg! Uakor Turg! Uakor Turg! Uakor Turg!"

The threatening clouds parted, and a Dark Rider mounted atop an armored black ajatar swooped down through the rift. The beast gave a piercing howl and rose over the army, high, high into the air. Inhaling with a great dragging pull on the fowl air, and stretching its neck forward it let out a burst of fire that decimated columns of elven warriors. Amidst the horror the White Star held its position, standing steadfast while elven archers and Vilyarok darkened the already black sky with arrows. But the heavily armored ajatar with impenetrable scales on its body and rows of back plates along its back and tail simply laughed.

The Dark Rider turned the ajatar's head and began a second descent. Vilyarok attempted to impede its path, but the mighty beast simply flicked the winged horses away with its spiked tail. Many of the Vilyarok came crashing down upon the columns of elven warriors who remained still with unflinching courage. A second blast of fire came from the ajatar's belly annihilating hundreds more and setting ablaze trees and shrubbery along the river. Dalgaes and Col Shas stood in dread. They knew that only a lone arrow finding its mark in the eye of the beast would fall the monster.

"More archers! More archers! The eye! Aim for the beast's eye!" shouted Col Shas.

The Dark Rider turned the ajatar's head for another descent amidst a cascading sea of arrows. As the ajatar sped onward taking aim at more columns of elven warriors, Dalgaes caught a glimpse of a green bolt of light from the corner of his eye, streaking down from atop the southernmost mountain peak. It surrounded the massive ajatar and Dark Rider in a mist of green. Then there came a brilliant flash and a massive explosion which shook the defile and fell the demons. There was a booming crash. The ajatar lay before the White Star, writhing and coiling in the endless green light, its body split apart and scorched, while the Dark Rider lay dead, its severed head at the feet of the Elf-King.

The clouds began to clear. Dalgaes turned to the southernmost mountain. He saw a small cat, light grey with darker grey stripes at its peak. Col Shas also spied the cat. The cat looked down from the mountain's misty heights and ran off followed by two other cats.

"My liege, what was the feline?' asked Col Shas. "Guild Lord?"

"That was no Guild Lord. They do not have such power, such magic," said Dalgaes quietly.

"If not a Guild Lord, then what?'

Dalgaes dared to speak the words. He took a deep breath.

"Tar Shor," he said. "The feline was Tar Shor."

The words spoken harkened back to a period of great unrest in the Harrow.

"Tar Shor?" said Col Shas. "The Fifth Guild?"

"Yes, the Fifth Guild, the Guild of Witches."

"The Huntress? But it cannot be her," said Col Shas in disbelief.

"I know of no other cat that can wield the power of the green light, other than the Huntress herself."

"But the Tar Shor and the Huntress were eradicated long ago by the other Guilds as N'alaquel."

Dalgaes kept his stare on the mighty mountain, looking to perhaps catch one more glimpse of the cat.

"You speak of a tale, told by many to mislead," he uttered.

Col Shas could sense a gleam of secrecy in the Elf-King's eyes.

"Mislead? How so?" he asked.

"What was given as truth was, in reality, an untruth, my friend," said Dalgaes. "The Huntress and many of the Tar Shor survived the purge. This I know."

Col Shas could sense his King's uneasiness. He chose his words wisely.

"My liege, if it was the Huntress then why has she returned now, at this place?" he asked. "Why would she use her powers to save us?"

Dalgaes put a hand on his friend's shoulder and shook him slightly.

"In time you will know all," he said. "But, on this day, know that she has allowed us to fight another day. She has been our savior and has delivered us from this trial. She may yet help us in the days to come. But tell no one of this, no one." He looked into the deep black eyes of Col Shas. "If our warriors ask, tell them the Maker looked fondly upon us this day. For now, let us not worry about the unknown but focus on the known. We have much to do and have already lost precious time. Let us continue onward."

The terrain of trampled brush looked as if a horrific storm had swept over it, strewing armaments, and scattering the bodies of fallen elven warriors in dark spots over the field. There was discipline and order as the great army collected their dead fellows, covering each with white silken sheets and carefully placing them upon golden caravans bound for Huur Shec. From there they would be taken over the great seas on their final journey home. At death, fallen elven warriors were to be buried in their homeland and offered a ceremony that accorded them the special status of Eir Shasos, or *great warrior*. As the long morning wore to an end the army had cleared the battlefield and took fire to the carcass of the black ajatar and demon rider. In time, the great army left the Draaklel' Daan, starting its long march south to the citadel city of Chyh-Mehm.

$$* * *$$

As the day wore on, the constant drumbeats of the Kyr Thysaer grew closer to the Thorndell Fields where the great armies of the Harrow and their leaders had gathered. By nightfall and from the north, the great feline army flowed as one joining with the other armies of the Harrow.

In his white command tent, high atop a hill overlooking the valley of jagged rock, Erol Carrick spent most of the day thinking of the news he had heard, trying to make sense of it. The more he thought about what he had heard, the more he became convinced that the journey ahead, and his future, would take a very different course.

Life is never simple, he thought. *It is always full of complications. And with every complication, the potential for a complication that has not been anticipated rises as well.*

He knew war was a daunting prospect, with its uncertainty and its risks. But so far it had been a necessary thing.

If it was not for war, many would be enslaved, and many more would be killed for their beliefs. Better to die for what you believe in than to live and let your beliefs die.

He felt restless and suddenly unfocused. He needed to get some air and stretch his legs. He put on his boots and laced them up.

He left his tent. With a mug of mead in a hand and the wind playing with his long white hair and beard, he saw his friends, those of the many armies below - Waywyn I'Kinillel, Bombadorn Roundthaler, Ranagul Dithil, Entur Donduin, Lil' Man, and Chumsey.

Noting the appearance of the two cats, the Balor Guild emissaries, he bent to one knee and welcomed them. There was a calmness in the way he moved, the way he stroked them, and how he scanned the landscape, even with all the calamitous news. It was as if he was seeing something else, something more, something others could not see.

In the cold of the night, the group looked over the great armies of the races gathered below; the men of Eldor under the banner of the Fist, the dwarves under the banner of the Axe, the men of Ahlgren under the banner of the Tree, and the powerful Kyr Thysaer under the banner of the Claw. The armies were formed into their units, companies and regiments, brigades and divisions.

Enormous war machines towered within the wide valley, as tents and fires drew the activity of thousands of warriors. The smell of embers wafted over the land, illuminated by the fires of smithies who forged weapons and armor, unlike anything that had been seen before.

From the hilltop the sounds were muted, low conversations, a calm that surprised Carrick.

"Too quiet," he said.

"Ah, it's always quiet before a big push," said the stout and doughty Roundthaler.

Those in the group spoke of the many movements and occurrences now taking place. They talked of Fairfax traveling to the east, to the Rakl. They talked of how Ras Amon had been ripped from the clutches of death, and how he now traveled west to face the demon librarian and resurrected Foulhand. They spoke of a third group that also traveled east. This was the group that brought with them an orc and the Lia Fail held by the Professor's niece Molly, and a second shard carried by a man descended from the time of kings. This was the group that planned to face the evil master of the Crag. Lastly, they spoke of the White Knight, of the vision that came to the Guild Lords.

During it all Carrick said nothing. His look remained calm and serene as he gazed upon the great armies and then off into the distance and the far horizon. As the talk died down and there came silence, the sound of a breeze was heard. It was like the sound of an old man who was whistling a dirge. It stirred an instant melancholy in the heart of Carrick. He felt a sudden chill as if he had just been in contact with a dead person, and for a moment he shivered.

"So, death has eluded the Learned One," he said. "It ignored him, stepping aside, leaving him to fight yet another battle. And my friend the Professor gives us his nieces and the Lia Fail along with a second shard and an orc. There is much strangeness but the forces of good are aligning as one. The battle lines are being drawn. A maelstrom of pain and blood will soon be upon us, my friends. Our task is a simple one - victory over the menace!"

"Here, here," the others said.

"What about the White Knight?" asked Roundthaler. "A vision most unusual from the cats."

"A fable my friend, just a fable, the stuff of storytellers," he said in a frosty tone. "I am afraid a legend cannot win a battle. The blood spilled in the upcoming days will come from those living and not from one born of the Maker's spirit. The fate of this land is in our hands. We cannot fail the races. I am afraid there will be no divine intervention. Oh, there may have been some of that in the past, as history tells us. But we did not understand the Maker's message then, and I am afraid we surely do not understand the message today. No, there will be no divine intervention this time, neither judgment nor mercy."

I'Kinillel looked at Carrick.

"My liege, what does tomorrow bring?" he asked.

Carrick took a sip of mead.

"We shall begin our march to Chyh-Mehm," he said. "As my rotund friend here said, the big push begins tomorrow. And who knows better of such big pushes than our big friend."

He rolled his eyes while taking another sip of mead.

Everyone gave a hearty laugh.

Roundthaler rubbed his protruding belly.

"Just let me lead the way," he bellowed. "I will take the fight to the cruel darkness!"

"What of the elven army?" asked Entur Donduin. "As they travel from Elandrake surely they'll attack the brood in the west."

Carrick became serious.

"No. They do not travel from the west. The White Star has journeyed via great ships to Huur Shec. I expect that as we speak the Elf-King has taken his forces through the Draaklel' Daan."

"The defile?"

"Yes. We will join with the army of the White Star at Chyh-Mehm. The darkness we face comprises the breadth of evil. We'll need their strength."

Donduin was skeptical.

"I don't understand," he said. "With the greatest of respect, the brood presents terror across the whole of the Harrow, on many fronts. We must meet them wherever they are."

"We cannot disperse our forces and fight on so many fronts," said Carrick. "That is the trap the brood would have us fall into. Unlike past wars where we could defeat them with extreme force, I am afraid the times have changed. They have added the Ra Draug as an ally, strong in strength and numbers. I fear the brood has become wiser in the ways of warfare. In time even evil learns from experiences and mistakes. No, my friend, we will meet them in battle but on our terms." He turned and pointed to the east. "We must meet them as they spew from their evil land. The only way to stop a flood is to cut off the flow."

"Are we then to concede parts of the Harrow?" asked I'Kinillel.

A slow smile spread over Carrick's cleanly sculptured features.

"Hardly. We will go about things methodically and first defend the heart of the Harrow and that part where the evil churns forth its doom," he said. "But we will have forces elsewhere. Thaken will take some of his men and meet up with the Learned One. They will face the evil in the west, while Mirandell journeys to the Rakl. Each will give us the time we need to defeat the brood. It will also give time for the Lia Fail to defy the wickedness that dwells in the Drueger. We are tasked with securing the heart of the Harrow, and we will."

"But isn't Thaken's force small?" asked I'Kinillel. "And the good wizard has only one Fenri pack to face what surely will be a formidable Ra Draug force at the Rakl. I fear they'll be slaughtered."

"Let's not forget Mistmere is already lost," reminded Donduin, "and the land swarms with Dark Wizards."

"Ha, even a Dark Wizard can fall at my axe!" roared Roundthaler. "Do you not believe that a plan has been devised? Fools!"

"Friends, friends," said Carrick raising a hand, "the art of war is the art of deception and by always giving an appearance contrary to what one is, one increases the chances of victory. We will play on the brood's emotions, their impatience, and their insatiable thirst for blood. This is their weakness. We will bring our forces south of Chyh-Mehm, all that is except the Kyr Thysaer. They will be positioned to the north of the city, a position well covered by the city's walls and spires. Meanwhile, the White Star shall extend one flank to the south of Mistmere. The other flank will proceed south along the Old River and hold until the trap has been sprung."

"What's this deception you speak of?" asked Dithil.

"Were you not listening?" said Roundthaler in a tone and loudness of voice that made everyone tremble.

Carrick took another sip of mead.

"The deception I speak of will be of historic proportions," he said. "While this deception is the foundation for our eventual victory, our tactics will play into the brood's emotions. First, our archers from the southern force will make the sky black with arrows. This will give us cover to begin to cross the river. The brood will respond and attack as they believe us vulnerable while we make the crossing. They will look to make a hasty victory. We will suffer losses but the archers will continue to blacken the skies and our armies will continue to surge ahead. And the enemy, in all their blood rage will commit more of its forces.

"It is at that point that the drums of the Balor Guild will begin and release the Kyr Thysaer. The great army of the Claw will heave into the brood. They will split the demons in half. The brood will be confused and turn to fight the Kyr Thysaer. We will then bring the full force of our might from the south, over the river, and fully engage the enemy. The Kyr Thysaer will further divide the brood, making pass after pass after pass. As we continue to take the fight to the enemy from the south, the White Star will then attack from the north. We'll have the scum circled, in disarray, and ripe for the kill."

I'Kinillel was not convinced.

"Much too easy," he said. "You've forgotten one thing. What of the Dark Riders? The brood will be accompanied by the winged evil. How will we defend against such vileness?"

"Dark Riders? Hmm . . . Carrick, how will we defend against such hideous beasties?" asked Roundthaler sarcastically, raking his fingers through his beard.

Carrick smiled.

"My friends, what I have not told you is Dalgaes brings the whole of the White Star to include the Vilyarok," he said. "The Vilyarok and our own Moondancer shall defend against such evil. Once we have broken the brood here in this place, we will set our armies across the land to finish the deed. So, there you have it."

"And if the elves are delayed?" asked I'Kinillel tersely. "What then?"

Carrick stared at the man, his eyes wide and blazing.

"We fight and die together," he said.

Roundthaler had an angry look about him.

"Any other questions?" he asked. With no response, he laughed. "I thought so!"

A herald then approached them.

"Sir, a black horse, and a young man wish to speak with you," he told Carrick. "I told them you were very busy, but they are insistent."

Carrick gave a glance to the herald and nodded.

"I will see them."

The herald beckoned into the darkness. There came the sound of a horse coming at a trot. Emerging through the misty night was a tall and sturdy black horse with a young man saddled atop. He appeared tired and cold. He was pale, almost pallid under what seemed to be a usual healthy complexion.

Carrick immediately recognized the magnificent horse as one of the Ure Rokko. He smiled.

The horse bowed his great neck.

"My friend Erol Carrick, it is good to see you," said the horse in a strong voice.

Roundthaler also recognized the horse.

"By the Maker," he said with a broad smile. "The stars are aligning in our favor, my friends. The great warrior horse of ages past has returned."

Carrick walked over to the horse, rubbing the horse's neck. He let the horse nuzzle the side of his face.

"Saraanth," he said softly, "you bring warmth to my heart in this most difficult of times. I know of the decimation of Portmoor. I am saddened by the loss of Master Harwell. I wish he were here with us."

"His spirit will always be with us Erol," said Saraanth. "He will never be forgotten."

A surge of emotion welled up within Carrick, and he struggled to contain it. Seeing the great horse brought memories of battles past when he and Harwell fought together. The silent visions flashed to him, of forgotten hopes and fears, of long-dead friends in faraway graves, remembered only by fellow warriors. Those were times long past, but they lived on through harsh and cold memories.

He turned to the young man.

"And who is this that rides with the mighty Saraanth?" he asked.

There came a burst of energy from the young man. In front of him stood the great Erol Carrick, a legend and hero to all the good races.

"I'm Elban Miragrin, sir," he said with excitement, his voice strong and daring. "We've traveled a great distance to be here. I want to join the fight against the darkness. They destroyed my home, they endangered my family, and they killed Master Harwell."

Carrick looked into Miragrin's eyes in a way that could be interpreted as a test. But the young man was unyielding, meeting the glare.

Carrick found just what he had hoped for. Miragrin's eyes were serious and deep. There was no fear or rage, only unwavering courage.

He knew what he had to say.

"Young Miragrin, then fight you shall!" he told the young man. "You shall fight alongside me under the banner of the Tree. Now get some rest. Tomorrow we begin our march east."

"Thank you, sir. You will not regret this."

Excitement filled Miragrin's face. He and Saraanth trotted off into the darkness.

"So, it begins," said Carrick with ease. "We who live in the shadow of war know of only one end - victory!"

He took a last sip of mead and returned to his command tent followed by Roundthaler, leaving the others to the chill of the night air.

There was a quiet astonishment in the group. Never had the whole of the White Star been assembled, for during times of war much of the great elven army remained at Tir Nan Og to defend the motherland. And now, one of the greatest Ure Rokko warriors joined the fight. There was no doubt, no denying the simple fact that the greatest war in history was about to be undertaken, the tragedy of which would unfold itself before their eyes.

Chumsey looked at Lil' Man. They sped from the hilltop and to the Kyr Thysaer below, preparing for the next day's travels. Few words were spoken between them, for they understood each other and there was clearness and simplicity in what Carrick had presented. Still, the silence had nothing to mark it as gloomy; there was merely quiet recognition of the trials before them.

* * *

In the darkness of night, something within the black recesses of the great mountain Drar Druul stirred. Not a living soul in the Harrow felt or sensed the tremble; for it was slight, barely apparent, and yet it was there. It was as if silken threads of cobwebs were brushing across one's flesh, hardly noticeable unless one questioned what had just happened. It was an evil so great, so horrible that it surpassed all the temporal and even eternal evils of all realities combined. The destruction, or above all the damnation, of the Harrow's races would easily and quickly succumb to this darkness. Yet, it stirred but for a moment, for one moment in time, and then it was gone, receding into the darkness. Doom remained asleep.

So ends the first part of the history of the Second Shadow War as written by Tollen Popperdock . . .

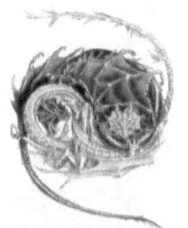

APPENDIX I
SINOME A' ELLER
THE GREAT UPHEAVAL
AN EXCERPT FROM THE I' QARMA EN' ILYA
THE BOOK OF HISTORIES

Note: The I' Qarma En' Ilya is a compilation of writings from the many scribes, scholars, and historians over the ages. They are known as the Coiasira. The Sinome A' Eller is the first section of the great book. There are three textual witnesses to the Sinome A' Eller: the fragments of history from the Mur' Edan, the elven book called the Edhel Yena, and the historical writings of the En' Naug. Over the ages, the Sinome A' Eller has been translated many times rendering several versions. The following is the composition by the historian Ishaq bul Hune of the Age of Kings and is structured around the recurring theme *ie' i' yesta*, or with the new reality.

AT THE START OF IT ALL was darkness and within the darkness a great mirror, the Madh Nauk. And the Maker looked within the Madh Nauk and from its reflection was great disorder. This was the beginning of the great upheaval. From the disorder, the Maker wrought new life and called the new life En' Coia. There were those that lived in the reality just before the great upheaval, those that somehow survived the disorder. These were small creatures, those able to seek safety within the clefts of rock and stone. These were of the En' Coia and called the I' Atya. There were others, those that were altered, creatures already of bone and flesh, their bodies twisted into new shapes, tortured anguish from the old. These were of the En' Coia and called the I' Naru. There were some, those born anew from the darkest of elements of the new reality, from rock and fire, of ghastly winds. These were of the En' Coia and called the I' Mortu. And in time places where secrets and evil held dominion became known to the En' Coia, and these places were called the I' Drar, and from this gloom there came the I' Ksh. The I' Ksh were horrible things, ancient creatures, born of evil, and hatred, and greed. All this happened over time, but time is a finite resource and not to be wasted. To understand time is to understand its passages. So, we shall start at the start of it all.

1. Before time there was darkness and the great mirror, the Madh Nauk.

2. All that has ever existed or will exist is but a reflection from the great mirror, and it is the Maker who looks within the mirror and controls what is reflected.

3. And the Maker saw reflected great disorder, and in an instant, a blink of an eye, the Maker brought forth a great transformation within the great mirror's reflection.

4. The very fabric of existence changed in a single moment, and it was called the Ay' Panul, and from it, a new reality was formed.

5. There was no warning; at once, what had been was cast in ruin.

6. The firmament changed from pale blue to black, and the Shyjael Tyl was torn asunder and caressed the land, rising breaths creating great wisps of white therein.

7. Mayhem of rock and earth brought forth fire and filled the firmament with deadly smoke. Mountains were flattened while new peaks jutted from the chaos. Rivers and oceans were lost in a sea of fire and molten rock.

8. The heavens rumbled and darkness filled the sky, blotting out the light, while fire spewed from the core of existence. A powerful wind of fire sprung up, battering all.

9. The waves of death swirled about the land; the torrent of destruction overwhelmed as a new reality was made.

10. What was became what is.

11. When the Maker was done with the new reality he gazed into the Madh Nauk and from its reflection decided to form two more realities. There was the Tau Menel for those souls that would live forever near the Maker, and the Mori Assa for those souls that would live forever in darkness.

12. For only the Maker knows, and for only the Maker can look within the Madh Nauk and bring about life and death, and in death, only the Maker can know the heart and judge fairly.

13. And when he was done fashioning the Tau Menel and Mori Assa, the Maker gazed within the great mirror and saw his reflection, but his reflection morphed into strangeness, a twisted and contorted image. The Maker called this image Zi Illsku and banished it to eternal darkness in Mori Assa.

14. The Maker was troubled by Zi Illsku but looked upon the change with delight; for the existence reflected is random, in all its ways, something to be believed, in every incidence.

15. As the Maker looked over the disorder he saw that the new reality was ready for life; and the Maker brought forth the elements to make such life, from the cracks of rocks, from the surface of still waters, from shimmering slime, did life begin to emerge.

16. From the disorder wrought by the Maker, the beginnings of life began to progress and take new shapes. The Maker spoke and called the new life En' Coia.

17. There were those that lived in the time just before the great upheaval, those that had survived the disorder. These were the ones hidden away in crevices, for they were small enough and required little. These were of the En' Coia and called the I' Atya.

18. There were those that were transformed. Bone and flesh cracked and tore, as new life contorted and twisted from the old. These were of the En' Coia and called the I' Naru.

19. There were others, those that sprang anew from the darkness and fire. This was life born of slime and rock and fire, and of the deathly air. These were of the En' Coia and called the I' Mortu.

20. Time knew no boundary for it passed without record, ages upon ages of cycles.

21. Then rains came and the fires were cooled.

22. The rains lasted for ages and new seas were formed while landmasses were apportioned.

23. Finally, the moment came when the I' Urnu broke through the clouds and to the ground, and warmth came to the new reality.

24. The En' Coia rejoiced in the warmth and saw that it was good.

25. The I' Urnu produced a brilliant but soft ring of color in the firmament, and the Maker appeared within the color and seized the brilliance and filled parts of the ground with hardened stones of brightness, and sowed seeds of light in drills and broadcast over the land.

26. The Maker called the stones Ondo En' Tir, and the seeds he called Qual Ered, and each was given a power known only to the Maker.

27. And the Maker said unto the En' Coia that such was the glory and power of what he had done, and that the stones and seeds were to be untouched, and that if his

words went unheeded all would be placed within the darkness of the Mori Assa.

28. The En' Coia cowered under the words as if in fear of death but as time passed the brilliance of the firmament faded and the Maker's words and good deeds were forgotten.

29. But the Maker had not lamented the new reality for in his wisdom he withdrew into different places and went about creating opportunities for more randomness, for coming times and in those places yet discovered.

30. And so it came to pass that variations of the En' Coia took shape and began to populate the new reality.

31. From the I' Atya, I' Naru, and I' Mortu races were formed in response to the environment in which they found themselves. They found places where they could be sustained but fed off each other. Soon war came to the new reality and with it change.

32. Some of the I' Naru began to gain powers, abilities to manipulate existence, time, and space. For these few, their special powers grew in intensity and soon they dominated their kind and those of the I' Atya and I' Mortu.

33. War prevailed and battles were fought, and those who were bone of bone and flesh of flesh sought to be bound to each other.

34. And the land fractured under the many battles, and war was made by many and great rivalries formed.

35. And of war, there can be no conquest made: and where conquest has not been made or no longer exists, the right of demanding possessions cannot exist, since a claim cannot be made to retain that which one has not, or that which he no longer has.

36. Battle upon battle raged as a great sorting of things occurred.

37. Places were filled with slaughter, bloodshed, and destruction; for when the Maker brings battle, pestilence and famine are also wrought upon the land, the innocent suffer equally with the guilty.

38. Alliances were forged between the strong, and the weak trembled.

39. Time passed and some alliances were strengthened while others faded and new alliances were born.

40. The rampage of battle and death continued in those places known to the races, but there were many places yet explored that held dark secrets and evil.

41. In time places where secrets and evil held dominion became known to the En' Coia, and these places were called the I' Drar, and from this darkness there came the I' Ksh.

42. The I' Ksh were horrible things, ancient creatures, born of evil, and hatred, and greed.

43. The evil struck at the En' Coia and withered all that was good.

44. Yet, where there is darkness there must be light, for the night cannot exist without the morning; for the Maker has devised it in this manner.

45. So there came to the new reality the Anar Ere, or Enlightened Ones and they brought knowledge and understanding; for they were the messengers and attendants of the Maker and pure and incorruptible.

46. And the Anar Ere were sent amongst the En' Coia with the words of the Maker.

47. There was Alu who held dominion over the water and seas; Menel who brought the warmth of the I' Urnu and the cold of night; Kemel who shook the land and raised mountains and furrowed deep valleys; Sil who stirred the winds and brought the seasons.

48. But the races were ignorant of the messages brought by the messengers, and they were mocked, and the Maker's words despised and the messengers abused, and there seemed no remedy.

49. This darkness in the minds of the En' Coia, this ignorance of the Maker's words, of his nature and his will, was and continues to be the origin of all evil in the land.

50. Thus, did the ignorance of the Maker's words produce that consummation of all wickedness and despair, a darkness so black that reality seemed to vanquish. For it was on this darkness of mind did the I' Ksh erect their kingdom and throne, for such darkness became more commanding than light.

51. While the I' Ksh feasted on the souls of the En' Coia amid the horrors of the burning land did the Maker contemplate a correction.

52. For the Maker saw that the new reality would have limited randomness and therefore brought forth another messenger who was called Nim Dagora; he had been of flesh and bone and was joined with the Anar Ere.

53. And the Maker made Nim Dagora hold dominion over might and justice; he appeared as white within a light.

54. Nim Dagora slew the darkness of the I' Ksh and brought peace and comfort to those panicked and of worrisome hearts.

55. And when calm was restored to the land did Nim Dagora return to the Maker who said unto him that he would be the messenger of light whenever darkness would prevail.

56. The En' Coia were reawakened to the messages of the Anar Ere, and they entrusted the Anar Ere with the responsibility of bringing forth new decrees from the Maker and in his name.

57. In later times the Anar Ere would be known as the Fae Tari, or Spirit Kings and they looked to bring peace to the land through their actions, and as ordained by the Maker.

58. So marked the Sinome A' Eller and a time of savagery.

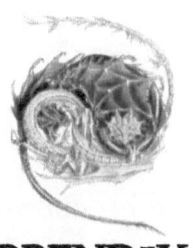

APPENDIX II
THE ORN EN' COA
OF THE RACES

AN EXCERPT FROM THE I' QARMA EN' ILYA
THE BOOK OF HISTORIES

Note: The I' Qarma En' Ilya is a compilation of writings from the many scribes, scholars, and historians over the ages. They are known as the Coiasira. The Orn En' Coa is a section of the great book that provides a graphical depiction of the Harrow's races. Its textual witness is the Sinome A' Eller, the first section of the I' Qarma En' Ilya that describes the creation of the Harrow. The following is the composition by the historian Zuha Ben Berna of the Age of Kings. It is based on an interpretation of the Sinome A' Eller or The Great Upheaval, the first section of the I' Qarma En' Ilya.

THE MAKER CREATES ALL LIFE, and all life is created for a reason, a purpose, to live in his light which is the light of his glory. So too did the Maker create awareness, and gifted awareness to some of his creations to progress through. It was this awareness that fashioned the first word, and the first word became the foundation for language, which formed the new reality. Of special consequence did the Maker give some creatures the ability to reason and make choices, and this too was part of the gift of awareness. The Maker gave his creations everything needed from the beginning of life to eternity. Everything was already set in life, to give life what it needs as it advances. The reality has been created for all creatures to live, awakening to higher levels of awareness with the ability to expand life infinitely.

The Maker created his creatures, not because of any need for them, but because of his magnanimity and generosity, and a desire for difference and change. His creations are based on truths and imaginative ideas. It is modified again and again. All started as a simple life form, and over time changed into complex forms and on and on until life progressed to its current state.

It is truth there are some changes and variations within the same plant or creature groups over some time, and there is truth that some in one group progressed and changed into another form of life, forming different groups of creatures. Because there is a likeness in anatomy and structure among some of these different creatures, it is a mark of the Maker's creativity, of his wanted desire for randomness and variations within his creations.

It is also truth that over time creatures served many uses throughout the Harrow. Some served as beasts of burden for carrying others and cargo, while others were used for war, and yet others were used as summoned creatures to defend wizards and sages and armies. It is common for some creatures to be hunted as food or for their fur, or alchemical properties, those creatures without the gifts of speech or thought, or choice. For some, they were used as a workforce and enslaved. While a creature may serve one primary purpose, this does not mean its role is final, for as it is known the Maker values randomness.

OF THE RACES, BESTIARY:

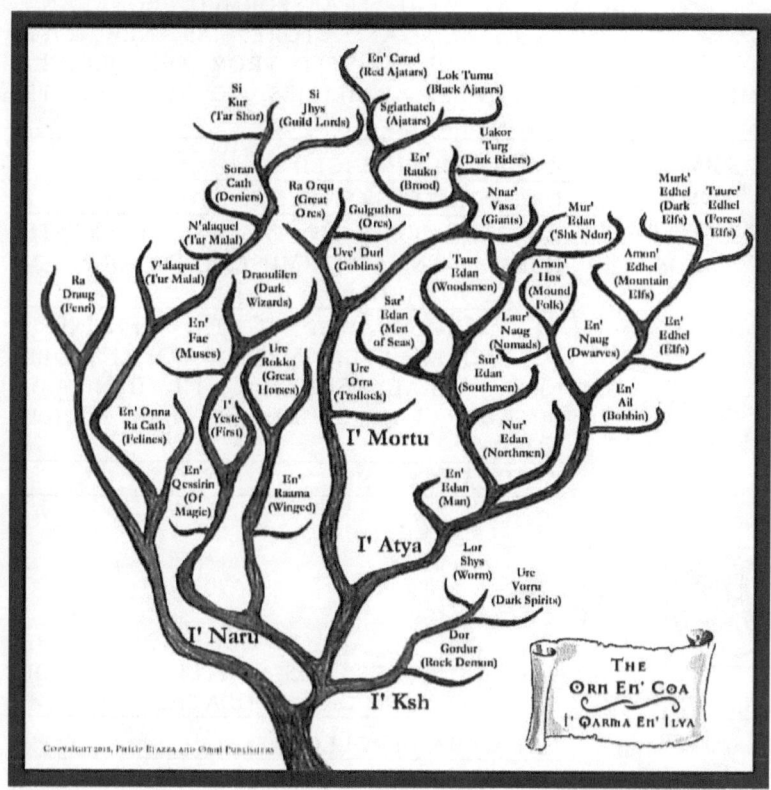

En' Carad (Red Ajatars)
Lok Tumu (Black Ajatars)
Si Kur (Tar Shor)
Si Jhys (Guild Lords)
Sglathatch (Ajatars)
Uakor Turg (Dark Riders)
En' Rauko (Brood)
Soran Cath (Deniers)
Ra Orqu (Great Orcs)
Gulguthra (Orcs)
Nnar' Vasa (Giants)
Mur' Edan ('Shk Ndor)
Murk' Edhel (Dark Elfs)
Taure' Edhel (Forest Elfs)
N'alaquel (Tar Malal)
V'alaquel (Tur Malal)
Draoulilen (Dark Wizards)
Uve' Durl (Goblins)
Taur Edan (Woodsmen)
Amon' Hos (Mound Folk)
Amon' Edhel (Mountain Elfs)
Ra Draug (Fenri)
En' Fae (Muses)
Ure Rokko (Great Horses)
Sar' Edan (Men of Seas)
Laur Naug (Nomads)
En' Naug (Dwarves)
En' Edhel (Elfs)
En' Onna Ra Cath (Felines)
I' Yeste (First)
Ure Orra (Trollock)
Sur' Edan (Southmen)
En' Ail (Bobbin)
I' Mortu
En' Qessirin (Of Magic)
En' Raama (Winged)
Nur' Edan (Northmen)
En' Edan (Man)
I' Atya
Lor Shys (Worm)
Ure Vorru (Dark Spirits)
I' Naru
Dor Gordur (Rock Demon)
I' Ksh
COPYRIGHT 2015, PHILIP BLAZZA AND OHMI PUBLISHERS

THE ORN EN' COA I' QARMA EN' ILYA

I' ATYA

THOSE THAT LIVED IN THE TIME JUST BEFORE THE GREAT UPHEAVAL, HAVING SURVIVED THE DISORDER, HIDDEN AWAY IN CREVICES, FOR THEY WERE SMALL ENOUGH AND REQUIRED LITTLE.

ANONA	EN' EDAN (MAN), NUR' EDAN (NORTHMEN), SUR' EDAN (SOUTHMEN), SAR' EDAN (MEN OF SEAS), TAUR EDAN (WOODSMEN), MUR' EDAN (MEN OF 'SHK NDOR)
NAUGRIM	EN' NAUG (DWARVES), AMON' HOS

	(MOUND FOLK), LAUR' NAUG (NOMADS)
ANNATH	EN' AIL (BOBBINS)
QUESSN	EN' EDHEL (ELFS), AMON' EDHEL (MOUNTAIN ELFS), TAURE' EDHEL (FOREST ELFS), MURK' EDHEL (DARK ELFS)

I' NARU

THOSE THAT WERE TRANSFORMED. BONE AND FLESH CRACKED AND TORE, AS NEW LIFE CONTORTED AND TWISTED FROM THE OLD. IN TIME SOME GAIN POWERS, ABILITIES TO MANIPULATE EXISTENCE, TIME, AND SPACE.

KRAE	EN' RAAMA (WINGED)
HORUKE	URE ROKKO (GREAT HORSES)
UKPELL	EN' QESSIRIN (OF MAGIC), I' YESTE (FIRST), EN' FAE (MUSES), DRAOULILEN (DARK WIZARDS)
CAAV	EN' ONNA (RA CATH, FELINES), V'ALAQUEL (TUR MALAL), N'ALAQUEL (TAR MALAL), SORAN CATH (DENIERS), SI KUR (TAR SHOR), SI JHYS (GUILD LORDS)
HUNDUR	RA DRAUG (FENRI)

I' MORTU

THOSE THAT SPRANG ANEW FROM THE DARKNESS AND FIRE. THIS WAS LIFE BORN OF SLIME AND ROCK AND FIRE, AND OF THE DEATHLY AIR.

AVROL	URE ORRA (TROLLOCK)
GREAAV	UVE' DURL (GOBLINS), GULGURTHA (ORCS), RA ORQU (GREAT ORCS)
AVALL	NNAR' VASA (GIANTS)
AVHERUKO	EN' RAUKO (BROOD), UAKOR TURG (DARK RIDERS)
SGIATHATCH	LOK TUMU (BLACK AJATARS), EN' CARAD (RED AJATARS)

I' KSH

IN TIME PLACES WHERE SECRETS AND EVIL HELD DOMINION, THERE CAME ANCIENT CREATURES, BORN OF EVIL, HATRED, AND GREED.

DOR GORDUR (ROCK DEMON), URE VORRU (DARK SPIRITS), LOR SHYS (WORM)

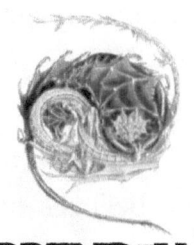

APPENDIX III
PARMA EN' QUENTA
OF TIME AND THE AGES

AN EXCERPT FROM THE I' QARMA EN' ILYA
THE BOOK OF HISTORIES

Note: The I' Qarma En' Ilya is a compilation of writings from the many scribes, scholars, and historians over the ages. They are known as the Coiasira. The Parma En' Quenta is a section of the great book dealing with the concept of time and the ages. Its author is Daibheid Terrad of the En' Naug. His work was commissioned by the Paragon Boidac Aldril during the Age of Kings. The foundation of the information contained in this section is based on the writings from the Harrow's many scholars, including Paart Os, Master Sage of the Sur' Edan.

A LETTER TO THE PARAGON: Venerated Paragon Boidac Aldril, Grand Protector of the En' Naug, and servant to the Maker:

This book I destined for you, my very dear Protector, as soon as it was complete, for you and you alone shall be the first to read its contents, in its fullness, and I am convinced that it could be read by no one except yourself.

As I am fortunate to be a member of the Coiasira, this book shall be numbered as one of many in the collection of books so named the I' Qarma En' Ilya. I have named this book the Parma En' Quenta for it deals with the understanding of time and history, and as you so generously entrusted. Be it known that the Grand Sage of the Coiasira, Juel Lotknie, has asked for an opinion by letter of my work from other contributing authors. He has sent portions of this book from which he believes others would be able to read the remainder in due time. To its understanding, he devoted unfaltering toil, as is apparent from attempts of his which I send you herewith. But Lotknie's toil was not in vain for such is the Coiasira as the many scholars obey no one but their master, knowledge itself. Accept now this token, such as it is and long overdue though it be, of my devotion for you, and burst through its restraints, if there are any, with your wonted grandness.

Paart Os, Master Sage to his Highness Urm Riorn of the House Riorn, as his eyes gazed upon portions, told me the said book captures the knowledge you have requested and in great elegance. On this point I suspend judgment; it is your place to define for us what view we should take thereon, to whose favor and kindness I unreservedly commit myself and remain.

> At the command of your Veneration,
> Daibheid Terrad
> Ronwe, Year One, Age of Kings

* * *

TIME IS A TRAVELER. It walks alone down the pathway and its journey is never-ending.

Time has its own nature, independent of the existence or non-existence of the created world. It is forever and eternal. It is neither the number of motions nor the duration of things, their amount of being. It is not an actual existent, for the past is no longer here, the future is not yet, and the present is merely the now which binds the past to the future.

All have been made in the service of time, both living and dead, and there can be no precise interval by which time can be measured as it is fluid. But it is time that helps to note the passing of itself and the events that occur within it.

Since the Ay' Panul, the En' Coia has looked to mark the passing of time based on the movement of the I' Urnu in the firmament. The origins of today's time measurement resemble the description of passing time first used by the Taure' Edhel (Forest Elfs). It is this measurement that is used as a foundation for reckoning time in ordinary affairs.

For most races of the En' Coia the most common segment of time is measured by the rise and setting of the I' Urnu. This is called a Bur Re, or small moment. Within a Bur Re are the Saurn and Caurn. The Saurn is the point when the I' Urnu first appears and travels high into the firmament. The Caurn is the point when the I' Urnu travels low and disappears thereby manifesting darkness.

As time passed over the ages, a method to measure the passing of several Bur Re was adopted by some of the En' Coia. This measure is referred to as a Tur Re, or large moment. It is also sometimes referred to as a cycle. The Taure' Edhel referred to this cycle, to the movement of the I' Urnu over a large expanse of time, as Re Anar. For the Taure' Edhel this large expanse of time comes in four segments that repeat. First, there comes the time of Ered, or unfurling of tree buds; next comes the time of Lazqe, or when the forest trees are full; next comes the time of Lanta, or when the trees drop their leaves; finally, there is the time of Rudh or the hardening of tree bark. A cycle is therefore the passing of a set of the four segments of time, each of which may vary in length of time.

Similar to the Taure' Edhel, the Sur' Edan (Southmen) marked a cycle of the I' Urnu in four segments; however, the segments were defined by the planting, growth, and harvesting, and storage of crops. For the Sur' Edan, the start of a cycle is Talar, or that time when furrows are formed for planting. This is followed by Ehtele, or that time when seeds sprout and flourish. Next is the Yavan, or that time when the harvest is made. Lastly is the Ronwe, or when the harvest is stored and the ground hardens. So too did the other races within the En' Edan assume this method.

The Ra Cath formulated a different method of measuring a cycle. Instead of four segments, the Ra Cath came to mark a cycle in only two segments and based on the thickness of fur. The first segment is called Laire Findl, or that time when the Ra Cath's fur sheds and is the thinnest. The other segment is called Hrive Findl, marking that time when the fur is thickest. Like the Ra Cath, the En' Raama came to mark a cycle in two segments, the Urnu

Hwesta or warm winds, and the Dorn Hwesta or time of cold winds.

As it regards the Brood or the Sgiathatch little is known as to how such evil marks cycles. What is known can only be suggested from lore where time seems to be segmented into two parts, Dor Toha or great battle, and Dor Seere, or preparation for battle. Here, the cycle is not dependent on the I' Urnu as each segment can expand over several cycles as would be marked by other races of the En' Coia.

With the advent of numbers and counting by the Ra Cath, and having become an integral part of everyday existence, the measurement of time took form. The Ra Cath first began noting time in a numeric sense with the death of Ra Carathor who is known as the Prime Heru and first Guild Lord. The great feline had perished on the battlefield, the last battle of the Great War (Ra Ru Dagora), and he had done so in grand glory taking with him the soul of the evil Zeph Drach.

The death of such a great being brought forth tribute from each of the En' Coia, save those of evil spirit and intent. Masses of En' Coia including each of the great chieftains of the time converged on the Ra Cath's homeland, known as Ra I' Ru. Later the homeland would be known as Dagda, named so in honor of the second Heru and son of Ra Carathor, Ra Dagda. At the time of Ra Carathor's tribute, a great meeting of all the chieftains of the righteous was held and this was known as the I' Ra Omenta. As it were, each chieftain brought with them their most trusted scribes and scholars to mark the occasion. Foremost of the scholars was the man of the Sur' Edan called Paart Os, and it was he who was called by the chieftains, under the direction of Urm Riorn, to direct the meeting and bring forth new ways. Here, and for the first time did the congregation of scribes and scholars meet as one, and henceforth were called the Coiasira.

Decisions of great consequence were made at the I' Ra Omenta, decisions that provided the foundation of the current state. First, it was decided to use a common tongue and a common set of time measurements. The small moment or *Bur Re or e' daye* in the old tongue would be called day. A grouping of four days or e' yweke would be called a week. The large moment or Tur Re or e' yare would be called year. Each of the En' Coia would retain their method of segmenting a Tur Re, or year. It was also decided that because a year could expand based on how it was segmented, the Coiasira would meet once each year to declare the end of one year and the start of another. The Coiasira would also retain the chronology of historical events and do so in terms of time elapsed from the noted death of the great Ra Carathor. They decided on the delineation of larger segments of time, or e' ayene and called such segments of time ages. The death of Ra Carathor would therefore mark the end of the Age of Fire and the start of a new age. It would be known as Year One of the Age of Kings.

* * *

CHRONOLOGY OF TIME: AGE OF FIRE, OR COIASIRA EN' NAUR

i. The Maker brings forth the great transformation, the Ay' Panul, and from it a new reality forms.

ii. The elements to make life are given; the En' Coia takes shape in a rudimentary form.

iii. The I' Urnu warms the new reality.

iv. The Maker fills the rock with stones called Ondo En' Tir, and plants seeds called Qual Ered in furrows; the Maker gives each a power known only to the Maker.

v. Variations of the En' Coia take shape and begin to populate the new reality - the I' Atya, the I' Naru, and the I' Mortu.

vi. From the I' Atya, the I' Naru, and the I' Mortu, races are formed.

vii. Some of the I' Naru gain powers and the ability to manipulate existence, time, and space. They dominate their kind and the I' Atya and I' Mortu.

viii. Great battles are fought, alliances and rivalries are formed.

ix. The Ure Orra leave the I' Mortu and migrate to the vast northern mountains to the west. Great cities within the mountains are constructed.

x. Of the Sgiathatch (Ajatars), the En' Carad disavows the I' Mortu while the Lok Tumu remains loyal.

Both maintain existence at 'Ksh Nierwes, but battles are waged for dominance.

xi. Battles bring about displacement and migration of the races. The I' Mortu find refuge in the east, beyond the great mountains; the I' Atya find places to the north and south, and some parts east; the I' Naru exist nomadically in the west and parts east.

xii. The I' Ksh are discovered in the place called the I' Drar in the mountainous east and make their way west to a great river called Iant Duin (The Old River) and mountainous regions north and central.

xiii. An alliance is formed by the I' Naru and I' Atya to drive the I' Ksh farther into the eastern mountains. The I' Ksh ally with the I' Mortu. Battles are waged.

xiv. The Anar Ere appear and look to guide the I' Naru and I' Atya, but the I' Naru and I' Atya have darkness in their hearts.

xv. The I' Ksh prevail in battles over the Anar Ere and assume dominance, erecting their kingdom called Greev Osku in the east. They are led by the one called Ukaavan.

xvi. Ukaavan and the I' Mortu enslave the Anar Ere and many of the races. The I' Mortu plunder the land of its riches and slaughter many of the races.

xvii. The nomadic Ra Cath unites under the leadership of the one called Ra Carathor.

xviii. Nim Dagora appears and frees the Anar Ere. A great battle called Ru Torgru takes place. The Ra

Cath and the En' Raama join the Anar Ere and Nim Dagora. Nim Dagora slays Ukaavan of the I' Ksh. Few I' Ksh remain and withdraw into the darkness of the east. The remaining I' Mortu protect the I' Ksh. The northern reaches of the eastern wastelands is called 'Shk Ndor, a place also populated by men called the Mur' Edan.

xix. Nim Dagora restores the races across the land. The Ra Cath settle south of the mountains Iant Amon (The Old Hills). The En' Raama settle in the ancient mountain called Yaara Orud (Muul Duul Durra). The En' Edan settles in places North (Nur'), South (Sur'), and East (Taur). The Mur' Edan endures in the east. The En' Edhel remains in three sects – Taure' (Forest), Amon' (Mountains), and Murk' (Dark). The En' Edhel Amon' settle in a land they call Tir Nan Og and build the grand city Eilthir. The En' Naug settle in the central mountains (Amon' Hos) while a group remains nomadic (Laur'). The Ra Draug mark their land in the mountains of Ragmorok. Each of the races selects its leader and leadership structure. The leaders are referred to as chieftains.

xx. The Sgiathatch (Ajatars) remain fragmented as the En' Carad (Red) settle at Sar Vael while the Lok Tumu (Black) remain at 'Ksh Nierwes, led by the Tura.

xxi. Shade Stonehelm, the great chieftain of the Nur' Edan gains great wealth and riches from mines in the northern coastal mountains. His people prosper and gain numbers.

'NER ADUR – WAR OF LAND

xxii. Stonehelm desires more wealth and expansion for his people. He declares 'Ner Adur (War of Land) against the dwarves of the central mountains and the Sur' Edan to the south.

xxiii. The En' Edhel and Laur' Naug ally with the Sur' Edan and defeat Stonehelm. Stonehelm is allowed to retain a leadership role of the Nur' Edan but they are subjugated by the victors.

xxiv. Stonehelm passes of old age but not before appointing Adr Rile as leader of the Nur' Edan.

xxv. Over time Rile foments a nationalistic pride within the Nur' Edan and begins to muster a great army and build war machines.

RUTHR' AHTAR – WAR OF REVENGE

xxvi. Rile aligns with demon worms and wages war against the Fenri and conquers Ragmorok.

xxvii. Eligor Riorn forges the fire swords, assisted by a conjuror.

xxviii. Rile marches upon the city-state of Mistmere and quickly subdues its forces.

xxix. Rile forms an alliance with the Lok Tumu. Sar Eldor of the Sur' Edan allies with the En' Carad.

xxx.   Rile opens war against the Sur' Edan, while also marching part of his forces west against the En' Naug. The En' Naug leadership is disjointed, but the strongest of their leaders is called Paragon, and his name was Driado Aldril. The nomadic Laur' Naug are defiled by Rile and his armies. Driado Aldril leads the En' Naug in battle after battle against Rile, but eventually dies at the hands of Rile.

xxxi.   Seeing the evil in Adr Rile's heart the En' Carad, En' Edhel, and Mur' Edan aid the En' Naug in the west and push back Rile. Eligor Riorn uses the fire swords in a battle in the west. He and his steed Ravenscar perish in the battle. The fire swords are given to Zurq Riorn, Eligor Riorn's son. Sar Eldor defeats Rile's army in the south. The Lok Tumu's Tura loses an eye in the battle. Adr Rile flees to the north, to Aldkeep Point.

xxxii.   As the Nur' Edan sense loss they rise against Adr Rile and hang him by his wrists from the topmost turret of Aldkeep Point. Rile's body severs and falls into the sea. Demon worms are decimated.

xxxiii.   Sar Eldor and his forces push north. He is treated as a conquering hero by the Nur' Edan. The Fenri are given their freedom; Ragmorok is restored.

xxxiv.   The great mount 'Ksh Nierwes and Sar Vael boil in turmoil and war as the Lok Tumu battle against the En' Carad.

xxxv.	The En' Carad are devasted by war and pestilence.
xxxvi.	The Aina Dur grows and blossoms in the west. The En' Ail construct the library; doors are fashioned and the eternal fire or Tella Runya is lit.
xxxvii.	Sar Eldor passes. Zurq Riorn passes; the fire swords are given to Urm Riorn
xxxviii.	Ra Carathor establishes the Si Jhys (Guilds).
xxxix.	Zeph emissaries visit the Harrow and secretly meet with elements of the I' Mortu. An alliance is formed.
xl.	Under the watchful eye of Zeph conjurors, the I' Mortu of 'Shk Ndor breed a demented variant of brood called the Ru Gwaith.
xli.	Zeph forces overwhelm the Sur' Edan, conquering the land's southern regions. The Sur' Edan is ravaged, but its leader Urm Riorn remains and leads the resistance which carries out small attacks on the Zeph.
xlii.	The Nur' Edan, Taur Edan, and Ra Cath form an alliance against the Zeph.
xliii.	The Zeph Drach is created from dark magic.
xliv.	Thousands of Ru Gwaith are sent to battle alongside the Zeph, to honor the alliance between the I' Mortu and Zeph.

Ru Ahtar (Ra Ru Dagora) – War of Rage

xlv. The Zeph and Zeph Drach wage a great War of Rage, or Ra Ru Dagora as called by some, and Ru Ahtar by others.

xlvi. The Harrow is devastated by the Zeph and Zeph Drach. Central, eastern, and northern lands fall. The Red Death overcomes. Pestilence and contagion concur with a peculiar state of air.

xlvii. Ra Carathor implores the I' Ra Heru for guidance. A vision comes to Ra Carathor called the Olos Naq by the Ra Cath, an interpretation of the Kainen Sanye Cath. The vision is given to the Si Jhys.

xlviii. The great Balor Guild warriors form the Kyr Thysaer for the first time, as summoned by the Si Jhys, to dream about the moment of being as one.

xlix. In a great battle known as the Uru Daqoru, the Ure Orra joins the side of the righteous. The Kyr Thysaer injures the Zeph Drach alongside Urm Riorn and the fire swords. Ra Carathor slays the demon, taking its soul, but perishes in the fight. The Zeph and Ru Gwaith are decimated; evil recedes to the eastern lands.

l. Ra Dagda, son of Ra Carathor, ascends to lead the Ra Cath as Sil' Heru.

li. The great chieftains of the many races gather at Ra I' Ru to honor Ra Carathor. They meet as one to form a lasting alliance against future threats, and this meeting is called the I' Ra Omenta. From the I' Ra Omenta, Urm Riorn of the Sur' Edan is appointed to direct the proceedings. Urm Riorn directs the land's great scholars to form what is called the Coiasira and to propose new structures for the races. Juel Lotknie is selected as the Grand Sage of the Coiasira. The reclusive Mur' Edan is unrepresented.

lii.   Power consolidates throughout the land. The En' Edan forms two great Houses – House Eaniel and House Riorn. House Eaniel rules the land west of Greenvale, stretching north of the Deep Thicket, and to the northern land of the Shadow Barren; House Riorn rules the land west of the Old River and lands south to Loch Shore, that which is called Ahlgren and the Eldor. Each House ordains a King – King Dorl Eaniel of House Eaniel and King Urm Riorn of House Riorn. The En' Edhel unites under one King, King Ilikalyn, who rules from Eilthir; the En' Naug unite under one Paragon, Boidac Aldril, ruling the lands of the Old Hills known as Mortha; the Ra Cath ordain Ra Dagda as its Sil' Heru; the Ra Draug ordain Vesular as King of the Rakl. The city-state of Mistmere ordains Proko Larver as King.

liii. Blackstone Keep and Elandrake are constructed by the Trollock.

liv.   Ra I' Ru is renamed as Dagda.

lv.   Ra Soran forms the Soran Cath sect, the Deniers. Ra Soran is chosen as the Grand Denier.

lvi.   Decisions of great consequence are made at the I' Ra Omenta that provide a foundation for the current state.

lvii.   Ra Carathor is proclaimed the Ra Cath's Prime Heru and entombed within the center of Dagda. The Trollock constructs the golden city of Katzhu Pu around the tomb.

So marks the end of the Age of Fire and the beginning of the Age of Kings

CHRONOLOGY OF TIME: AGE OF KINGS, OR COIASIRA EN' ARAN

1. A time of great prosperity. The first books of the I' Qarma En' Ilya are written. Several books are later added to the great work. King Ilikalyn passes. His son Tasartir reigns.

8. Rimprandzist petitions King Eaniel of Cairn to bring all the land's conjurors together to form an Order.

10. The Edainar, or Order of Wizards, the protectorate of the Harrow, is formed by King Eaniel at the urging of the four great conjurors of the time. The Edainar is housed at Eaniel Castle.

11. The Si Jhys (Guilds) start the process of N'alaquel as instigated by the Soran Cath (Deniers). The Tar Malal and

Tar Shor are expelled. A conjuror creates the Tangle to protect the outcasts.

23. Ra Soran challenges Ra Dagda for Sil' Heru. Ra Dagda kills Ra Soran in a fight. The Soran Cath (Deniers) are banished from the Ra Cath.

25. The Professor and Erol Carrick first arrive from the Aina Dur. They are met by Fairfax the Good.

26. Big Grey and Lil' Man first arrive from the Aina Dur.

37. Ra Dagda passes. Several felines ascend over the years as Sil' Heru.

59. Trade routes are established throughout the Harrow.

65. Dark Wizards first appear. Paragon Boidac Aldril passes. The En' Naug begin to construct the massive Bagnar Pelaithis.

66. An aged King Urm Riorn gives the fire swords to Erol Carrick. Urm Riorn passes. Aelis ascends as King.

67. Brood appear throughout the lands, but their numbers are small.

85. The Fail stone is discovered in the Old Hills by the dwarves of Mortha. The stone is brought to the elders in the city of Volemill. The elders decree that the Fail stone is blessed by the Maker and of the Ondo En' Tir, and order it taken to the elven city of Eilthir.

86. The Fail stone is taken to Eilthir and placed in the rotunda of the great elven castle Kaer Tari, under the guidance of the elven King Tasartir. The Kings of the great Houses journey to Eilthir – King Aelis of Ahlgren (House

Riorn), King Zare of the Cairn (House Eaniel), Paragon Troidoc Aldril of the En' Naug, the Ra Cath's Sil' Heru called Ra Gruml, and King Pargu of the Ra Draug.

87. Princess Arakarra, daughter of King Aelis of House Riorn, touches the Fail stone and a small shard, the Lia Fail falls from the stone. Other shards fall and are unaccounted. The Lia Fail has magical powers and is forever the mark of the Queen of Ahlgren.

87-100 Great wealth is amassed by House Riorn in the south because of trade and what many believe to be the gratuitous use of magic from the Lia Fail.

104. Descendants of the warriors who fought beside Shade Stonehelm, the great chieftain of the Nur' Edan, begin to speak of uniting the Northmen against the union under House Riorn. The En' Naug finish the Bagnar Pelaithis

110-119. The Nur' Edan noblemen and lords refuse to pay tariffs on goods purchased from the south. In retaliation, they impose high tariffs on incoming trade. Economic strife occurs related to trade tariffs.

119. House Riorn imposes tariffs on the Nur' Edan crippling the Northmen's economy. A Nur' Edan nobleman, Tyrus Turl, is visited by a Dark Wizard named Rave Morgan. Turl is corrupted by Morgan.

120. During the economic strife, Tyrus Turl rises to lead the Nur' Edan. Turl brutally quells Nur' Edan opposition to his rule.

121-125. The Nur' Edan enslaves many and craft great war machines in preparation for battle against House Riorn.

126. The Nur' Edan forge alliances with the Ru Gwaith and the Lok Tumu against House Riorn. House Riorn forges an alliance with the En' Carad and the dwarves of Mortha.

127. The Edainar form the Hulnur Istare, or warrior wizards. Tyrus Turl requests an audience with King Aelis of House Riorn, to avoid possible war. Aelis grants the audience.

128. Tyrus Turl visits Riorn Castle and King Aelis, bearing gold coins and flowers, an offer of amends. Turl slays King Aelis of Ahlgren upon his throne. Turl escapes using Morgan's magic. The eldest son of Aelis, Celis is crowned King of Ahlgren.

LOT AHTAR – WAR OF FLOWERS

128-136. The Lot Ahtar (War of Flowers) is waged and the lands are devastated. The Nur' Edan takes most of Ahlgren and the South Eldor.

137. King Celis decides to appoint Erol Carrick as Supreme Commander. He is assisted by Bombadorn Roundthaler (Mortha) and Torn Ronin (House Riorn).

138. Princess Arakarra uses the Lia Fail in battle on the Snowwynne Barrens, screaming vengeance for the death of her father. Rave Morgan, the brood, and Ru Gwaith flee to the east. Tyrus Turl is killed in battle.

139. House Riorn installs a steward at Aldkeep Point to oversee the Nur' Edan.

140. House Riorn asks Torn Ronin to build a city to the east, over the great southern plains land as a means to protect the south. The city is called Gortha Losh and the plains are referred to as the Ronin Plains. In later years, the plains are renamed the Foghollow Barrens.

ER' SEERE – GREAT TIME OF CALM

138-336. Er' Seere, or Great Time of Calm prevails over the lands.

GURTHA AHTAR – WAR OF DEATH

337. Kern Durned ascends in House Riorn and is crowned King. He is viewed as having dark powers and unstable by courtiers. Durned amasses a great army. Durned crafts the doctrine of Veer' Un (Unite as One).

340. Durned besets House Eaniel asking to unite under one house. King Eurak of House Eaniel refuses.

342. Durned takes his army and marches it along the southern coast and invades Portmoor.

344. Durned marches his army north taking the southern region of the North Sage Barrow. Durned leaves a path of destruction and is known as Durned the Vicious. House Eaniel wages counter attacks that fail to push back Durned's forces. Hycis, Queen of Ahlgren speaks out against Durned. Durned plots to imprison Hycis.

345. Hycis flees Riorn Castle upon learning of Durned's plot.

346. Another army of Durned takes Laurel Glen and the Cairn Dale. Eaniel Castle is surrounded by Durned.

347. Carrick leads armies of dwarves and elves to combat Durned. Hycis joins Carrick in battle but does not have the strength to use the Fail shard against her kind. Hycis leaves the Fail shard on the battlefield and disappears.

348. Elves battle Durned's forces in the west; Carrick and the dwarves wage battle in the east. Carrick pushes his army south along the Old River.

350. The dwarves of Mortha free Eaniel Castle and push back Durned's forces south.

351. Durned is killed in a battle in the lake region of Adu Alu.

352. House Riorn is restored. Alwin ascends as King of House Riorn over his brother Dalrick who is ostracized by some for taking an Elven wife.

354. Dalrick leaves House Riorn and moves to a western part of the Tangle forest referred to as Dunhollow. He takes the name Arundel.

425. Reports surfaced of a shadow that consumes part of the east.

437. Ras Amon commands his students to find ancient relics from the great upheaval.

438. Brighthand joins with Bentgibber to seek a relic of great power.

440. Brighthand finds an evil relic at Drar Druul. The relic corrupts Brighthand transforming him into the malevolent

Foulhand. Bentgibber attempts to fight the corruption but to no avail.

442. Foulhand and Bentgibber recede to the dark places of the east. Ras Amon begins a journey to seek out and confront his once student.

444. Ras Amon confronts Foulhand at Drar Druul.

458. The evil tower Ug' Cthuth appears in the east.

461. The Ru Gwaith grow in numbers and construct the stone caves of death or Gon Durth where they systematically attempt to extinguish the Mur' Edan.

RA AHTAR – THE GREAT WAR (FIRST SHADOW WAR)

470. Foulhand and Brood form an alliance with the Lok Tumu and wage war throughout the land. The Ra Ahtar, or Great War, or Shadow War begins. Carrick joins with the forces of good to lead the battles.

471. Straya is born.

475. The Battle of the Ronin Plains is waged; Aerin uses the Lia Fail.

475. Bur Shas is killed by Drogur Vorn in a battle in the Eldor.

475. Aerin dreams of her death and fashions the Lia Fail into a necklace. She gives the necklace to the Professor.

475. The Night of Death, or as it is called the Dome en' Gurtha, occurs before the final battles of the war. On one brutal and menacing night, every possible member of each

royal family is killed except the elven king and his heirs as they were protected by magic. The beloved Aulfuren, King of Ahlgren perishes in defense of his family. Eaniel Castle and Riorn Castle are left in ruins. The Aina Dur is burned. Aerin, the Queen of Ahlgren of House Riorn perishes. There is great mourning throughout the Harrow over the loss of two royal families. Fighting continues. The armies of the good fight with renewed strength.

476-478. Erol Carrick and Merira lead more battles as evil is pushed back. The land and its great cities are devastated.

479. Merira passes on the battlefield. The forces of good prevail and at the end of the Great War of the Second Age. The brood withdraws deep into the Drueger.

479. The Aina Dur heals and blooms.

480. Foulhand is destroyed at the hands of Erol Carrick and the Hulnur Istare. The tower Ug' Cthuth is destroyed.

481. Bentgibber is banished from the lands.

481. The Trollock rebuild the great cities of the land.

484. The Elf-King decrees the Trollocks' gifts of Elandrake (En' Edhel), Blackstone Keep (En' Edan), and Katzhu Pu (Ra Cath) as sacred places and belonging to the races. The Edainar locate at Blackstone Keep.

486. Varul Teardash attempts an insurrection of the Edainar. He fails and flees to the east.

489. The Trollock disappears.

So marks the end of the Age of Kings and the beginning of the Age of War

CHRONOLOGY OF TIME: AGE OF WAR OR COIASIRA EN' DAGORTA

500. Talon Bane is chosen as the Soran Cath's Grand Denier and is called Ra Bane.

501. The tower Ug' Cthuth is rebuilt.

503. Morna Anya informs the Dominar of a premonition of evil. She is imprisoned to the depths of Blackstone Keep.

503. Gortha Losh is overcome by the shadow.

503. Molly and Elizabeth, nieces to the Professor, arrive from the Aina Dur.

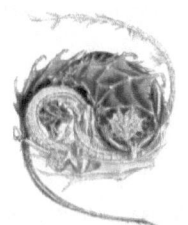

APPENDIX IV
SANYE A' OLWEN
MYSTICAL TENETS OF THE I' RA HERU
AN EXCERPT FROM THE EN' SANYE CATH
BOOK OF TEACHINGS OF THE HERU

Note: The En' Sanye Cath, or Analects of Ra Carathor and the Si Jhys, is a collection of sayings and ideas attributed to the Great Feline and his contemporaries. The Sanye A' Olwen is but a part of the Analects and a record of the words and acts of Ra Cath thinkers and philosophers. This excerpt provides the foundation of Ra Cath law, or Kainen Sanye Cath, as given to Ra Carathor in the Olos Naq.

IT CAME TO ME in a dream. Everyone knows the I' Ra Heru speaks to us through dreams. And in the dream, from within a fiery sky, visions were shaped and presented. With my mind's eye, in a moment in time, a great transformation occurred. There was no warning. The I' Ra Heru had changed reality with fire and ice. What was, was gone forever. For it is said, life is but a vapor in time, so quickly passing its course. One can live our given moments from the I' Ra Heru in a state of true peace if one will. But one must understand that one's reality is fluid like the waves of a roaring sea. From the disorder and through the mists of time words bellowed forth in my dream, words that brought clarity to the chaos. It is these words that are the

Decalogue, the Kainen Sanye Cath, words that serve as principles of virtuous behavior for the Ra Cath. And the I' Ra Heru said unto me . . .

1. Only from Noise can there be Quiet, and from Quiet can there be Noise.
2. To understand each, one must understand the other.
3. All creatures come from the One, the Father Creator (I' Ra Heru) for he is divine life.
4. Dream about the moment we are one.
5. The wind brings scent from one direction alone.
6. Create meaning for a meaningless world.
7. Discern the Cestal (not of the same).
8. Honor those which time has touched.
9. There is no one path through life.
10. The claw can only draw blood.

Note: A sect of the Ra Cath called the Soran Cath, or the Deniers, came to popularity at the end of the Ru Ahtar. Its central figure was Ra Soran who opposed Ra Dagda and the canon of the Kainen Sanye Cath. The Soran Cath understood the I' Ra Heru's teachings in a different manner, primarily denying the traditional interpretation of the I' Ra Heru's Decalogue. Soran Cath philosophers published their canon based on the premise of *mani er' tu*, or *what one is*, which became the foundation known as the Sanye e' Soran Cath. The publication was later banned and the Soran Cath was banished from the Ra Cath. The basis or *talma* of the Sanye e' Soran Cath are the five laws for feline life. They are . . .

1. Noise is both the beginning and end.
2. Wind is a force of disruption against the calm and cleanses all.
3. Action creates meaning and prevails over thought.
4. Cestal are weak and lesser creatures.
5. The claw is for seizing and taking.